THE OCOOSA
COUNTY BURDEN

"The Ocoosa County Burden," by Arthur H. Heath. ISBN 978-1-60264-006-1 (softcover); 978-1-60264-005-4 (casebound).

Library of Congress Catalog Number: 2007922865.

Manufactured in the United States of America.

THE OCOOSA COUNTY BURDEN

BY ARTHUR H. HEATH

DEDICATION

To Cullen and Mary- Your encouragement and enthusiasm for this work were all I needed to pursue it to publication. Thanks for your confidence and all your help.

To Michael, Boo and Kirsten (the "Dolly") - If you hadn't been there, this wouldn't exist!

To Brittany- Thanks for all your technical help in getting this on paper in a readable form!

The land remembers what evil has been done upon it.
Impartial, it does not judge; unblinking,
it is the perfect witness of history and time.
Learn to listen, and it will whisper tales
of great shame and sorrow.

- Randolph Martin, 1935

PROLOGUE

June 6, 1905
10:14 PM
Pebble Stretch Road

As her husband struggled in futility to raise himself up from the floor on his remaining good arm, Agatha Ring turned to him once more to point the bloodied hunting knife she held down at his face, brandishing it in a final, silent warning. Mason Ring's hand slipped on the wood floor, now slick from the blood lazily spurting from his left shoulder and arm, dully realizing if he failed to lift himself up to his feet now, his wife would escape the house and he would certainly bleed to death where he lay. His focus fading with his consciousness, he looked up into Agatha's face, into the unblinking eyes that had been the color of robin's eggs, now almost black in dilation and hate. He weakly extended his right arm in a last effort to stop her as she turned away from him to stride from the candled parlor with purpose, through the front door and out into the moonlit yard, the knife clenched tightly in her right hand, her four-day-old son Jacob dangling from the other; the baby instinctively crying with all its strength, helpless and quivering.

She made her way through the clinging wetness of the grass toward the crumbling remains of what had once been an enormous stone chimney, looming up from the ground where the semblance of the undefined yard met the encroachment of the deep woods, casting an ominous shadow toward her in the bright moonlight. Falling to her knees in the square of darkness, she dropped the panicked infant to the ground and stared down at it, a menace growing with her breathing.

Mason lay sprawled on his side only feet inside the open door, unable to speak, motionless in a darkening pool of crimson, blankly staring at his last earthly visions of a room so familiar, so warm and safe to him. His eyesight failed at the words Agatha had hastily drawn with his blood on the floor beside him in her determined exit. He took his last shallow breaths while somewhere outside in the dark his newborn son's pulsing squall suddenly stopped, followed seconds later by a single choking cry from a young mother overtaken with an anguish she never understood.

***

As the crickets and frogs gradually resumed their songs of lust from the moist recesses of the land, the trees and fields of Ocoosa County observed the scene in the same perpetual silence they had in the past; as they would again in times to come.

CHAPTER 1

Monday, September 4, 1995

H abits, patterns, idiosyncrasies, things like that," Loretta Carmichael said to the receptionist who was showing some confusion with the conversation they were having. "Myself, I think they're fascinating. Life is full of them if you just look, and to me, really boring without them."

Vanessa's face showed she was still puzzled. "Such as? Give me an example."

"Okay," Loretta said, "I've been here, what, three months? And I've already picked up on a bunch of patterns and habits of the patients here, especially in the waiting room. That's an easy example. Come here, I'll show you."

Vanessa looked through the open waiting room door at the expectant women and mothers with children seated in the large, brightly lit room. The waiting room of the Watsonville OB/Pediatric Clinic was designed big and roomy, industrial-but-soft carpet wall to wall, and contained twenty-two available seats for patients waiting to see the two doctors who staffed it.

"Here's what I mean," Loretta said, pointing to the

assortment of chairs and small colonial-style benches. "Any time there are eight or more people out here, patients and husbands, moms and kids, whatever, the seat selection is about even; they spread themselves out to keep their personal space. Make sense?"

"Yeah, that makes sense," Vanessa agreed, "but that's easy to figure. So what?"

"Okay, but here's where it gets interesting," Loretta said, smiling, her enthusiasm for her subject showing in her voice. "At any time there are seven or less *females*, and this hasn't failed yet, they'll all sit on the left side of the room, facing the bay window. Every time."

"Why?" asked Vanessa. "Why do you think that happens?"

"I say it's because the window has those cartoon duckies and squirrels on it. If there are kids waiting to be seen in peds, the characters probably keep them calmer and the moms know it. If it's just an expectant mother by herself, waiting for OB, and she's got the space, she'll sit there too because it's more pleasant for her to look out a window than to stare at a wall. Women like that, you know," she said to Vanessa, nudging her.

Loretta held up her index finger to emphasize her next point. "But – if husbands or boyfriends are with them, they'll sit against that wall, facing the door," she said, pointing to the other side of the room. "It's the guys. Guys do that; it's the 'saloon' mentality. Men have it. Goes way back, maybe even to caves."

Vanessa nodded her head in apprehensive approval. "You put a lot of thinking into this?" she asked.

Loretta shook her head. "No, not really. It's all mostly

subconscious. I see it but I don't, you know what I mean? It's like, I don't know, like riding a bike or driving a car, maybe. You're doing it, but you're not really aware you're doing it. Does that make any sense?"

"Yeah... yeah. That's pretty cool anyway, girl," Vanessa said as she began to walk back to her reception desk.

"I picked up on a little something about you, too," Loretta said with a mischievous inflection in her voice, intentionally staring down at her patient list and smiling.

Vanessa stopped abruptly and spun on her heel. "Me? What? Is it bad?"

Loretta grinned. She knew she had the receptionist where she wanted her, on the spot. "No, it's nothing bad. You like to tell stories; you have a lot of stories about you, your family and friends and everybody loves to listen to them. And you know it too, don't you?" Loretta said laughing, goading Vanessa and poking her.

"Things just happen to me that turn out funny, I guess. And I like to hear people laugh; I always have. So what do I do that you see?"

"Just this: You never tell your stories standing up. You can't. You always sit, mostly at your desk, and let people gather around you like an audience, I guess. And there's something else that goes with it," Loretta said

"What else?" Vanessa asked, showing almost a mild panic. She was embarrassed already, but felt she needed to hear it all.

"I've never seen you tell a story without a pencil in your hand. You can't seem to do that, either. The whole time you're talking, do you know what you're doing? You're thumping a pencil on your desk, eraser down. You're not even aware of any of this, are you?" Loretta asked.

Vanessa looked mildly stunned and furtively glanced around the room. "Damn, girl, I'm afraid to think how well you got me figured out, seeing little stuff like that. Don't tell anybody about this, okay? You got me paranoid now!"

"Don't be, Vanessa," Loretta said, laughing and patting her on her back. "It's all in fun, it doesn't mean anything! I won't say a thing to anybody if it's going to make you feel self-conscious."

She smiled and looked back down at her patient appointment chart, taking the added job this Monday of calling the patients in to be screened and "roomed" for the two doctors. Leanne, another of the four nurses at the clinic, was out with a summer cold, but Loretta was actually happy to do the job. It gave her the opportunity to meet many of the OB patients she wouldn't ordinarily come in contact with, except to pass in the hall.

Though they were located in the same clinic, the Obstetric and Pediatric departments were run as two separate areas, Dr. Anthony LaStazzi in charge of peds, with whom Loretta worked, and the very talented Dr. Leonard Harkness heading up the OB duties. Tall, with an abnormally full head of straight black hair and hawkish face, Dr. Harkness had a lean, assertive look to him that suggested a capability. A graduate of Duke and Johns Hopkins, Len Harkness was considered one of the best in the Southeast when it came to bringing babies into the world. Before coming to Watsonville to "slow down a little," as his wife told those who asked, his practice at Athens General was booming. Everybody seemed to want Lenny Harkness to

4

deliver their baby. "Leonard Harkness, Obstetric Superstar." And some mothers-to-be really needed his skills. He was the doctor of choice for suspected problem births. He had a knack for knowing soon in a pregnancy who would most likely be having what difficulty and at what stage, and therefore, how to successfully manage the coming months. His deliveries, like any work by an expert, were fine-tuned.

Without thinking much about it, Loretta played her "placement" game in her head before she opened the waiting room door. *Let's see,* she thought. *Four patients on the list to be seen in the next hour, that means if Danielle is out there by herself, she's looking out the window. If she's with her husband...*she swung the door open and scanned the room for the face she only knew casually by sight. Danielle Hyder and her husband, Bo, were right where she had expected them; sitting against the wall, facing the door. *Never fails.*

"Danielle, come on in, girl! My goodness, you're big!"

Danielle *was* big; huge, in fact. Dr. Harkness had told her the week before that if she hadn't gone into labor by September 6, he would induce her. Things were getting down to the wire and this was going to be her last office visit one way or the other. Her husband always came to the clinic with her since her sixth month of pregnancy, not so much because he was worried, but because his whole interest in the "parent thing," as he called it, was growing along with Danielle's tummy. And, as she neared her due date, she welcomed his company if for no other reason than to help her up. She struggled to stand when she heard her name called but the look on her face told Bo that she wasn't going anywhere without a good tug from him.

"How y'all been? I'm Loretta," she said, extending her

hand to them, finally getting the opportunity to formally introduce herself to two people she had seen in passing on a regular basis for the last three months.

"Hi, I'm Danielle and this is my husband, Bo. I'm so glad to be meeting you; I've seen you here so much! I guess when this baby is finally born we'll be seeing you a lot more often," Danielle said, all smiles. "Doctor LaStazzi is going to be our baby's doctor."

She was a pretty girl, Loretta had always thought; big blue eyes, fair skin with freckles on her cheeks and nose, and long, curly dark hair, full and down to her waist. *She'll probably cut that hair real soon after the baby comes,* Loretta thought. *Too bad.* "I'm happy to meet both y'all too. We've been seeing each other here for so long, now," Loretta said, her eyes falling to Danielle's oversized stomach. "Girl, you are HUGE! It's gettin' to be about time to have that baby, isn't it?"

"Oh yeah, and I'm ready for this young un' to be out, too!" Danielle said, gripping her huge belly as well as she could. "It's time to stop carrying this thing around and be a momma!" she said, laughing.

"Uh huh, I'll go along with that," said Bo, chiming in to confirm her desire to finally have this baby. "All she does anymore is bitch about how big she is and how uncomfortable she is…"

Danielle punched his arm. "That's okay buddy-boy, next time it's *your* turn to carry a big ol' thing like this around. We'll see who's bitchin' then!" Danielle and Loretta both laughed, looked at each other and chimed in unison, "Men!"

"Had Doctor Harkness said anything about twins at all, at any time?" asked Loretta. "This sure looks like twins to me."

"For a while, but he figured from four months on, it was going to be just one big baby!" Danielle replied. "All he's heard for months is one heartbeat and the sonogram showed only one."

"You planning on having more after this?" asked Loretta.

"I don't know; we'll see how this goes. It's our first, and we both love kids, but I told Bo I'm not making any promises till we see how this goes. Maybe."

"Do you know yet what it's going to be?" Loretta asked.

"We had the chance to find out, but we decided no, we wanted to wait and find out when it's born!" she said, excited by the thought.

They came to the exam room and Loretta helped her up to sit on the table and did some minor preps to the room while Bo sat in the corner chair and reached for a Popular Mechanics magazine from the rack on the wall. Loretta glanced at his arms and noticed perhaps a dozen small, localized burns scattered around from approximately his elbow on up to where his shirt sleeve would be, burns perhaps the size a cigarette would make. The tank top he was wearing showed a dramatic line between the white skin of his shoulder and the dark, reddish tan that stopped at his bicep. The red sunburn was also underneath his arm. She examined his arms for a few seconds from where she was standing. *He's a welder, I'll bet,* she thought. "Bo, what do you do for a living?" she asked.

"I work at J&B Fabrication in Ludlow," he said. "Been there for a while, now. It's alright. The money's okay; it pays the bills, I guess, but I don't want to weld forever, you know? I'd like to own my own business someday, maybe tower erecting. That's getting big."

Loretta looked over her chart, making sure she had all the information up-to-date. "Any changes we need to know about?" she asked.

"Just our address, we moved three weeks ago. Got a good deal come up. We're in a doublewide on Black Nate Road now; number thirteen thirty. It's down in a hollow, it's so cute! The landowner cleared out a lot of brush that had growed up over the years and left the small scrubs. He thought he wanted to live there hisself but decided to rent it out instead. And since we decided to chance it and stay in Ocoosa to have this baby, we went ahead..."

Bo's eyes flashed up from his magazine and caught Danielle's with a fixed and reprimanding stare. Seeing his intensity, she stopped mid-sentence.

Loretta paused her notations long enough to ask, "Stay? Where else would you go? Why wouldn't you have it here?" Quickly noting the silence, she glanced up at the two of them and scanned both faces, sensing an immediate and palpable tension that had not been present between them moments before. She felt it fill the room and penetrate her. Bo's glaring had made its point and his eyes drifted back down to pages of his magazine. Danielle quickly shifted the conversation back to their recent move.

"Bo and a friend of his had to do all the moving, I'm about useless. And besides, Doctor Harkness told me not to lift anything over *five* pounds about two months ago! I think that's a little too dang strict, don't you?" she asked.

"Well, that's a new one for me," Loretta said, still going over the chart. "The address, I mean. Then again," she said, looking up again, putting the peculiar shift in conversation on

8

the back burner of her mind, "most addresses I hear *are* new to me. I've been here all of three months and I still don't know my way around much. That's the hardest thing about picking up and moving somewhere completely different; you're lost for so long, it seems. As big as Atlanta is, I knew my way around; knew where everything was, I'd been there so long."

"How long did you live in Atlanta?" Danielle asked. "I've been there a few times, but I don't like it at all. Way too hustle-bustle for me."

"All of my life till I moved here. Yeah, it's fast alright," replied Loretta. "I think that's what I liked about it for so long. I came through here once a while back and I just felt good here, really fell in love with the place right off. Figured it'd be a good town for me to slow down a little when I was ready to, kind of settle in where people are friendlier, more predictable, you know?"

"That's us, Watsonville: slow and predictable!" Bo replied in a resigned tone of voice. The room was all laughter and it felt good to the three of them.

"Is he going to 'induct' me?" asked Danielle, changing the subject, a slight pleading in her voice that told Loretta she was getting predictably worried as her time approached. Loretta laughed slightly, but not enough to make this simple Georgia girl feel awkward about her choice of terms.

"You mean 'induce?' Well, Doctor Harkness said he would if you hadn't started labor by... tomorrow, so...yeah, unless you go in between now and Wednesday, I believe he has you scheduled for Thursday morning to induce or take it Caesarian if he has to," she said, looking intently at the latest orders written in the chart. "That decision he'll make at the last minute. It'll be up to him what he thinks is best for you and the baby at the time of delivery."

"He does? He's got me down for Thursday?" she replied, her pleading tone replaced with surprise. She glanced over at Bo who looked up at the mention of a Thursday delivery.

"I know, I know," Loretta reassured her, realizing full well the apprehension all mothers seem to slip into as the delivery date finally comes into sight. They all want it out, but they've become so accustomed to this growing lump in front of them that the idea of a change scares them. "It's come to a head now, excuse the pun, and you're going to finally have this baby, and it will be beautiful boy or girl and you're going to love it and spoil..."

"And be up all damn night with it," injected Bo, trying to be funny and do what he could to ease the anxiety his wife was feeling.

"Doctor Harkness will be here in just a few minutes, so just sit back and take it easy. He'll most likely want to talk over Thursday with you and you just listen to him, listen to what he tells you, he's really good, y'all know that. You couldn't ask for a better doctor. Don't be afraid to ask him any questions you've got, he's got the answers," Loretta assured them. "This whole procedure about birthing babies doesn't get too far off the main track very often and chances are whatever questions you have, he's answered hundreds and hundreds of times. You seem to be progressing fine right up to now, I doubt you're going to have much trouble at all, okay?"

"Thanks, thanks for your help," Danielle said as Loretta turned to leave the room. "You've been just super and we'll be seeing you again soon, I guess. Wish us luck!" she said as she bit her fist in mock panic.

"Y'all gonna be just fine, really! I'll see you next week, maybe the week after when you're in to see Doctor LaStazzi for your first visit with your brand-new baby," Loretta said, sounding as upbeat as she could for the concerned young woman. "I'll give your address change to Vanessa at the desk so she can make note of it, so don't worry about it. Bye!" She closed the door and knew that even though it seemed so crucial and important to the soon-to-be parents in the room, the scene had been and would be repeated day in and day out at the clinic. Delivering babies was a business and the OB department went about that business in a controlled, conscientious manner. After all, that was the best way to ensure a consistent, quality product: a healthy new baby, ready to take its place in the world with the help of nurturing, informed parents. At least that was the theory.

CHAPTER 2

Hey, y'all know where I can get a map of this place?" She looked around and noticed none of the employees were interested enough to look up.

Becky, one of the other nurses, finally glanced up at her and said, "What, Watsonville? You need a map of this tiny town?"

"No, the county, dummy. Of course Watsonville's easy to find your way around in; it's small enough. I'm talking about a county map so I don't get lost when I drive out of town."

"Why you want to drive out of town?" Vanessa spoke up. "You lookin' to find a man out there for yourself? A farmer? There's a lot of them out there. 'Bout all there is in this county once you leave town."

"How would you know *that*, Nessa?" asked Becky, grinning at her.

"Oh, I got stories, child!" Vanessa replied, pointing at Becky with her index finger before she turned her back and swayed her ample hips in an exaggerated manner.

"I bet you do!" laughed Becky.

Dr. LaStazzi had wandered into the room for coffee and

joined in. "Do you want to find some good places to bass fish? I can show you those," he said, only half-joking.

"No, I don't fish, thanks," Loretta replied, sensing the room was not taking her request very seriously.

"Hey, maybe you should, really," countered Dr. LaStazzi, taking a sip of coffee and registering a sour look as if the infamous break room coffee was living up to its reputation. "A.J and I go out whenever we can, even if I'm on call; we just don't go very far off. Fishing's really great, so relaxing. You do a lot of talking to who you're with. A.J.'s only ten but we talk a lot about what's going on in his life and stuff; I really look forward to our trips. It's a real opportunity to bond. You get to know the county, at least where the bass are biting and how to get there!" he said with a laugh.

Vanessa went to the coffee pot and poured herself a cup. She liked it black, no sugar or cream, and the rest of the office wondered how she could get it down like that. They had all joked with her on occasion that she didn't like her coffee brewed, she preferred it "rendered." Watching her drink it made them cringe. "A map might not be a bad idea, really," she said as she filled her cup. "My sister went out and got one once after she got stranded and didn't know where she was."

"How did that happen?" asked Loretta

Vanessa turned and leaned against the counter and took a sip of coffee. "Well, she had been to church one Sunday, and, uh... she was all dressed up and everything... um..." She stammered and hesitated and made unconscious glances toward the table, not able to continue her story and not having a clue as to why.

Loretta got out of her seat, casually walked up to her and

whispered as inconspicuously as she could, "It's okay, go sit down! I want to hear this story!"

Vanessa smiled a small, embarrassed smile and hurried over to the break room table like a little girl that had been granted permission to do something special. She sunk into a chair, picked up a pencil and started to thump and talk all at once, both rapid-fire.

"See, it was a Sunday after church, my sister Tonya had dressed up real special; had on this real pretty royal blue pants outfit she had bought in Athens when she was up there. She had worn it because there was a fella there in church she kinda had her eye on, you know? And she had caught him lookin' at her too, so she dressed up for him that Sunday but he wasn't there. So that put her in kind of a bad mood to begin with. She left church to go to our Momma's house in Dwyerton, and that's a long drive from Watsonville 'cause you got to go way out forty-one, then take some side roads, well, you know." Her pencil was drumming up a storm now. "And this was a different way than she had been used to going, so, wouldn't you know it, her car breaks down in the middle of nowhere..."

"See? That's what I'm talking about!" Loretta said, turning to those in the room, attempting to justify her need for a map.

"She gets out," Vanessa continued, "doesn't know where in the hell she is anyway, so she don't know which way to go for help or even how far 'cause she doesn't know where she is to begin with!" Her audience laughed and it made her feel good to be entertaining them. "Now, I'm a big girl, y'all know that, but my sister Tonya got a *big* ol' butt, she's bigger than me, and there she was, lost, walkin', the middle of July, got on her best outfit, sweatin', and no traffic to even flag down out there 'cause its Sunday."

Becky was the most engrossed and asked, "So what happened? Did someone give her a ride finally? She must have gotten a ride with somebody; she's still not out there!"

"Yeah, she said first an old beat-up Mercury slowed down with two crackers…"

Vanessa stopped mid-sentence and her hand flew up to her mouth. Her eyes widened as her face registered shock and scanned the faces in the room, quickly passing from one to another, ready for scorned reactions that amazingly didn't come.

"What? What happened to Tonya? What's the matter?" asked Dr. LaStazzi.

"I am *so* sorry y'all, that just slipped out, really, I didn't mean to…" Vanessa spoke from under the hand that still covered her mouth, her head shaking from side to side in embarrassment for the racial transgression she felt she had just made.

"Nessa, what? What's wrong?" asked Becky, confused with the circumstance that was so very clear to Vanessa.

"I said 'cracker' and I'm so sorry!"

"Is that all? Finish the story. What happened to your sister? Two white people slowed down to, what, offer her a ride, right? Didn't she take it?"

Vanessa was puzzled at this lack of concern for what she felt would be at the very least a minor insult to these white people in the room with her. "Wait a minute, y'all not mad? I don't get it."

"It's no big thing Vanessa, it's just 'cracker'," assured

Loretta, trying to keep her friend from feeling on the spot.

"But that's a bad word, like 'nigger' is, isn't it?" Vanessa asked. "My folks always told us that if white people were polite enough not to say 'nigger' around us, we ought to return the politeness and not say hurtful things like 'cracker' and 'honkey', and the like, around them."

Dr. Harkness had entered the room during the conversation and had heard enough to be aware of the nature of the situation. Race had never been an issue at the clinic and he saw no reason for it to start to be one now, not over this. But perhaps this was the opportunity for some social clarification and definition for everyone.

"Vanessa, do I understand you to say you were brought up to feel that if you called a white person 'cracker' or 'honkey' or 'ofay'…"

"You heard that one? 'Ofay'?" Vanessa asked in surprise. "That's a OLD one!"

"Oh, yes, once or twice," he said, smiling. "Your folks told you it was wrong to say those around white people and you didn't, is that right?"

"Uh-huh, and that's why I stopped myself…"

"Hon, I think I might know where Doctor Harkness is going with this because I feel the same. Correct me if I'm wrong, Doctor, but what he's, what *we're* trying to tell you here is that those words don't really hurt whites the way 'nigger' hurts black people; it's just not the same thing," Loretta said as she sat on the edge of Vanessa's desk and looked down at her wondering face. She had gotten the feeling in the past that this was something black people evidently didn't understand.

16

"They don't bother you?" Vanessa asked as she looked around the room at the faces that were unanimously shaking their heads to the negative. "How 'bout 'white trash'?" Vanessa asked, her face almost lighting up in the hopes that she had pulled out the 'big gun' that she had always been told infuriated whites.

"No. Close, but not really that either," said Len Harkness, gently shaking his head, almost sorry to be disappointing her once more. "Look at it like this: if you were to call me 'white trash' out of anger, or even joking around…"

"I wouldn't do that, Doctor Harkness," she interjected, showing an honest esteem for this acclaimed doctor who happened to also be her boss.

"I know, and that respect is great. I thank you for it, but my point here is, if you did, you know I'm not white trash and so do I, so the hurt kind of, well, 'bounces off', for want of a better term. You don't really think I am and I know I'm not."

Vanessa thought for a few seconds. "Then, what if I called somebody 'white trash' who *was* white trash? How do they take it?" she asked, sounding almost hopeful.

The room replied practically in unison, laughing; "THEY DON'T CARE!"

Loretta sat on the table and laughed out loud as the absurdity of the situation dawned on her for the first time. She was going to educate Vanessa with a fact that white Southerners took for granted. "White trash, REAL white trash, *know* they are, Nessa," she said, "and if you accuse them of being that, they'll usually say, 'Yeah, so what?' and that's the extent of it. They pop another can of Bud and go their way." A bit of seriousness crept across her face as she attempted to make an important point through all this. She looked down at Vanessa and said, "Sweetie, the point here, I guess, is that intelligent white people, polite white people, don't say 'nigger' to you because, first of all, it's wrong to do and they know it hurts you. And secondly, you, a black person, really have no verbal ammunition to fire back at them. That makes it unfair, and good people, good people of *any* color, don't take advantage of unfair situations that hurt someone else, be they black or white or whatever color. Maybe that's something decent white people carry around in the back of their minds and don't ever really think about. I guess I really didn't until just now. Maybe it's really that simple."

Vanessa had a look of mild revelation on her face. "Damn, I never knew that. Never thought about it that way."

"I don't think most of us did either, consciously anyway, until right about now. Hey, what about your sister? How'd she get home?" Becky asked.

"Oh, she finally got a ride with a black couple and that was probably a bigger mistake than refusing the ride from the white folks 'cause these black folk were farmers, she could tell that, no doubt about it. They must have just been out fertilizing their fields, they smelled like manure!" The room erupted in laughter. "They got her to a payphone, she called our brother Andre, and he came and got her in his truck, but he got lost too and it took him an hour and a half to find her. He was prob'ly high, if I know him! Damn, she was **so** mad! 'Specially when he made her ride in the back in the hot sun 'cause she smelled like cow shit!" Vanessa had managed to practically flatten the eraser on a new pencil with her story but the laughter she brought out boosted the spirits of the staff of the Watsonville

Clinic as always. And, as a bonus, they left there that afternoon a little more conscious of themselves, perhaps a little kinder, now that they all were aware of why they should be.

CHAPTER 3

Friday, September 8

H ey, did anybody figure out where I can get that map I'm after?" Loretta shouted into the break room again, sticking her head in from out in the hall. She had not been anywhere but work, but the weekend was coming and a map would be a welcome peace of mind to have in the car if she decided to go exploring. The weather was beautiful and Vanessa had told her of a fruit stand just out of town on the Miller Bridge crossroad that always had fresh fruits and vegetables which seemed better than everyone else's and were cheaper to boot. *My kind of place*, Loretta thought. *Just don't need to get lost going there.*

"Hey, your hair!" Becky shouted, smiling at Loretta's new hair cut. "When did you get *that* done?" She got up to meet her in the middle of the room to inspect it.

"Last night. I figured, 'it's time for a change,' so I just went into Carmen's and told them what I wanted. I thought 'new place, new look'."

"A 'page boy'! Good choice! You look so different!"

Dr. Harkness walked by the door to the lounge on his way down the hall but immediately walked backward into the doorway to look in to see what the commotion was about. "Whoa, look at that! Very nice, Loretta! I like it!" he said. Len was not the type to dole out false praise; he was too busy to be anything but straightforward. If he said something, he meant it.

Loretta was eating it up, basking in the attention. She had taken a chance getting the shorter cut that framed her face. It was a big change for her to make and she had to swallow hard when the scissors took the first cut of her long auburn hair. Not as tall or thin or as sleek as she would have liked to have been, she was who she was. She had always been a bit dissatisfied with her shape, but figured it was something she must have inherited from her father's side. Her mother had been taller than she, and rail-thin all her life. A longer hairstyle, shoulder length, had always worked out well for her, adding some inches to her height and lengthening her face. No one could hear the silent breath of relief she was exhaling with every compliment. Dr. Harkness was about to leave when Loretta drew his attention away from the chart he was studying. "Doctor Harkness, do you have a minute? I've got a couple of questions to ask that I think you can help me with."

"Yeah, I've got a couple of minutes, but I do have Mrs. Bradley waiting in six. What do you need?" He put the chart under his arm and shoved his hands into his pockets. Loretta knew this was his "make it quick" posture. When Len Harkness didn't have the time to spend to listen, his hands would go in his pockets and play with whatever change he was carrying. The "I'm all ears" look was characterized by him immediately finding a wall or desk to lean against and crossing his arms in front of him. Granted, he was a busy man, and everybody seemed to want part of his time. And being the good doctor that he was, he gave them as much as he could. Today was a coin day. Loretta could hear them jingling. She knew she'd have to be fast.

"First, do you want to hear a short OB joke?" she asked.

"Yeah, go ahead," he replied, smiling in anticipation.

"Okay, this guy's wife is pregnant and getting real close to her due date, and she goes into labor at the house. He gets panicky and calls 911. The dispatcher answers and asks him what the trouble is. He says, 'My wife is going into labor and her contractions are almost a minute apart! What should I do?' The dispatcher says, 'Calm down! Is this her first child?' The guy says, 'No, damn it, I told you; I'm her husband!'"

The doctor's head reared back and she got the laugh she wanted out of him, and then some. It was good to see him laugh like that. He had the serious personality that caused him to neglect to laugh even when he had the chance. "Oh, that's good! I've got to remember that. What do you need to know?" he asked, still beaming.

"Did you deliver the Hyder baby yesterday? Danielle and Bo Hyder?"

"Yes! Yes I did! And she came through beautifully, no trouble, no complications. I thought for a while I'd have to take it C-section, like I had said, but I saw she was going to be able to deliver on her own with just a block and she went ahead and delivered a real pretty girl about ten or so yesterday morning. Baby is fine, all the fingers and toes; she's going to have a full head of dark hair just like her mom. Mom's doing well too."

"Oh that's great," Loretta said. "What'd they name her?"

"They hadn't by the time I left them. They were still undecided, had a couple of names they were still considering."

"I like them. It's going to be nice taking care of that baby when they come in. The other thing, and you probably think I'm dumb for still harping on this, but I never did get any good suggestions as to where I can get a county map. Would you know where?"

"If it's a county map you need, go to a government office; a county office. One around here in Watsonville should have one."

"Good idea," Loretta nodded. "Why didn't anyone else think of that? Like me for instance?" She shook her head at the simplicity of the answer. "Oh, and *one* more quick question; you just had some work done on your house, right? Who did it?"

"A guy named Luke McClain, really good, does great work, and he's not expensive, either. Do you need some work done on something?"

"I do. Have you got his number?"

"Uh-huh, and that reminds me," Dr. Harkness said, perking up at the thought. "I need to call him today anyway, I'm glad you brought it up. He was supposed to come over tomorrow morning and give me a quote on building a shed, but we're going out of town tonight. Charleston, for the weekend, to see Patsy's family. Tell you what. Since I won't be here and you will, why don't I just call him and send him over to your house instead? He's got the time reserved for me anyway."

Loretta agreed. "That sounds like a plan to me. What time was he going to be at your place?"

" 'Bout eight or so."

"Good, tell him to make it eight at my place too, then. My address is eleven twenty-one Bessemer Court. Watsonville, naturally. Cool! This should work out well," she said, feeling happy about all the news she had just gotten from the doctor. "Hey, have a great time in Charleston!"

Len Harkness smiled and waved as he walked off down the hall.

"Huh, a girl! Good for them!" Loretta muttered to herself and smiled as she turned and headed to the next patient's room.

CHAPTER 4

Saturday, September 9, 1995

T he air was just starting to change; at least Loretta thought she could feel it. It was different; cooler, drier. Now and then, you could smell autumn in the air for a little while, especially in the mornings. It wasn't long enough for Loretta. Not yet. She loved the fall. It was her favorite season. She looked up from her coffee as she saw the truck pulling up in her drive. A dirty, white '82 Chevy pickup that looked like it was on its last leg. A man got out, fiddled with something back in the bed, and started up her walkway toward the screened porch where she sat. Thick salt and pepper hair and matching moustache, weathered face, wearing faded jeans and a plaid shirt. She rose to meet him at the door. Looking up, he saw her standing there and attempted to introduce himself from the bottom step. "Good morning, ma'am, are you Loretta Carmichael?" he asked with a slight smile.

"Maybe. What if I'm not?" she replied, smiling back.

Luke broke into a full grin, realizing the joke. "Then I guess I don't have to be Luke McClain!" he said, as he pretended to turn and walk back to his truck.

"Ha! Ha! Yeah, I'm her, come on back!" she laughed and skipped down the three steps to greet him.

He stopped, turned, and still smiling, said, "Good, you're who you're supposed to be and I am, too. Luke McClain. Glad to meet you, ma'am."

They shook hands and Loretta could feel they were rough and strong. *He does a lot of outside work with these*, she thought. "I'm Loretta, and it's good to meet you too. Doctor Harkness highly recommends you. I'm glad you had the time to come over this morning."

"Yes, ma'am, I've done a lot of work for Len in the past few years, he's been doing a lot to his house, changing this, adding to that. It's worked out well for us both. He's a good guy, I like him."

"I can show you what I want done, but would you like to have a cup of coffee first? It's already made. I'd be happy to get you a cup," she asked, trying to be polite, and trying to be something else she couldn't quite put her finger on. She looked up into his face and all she could think of was *cowboy. My God,* she thought, *I'm getting coffee for the Marlboro Man.*

"Well, I left without having mine at home, so sure! Just a little cream please, if that's not a bother."

"Not at all," she said as she turned to go up the stairs. "Please, come on in, have a seat. I've been enjoying the fall morning," pointing to a chair. Luke took a seat at the small table on the porch and was immediately joined by a friendly Calico cat walking on the table in front of him, obviously looking for attention. "Is she supposed to be up here?" he called back into the house to Loretta.

"It's okay, that's Peach. She goes where she wants to," Loretta shouted back. "How'd you know it was a 'she'?"

"Because she's a Calico, they're all female; everybody knows that, don't they? Besides, I grew up on a farm; we had different cats from time to time."

Loretta came back through the doorway with two coffees, spoons and a creamer, a creamer she scrambled to dig out of her modest hutch, the creamer she hadn't used since she had left Atlanta. *Why am I making such a fuss all of a sudden?* She asked herself. She put the coffees on the table, picked up Peach and dropped her unceremoniously onto the floor. Luke stirred his coffee while she sat down.

"So you need some work done. Can you tell me what you think you have in mind?" Luke asked as he continued to stir.

Loretta worked to tick off the mental list she had accumulated. "Well, I know the soffits need replacing, at least the side and back. There's some fascia board in the front here that's going bad, dry-rot I think. Those are the things I can think of, mostly exterior; but you can look around too, please, and tell me what you think."

"You seem to know something about construction; how'd that come about?" Luke asked, a little impressed by her knowledge. He liked a woman who could speak his language. It made socializing a lot easier and was always a potential topic of conversation when things got uncomfortably quiet. Unfortunately, women like that were hard to find.

"I had a brother-in-law who was a contractor; I listened."

Luke spoke up for a clarification, one with a hidden agenda he tagged on since he was inquiring anyway. "So your sister's husband was in construction?" he asked.

27

"No, my ex-husband's brother," she said. "He built all my ex's dealerships." *Oh, well, I might as well throw this out there now, it looks like it's going to come up sooner or later*, she thought. "I used to be married to Jeff Carmichael," she said matter-of-fact, and settled back in her seat, crossed her arms and waited for the name to sink in.

The name bounced around in Luke's memory for a second or so. Then his eyes widened in recognition. "Jeff Carmichael, the 'car guy'? The guy with all the dealerships in Atlanta?"

"Yep," Loretta answered, not nearly as impressed with the fact as Luke seemed to be. "That'd be the one."

"Well, how about that! I see him all the time on his TV ads, running up and down in front of his cars, tearing up the price sheets..."

"Acting the fool," Loretta interrupted. "Bet you never thought you'd be sitting having coffee in a small Georgia town with the ex-wife of a hot shot like Jeff 'Car-Crazy' Carmichael, did you?" she said in a dry tone.

"Ma'am, look, I'm sorry if..."

"No, no, it's okay, I volunteered the information. Here's the story about that, for the record, 'cause I know you're probably wondering; everybody does when I tell them. Jeff and I got married back in eighty-nine. I met him when he was a struggling car salesman, full of energy, a real go-getter. He was a fun guy back then. He developed a real knack for selling cars and pretty soon he swung his own dealership. He got on the fast track and just took off like a rocket. Then he bought another dealership and then another. Pretty soon there was no time for anything else but work."

Loretta gazed at her coffee while she absent-mindedly

stirred it. "I was a nurse with a lot of hours then and we, well, we just drifted apart. There were other issues too, I guess, but that was the big one. We split two years ago; I got absorbed in my work at the clinic I was at, not having the time to get back into the dating scene at all like I thought I would. I moved here three months ago, started working at the clinic. And that's about all there is to tell. That's my story." She looked up at Luke's face and managed a weak smile.

"Well, I am sorry. But why here?"

"Come again?" Loretta asked, confused by the question.

"Why Ocoosa County? Watsonville? What brought you out this way? You know anybody here? Got kin?"

"No, neither one. I don't know, really. I had driven out here once years back looking for a certain antique for a friend that someone told me I'd probably find in one of the shops here. Y'all got a lot of antique shops in this little town! I liked the place right off. It was like there was a subconscious thing going on; a 'pulling' on me that said this is where I ought to be. I still feel it."

Luke nodded. He knew women often felt these things even though there was no rational reason for it. Luke stayed quiet while absorbing her story. Loretta quickly changed the tone for both their sakes, feeling awkward about the mood she set with the story of her past.

"Hey, I drove some fine cars in those four and a half years I was married! That was a big plus!" she said, getting more animated, attempting to lighten things up.

"I'll bet you did, too," Luke said, and took her lead, sensing she had been heading in a direction that could have dampened the rest of the conversation, one he was beginning to enjoy. "What was the nicest? No, what was the fastest you had?" he asked, hoping it was some exotic sports car; one he could never imagine driving. Luke always had a thing for sports cars, though he had never owned one. It was the one romantic dream he held onto through the years. The time never seemed right to buy one, or the need for a utility vehicle like his truck always took precedence. Now he felt his time for buying one was quickly passing him by. His fast motoring along deserted country roads was going to have to be vicarious, he was afraid.

"A Viper," she said, her face boasting an impish grin. "Jeff wangled one from Dodge. They weren't even out yet."

"No! Really?" he replied, sounding like a teenager. "How was that to drive? I've heard they're great to drive."

"Scary. Dangerous-scary. I don't know what you've ever driven," Loretta proclaimed, allowing herself to become a little authoritative, "but I can just about guaran-damn-tee you you've never been in a car that gives you more of a feeling of pure, raw power than a Viper."

"Wanted to break the wheels loose, did it?" Luke asked, eating this up.

"*Oh*, yeah. 'Bout the first time it got sideways on me I gave it back to Jeff, told him to get me something more sensible. So I got that Camry over yonder," she said, motioning to her car sitting in the driveway in front of Luke's truck. "And that's what I've been driving ever since, that same one. Good car. So. How about you, Mr. McClain? You married?"

The animation Luke showed with the car subject waned quickly when Loretta asked him about his own life, at least this part of it. He became noticeably somber and began to stare at his coffee as he spoke. "No, I was, but that ended back in '90."

Loretta started to notice a subtle but definite shift in Luke's body language as he started into his marital history. He began to lean forward and back, as if trying to get comfortable in his chair by shifting his weight. He crossed and uncrossed his legs as he adjusted his seating and the combination of movements started to make him resemble a ten-year-old in need of his Ritalin. *Christ*, she thought, *he's so nervous, he's going to fidget right off his chair!* "Okay, it's my turn to be polite here..."

"No, it's okay; I don't mind talking about it. It's just that hardly anyone I know asks anymore, they've all heard it, so I'm not all that used to talking about it, you know? Besides, you were good enough to share..."

"Okay, then shoot, if you really want to. I'd like to hear it. Tit-for-tat."

"I was married for twenty years to a girl I dated in high school, Betsy Masterson. Time went by as it does, I worked for the Postal Service..."

"You were a mailman?" Loretta asked.

"Yeah, a letter carrier, yes ma'am. I did that for twenty years until I retired in '90. I guess things between us had been going downhill for years before that, I just didn't notice. That s me. Maybe because I worked for the Post Office; that's not easy, you know? People think there's nothin' to handling mail, walking house to house, dropping letters into slots, boxes, and maybe that *is* the easy part. But going there day after day...people don't know what kind of an environment it is. There is no doubt, in *my* mind at least, where the term 'going postal' came from. I know why those things happened. I was luckier than most, though, I had rural routes much of the time. That kept me out of that environment, but away from home too. 'Deadland' mighta saved me one way, but cost me my marriage in the bargain." There was a reflection in his voice that was hard to miss.

Loretta cocked her head in question. "Deadland? What's that?"

"It's just a name my daddy always called the real remote parts of Ocoosa County."

"Odd name."

"Odd reason," Luke replied in a tone that suggested to Loretta it was the only explanation he was going to give her.

"Maybe it all went to hell because I drank a bit, too," he said, going back to the topic of his marriage. "I don't kid myself any, I figure that was a big part of why she left. I stopped drinking right after we finalized; bad timing, huh?" Luke said, becoming pensive as he talked, as though he had not thought these things for a long time, and each time he did they explained it all a little clearer to him. "The biggest thing, to me, is that I was the kind of guy who never really needed much, and she became the kind of woman that always wanted more."

"I think I know just what you mean," said Loretta, thinking back on her own marriage. "Do you see her at all anymore, I mean around?"

"No, she moved to Atlanta. Wanted more than Watsonville could give her, or even Athens, for that matter." Luke's reply was matter-of-fact, neutral. He didn't miss her.

"No kids?"

"Naw, she never really wanted any; it just wasn't 'us' I guess. I suppose, in all, that worked out for the better."

There followed an awkward silence where each seemed to be reflecting on that segment of their lives they considered to be a failure, justly or not, and how the story they had just heard from the other more or less paralleled their own. Without saying it, they both found it strange, and a little comforting. "Do you mind if I smoke?" asked Luke.

Loretta was taken completely off guard by his request. "You smoke? I didn't know...I couldn't..."

"Yeah, I do, some," he said as he took a pack of unfiltered Camels out of his shirt pocket. "What? You couldn't smell it on my clothes, right? They're clean, that's why! And I mostly smoke outside, anyway. Cuts down on the smell on me and in the house."

Loretta was at a loss for words with this unexpected revelation. "I guess I just didn't expect it, that's all. Yeah, go ahead if you want, we're outside, it's okay." Luke lit the cigarette and took a long, deep drag as he sat back in his chair, appearing to Loretta to be thoroughly savoring it.

"You seem to really enjoy that," she said, cringing slightly at the damage she, and certainly he, knew he must be doing to himself.

"I do, that's why I smoke. It's not a habit, at least not yet. I only started twelve, maybe fourteen months ago."

"You what?!" she said, spitting out her amazement at what he was telling her. "Why? You waited until you were..." Loretta halted, realizing she didn't know how old he was.

"Fifty," Luke said proudly, having no reservations about revealing his age to this woman. He was what he was.

"Okay, fifty, to start smoking? Why? Why didn't you smoke earlier while you were a mailman?"

33

"'Letter carrier'," Luke said, correcting her again. "Like I said before, I drank then. I had a different vice!" he said laughing.

"You know, when you got here and came up the walk, I thought to myself you looked a lot like the Marlboro Man."

"You think?" Luke responded after taking another deep drag, impressed with what seemed to him to be a compliment. "Thanks! He was a really good-looking guy!"

"Uh-huh, *was*, that's a key word here, Luke; he's dead," Loretta said, emphasizing a fact she was sure he knew also.

Luke forced a fake, mocking smile. He knew he was in for a lecture if he let this go on. "Everybody dies, Loretta," he replied.

"True, but not everybody decides late in life to pick up a habit known to speed the process along," she replied quickly, trying to hammer home what should be obvious to any responsible adult.

"I suppose you have a point there," he acquiesced. "I'll put it out if it bothers you that much, and it seems like it does," Luke offered as he looked around for an ashtray, immediately realizing he wouldn't find one. He started to get up when Loretta stopped him.

"No, no, go ahead, you're a big boy; it's your choice," Loretta told him and waved her hand to let him know he didn't have to move. Luke finished the last few puffs and got up to crush out the stub outside on the steps, field-stripping the remaining paper and tobacco. The ashes he had saved in his hand were flicked off the side of the steps. He returned to his seat only to look at Loretta like a little boy who had just gotten away with something he shouldn't have done. She pretended to glare back at him. *Time to get on to something else*, she thought.

"'Luke'", she said, as a proclamation of sorts. "Where did that name come from?"

"My folks read the Bible a lot. It came from the Bible. It could have been really bad, like 'Ezekiel' or something. I thought it was kind of cool as a kid, the name 'Luke', having watched 'The Real McCoys' on TV."

"Who?"

"You don't remember The Real McCoys, the show with Walter Brennan as Grampa and Richard Crenna as Luke McCoy? How old are you? Oh, I'm sorry! That just...I just meant..."

"Thirty-five," she blurted out. *There, I said it, it's out, I don't care, now he knows,* she thought, defiant with herself for saying it. *If he can do it, so can I.*

"Oh... then you wouldn't remember it. What was I thinking? Thirty-five, really? You look, maybe, twenty-five, late twenties, max. You'd a-had me fooled," he said, being truthful with her, and while trying to be complimentary, realizing as he said it, he couldn't avoid it sounding like bald-faced flattery.

***

Loretta Carmichael could be shy sometimes though it wasn't the problem now that it had been in her past. It was a trait she had tried hard to deal with as a little girl growing up in Atlanta. When she felt cornered in a situation, threatened with her own feelings and insecurities, she would try to run away rather than stay and face things. Relationships had been difficult for her as a child, with friends as a little girl and boyfriends as a young woman.

The day she lost her chance to have Danny Mobley as her boyfriend set things in motion to change all that.

They were juniors in high school. He was blond, boyishly handsome, and had his own car. All her friends were envious that Danny had called Loretta late one night, out of the blue, and said, in the course of the unexpected conversation, that he had always thought she was 'cute,' and would like to take her out sometime if she would like to go. From that phone call on, she avoided talking to him in school, refused to talk to him on the phone ("I'm not here! Tell him I'm not here!" she would instruct her mother to say), and would go the other way in panic if she saw him in the halls.

"Why don't you want to go out with him?" "Are you crazy, girl?" her girlfriends would ask. "He's yours if you want him." "You better quit playing hard to get if that's what you're doing, he's going to lose interest if you keep it up! What's wrong with you, girl? Talk to him!"

The day she mustered the nerve to walk up and talk to him, the very day she decided to stop telling herself she wasn't pretty enough or popular enough to date someone like Danny Mobley and to meet him head on in the hall and talk to him like the girl inside her had wanted to do from that first phone call, was the very same day Danny decided Loretta was not worth the time and trouble to pursue.

Her avoidance had made him look bad in front of his friends, he felt, and all this failed attempting to get her to "just go out for some damn Krystals, for Christ sake," was too much

36

for his adolescent psyche. He was not going to give himself the chance to understand this strange school-girl mentality. Life moves fast for a junior with his own car and boyish good looks. When she stood in front cf him, shy, smiling, that very day of her decided courage and determination, Danny looked at her deadpan, emotionless, and walked on by. That night, hour after teary hour passed until she had her mother crying, too, for her heartbroken little girl.

Finally her mother, tired of this endless weeping, took Loretta by the shoulders, faced her and explained that she had to have confidence in herself, that she would never have anyone or anything worthwhile unless she believed she *should*. "If you think you don't deserve nothin', nothin' is what you're gonna get," her Momma told her, dabbing at her daughter's puffy eyes with a wadded-up Kleenex. "That's a mistake too many women in this world make. Me too, I'm ashamed to say, and it's just not right. That's the 'shadow side' of being a woman. It just doesn't have to be like that, Sugar, you hear? We can see it for others, just not ourselves. That's our problem. I can see it for you; you're my baby! I have a saying of my own, and this is it: 'If a woman is poorly bred, poorly raised and poorly schooled, when it comes to matters of the heart, she's pretty stupid. If a woman is well-bred, well-raised and well-schooled, when it comes to matters of the heart, she's pretty stupid.' What I'm trying to say, honey, bottom line, is that you're an attractive and intelligent young woman. No one, no 'thing' you should consider out of your reach. Never! You want it, you square them shoulders, bow yourself up and you go get it! You do it!"

There were times after that night when Loretta had doubts

about things, felt a bit awkward in certain situations. She knew that was only being human. But from that night, from the moment her mother wiped the last tear from her swollen eyes, she promised herself she would try to be the woman her mother, in her mother's wisdom, knew she could be. If pushed hard, when she felt her most vulnerable, she would always retreat to her last mental refuge and come up fighting. "I'll do it for Momma, 'cause she said I can."

***

Loretta felt the red glow of embarrassment start at her neck and flash up to her face and there wasn't anything she could do to hide it. *Just gracefully sit here, say 'thank you' and act thirty five*, she told herself. "Thank you, Lucas."

"'Luke', please. I only get called Lucas when I'm in trouble! Since we're on the subject, how'd you get the name 'Loretta'? That's a very pretty name." Luke sat back and waited for her response. He was relaxing again now; no more talk of a dead marriage allowed the tension to drain away.

"My dad saw a photograph of Loretta Young when she was a young actress and he thought she was the most beautiful woman he had ever seen. So when I came along, he named me Loretta. That's the story I was told, anyway. Then, when I was eighteen months old, he left us, my mom and me. Figure that, huh?"

Luke could see they might be drifting back into 'blue waters' again and offered another apology. "I have to apologize, if that's a painful memory for you, because if it…"

"No, not at all anymore, I mean, I never knew him, so it's

38

not like I could miss something I never had, you know? Not ever having had a father is part of who I am, for better or worse. It shaped me. Did you grow up with both parents? Count yourself lucky if you did, it doesn't happen much anymore."

Luke felt a sudden small ray of pride in being able to answer "yes" to her question. He knew she was right. "Yes, both parents, my whole life. They're still married, in fact, in their early seventies, living in Florida now, Boynton Beach. And I do feel lucky, whenever I stop to think about it. I just consider it normal, but I know it's not, not now, especially."

"Just you?" She asked. "No brothers or sisters?"

"Just me. We had a lot to do on the farm. There wasn't much time for playing or feeling sorry for myself that I was alone. Like you said, you really don't miss what you never had." Luke finished his last sip of coffee and pushed his chair back away from the table. He was ready to change subjects. "You ready for me to take a look at this house?" he asked as he stood and stretched.

"Sure, let me show you what I think it needs," she said as she stood and led him through the screen door and down the steps. She turned to look up at the front soffits. "Don't they look like they could use replacing? See them? The sides are even worse, come look."

Luke followed her as she walked around to the left side of the house. For the first time, he had the chance to study her as a man would study any woman he had just met. *You might not have been a contender in Hotlanta, honey, but you're gonna do just fine in this little town,* he thought as they made their way around the house through the sparse grass. *Nice butt, pretty face, pretty hair. Smart, too, got something to say when you talk. Okay, ease off; best tend to business.* "Yeah, you're right, they could come down. Won't be much to it. I been looking at the fascia, too, and that seems easy enough, just one-bys. Replace them, a little paint, and this house will look real good from the street," Luke said, his hands on his hips, motioning now and again at the work to be done. "Tell me something; did you buy this from Billy Treadwell or is he renting it to you? I never heard about it being up for sale. Billy likes to keep property until it falls down around people from neglect!"

"I know, he showed me a couple of his other houses," Loretta said, shaking her head and making shivering motions with her body. "They were disgusting! But this one was different. I took it, saw what needed to be done, and offered to get the work done if he'd apply the cost to my rent; give him the receipts. He said fine."

"Well from what I've seen, I think I can get you started. It's all pretty straightforward, but you seem to know that," Luke offered. "Give me a few days to work up a price, materials and labor, and I'll stop by. Or I can call."

"You can stop by if you like," Loretta said, trying not to sound too enthusiastic. "Stopping by would be fine!"

They turned to walk back to the front of the house and this time she followed Luke. *This guy wears his jeans better than Springsteen,* she thought as she watched him walking with a smooth, relaxed gait. *He moves like somebody that's already been everywhere he's ever needed to be. Momma always said 'age is good for one thing only: experience; it makes everything else ache, fade, or sag'. Everything about him says, "been there, done that."*

40

"So, I'm guessing you paint, plaster, and roof besides the carpentry? Do it all, huh?" she asked him as they arrived back at the front of the house. Luke turned and looked a little surprised.

"And you would know that...how?" he asked.

"You want me to tell you? Okay, well, even though your clothes are clean, like you said, some things just don't wash out. Your shirt has white and green paint spatters on it, love that plaid by the way; your boots have plaster or drywall on the tops and there's tar or roof sealer, 'bull' maybe, down by the soles. And to 'nail' that assumption, pardon the pun, you've got a Simplex nail in the heel of your right boot. Can't you hear it click when you walk? Why don't you take it out?"

Luke stared down at her, not wanting his incredulousness to show. "You took in all that since I've been here? You are something else, Miss Loretta!"

"Loretta," she said, "please." She had always had a problem with the "Miss" title. It was a small thing but one that bothered her, a pet peeve. "The only women that prefix their first names with 'Miss' are daycare workers or topless dancers. At least that's the way it is in Atlanta!" They both stood in front of her house on a beautiful September morning and laughed an easy laugh at her comment. Everything seemed magically correct with right then, right there. And both were hesitant to admit it to themselves. "Do you want some more coffee before you go?" she asked, trying to do something, anything, to prolong how good she was feeling right then. "I've got more made and I won't drink it all. If you don't help me. it'll just go to waste. You know, 'kids in China'?"

"Yeah, okay. I can stay a bit longer. It is good coffee, I

meant to say something before," he said as he followed her back up the steps onto the porch. Peach ran up to him from out of "cat nowhere" and started criss-crossing back and forth on his shins. "I can help if you need me to," he offered, petting the cat.

"I've got it, thanks," she answered as she came back with two more cups. "Here's your cream again."

"Thanks. What kind of coffee is this anyway? I don't think I've ever had this before, it really is good. Different tasting."

"I get it at a specialty store in Athens when I go there. It comes from a small coffee plantation in Ecuador, they say. Kind of hard to get, they don't have it all the time. The beans grow on the side of a certain mountain, they call it…'Montana del Guano'", she said, watching his face with apprehension, hoping he didn't know enough Spanish to fully comprehend the implications of the name. He did, just barely.

Luke looked up at her, then back down at the coffee, and started stirring it with a purpose, trying now to look into it. "Loretta, I don't understand much Spanish, and that's by choice, but I under…"

"I know, I know!" she said, her face cringing, her hand waving to cut him off. "But doesn't it taste good, though? I mean, it makes me feel a little queasy too, when I think about it, but I just try not to! I've been drinking it for a couple of years now, and I'm okay! Here's the story they gave me about how it's grown and why it tastes the way it does," she offered.

"Do I really want to hear this?" he asked, still staring intently into the cup.

"It is interesting if it's true; listen: this plantation where

42

the coffee bushes are, or whatever they are, trees, shrubs, is on the side of this mountain. Well, near the top of the mountain is a really, really big bat cave; supposedly millions of bats in it. Have you ever noticed that there's never just a few bats in a cave? There's always millions? It's like there's a permanent 'vacancy' sign out front or something. Anyway, when they wake up at night to leave the cave and go fly around looking for food, they... well, they poop, I guess, as they come flying out. You know, they just woke up and all...." She looked at him wide-eyed and hopefully, as if this explanation she was offering might somehow ease his concern. "And I suppose all this poop hits the bushes and beans and eventually gets washed into the ground by rain. I guess."

He stared back up at her. "Is that supposed to make me feel better?" he asked her. "Bats 'pooping' on the coffee beans I'm drinking right now?"

"But don't you think they sterilize them?" she asked him, hoping he could add a sanitary confirmation on the production of this 'bat-poop' coffee.

"What, the bats? What difference would that make?" he asked

"No, the beans! Aren't they sterilized or 'sanitized' or something like that?"

"Loretta, think about it," he said, giving up on finding anything solid floating in his coffee. "It's Ecuador! I doubt *anything* gets sterilized in Ecuador!" He looked at his coffee for a few more seconds then cautiously took another sip. "You know though, I can't argue with the taste; it *is* good coffee. Well, what the hell, I've had worse in my life, I'm sure. Just didn't know it. And probably paid good for it! I'll have one more cup for the road, then I've got to be going. 'Bat poop,' whatever, it's waking me up and that's the point."

Loretta came back with the pot, almost empty, and poured the last in Luke's cup. He watched intently as it poured in, looking one last time in the chance something observable might be sliding in along with the dark coffee.

"Is your mom still in Atlanta?" he asked.

"Kind of," Loretta said, forming a weak smile as she replied. "She died when I was eighteen. She's buried there. Breast cancer. It runs in her side of the family, so I have to be careful, you know? Screenings every year."

"I seem to be asking all the wrong questions…"

"No. Don't feel bad; honest, don't. I did take it hard for a while, but she and I had a long talk before she went, about life and death and letting go. Momma said: 'let go of the things that you really need to let go of, but fight like hell to keep the things that need to remain.' She was so good about it, so strong. She made me strong, too. She had in the past, when I was younger, about myself. That's the one thing I miss most about her; her strength. She wasn't an educated woman, just a lot of character. We're all each other had, in my life, anyway. She never remarried after my dad left us, never really dated."

"So you never knew your dad. Have you ever heard from him? Know much about him, what kind of man he was?" Luke asked. This was a phenomenon he never had to deal with in his life and he was curious how a person must feel about an abandonment he found so foreign.

"Never heard from him; don't know a damn thing about him, actually, except he came from northeast Georgia somewhere. They met in Doraville, that's all I know. Momma never talked much about him at all. I used to ask her, as a little girl, and she'd tell me there wasn't much to say; said she hardly knew him either, they were married such a short time. I always kind of figured she felt it too painful to go into. So I just let it fade as I grew."

Luke admired the way she talked so openly and frankly about what must be a truly vacant aspect of her life. It did show strength. Wherever she got it from, she had it.

"And you grew up on a farm? What was that like? What kind of farm did you have?" Loretta wanted to know. She was city-born and raised and she always felt the country had gently called to her in some way. After all, that was why she was here.

"We had peanuts, mostly, and cows too, but not for dairy; we didn't have enough acreage. We raised calves to a year or so and sold them. Yearlings. It was alright," Luke continued. "Farm life is hard, harder than most people think. It's where I learned to fix things, do carpentry work. There's certain things you just have to do, even when you don't want to. Crops need to come in, all that. Those things can't wait. There's really no days off. And not only did I have to help my dad, I had to help my uncle John, too."

Loretta saw him begin to fidget again when he mentioned his uncle. She asked a purposeful question to see if her observation was right. "He was your dad's brother, your uncle? You didn't mind helping, did you?"

"He, uh...he had suffered a heart attack when he wasn't very old," Luke said as his discomfort signs were starting to creep into his mannerisms again. He shifted and crossed his legs again as he spoke. "He couldn't do much, although I always suspected he could do more than he did. I never have liked being taken advantage of – no one does I suppose – but there wasn't much I could say." The stress and resentment he was showing with this subject was beginning to tell in his voice. "I did it for my dad. I knew it was important to him."

"What kind of farm did your uncle have?"

"He grew alfalfa.... and he raised dogs," Luke said looking away.

"Dogs? That must have been fun! What kind of dogs? What did you do?" Loretta asked, not being able to envision any earthly problems in a past in which one raised dogs.

When Luke turned his head back toward her, it was clearly evident his eyes were misty. She immediately felt bad having put this man she was quickly growing to like intentionally on the spot like this, without him even aware of what she was doing. *I can't imagine what the hell happened with dogs,* she thought, *but this little experiment's over.*

"Fox hounds. Can we talk about something else?" Luke asked. The strain in his voice was uncomfortably apparent to her.

"You bet," she said, more than willing to help him escape the recollection of what was obviously an emotional time in his past. "Hey, know what? There's something else you might be able to help me with besides this wood work," she said, attempting to sound upbeat with a totally different subject. "You know this town and the area as well as anybody would. I've been looking for a map to help me learn my way around this county. I've got a couple of places I'm going to try when I get the chance, but do *you* have any good ideas where I might go?"

"Find yourself getting lost when you head out of town, do

you?"

Luke asked, visibly recovering from his stress. "There's a lot of roads that go on and on. It's pretty easy to lose your way at first."

"That's what I'm trying to tell the damn people I work with!" she exclaimed. "They think I'm being a baby about it!" Loretta felt vindicated a second time about her directional ignorance.

"I know just the place to go, fix you right up. Go to the courthouse and go to the county clerk's office, real nice guy in there, Tom Billingham. He's the clerk of Ocoosa County. I've done work for him before. He's got maps in there, it's a county service. They cost, but not much; just covers the printing." Luke stopped talking and rubbed his chin in thought. "You know, I could pick one up for you…no, that's right too, I've got a remodel job I'm starting on in Thomasville early tomorrow morning; take most of the week. With the driving to and from, I'll be gone early and back late all week. Sorry."

"Hey, that's okay; at least I know where I can get one now. Thanks for the tip, anyway."

Luke rose to go, looked around to be sure he wasn't leaving anything, and looked down at Loretta who stood up also. "It's been a pleasure to meet you, ma'am. I'm looking forward to getting this job done for you," he told her.

"Just Loretta, please," she said.

"Of course, Loretta," he repeated. "Or 'Viper Babe', how about 'Viper Babe'?" he asked, laughing.

She laughed back. "Viper Babe," she said, as she weighed the sound of it. "I don't know. Three years ago that would have been me, for sure. I'll let you know when you get back to me with the quote, okay?"

"Okay, take care," said Luke as he turned to walk to his truck. His right heel clicked as he made his way down the concrete walkway. *Gotta take that damn thing out*, he thought as he opened the door and got in.

Loretta watched as Luke pulled out of her driveway and disappeared down the street. Her mind was swimming with a hundred thoughts as she turned to climb the steps to the porch. Two hours had passed since Luke had first arrived, but it seemed like a matter of minutes. *That's got to mean something,* she thought. She was glad she met him. He would be a good person to know for help around the house; that was for sure. And, she had to admit to herself, she liked his company. Loretta hoped she had managed to keep that from being blatantly evident to him while he was there. *A little evident would be okay,* she thought. She made a mental note to be sure to hit that specialty store again the next time she went to Athens.

CHAPTER 5

Thursday, September 14, 1995

For whatever reason, Thursday was slow at the Clinic and the staff found themselves looking for work to keep busy. Vanessa helped file old records, the same old records the nurses were trying to sort and update. Loretta noticed Dr. Harkness pass by the chart station and left her work to catch up to him in the hall, almost running to chase him down. "Doctor Harkness, wait up! Where you going in such a hurry?"

"Hey! Nowhere, I just move too fast for this small place, I guess. In Athens, you had so much distance to cover in the hospital, you just got in the habit of 'hoofing' it in the halls. I think I'm still programmed to accelerate when my feet are on industrial carpet or endless linoleum! What can I help you with?" He leaned back against the wall and folded his arms in front of him, his 'I have time' stance. *Good*, Loretta thought, *you need to slow down anyway.*

"I just want to thank you for sending Luke McClain over last Saturday, I haven't had the chance to do it yet. I haven't seen you long enough! So thanks!" she said, a little short of breath from chasing him. "He was over, checked out what I need done, and he got back to me with a quote last night on the phone. Way less than I would have thought. He says he'll start Saturday morning. Should work out well, I think." Loretta beamed at Dr. Harkness, proud of the progress she had made, and the friend.

"Well, good! I'm glad it did, he's a good guy."

"You'll be happy to know he says the same about you," she told him.

"Super! What did **you** think of him? Easy to talk to, isn't he? Real down to earth guy. Knows a lot about this place, too. You can ask him any thing about Watsonville, he knows the answer. He was born and raised right here."

"Speaking of which," Loretta burst in, "he told me where I can get a county map, like I asked you about. He said the same as you, go to a county office and they would have one. He knew right where, the county clerk's office. So, can I go?" Loretta started shuffling her feet and acting like a little girl trying get her father to let her do something she wanted to do, an act she was pulling off remarkably well for a woman who never had the opportunity as a child to actually play the part. "Doctor Harkness, can I go to the county clerk's office today and get a map so I don't get lost anymore and so nothing bad happens to me out on some dumb 'ol desolate road somewhere in the middle of a snowstorm, or..." she said in a sing-songy voice. She tried her best to sound cute. Evidently, Len Harkness thought she did.

"Yes! Go ahead and go! Stop it, you sound like a whiny little girl! We're not busy, go ahead and take off," he said as he smiled and shook his head.

***

Loretta left the clinic and decided to walk to the county clerk's office rather than drive. Only three blocks from where she worked and the weather being what it was, she thought the walk would be good for her. She needed to explore the town a little more anyway. After all, it seemed the town was why she had moved here. It was ideal for the lifestyle she had been picturing for herself, for the last several months at least. And she was still at a loss as to exactly why. Born and raised in Atlanta, her rather sudden yearning to escape the big city where she had felt comfortable and familiar for so long seemed strange to her at first, and even stranger to her friends, many of whom she had known most of her life. "I'm only an hour and a half away, tops," she would say when they would press her for the reason she was moving, never giving an explanation for her move. *Hell,* she thought, *I don't even know the reason myself why I'm picking up and moving way out here. Just seems like where I ought to be in my life right now.* And that was what she told anyone who asked, friend or stranger, when questioned why a single city girl would up and move to a town she had been through once in her life on an antique hunt, where she knew absolutely no one. "This just seems where I ought to be in my life right now." It was the answer she had to settle on for herself and it would have to suffice for the others. Loretta had never admitted to anyone what at least a part of that reason might be, simply because she couldn't explain it to herself.

Years before, on her one and only visit to Watsonville, she was acutely aware of what seemed to be a subdued tingling, almost a low-voltage current going through her the entire time she was there. As a stranger, she didn't want to appear crazy by approaching anyone to confirm if they felt anything odd also. She had tried to pass it off as something in the fast food she had eaten that afternoon, and she would have let it go at that, except for the fact that she distinctly felt it fade the further she got from town on her drive back home to Atlanta. *What the hell was THAT,* she asked herself as she passed the city limit sign out of town. *That felt like a low humming right in the pit of my stomach. Can't say it felt bad, though. In fact, it felt kinda... warm, almost soothing. That doesn't make any sense at all. Loretta, girl, you just better hush up about this and keep it to yourself, or they'll be **keeping** you in the big city in a WARD!*

And keep it quiet she did, even though she felt it begin again as she passed the welcome sign to Watsonville the day she arrived to start her new life there. She had thought after her move about enquiring around about power lines and such, but until she could formulate an accurate description of what she felt, she thought it was best just to let it go for awhile. *Maybe it's the water or something,* she told herself. Whatever it was, whatever the nature of it, might always remain a mystery. But the fact that it was there and real to her was always just under the surface, and since she was walking to the courthouse this fine day, she was going to take a few minutes to explore it a little more thoroughly.

The intersection of Gilmore Avenue and Garden Street was a place in the heart of Watsonville that Loretta drove through with frequency, going to and from the clinic. A typical small town intersection of paved streets with certainly nothing spectacular to distinguish it from any other, except for the one small fact that Loretta noticed the first time she drove through it on her way to work: the low humming sensation she felt while in town intensified there.

Walking up to the crossroad this morning, she could feel the sensation getting more noticeable, more widespread in her body. She approached slowly, experimentally, to let the growing feeling do whatever it was going to do. She didn't fear it; it was, after all, a pleasant feeling, one of well-being and lightness, and one that made absolutely no sense.

Loretta stood in the bright sunshine of the otherwise unremarkable intersection and took the time to drink in what she saw and felt. A small, red brick professional building lie to the left across Gilmore from her; a grimy little gas station hurting for business occupied the opposite corner. Right in back of her was a postage stamp sized parking lot for a store that sold braces and prosthetics. And directly across Garden Street from where she was now standing stood an innocuous, tall, pale yellow one-story building with no visible windows and two garage-type doors that opened right to the street. The only identification she could see was the street number above the solid wooden entry door at the far right end of the building front: 918 Garden, the chipped black paint read.

This isn't telling me anything, she said to herself, looking around, hoping to see something else that might shed some light on what she was feeling. *There's nothing here any different from any place else in this little town. I guess expecting to find some obvious microwave emitter or homegrown nuclear power plant was asking too much. Well,*

I'm just going to have to ask around about it sometime. Right now, I've got to get going.

Loretta turned and began walking toward the courthouse, stopping briefly to wheel around one last time to look the intersection over again, just in case something had escaped her inspection. Her eyes took in the entirety of the scene then quickly darted to the entry door of the yellow building across from her. There, just brief seconds after her last inspection, a short, balding man stood in front of the door, feet together, his hands apparently clasped behind his back. A pleasant, almost anticipatory smile filled his face as he leaned slightly forward, his eyes fixed on Loretta. His body language told her he wanted her to see him, to acknowledge him, to say something to him as he stood motionless and remained unnervingly silent.

*I **know** he wasn't there a second ago*, she told herself. *Where in hell...*she thought as she stared at this little man whose sudden presence was startling, yet at the same time strangely familiar and soothing. Loretta wanted to speak, step across the narrow street and approach this person and introduce herself, tell him her story of why she was there at this particular intersection on this sunny day. Instead, suddenly unable to find her voice, all she could manage was to simply smile back at him in her own friendly manner, slightly nodding her head at him, hoping her visual reply would prompt some response from this dark little man whose ample forehead gleamed in the bright sun. No reply came from him as he remained stationary, continuing his cheery, silent smile. *He looks so pleased, so happy*, she thought. *He's glad about something.*

The wordless exchange had been more than sufficiently made and Loretta felt the time had come for her to turn and depart when she became increasingly aware of a small dust-devil that struggled to form by her feet where the curb met the sidewalk. She dropped her eyes away from the man to observe the whirlwind swirl the dirt and litter of the street into a gentle spiral as it moved back around her through the lot, fading away half a minute later and leaving traces of a sweet smell she subconsciously recognized as the fragrance of flowers; jasmine, perhaps, with a lavender note.

Loretta looked back at the man with a final small nod of acknowledgement and she turned to walk to the courthouse. She intentionally stared down at the cracks of the broken sidewalk as she hurried her steps away from the intersection, feeling the intensity of the humming in her stomach fade just slightly. She fought the temptation to look back once more, a slight uneasiness taking over her consciousness. *No, don't do it*, she commanded herself. *This damned feeling you've got is hard enough to deal with. What are you gonna do if you turn around and there's no little man standin' there?* Though she knew better, knew what she had, in reality, just seen, for her own sake Loretta set about the mental task of convincing herself that nothing had been the least bit unusual there at the sunny, small town crossroad of Gilmore and Garden.

CHAPTER 6

Watsonville, founded in 1822 by Luther Watson, was at first a thriving small town whose initial claim to fame was tar and pitch, derived from the abundant pines that surrounded the area. As the trees were cut and not replanted, the economy shifted to dairy and poultry, making use of the cleared land, most of it owned by Luther and his family. Luther prospered, the town was named after him in 1827, and Watsonville settled in to earn its place among the dozens of small, unremarkable Georgia towns that fanned out from Atlanta. People of Watsonville seemed happy then. They seemed that way now. It helped that the town was reemerging as a quaint antique and bed and breakfast haven, with couples from as far away as Atlanta driving the distance just to walk the oak-lined streets and eat old-fashioned ice cream on weekends, discovering this new 'old' town, wandering the new 'old' shops that were opening all the time. Sometimes by just strolling down the streets and looking in the windows of the stores, it seemed that all the antiques in the country were somehow finding their way to Watsonville, a migration of the old but valuable. The unstated plan seemed to be that, in time, the notoriety would grow by word of mouth between Atlanta and Watsonville and a stream of yuppie-types would make the drive out to buy just the piece they were looking for to complete their upscale condos in Buckhead.

***

The clerk's office was practically empty when Loretta entered and walked up to the desk. The clerk seemed very friendly. Odd, Loretta thought, for a government employee. Most she had dealt with in the past, in any capacity, seemed to have had a chip on their shoulder, a grudge, or were just simply unpleasant people to begin with. She had always thought that there was a place on the job application for 'Crab,' and those that got hired had checked it. *Government service,* she was fond of saying, *the last bastion of the incompetent and cranky.* The clerk introduced himself as Tom Billingham and asked what he could do to help her.

Loretta's mood cheered to match his. "Well, I'm kind of new here, three months really, and I'm embarrassed to say it, but I get lost when I drive very far out of town. What I think I need is a map so I can at least look at something and get my bearings, you know what I mean? Luke McClain told me to come in and see you, said you'd fix me right up."

"Oh, Luke! Luke's a good guy, and a talented carpenter, too. How is he? I haven't see him in a while. He's fixed my place up so that I hardly know it's the same house I bought a year ago. New windows, repaired around the gables, everything."

Tom also agreed with Loretta's direction problem. "I

57

know just what you mean about not being sure where exactly you are sometimes. I've only been here a few years and I'm okay now, but at first I was mixed up by a lot of these long country roads that go on and on and if you're on the wrong one to begin with, you don't find out about it till you're way out of your way, really lost!" He leaned forward and whispered, "I'm really supposed to keep that a secret; I'm a man! And you *know* we don't stop and ask directions!"

Loretta laughed and said, "That's exactly what I'm talking about! My co-workers…"

"Where do you work?" asked Tom.

"The OB/Pediatric Clinic, just down the street."

"Oh yeah, I go by there all the time," he said. "Are you a nurse?"

"Yeah, I am." She continued, "My co-workers all think I'm crazy, always worried about not being able to find my way around, but hey, you know, like you said, who wants to get stuck out in the middle of nowhere, not even sure of where you are, right? Don't men feel that way?" she leaned forward, mimicking his confidentiality.

"Not that we'll admit!" Tom said with a laugh, and Loretta laughed with him. "I've got a county map here," Tom said, turning around and walking back to an old desk in the corner. He opened a bottom drawer, long and deep, and drew out a rolled map. "It's an older one, the newest edition won't be out, or here anyway, for a few weeks. Do you think you can do for a while with this old one? It should contain most everything you want to know, main and side roads and all. I won't charge you for it, it's old."

She slipped the band off the map and unrolled it, laying it

58

down on the wide counter. Her eyes wandered over it, a black and white tangle of squiggly lines going everywhere. It was almost as disheartening on paper as the actual roads were to her in reality.

"Hey, this is pretty cool," she said smiling. "Oh my God, look at all this! Am I ever going to be able to find my way around here?" she asked Tom as she shook her head.

"Oh, yeah. Give it some time. Much of what's there are dirt roads you wouldn't use anyway. You've got this now, and if you keep this with you in the car, you'll be just fine."

"Well, thanks so much for your help, 'Tom,' right?" Loretta said, shaking his hand.

"Yes, ma'am, Tom Billingham. It was a pleasure meeting you and I hope you come to think of Watsonville as your home."

Loretta laughed. "I already do," she said. "It's just that I can't seem to find 'my home' again if I drive too far out of town!" Walking out of the office and down the street back to the clinic, Loretta noticed that the sky and the air matched the mood she was in; sunny and bright. *Damn, I like this place!* she thought.

CHAPTER 7

L oretta entered the clinic through the back door and went to the employee lounge in the rear, putting her purse in her locker and opening the map again just to show anyone who was interested. "Hey y'all, 'lost Loretta' got herself a map, and it looks like a doozy!" she called out to whomever might be close by. "Come check it out!" As she looked it over, scanning the entire county that had been reduced to a flat, tangled mass of white space and thin black lines, two curious notations suddenly caught her eye. Small, handwritten additions to the map, each at opposite and remote areas of the county, were tucked in unobtrusively among the thin, broken lines that represented dirt roads. "INFANT BODY FOUND THIS LOCATION '89" the writing said at one side of the county, the other entry exactly the same, but with the date of '87; both entries very legible, very neat. A small "x" marked the spots. The entries would have been easy to miss except for being lettered in a blue ink that slightly contrasted with the black ink of the map. That slight contrast was more than enough for Loretta's eyes to notice. "What the hell...? Hey, y'all, somebody come in here and look at this and tell me I'm not seeing what I think I am," Loretta called out to anyone within hearing distance. She took coffee cups that were on the table and put them on the four corners of the map she had just spread out. Her finger alternated back and forth between the two inscriptions, as if to confirm what her eyes were telling her.

Vanessa wandered by and then Becky, each glancing at the map.

"What you got there, your map? What's up?" Vanessa asked casually, looking it over.

"This! This is what's up! Somebody wrote on here on purpose that these two places are where babies died, or where their bodies were found anyway. Is this true? Do you guys know anything about this? This is too weird, being on this map I just got," Loretta told her friends, her voice showing a marked concern.

"You know what? This one here, I remember this one when it happened, if it's what I'm thinking of," Becky said pointing to the site with the '89 date. "They were both patients here."

"Both? What do you mean, both? Did someone else die besides a baby?" Loretta asked, stunned at Becky's recollection. "What do you mean? What happened?"

Dr. Harkness entered the room just at the time Loretta was asking her question and Becky said, "Here's Doctor Harkness, ask him, he'll probably remember more that I can, I forget the details. He delivered the baby."

Loretta swung around to meet Dr. Harkness as he came in. "Doctor, do you know anything about babies dying, a mother and her baby dying in '89 that were patients here? Becky said they were patients. It's written on this map where they found the infant's body, and another one two years before that. What's going on?"

Len Harkness walked to the table, folded his arms in front of him and looked down at the map, studying it in its entirety. He nodded his head at the entries without saying a word. Loretta could not wait for his answer and was just about to speak. "Where'd you get this map, the clerk's office, like you said you were going to?" he asked Loretta.

"Uh-huh."

"This must have been used by some professional; police or investigators, maybe. My guess is it got put out for public sale by accident. Did you see where the clerk got it from?"

Loretta recalled the old desk the map came from. "You might be right," she said. "He took it from an old desk drawer, said it was an older map. Do you know about these? Do you remember these deaths when they happened?"

Len Harkness looked serious as he answered her, not looking up from the table. "Yes, I do. It was in the papers for days, police definitely thinking it was foul play, wanting anyone with any information to come forward, but no one did. This is way out in the country, the middle of nowhere. They finally assumed no one knew exactly what happened. Her husband was devastated when he found them that night when he got home. Police cleared him right away; he was in Ludlow working, had an alibi."

Loretta was beside herself with disbelief and questions. "Wha... what happened? They were *killed*, you mean? Did they find out who did it? Who was she? It was her baby, right?"

Dr. Harkness put up his hand and gently waved her back to get her to calm down. "Hold on, hold on, calm down and let me think a minute. One question at a time, it's been a while. Her name was... Melissa Shilke, and the baby's name was..." he rubbed his temple in an effort to recall the name of the baby that had died six years before.

"Tyler," Becky jumped in. "Tyler. I remember, he was cute. Eight, maybe nine days old when he died. Doctor Harkness delivered him. Good delivery, no complications."

"Yeah," he said, "Just another regular couple having a normal baby in a normal manner, getting ready to live normal lives; except something obviously went abnormal, somehow, for her to kill her baby and herself." Len crossed his arms again, shook his head and looked back to six years ago, trying once more to make sense of the abrupt and tragic event that had cost him many nights of sound sleep.

Loretta's eyes opened wide. "*She* killed the baby? The mother? And herself? You must be shitting me!" she said. She didn't curse out loud very often, not while at work anyway, and the people in the room turned their heads to look at her. Loretta was visibly upset. They didn't say a word to her about her language.

"The deaths were ruled a murder-suicide from the appearance at the scene by the examiner and the lack of any evidence to the contrary," Dr. Harkness explained, shrugging his shoulders. "The weapon was found by her body, a .357 magnum revolver. The husband, William, took care of the arrangements, buried them, and left the state. Went to Tennessee or somewhere. He wasn't a suspect, so he was free to go."

Loretta sat down in one of the break room chairs, motionless, stunned. "I'm finding this hard to believe, y'all. Don't you?" she asked, looking to her co-workers for agreement. They nodded their heads and looked solemnly over at the map. "What about the baby in '87? What happened then?" Loretta asked the group before anyone could leave. She looked up at Dr. Harkness for an answer.

"That mother and baby were not patients here; I didn't know them so I only remember what I read in the papers about that," he continued. "The mother was alleged to have had a history of mental illness, being treated for psychosis. Mother and baby were both found dead there outside the house. It was a brutal scene, the paper said. The mother and baby were patients of Doctor Stimson, Wendell Stimson, an old GP here in town; been here forever." Dr. Harkness walked slowly around the room, pacing to help himself remember. His hands were in his pockets and Loretta could hear the tell-tale jingling of change, but she knew from his demeanor that Dr. Harkness wasn't going anywhere, not quite yet. Habits and idiosyncrasies are never hard and fast, just a predictable guideline. "Wendell Stimson delivered a lot of babies around here before the clinic was built. Half the young people here in town probably had him as their pediatrician too. He did everything back then." Dr. Harkness said to the room.

"He's a nice old man, too," said Becky, "the kind of old practitioner you'd have liked to have had as your doctor growing up. Nice guy to talk to, he always has been when I've run into him."

Loretta turned toward Becky with some surprise. "You know him? Know him to speak to? How?" she asked.

"You see him around town, his office is, was, over on Dowling, right in the middle of town. He's involved with Watsonville functions and things sometimes still. He's a fixture here." Dr. Harkness replied.

"You said his office *was* on Dowling. Is he not there anymore?" Loretta asked.

"He retired a few years back. He's old, in his seventies. He wanted to enjoy the time he has left, I guess."

Vanessa, who had finished the last cup of bitter coffee in the pot, stood up to go back to her desk. "I've spoken to him too, from time to time when I've seen him at the store or the pharmacy," she said. "He mostly goes to the old drug store, Martin's, but when I've seen him he's always been nice to me; he knows I work here at the clinic and he seems to like people that work in the medical field, even if you're not a doctor."

Becky spoke up to confirm what Vanessa had just said. "Yeah, he seems to know all the medical people in town, somehow, and he's nice to us all. I've noticed that. I haven't ever heard anything bad about Doctor Stimson from anyone. Just a nice old man."

"Do you think he'd talk to me, being a nurse?" asked Loretta, looking around at anyone that might give her an answer considering their past dealings with this old GP.

"Maybe. What about?" asked Dr. Harkness.

"This," Loretta said, holding up the map. "It's 'kids', y'all. Kids are our business; it's what we all do for a living and what I love more than anything else in this world! This scares me and repulses me, too, at the same time. *If* Doctor Stimson delivered this baby, the one that died in '87, and we're assuming he did, maybe he was the girl's doctor too and he can tell me more than I know right now about this whole mess. I'd like to go talk to him if he'll talk to me, and see what he has to say."

"Chances are he's not going to want to divulge patient history to you," Dr. Harkness said, shaking his head and thinking of what his own response would be to someone inquiring about one of his patients that killed her baby and husband and then herself. "But if you're so determined to find out about these deaths, give it a try, he may talk to you if he knows you're a nurse. Who knows? Or, you could whine to him like a little girl. That seems to work well on some people." Loretta gave him a sideways glance, the meaning of which was lost to everyone else in the room.

"That's what I'm hoping," Loretta said. "Does anyone know where I can find him now?" She rolled the map back up and put a rubber band around it, then went to her locker to gather her purse and keys.

Dr. Harkness stood shaking his head. "You're going *now*? Alright, go ahead, you might as well. You won't be much good around here until you get some answers. I'll tell Doctor LaStazzi you're gone for the rest of the afternoon. We don't have much time left anyway, or peds patients scheduled for that matter."

"So where is he?" Loretta asked.

It was uncustomary for Len Harkness to initiate humor, but he saw the chance to do it one more time, and also to slip in a comment about work. "Doctor LaStazzi? Oh, he's probably in an exam room waiting for his nurse to show up, which I'll go tell him she's not going to do for the rest of the afternoon!"

"No, Doctor Stimson! I know; I'm sorry this thing has me

all upset. Tomorrow is my half day, but I promise I'll bust my butt tomorrow morning. Tell that to Doctor LaStazzi for me, will you?"

"I will, but he won't believe me; he knows you!" Dr. Harkness told her, a big grin on his face. "Sorry, I'm just on a roll!" Loretta walked over to him and lightly punched his shoulder, acknowledging his point and giving him some payback. The smile she returned said 'thanks for understanding'. The coins in Harkness' pockets were jingling again as he told Loretta what she wanted to know. "You can probably find Wendell Stimson at his home. Do you know where they're building the new Super Target just out of town on 15? Go just past that and on the right is an old neighborhood called Dreamy Acres. Nice place, old, a lot of older houses and lots of big oaks. He's on Sandman Street. I don't know the number, but you can't miss the house. It looks like something out of a fairytale, all gingerbread. It's yellow. In fact, I think Luke McClain did the work. Come to think of it, there was a photo in the paper when it was done."

Loretta thanked him and headed out to her car. She was hoping this old MD would talk to her. She needed to get to the bottom of this infanticide-suicide thing. It was just too bizarre for her way of thinking. Big counties like Gwinnett, Cobb, or Dekalb might have a problem like this on a regular basis, but not a county the size of Ocoosa. The odds shouted a definite *no*.

CHAPTER 8

L oretta pulled into the neighborhood and immediately saw what Dr. Harkness meant by old. Watsonville and the small towns in Ocoosa County all had areas that had been long-established, some kept up, some neglected, just like any town. Dreamy Acres was a slice out of time gone by, quaint streets laid out in a proper order, each lined with tall, ancient oak trees forming a shady canopy for their entire lengths. The houses were of the old architecture, small simple structures, mostly two-story, with gables and filigree work everywhere. The front yards were small, neat, showing the individuality of the owners, with the backyards disappearing into what looked like a collective enchanted forest. It was old, homey, and comfortable looking; a place older people would live in a small town like Watsonville, a place young people would pay a fortune to live in and raise their families in larger cities, if they could even find such a neighborhood.

Loretta had little trouble locating the house of Wendell Stimson. It was exactly as she had pictured it from Dr. Harkness' description. Yellow with white filigree trim, working shutters on the small blown-glass windows. Twin oak trees on either side of the walkway shaded the walk and the house. *If Luke did this work, he's a lot more talented than anyone has let on. Joints are sharp, angles look clean and right. He's good,* Loretta thought as she paused briefly on the walk to survey the work. She walked up the steps that led to the opened, railed porch. A collection of potted plants lay at the right end, all fighting for the few rays of sunlight that struck there through the trees. At the other end of the neat wooden porch was a double porch swing with brightly colored cushions lining the back and seat. A table was next to it, covered with a lace doily and two coasters, one of them being available for the large dark brown wicker chair that sat adjacent to the front door. *They sit out here often, and use this swing,* Loretta thought to herself as she rang the door bell and waited for a reply. *The cushions are clean and there's no dust on the table or coasters. No sense in keeping things so clean out here if you don't use them very much.*

The door opened slightly and half the face of an old woman peered out at Loretta. The face was questioning but not fearful. Why should it be? This was an old house in an old neighborhood in Watsonville, Ocoosa County; not Atlanta. Loretta could feel herself wishing she had grown up in a place like this; safe, quaint, slow.

"Can I help you, dear?" The woman spoke in a friendly tone, as some old people do, no matter who they talk to. "If you're selling something, I'm afraid we don't really need anything right now, I'm sorry."

My God, she's not even closing the door in my face, she's waiting for a reply, Loretta thought as she smiled at the woman and began to introduce herself. "No ma'am, I'm not selling anything. My name is Loretta Carmichael and I'm a nurse here in Watsonville. How do you do?" she said as she offered her hand to her. The woman she assumed was Mrs. Stimson smiled a friendly smile, opened the door wider and shook Loretta's hand. It was the hand of an old woman, wrinkled and soft from age; from doing the things with yarn and thread and bake trays that old women do inside their homes for the people left in their lives. Soft from having left the hard, rough chores of life to others years ago.

"Well, my dear, what can I help you with? Are you here to see Wendell? He doesn't practice medicine anymore you know, he's retired now."

"Yes ma'am I know, they told me at the clinic where I work he was retired, but I thought I'd drive out this way to see if he would have time to talk to me about a former patient of his. Is he home? I won't take too much of his time, I promise!" Loretta said, trying to be friendly in the way only a woman can be with other women.

"I'll go fetch him for you, he's just watching TV. Please, wait right here, or better yet, have a seat in our swing over there, it's very comfortable. We're out here all the time in the evenings, it's just so peaceful!"

Thought so, Loretta told herself.

The door shut and Loretta turned to sit on the swing that did indeed look inviting. She sat down and gently pushed herself back and forth in the shady, pleasant air of September. *This really is nice*, she thought as the rocking motion immediately put her at ease. *No squeak to the chain, they do use this a lot. They wouldn't put up with a squeaky chain very long.* The relaxation she was sliding into was broken by the appearance of Dr. Wendell Stimson, who opened the door and turned his head to locate her on the swing. He approached her, smiling and said, "Well, I see you found our swing! Isn't it nice? How do you do, I'm Doctor Stimson."

Loretta rose to shake his hand and introduced herself all over again to this kindly old man. He was the epitome of how one would picture an old, country doctor; neatly dressed from having been so his entire professional life, recently cut white hair, another habit hard to break after so many years of keeping a professional image. A kind face with an expression of genuineness, a man that had listened to thousands of problems and complaints over many years and treated them all with similar concern. Dr. Stimson retained that certain 'bearing' so often found in older professionals.

"You sit over here," Loretta said, "I know how comfortable it is, I want you to be comfortable." Dr. Stimson sat down on the swing and settled back.

"Thank you for seeing me," she said, taking a seat in the wicker chair. "I won't take much of your time; I'm sure you have other things to do."

"Not at all, Loretta; may I call you Loretta? Now that I'm retired, I have the time to do what I want, when I want. What has surprised me is that there isn't as much to do as I thought there would be! Now, what is it that I can do for you, dear?"

Loretta laughed at his observation and thanked him again. Her mood segued into a more serious tone. "What I'm here to ask about is a former patient of yours, perhaps two patients. You were their physician, I think, until 1987."

"And who would they be?" Dr. Stimson asked.

"Norma Duncan and her baby," Loretta replied, watching

his face for reaction.

Though the pleasant smile did not evaporate completely, Loretta could see Dr. Stimson's face stiffen a bit at the mention of the names. He sat back slightly and gazed down at the floor as if recalling the two for the first time in a while. Seconds passed by before he spoke. "Yes, they were both patients of mine. I was the mother's doctor all of her life, and I had just delivered her daughter, Cassie I believe her name was, a week or so before it all happened." The recollection was working its way into Dr. Stimson's consciousness as he spoke. "Tell me, Loretta, why do you want to know about these people? This happened several years ago and it's not a pleasant memory. Are you related in some way?"

"No sir, I'm not related to them at all, you see, I'm new to this county. I've been here a little over three months and I just today found out about this, well… incident, and the one in '89 with the Shilke woman and her baby. I honestly hate to dredge up unpleasant memories for you, but there are things, facts, that I just feel I have to find out for myself about all this. I can't really explain it other than my own curiosity and the fact I love children." As Loretta talked to him, Dr. Stimson displayed interest in her story, the same interest and ability to listen that made him the popular general practitioner he had been for so many successful years.

"I'll answer what I can", he told her. "There was a great deal of information printed in the papers when these things happened. Have you read any of it? It might help you."

"No sir, I guess that would be the next step if I can find the old articles. I would like to read them. Do you have any I could look at?" Loretta asked him.

"Dear, no. I read them in the news when they happened, talked to some professionals concerning Norma and her baby because they were, in fact, patients of mine, and then I tried to forget the incidents as I suppose most people did."

Loretta knew her first question was the one Dr. Stimson would probably not be willing to answer. Asking a physician to share a patient's history of mental illness with a stranger, even if she was a nurse, was a long shot. She felt if she could at least confirm, by his admission, that Norma Duncan was mentally ill at the time of the murders, it would go a long way toward at least explaining to her how this particular incident could happen in this otherwise peaceful little Georgia County. "Sir, the people at the clinic where I work..."

"Oh, you work at the OB/Pediatric Clinic, with Drs. Harkness and LaStazzi? How nice! They're a great bunch over there. I know most of the staff." Dr. Stimson perked up slightly at the connection he had made.

"Yes, I do, and they all seem to like you very much also, sir; they all hold you in the highest regard." Loretta leaned a bit toward the doctor to emphasize the private and serious nature of her question. "The people I work with that were discussing what they knew of this particular case said they believed that Norma Duncan had been treated, or was being treated, for mental illness prior to the time she killed herself and the baby. Doctor Stimson, can you tell me if that's true? Was she, in your opinion as her doctor, mentally ill at that time? I know I'm asking a lot of..."

Wendell Stimson leaned forward in the middle of Loretta's sentence and for the first time his face reflected the gravity of the subject at hand. It was evident he wanted to speak. Loretta stopped talking to listen to what he obviously wanted to say. "Ms. Carmichael, at one time I would have considered your question a rude and unprofessional breach of ethics. And I would, at this point, have sent you away."

Loretta felt the warmth of embarrassment rushing to her face. She liked this old man and didn't want him to think badly of her, professionally or personally. "Doctor, please excuse me..."

Dr. Stimson raised his hand to stop her again. "I said 'at one time'. I've changed with time, as have circumstances, with this instance and others. These people you are inquiring about have been dead for some time; no family has come forward. There is probably no good reason, ethically or legally, to withhold information I may have that will help you toward whatever end you're seeking." He sat back in the swing and the pleasant look began to occupy his face again. "I was that girl's physician all of her life, and I can assure you that she was not mentally ill during the time I treated her, nor was she being treated for mental illness by anyone, at least to the best of my professional knowledge."

Loretta stared at the doctor, somewhat surprised at his declaration. This didn't help solve a thing. "Then why...what happened?" she asked, visibly confused.

"The 'why' of it we'll probably never know, my dear," Dr. Stimson said. "Something undoubtedly has to go very wrong very quickly in the life of an otherwise healthy young woman to cause her to kill her child, husband and herself so cruelly."

"Her husband too? I didn't know that! No one told me her husband died too!"

"They didn't tell you that? Perhaps they forgot. The paper talked about it at length. She shot her husband and then herself."

"And the baby? Then she shot the baby also?"

"No, my dear," the doctor replied, himself a bit surprised now. "The baby didn't die of gunshot wounds. Cassie Duncan died from blunt trauma to the head; massive trauma. Her cranium was crushed."

Loretta was shocked immobile at what she was hearing. She was just about to force herself out of her daze when Mrs. Stimson appeared to her immediate left, startling her out of her trance, carrying a tray with a Tupperware pitcher of iced tea and two glasses.

"Thought you'd like some refreshments," she said as she put the tray down on the small common table between them. "I'll leave these and leave you two alone to talk some more," she said as she spun to go back inside, sensing something important was being discussed. They both thanked the back of her as she disappeared through the doorway into the house.

Dr. Stimson could see Loretta had questions she could not verbalize and attempted to help her. "I was summoned to the crime scene. It was at their residence on Colman Crossing Road. The county medical examiner, Arlo Powers, called me out there. It was unusual for me to visit a crime scene, but he felt the fact that they were my patients, and the extreme circumstances, warranted it. I had my receptionist cancel my patient appointments for the rest of the afternoon. Later on that day, I was glad she did." Dr. Stimson interrupted his narration to pour a glass of tea for himself and Loretta. He was calm, actually at ease, as he asked her if she wanted sugar with hers.

All Loretta could manage at this point was to nod her head and stare at him, her face frozen in a frown. "What we saw there showed me, Arlo, and the sheriff, that the deaths were especially gruesome. It would almost seem that Mrs. Duncan could not have committed these murders by herself. But apparently she did; no other evidence was found to indicate, much less prove, that anyone else was involved. Norma Duncan was obviously quite motivated to have done what she did with such malice."

Loretta weakly spoke, needing to get past her shock and ask the questions she felt she must. "Did...did she kill her husband because he was trying to defend the infant? Did he happen on the situation and try to stop her?" she asked, feeling her throat tighten around her words.

"The examination of the scene told the M.E. and the sheriff, almost conclusively, that the husband, Richard Duncan, may have witnessed Norma abusing the infant or at least treating it in an unsafe manner of some sort. There was a struggle inside the house and blood was found; the husband's and that of the baby. Norma must have had the revolver, a .38, at that time because she used it at that point to kill Richard there in the living room. He was shot five times point-blank in the chest. He died immediately. We felt the reason she did not fire all six was she was intentionally saving the last round for herself, but not, as it seems, for the child."

The unfolding of this story had Loretta riveted, sitting on the edge of the wicker chair, alternately crushing and straightening a paper napkin that had come with the iced tea. "My God, why did you think that? Why didn't she just shoot the baby too, if she intended to kill it?"

Dr. Stimson slightly shrugged his shoulders and looked mildly perplexed at her question. "That's something we'll never know, most likely. At that point, the scene suggests she took the infant outside into the front yard. The house, as I said, is out on Colman Crossing, way out of town, remote even for Ocoosa County. They had no immediate neighbors so there were no witnesses. And no one could hear that poor infant screaming…" Dr. Stimson said, his voice trailing off and his eyes staring somewhere out beyond the porch. He turned his misting eyes back to Loretta. "You know what it sounds like, you're in pediatrics: that rapid, rhythmic wailing an infant does with all its strength out of instinct when it's in great pain or panic…" He stopped when he saw the tears streaming down Loretta's face. He knew she understood exactly what must have taken place in that yard; what it must have sounded like. Dr. Stimson composed himself and continued slowly, attempting to maintain control of his own emotions and the story. "Approximately twenty yards or so from the house, she stopped, threw or dropped the child to the ground, and then did something so bizarre that none of us have been able to come up with a good explanation for it."

Loretta was beside herself with intensity. Her face cringed in anticipation for what the doctor had to say next. "What did she do then?" she asked, breathless.

"The scene shows she then crawled around on the ground on her hands and knees, apparently purposefully trying to choose the right size stone from the yard with which to crush her baby's head. She loosened three, then decided on one about the size of a cantaloupe, for want of a better comparison, I apologize. It was this stone she used to crush the head with one blow."

Loretta put her hand up to her mouth to cover it, not wanting Dr. Stimson to see the anguish overtaking her. She stood and quickly walked the few feet to the top of the steps and there attempted to regain her composure. She felt she needed to maintain her professionalism in front of this man who over the course of his long practice undoubtedly had seen his share of death, much of it intentional and some, most assuredly, violent. She however, had not. She turned back to him when her breathing had subsided to normal again and asked, "No one knows why? What caused her to do this?" Loretta needed answers. She needed them before when she knew so little. She needed them even more now that she knew so much.

"No. Only Norma Duncan could have told you that," Dr. Stimson said in his calm manner. His voice had an inflection to it that told Loretta he had something else to say, something he had not yet told her. His body language said the same thing. He lowered his voice slightly and spoke his next words concisely, clearly so he would not have to repeat them. "What I'm going to tell you next I haven't discussed with anyone, not even my wife. This fact was not released to the public. The M.E. and the sheriff both felt it was best to suppress it, for fear it might start some sort of heinous copycat crimes or draw unwarranted connections to satanic groups as so often happens with such cases."

Loretta was now staring intently into his face. "What?"

"Remember I said that evidence of the baby's blood was found in the house prior to the actual death?"

"Yes," Loretta replied, the word barely escaping her lips.

"Norma..." he stopped to gather his composure, which

that he felt was about to slip again, as he weighed what he was about to divulge. He cleared his throat, took a deliberate breath, and spoke. "Norma evidently had taken a pair of scissors and carved the word 'EVIL' in the baby's back. It's unknown why. We know that she did it because the scissors were recovered with the baby's blood on them there on the floor. Her prints alone were on them. And the newborn's body showed the mutilation to have been very recently done, perhaps within the hour, judging from the freshness of the wound and the coagulation. Maybe Richard walked in and discovered her in the act of doing this, or found it later, but this most probably was the cause of his struggle with his wife and ultimately his death. I've not divulged that to anyone, but at this late juncture, I thought you should know everything since you are after all the facts."

Loretta recoiled and felt her legs get weak. She sat down on the top porch step and let her tears flow, not caring what the doctor felt about it. To hell with professionalism. She was a nurse and a woman that loved children and babies, and what she had been told by the good doctor that afternoon was the stuff her nightmares were made of. Dr. Stimson gently rocked back and forth in the swing and allowed Loretta to cry as she needed to do, to let the anguish she felt flow out with her tears. No one could blame her for breaking down under such circumstances, or do much to stop her. He finished the tea in his glass and poured more for her, anticipating she may want it when her crying was over and she settled down.

She slowly recovered, balled the wet napkin in her hand and stood to face him. "I don't know what to say," she said, her breathing still heavy. "I... as horrible as this all is, I appreciate your sharing this information with me, these details. I guess I found out a lot more than I came here for."

Looking at her with a neutral expression, Dr. Stimson nodded his head. As cathartic as it may have been for him to tell her these facts, the conversation had brought back vivid memories from the day he stood in that remote front yard of red clay and rock, looking down at a dead woman he had known since he had delivered her as a baby twenty years prior, her body next to her own infant he had handed to her only six days before. Fortunately, most men are not tested this way in their lives.

Loretta took one last drink of tea and thanked him again. "And tell your dear wife thank you for the tea," she said as she started down the steps. She reached the bottom and turned to see the doctor standing at the top. His expression suggested he had something further to add. "Was there something else, Doctor Stimson?" she asked.

He stood with his hands in his pockets, a look of curiosity on his face. "Perhaps one last thing. What did the people at your clinic tell you about the deaths in '89, the Shilke woman and her child?"

Loretta stared up at him while searching her memory for the facts she had just recently been told. "Doctor Harkness said that the mother had seemed very normal to him prior to the birth, that the husband had not been present when Mrs. Shilke had shot herself and the baby. Why? Is there anything else? Is that not accurate?"

Dr. Stimson walked down the steps and stood in front of Loretta, closely, so that she could clearly hear what he was about to say. "Ms. Carmichael," he said softly, glancing around briefly to ensure the privacy of what he was about to divulge. "I had hoped I was done upsetting you for the day, but, no, that's not entirely accurate. Arlo Powers informed me, as a professional courtesy a while after the case, that Mrs. Shilke did indeed kill herself with her husband's .357 revolver by putting the barrel in her mouth and pulling the trigger. Very intentional. Very final. And a very gruesome scene. Now, I don't remember if the papers mentioned this or not, but the baby did not die of a gun shot wound. The cause of death was, as in the Duncan case, blunt trauma to the head. Again, and we can't explain this either, a stone was used as the implement."

Loretta continued to stare at him while this new revelation sunk in and added further complications to her crusade for facts. Her senses were screaming to her mentality that this could not be happening, not in a small town, a tiny, peaceful county like this.

"Tell me, have you attempted to talk to the sheriff about this at all?" Dr. Stimson asked. "If you plan to, I would suggest at this point you forget about it. The sheriff that investigated both cases, Roy Kingrey, retired abruptly perhaps three years ago. Cardiac trouble; he's now in Arizona for his health. He did a great job with the investigations; he was a good sheriff for this town."

"And the present sheriff? Why shouldn't I talk to him about it?" Loretta wanted to know.

"You *can*, of course. His name is Lamar Franklin. He was Roy's deputy when Roy had to retire, so he got the job by default. Until the next election, that is. Then he'll be gone."

"What's wrong with him?"

Dr. Stimson smiled. "In my time, the old days, he'd have

been called a whipper-snapper. In today's vernacular, I think the word to describe Lamar Franklin is punk. I don't care for him. He's worthless as a sheriff."

"Punk?" Loretta asked, cocking her head in mild surprise, wondering if the doctor knew the current associations to the word.

Still smiling at her, the doctor replied, "I said I have a lot of time to occupy, my dear. I even find myself watching MTV sometimes. Yes, punk. I know what it means!"

She laughed slightly to ease her own tension and he joined her to walk her to her car. She opened her door and turned again to thank him for his help. "Thank you. I'm sorry you had to dredge up these old memories just to help me."

"It's alright, my dear, as long as it helps you find out what you want. Now if you want to see our illustrious sheriff in action, if you stop by the Midway Diner you can probably find him in there flirting with whatever waitress happens to be working; he doesn't seem to care who it is. I think you'll change your mind about asking him anything. It's up to you, of course. I will suggest one other source that may be able to shed more light than I have about these deaths: Gerald Martin."

"Of *Martin's Pharmacy?*"

"Yes, that's him; he's been around for a long time, I've known him most of my life. His store used to get almost all my pharmacy business. The store was a fixture downtown for many, many years. One thing about Gerald, he's difficult to deal with sometimes; a bit cantankerous when he feels like it. But catch him in the right mood and he's a wealth of information about Watsonville and the county. He has his own theory about these deaths, a bit unconventional perhaps, but that's up to you to decide, if he's in the mood to share it with you. Try him. I'm pretty sure he's there."

Loretta mouthed the words "thank you" and got into her car.

CHAPTER 9

Friday, September 15, 1995

From the time she arrived at the clinic that morning, all Loretta could do was talk about the conversation she had the day before with Dr. Stimson. She followed anyone that would listen, telling them the details as they had been told to her, all except the information concerning the mutilation on the Duncan child. She felt Dr. Stimson had told her that in confidence and did not want to break such a confidence if it did in fact exist. The reactions she received from her co-workers were concerned, naturally, this involving the deaths of babies. But she failed to see the same intensity in the others that she herself felt. Perhaps it was the fact that it had happened so long ago for these people, that time had softened the edges on all this to them; she wasn't sure. All she knew was that something was driving her personally to get to the bottom of all this, and that the morning hours were passing extremely slowly that day.

She worked until three that afternoon and already planned to stop by and talk to this Gerald Martin person as Dr. Stimson had suggested. She hoped he could add to what she had learned so far, though she found herself wondering from time to time that morning if she could actually handle anymore than she already knew. Three o'clock came and Loretta was headed out the door to find Martin's Pharmacy.

She drove a little faster than normal, taking the turns through Watsonville's downtown a little sharper than she ordinarily would have. The rolled map was by her side, and every time she glanced down at it, more questions came to her. Loretta was more confused now than when she began this search and considerably more concerned. *What does all this mean? What the hell happened to these women to make them do what they did? Is this all?* Her car swung down Main and off to the side her eye happened to catch the sign for the Midway Diner. There, parked in front, was a car marked **OCOOSA COUNTY SHERIFF**. *I've got a minute, I need to check this out,* she thought, *and I could use some coffee to settle my nerves. Think I'll go see my tax dollars at work for myself.*

Loretta pulled up and parked in front of the diner and noticed right away hers was the only other car in the parking lot. Entering, she looked left and right only to find one Lamar Franklin sitting at the far left end of the counter, busy flirting and making small talk with the one waitress she could see working. They appeared to be having a wonderful time, laughing and touching like two high school kids who had just started dating. Except he was the county sheriff, who undoubtedly had other things he could be doing, and she appeared to be the only waitress on duty, who definitely had plenty to do by the looks of the diner. Putting her purse on the counter, Loretta took a stool far to the right of the lovebirds, propped her elbow on the counter and rested her head on her hand, staring at the two purposefully to see how long it would take to get their attention. *Sooner or later they have to notice the only other person in here*, she thought. Minutes went by and finally her staring annoyed Lamar to the point that he stopped his flirting long enough to yell over to her, "Can I help you with anything?" The irritation in his voice was unmistakable.

Loretta calmly answered, "Yes you can, if you'd like to get me a cup of coffee. If not, maybe you can persuade your friend there to do it."

The sheriff said something inaudible to the waitress and she headed toward Loretta with a slow deliberate walk. *Ooookay, so this is how it's gonna be*, thought Loretta. The waitress stopped in front of Loretta and asked if there was anything she could help her with, her attitude matching Lamar's.

"Yeah, that cup of coffee I just mentioned would be good. Got any fresh?" Loretta asked.

"In fact I do, you're in luck."

"That's me, just lucky," Loretta said in a sarcastic tone.

"Anything else?"

"Maybe, depends on how good the coffee is." *Yes honey, I got you all the way down here away from your touchy-feely romance with Barney just to get me a coffee; deal with it.* The waitress put the cup in front of Loretta and told her if she didn't think she wanted anything else, the coffee was $1.06. Loretta looked in her purse, found a dollar bill and a quarter and put them on the counter. "Yeah, I guess that'll be all," she said, looking down the length of the counter at Lamar, visibly impatient with the waitress. "Everything I needed has been taken care of, I guess." She finished the last of her coffee and walked back out to her car. *He does seem to be a useless little punk*, she thought. *Dr. Stimson hit that character analysis right on the nose. Let's see if he's as accurate about this old pharmacist.* Her car rolled back onto Main and she drove the short distance to the onetime Watsonville landmark, Martin's Pharmacy.

CHAPTER 10

L oretta pulled up to Martin's Pharmacy and surveyed the front of it as she shut off her car. It was immediately apparent why the older residents of Watsonville made up most of the clientele that still came here. The big mortar and pestle above the door, the advertisements in the windows, all said "yesterday." Back when this was the only place to go for prescriptions and sundries, it had done a good business, she had been told, and recalled that fact as she opened the door and walked in. *Oh, this is too perfect*, Loretta thought, looking around the inside of the store. *This is history right here; living history. Well, kinda living, anyway.* A small, neglected soda fountain occupied the wall on the left side of the store, undoubtedly *the* place to be at one time in the distant past. Advertisements for products she hadn't heard of since she was a little girl hung from the ceiling and walls, yellowed and water-stained. Hunter fans, big and brown, hung here and there, rotating slowly, more now for appearances than for moving air, creaking and groaning from lack of oil. A few elderly men and women were scattered throughout the store, casually looking at the same products they likely had purchased here for decades.

One by one they took them from the shelves to slowly meander up to the counter to buy them at least once more.

Loretta located the pharmacy counter at the back of the store, a smaller counter that looked like the square entrance to a dimly lit cave. Shelves of drugs could be seen in the semi-dark in back of the man standing behind the counter, who was busy looking looking down at a brochure. Thinning gray hair, long-sleeve checkered shirt buttoned up to the neck, suspenders holding up brown polyester pants. This had to be Gerald Martin, proprietor, owner, local historian of Ocoosa County, one more person that might put some more facts to the locations on the maps she held under her arm. She walked down the worn green linoleum aisle that led to the counter and stood in front of it for an awkward thirty seconds or so before the man behind it acknowledged her presence. *What, am I friggin' invisible today?* she wondered. "Um, Mr. Martin? Gerald Martin?" she asked to finally break the awkward silence.

He slowly looked up over his half-glasses, almost perturbed as though she had interrupted something important. "Yes. What can I help you with?" Loretta was young. He knew he did not recognize her. "You don't have a prescription to pick up, do you?"

"Ah, no I don't, really. I, actually," she stammered, "I'm here to see if you can help me with something. You see…"

"Do I know you, missy? I don't remember seeing you in here before. I remember most of my customers, most been coming here so long, but I can't place your face. You new here?" Gerald's words poured out one after another, a soliloquy that would have been hard for anyone to interrupt. It was obvious he was used to saying what he felt he had to say all at once, and used to people letting him do it.

"Mr. Martin, my name is Loretta Carmichael, and, yes, in fact, I am new to Watsonville. The people I work with…"

"You like it here?" Gerald asked abruptly, cutting her off again.

"Excuse me?" Loretta responded, puzzled.

"Do you like it here? Watsonville, you like it? It's a good little town, used to be real good back when, but things change, you know. Most folks here still like it, that's why they stay, most likely. You been here long, missy?"

"It's Loretta, sir. I've been here about, oh, three months or so, and yes I do, I do like the town a lot, but I got this map…"

"A map? Of what?" he asked

"The county, Mr. Martin. Ocoosa County," Loretta replied, becoming a bit irritated with the one-sided course of the conversation so far. "You see, I've been getting lost when I leave…"

"You get lost easy? That why you think you need a map? Well, that's women for ya. I never seen it fail. This county ain't that big or complicated to find your way around in, but in my life, I've seen more women pulled off the side of the road…"

"*Mr. Martin*," Loretta interjected, "I just need some help with some writing I found on the map, not help with the map itself, or directions really. I'll get around okay in a while, when I venture out a little bit more."

"What writing?" Gerald asked, now more inquisitive than lecturing, looking down at the map. "Where'd this map come from, anyhow?"

Loretta felt it might now be her turn to get a word in edgewise with this odd old man and she proceeded with as much information as she could think of, attempting, for the first time, to dominate this conversation. "I got the map, actually, from the county clerk yesterday, just to be able to familiarize myself with the roads around here, and in looking at it closely yesterday, I noticed these handwritten notations here and here about baby deaths having happened at these locations. I asked the people I work with…"

"Where you work, missy?"

Damn it! she thought. "At the OB/Pediatric Clinic on Crossler Street. I'm sure you know it," she replied, trying to remain calm.

"Oh, yes ma'am, I know it alright. Never get a bit of business from them now that that Rite-RX got built. That damn store took more of my business than…"

"Mr. Martin, look, I'm sorry that the clinic changed accounts, but that happened long before I came here. Now, if I can just get you to look at these notations, see what you think or know, I'd appreciate it lot. You see, I find it pretty disturbing that a map has two…"

"Must have been a police map, sheriff's map or something like that to have this writing on it. Billingham give it to you by mistake, maybe?" Gerald asked.

"Tom Billingham, the clerk, yes, he gave it to me. He said this was an outdated map, that there were some he was expecting that would be updated. I took this one because I said it really wouldn't matter, just as long as it showed me my way around on the roads. Then I saw the writing. What do you think this means, Mr. Martin? Do you know? I'm sure you've heard of these before. I've been told you know a lot about the county, what's gone on here in the past and all. Doctor Stimson suggested I talk with you, he says you're the expert on this county and the things that have happened here. That's why I came here."

Gerald's expression turned even more serious. He looked at Loretta as though she had broached a subject that was off limits. "Yes, I know something about these dead kids. Most folks are familiar with it but don't really want to talk much about it. Mostly put it out of their minds, go on about their business. They've been in the papers, those deaths, the ones in '89 and '87. I doubt most folks prob'ly even give much thought anymore to the ones in '84 or '77 or before."

The shock of what she was hearing showed on Loretta's face. "There have been other infant deaths?" she asked.

"Four since 1977; others before that, scattered over time. They weren't just deaths either, missy, they were murders, did you know that?" Gerald said as he leaned forward to leer at Loretta. His eyes narrowed as he spoke.

Loretta stepped back and looked around for something to sit on, finding one of the old wooden chairs used by the customers to wait for prescriptions. She sunk down into it. "How can that be? What the hell is going on around here?" she asked him from the chair, waiting for some explanation she could understand.

"You been around this area much? Been driving around out of town, out in the country? Fields, pastures rolling out into tree lines and woods. Real peaceful looking, quaint, like a picture, ain't it? Well, those woods and fields are carrying somethin'; a burden."

"What burden?" she asked.

Gerald hesitated with his reply. Then quietly, with a matter-of-fact tone, he leaned and again squinted out his reply. "Ghosts, some might call it. Spirits."

"Ghosts?" Loretta replied, mentally rolling her eyes.

"That's right. I've felt it all my life when I've been out there, in the countryside. I don't know what else you'd call it. It's a feeling, like a presence. Ever since my daddy used to take me out there when I was little, he'd ask me, "Can you feel it, son?" and after a while I got so that I could, a feeling like something bad had happened where we were, out there certain places in the county. These things happened a long time ago, back before any of us were born, even before my daddy was born. But he felt all his life that things that went on here way back are still causing problems, making some people here in Ocoosa pay a price, a dear price."

Loretta was suddenly feeling she was being led down one of these country roads she had talked about by an old man who had found a new audience. "Sir, what does all that have to do with what I'm asking about? Are you trying to tell me ghosts killed those little babies and adults?"

"Plenty to do with it," Gerald replied, straightening, with a new tone of authority in his voice. "The land remembers what's been done upon it."

"What?" Loretta asked, the agitation clear now in her voice, her patience just about exhausted.

"The land remembers the evil what's been done on it; impartial, it doesn't judge. Unblinking, it's time's perfect witness."

"What does that mean? Is that from the Bible or something?"

"It's from my father," Gerald said, sternly looking at Loretta. "And I believe it too, now that I've gotten older."

Loretta at last found something to agree with. "Older, uh-huh, I think that's part of the problem going on here. Look, I'm getting a little impatient with this whole thing, sir. I came in here to see you especially, looking for some help, and I feel like I'm getting some kind of mumbo-jumbo runaround. Can you help me with this or not? Do you know why these babies have died? Or been killed?" she asked, her exasperation starting to raise the pitch in her voice.

"You just don't understand, missy," Gerald said as he shook his head.

"I guess the hell I don't, excuse me, but I want to know about baby deaths, not some spooky history of this whole damn county, now, can you understand *that*? And for the last time, damn it, it's LORETTA!" she said, shaking slightly.

She could see this was getting nowhere except to make her much angrier than she needed to be on what could have been a pleasant Friday night. She tucked the map under her arm and raised her hands up in defeat. "I'm out of here, sir, thanks for your time anyway," she said with mock appreciation. "I'll find some other way to get to the bottom of this, find out what's going on."

Gerald watched as she turned and walked down the aisle and out the door, closing it loudly behind her. *I truly hope you don't, missy*, he thought as she disappeared into her car. *We don't know; and it's probably too late now to find out.*

***

What the hell do I have to do to get answers around here? Loretta wondered as she wheeled her car through the last few streets of Watsonville. *The friggin' county sheriff is useless, that cranky old man is talking ghost stories. Jesus! Baby deaths, the map says baby deaths! And now I find out that even more than these two have been murdered! Is that such a casual, nonchalant item in this town that nobody wonders about it but me?* she asked herself, more and more incredulous as she drove. *I need to find that fruit stand Vanessa talked about, get some fruits and vegetables and go home, fix something to eat and calm down. I don't like this, not a damned bit. This is small town, country-ass bullshit!* She drove out of town on Route 10 just as the receptionist had said to do. The sun was beginning to drop quickly and the mellowing countryside was starting to take its effect on Loretta's mood. She felt her control slowly flowing back into her as she drove, mending her nerves. The sign for the Miller Bridge crossroad was coming into view. Loretta slowed to a stop at the intersection and looked both ways. Nothing. *Damn it!* she thought. *Which way am I supposed to turn?*

***

The trees and fields of Ocoosa County watched in silence as Loretta Carmichael drove past, so preoccupied with the here and now. This land was, as she had just been told, merely the indifferent harborer of memories.

CHAPTER 11

Ocoosa County, Georgia
Dawn, Friday, November 18, 1864

T he first red darts of cloud-fought sunlight cracked the tree line and spilled down into the open space, revealing an acre of undulating horse flesh and rope. Ragged men in disheveled blue uniforms coughed and spit and worked their way into the writhing mass of animals, their cursing vapor-breath mixing with the steam of urine and dung and a thousand flaring nostrils. The Union Army of General William Tecumseh Sherman was waking to another day.

***

The smoke of cook fires tentatively rose and choked the air, blending with the smell of burned bacon and boiling coffee. Privates and corporals, numb with cold, scurried to collapse and fold yellowing white tents of heavy canvas, still stiff with frost. Repeating rifles were unstacked and checked, fresh cartridges loaded into their breaches; muskets swabbed and nipples cleared for the caps to come, the stiff and grimy fingers of worn and tired men sticking to the frozen metal. The smell of the fires gradually gave way to the odor of wet wool and leather and the growing voices became shouts of orders and commands, louder and louder until all of Ocoosa County must have been aware the six hundred men of 14th Corp, 2nd Division, 1st Battalion of the New York Regulars were there, noisily preparing with impunity to continue their march to the city of Savannah.

Captain Zachary Beam hurriedly put the last of the personal effects of his major into the wooden chest at his feet, hoping his haste would not be apparent when the chest was opened again. He was about to extinguish the lantern in the major's tent, the last tent that would be packed up for the march, when his commanding officer ducked inside, still not completely in uniform.

Major Trevor Sean O'Sullivan, 33rd Massachusetts, was an impressive figure of an officer, fully dressed or not. Six feet tall, jet black hair with thick sideburns and moustache, he commanded the attention and respect of the men fighting under him. He was destined for greater things, higher rank, if this war didn't kill him first. Sherman favored him, had made him his aide-de-camp for a time, and had promoted him from it. O'Sullivan had impressed the general as a young and promising captain, and he had become a trusted and capable major at the age of twenty-four. The capturing of Savannah was to be General Sherman's Christmas present to Lincoln, and a successful march to that city was to be O'Sullivan's gift to Sherman.

Captain Beam came to attention as the major entered the

tent. "At ease, Zack. It appears as though you've gotten it all ready for travel. I thank you," O'Sullivan said as he looked around the tent. "Have you secured the brandy yet? If so, break it out once again, just for the moment; I should like to toast this endeavor with you prior to announcing marching orders." Captain Beam bent to unlatch another smaller trunk that he had just packed for the Major and extracted a bottle containing a few ounces of amber brandy. "This should be enough, sir, for a toast," he said, showing the contents to O'Sullivan while he pulled two small snifters out of the trunk. "I think the chances are great that we may find another bottle between here and Savannah!" he said, as both men laughed.

"Thus far, we seem to have appropriated most of what we have happened upon, captain!" replied the Major. "We were wise to have commenced this march with extra wagons and mules, what with the amount of material we have liberated from the populace. The extra livestock and horses we have acquired already have helped greatly in that respect. It should seem most probable by the time we take Savannah, we will be as large as the Union army was when this war began!" he proclaimed with pride. "Though we have considerable distance yet to cover, we have done exceedingly well to this point, captain. General Sherman will be well-pleased, I'm certain, with our progress. The reports should reach him by our runners today, perhaps by late afternoon."

The two sat in folding camp chairs, the tent empty save for the table, the lantern and both officers. The growing crescendo of coughing outside the tent told Major O'Sullivan the troops were being assembled in ranks, awaiting marching orders. Respiratory problems caused by the conditions of war and winter had affected almost all the men by now, contagiously spreading through the ranks so that first muster had become a cacophony of raspy throat clearing and hacking. It was becoming accepted as part of soldiering, the same as the stifling heat of the southern summer, the unexpected cold of the winter, and the ever-present blisters and foot soreness from marching.

"To the success of the Union!" Captain Beam said as he raised his glass to touch the major's. The glasses stayed held high as Major O'Sullivan agreed and added a toast of his own.

"As they say in Ireland, captain, 'To lives long and wond'rous; to deaths quick and clean'!" he said as the snifters parted and both men emptied the contents in a single gulp. "Don't bother to repack these, I'll wager we'll replace them somewhere before long! The 'landed gentry' of this area seem to like their brandy, I'm sure we'll find more than we can carry." The brandy warmed the two, and despite the presence of hundreds of milling, freezing soldiers just outside his tent, Major O'Sullivan leaned back in his canvas chair and relaxed, deciding now was a good time to clarify his thoughts on this march to his next-in-command.

"Captain, I am curious as to what is it that motivates you in this war we are engaged in, this march to Savannah we find ourselves on?"

Captain Beam was certain this question was not meant as a challenge to his sense of duty and honor. He had proved himself too many times in past campaigns alongside the major for O'Sullivan to doubt his dedication or bravery. Now was a strange time, he thought, for the subject of motivation to arise. "Sir, that poses as a simple question, but has, as I think you realize, a not-so-simple answer," the captain said, himself sitting back in his chair, positioning to enable himself to take a verbal stance. "First and foremost, my all-encompassing desire in this conflict is to survive it; to return to my home in Syracuse and to my prior life of farming. The seminary was where I felt my calling, but when the farm fell unexpectedly into my hands, the land beckoned the louder. I have embraced it, become friends with it. But in doing so, living to see this conflict through, it is my burning desire to see the Union preserved. I wake every day to gather my uniform, ready my weapons, and perform my appointed duty, that which the government of the Union has charged me to do, and that being to defeat the Confederate Army at any cost, in every battle, with all the strength and courage I can muster."

"Well-spoken, Zack! And you have fought with courage in every campaign we have joined," the Major said, nodding his head and smiling. "You distinguished yourself at Goldsborough Bridge and Fort Anderson in the Carolinas, to the extent that I still to this day must maintain you saved me from shrapnel in the latter battle. I shall always be indebted to you for that. I've made no secret of it since it is my belief I owe my life to you."

"Sir, your words are kind, but…"

"Do you not bear the pain of lead fragments in your legs every day? Fragments that, by divine will, or that of the Devil, were meant for me?"

"My dear major, divine Providence placed me between you and that canister charge, but I regret to inform you I did not leap there…"

"Then Providence holds our lives or deaths in its hands,"

O'Sullivan interrupted. "And the conduct of this war shall reveal in the end if we return to our loved ones and homes or perish into the hellish red soil of this God-forsaken land," the Major said, his tone turning acrid. "I have never revealed to you or to anyone, it occurs to me here and now, what forces me on in this conflict, captain. And it has welled up in me so that I must allow it now to pour forth. Would you like to know why I pull on my boots each morning, captain? Hear it from my mouth, what compels *me* forward through this wretched land in which we find ourselves?"

Captain Beam was now intent, leaning to listen to what obviously must be a heartfelt admission by the major. It was a strange time for catharsis, but he had found in the last three years that war turns the ordinary on its ear. Men took the time they were granted to do the things they deemed important, vital. And they did not always fit into the neat, ordered routine of peacetime life. Brandy at daybreak; the writing of letters home while bullets ricocheted past the ears of men bent on lying to loved ones they were safe and well.

Just as the major was about to speak, a voice from the other side of the tent wall yelled in a loud and congested manner, "Sir! Begging the major's pardon, sir! The troops are assembled and fallen in! They await marching orders of the day!"

"I'll give them the damned orders when the orders are ready to be given, Sergeant Major! Stand your troops at ease and await my command!" O'Sullivan barked toward the tent wall, clearly irritated.

He turned back toward the captain with a softer face and said with a calmer tone, leaning forward to rest his elbows on his knees, "This endeavor we find ourselves in, this march to the sea, is not so much a campaign as it is a demonstration; the sergeant major has not been informed of this, not as yet, and I have thus far felt it best not to inform him or the troops in general, for fear of a breakdown in discipline. Do you understand that, Zack?"

Captain Beam nodded his head at the procedure of command, at least. "Yes sir, I realize the need to only reveal to the men what needs be, at the time it needs to be. It is for the general good of the campaign. But as you have said, this, upon which we embark this morning, is not a campaign as such. Here you have me at a disadvantage, sir. I am, of course, puzzled. Are you authorized to explain?"

Over the noise of the rustling of horses and wagons, and the coughing of the men just outside, the major took this opportunity to inform his next-in-command of the nature of this venture through a state that had, until recently, been swarming with many thousands of well-armed Rebel soldiers. "Zack, General Sherman is attempting to march from Atlanta to Savannah quickly, successfully... and savagely. The city of Savannah he intends to offer to Lincoln as a cherished present for the holidays. We are part of that movement, wide on his immediate left flank. The Confederate resistance, as we have been informed to this point, will be minimal. Through battle attrition and the general cowardice of these southern..."

"You consider the Rebel troops cowards, sir? This comes as a surprise, inasmuch as we have engaged them, I have, with mine own eyes, seen them charge valiantly, without thought to life or death...

"Captain!" O'Sullivan interrupted. "I too have seen

episodes of valor and courage among the Gray; I have also occasionally seen it among rats in a chicken coop! I sat mounted alongside you as witness to these frays and battles, you would do well to remember! But the Rebels, by and large, as you yourself must bear witness, prefer now to snipe at us long range, ambush us from the hedgerows, atrit our regiments man by man. And that I see as cowardice."

"...Or the honed wit of survival, sir," Captain Beam replied. Beam had always perceived an underlying agenda that lie somewhere in the back of the major's mind, in an area he had not as yet been privy to. This seemed to be the time and opportunity to draw an explanation from him. Each soldier, from Grant and Sheridan and Sherman down to the lowest recruit, had his own personal reason for wanting the Union to prevail in this longer-than-expected war. Many would willingly admit it was simply to fight until there was no more fighting to be done, and then to go home to the farms and families most were so willing to leave just a few years before for the adventure of a war that "should only last two months, three at most." The glory of battle had faded quickly for the farm boys of Ohio and the pampered officers from Boston's elite. Glory was soon replaced with horror, when the first headlong charge into ten thousand muskets, all discharging death at once, brought about the immediate reality of what this war was about for them: carnage and slaughter on a scale no one could have imagined. Exhaustion, hunger, thirst, and wounds that festered and would not heal, both physical and mental, took their inevitable toll on soldiers of all rank and origin. For the tens of thousands that lay in rigor on the fields they had fought so bravely to secure and hold, the struggle had ended; they were at

103

peace. As has been the case since the beginning of man and his conflicts, it is the living who remain to suffer.

Bleary eyes on both sides of the struggle watched as exhausted surgeons, ever worked to the verge of collapse, attempted in vain to save the injured with the few instruments they were provided. The piles of amputated limbs outside the hospital tents, often as tall as the men that passed by them, bore witness that the suffering did not end on the field of battle. Each man that charged into the fray had his own reason for summoning again and again, day after day, month after month, the courage and sheer strength to fight each engagement. Beam was about to learn what it was that drove Major Trevor Sean O'Sullivan.

"The Rebel Army fights with what it has at its disposal, as do we, sir. We, by God's grace and good planning by our Department of War, have more of what we need to prevail," Beam said in an explanatory manner. "They have been a fiercer adversary than any of our leaders had thought possible, and they have done so with much less than one would expect. Lee, and his command, matches ours. As a military man, that must impress you to some end, does it not sir?"

O'Sullivan fixed a cold, unblinking stare into the eyes of his captain and said, while rising slowly from his seat, "I am *not* impressed with this vermin we combat, captain! I will tell you here and now what drives me on in this war: MY UTTER HATRED FOR THE SOUTH ITSELF! I despise the South and everything about this cursed region of our nation more than you or any mortal man can imagine or understand! The land, the heat, the vegetation, the way of life here; the inbred cretins that people this place! I loath the look of pathos in the eyes of these ragged, barefoot children we see everywhere. One could almost pity them and their dismal future, if it were not for the fact they are the enemy. I will tell you this; if it were mine to grant, I would allow these states the right and permission to secede forthwith and at great speed and be done with the lot of them!"

Beam sat astounded at the major's declaration. "You would allow the secessionists their victory, sir? This seems impossible coming from your lips! Secessionism is intolerable to our survival as a nation, as an American people. It is to be fought against to the last man, to the final volley fired. The unity of the Nation cries out for it! Nay, the survival of the Nation *demands* it!"

"Our politicians and industrialists do indeed cry out for us to stop the South from forming their own nation," replied the Major, "a sovereign nation that would border our own Union states. I feel there is more at stake for those people to lose than we are told, we soldiers and citizens. It is not so much about our loss as a sovereign nation that has these leaders so concerned as it is some other thing, something the people are not being told. Slavery is not the main issue; Lincoln has little real concern for the colored. And I for one have no real issue with a man that declares himself a rebel for what he considers a just cause. If he truly considers himself oppressed, rebellion be his only course."

"You would side with the secesh? This does not sound like you, major! Are you with the fever, sir?"

"Let me allay your fears, captain. I am not stating the confederacy is correct in their actions against the North. Our politicians and leaders have declared that if the South secedes, our nation will not withstand the loss. Perhaps... perhaps not. But we are soldiers, bound to carry out the wishes and commands of our leaders. We have little leeway in these matters, perhaps none at all. That being said, I understand the rebel mind. That is a fact I feel I need share with you. My great-grandfather was a proud rebel in Ireland. He died in an uprising against the hired British filth at the battle of Vinegar Hill in 1798 in the county Wexford. My father was told his grandfather fought bravely along with the Irish Freemen, all of whom were massacred by far superior forces that day in June. But still, they fought to the last man, much as we have asked our armies to do these last three years, as you and I are willing to do each rising day. The legend I have heard, and prefer to hold dear as truth, is that he died with his hand locked with that of Father John Murphy, the leader of the patriots that day. The British soldiers had to pry their hands apart so that they could burn the body of Father Murphy on a pyre, thus, they felt, succeeding in destroying his soul and legend. They did only the opposite."

"You would equate rebellion with patriotism?" asked Captain Beam.

"In the case of the Irish and the centuries of struggle against English rule, no doubt. In this case of the secesh in this manure pile we call the South, an unwavering 'no'."

"Then I, at this point, still do not under..."

"My hatred for the South is a personal one, Zack; I do not expect you to comprehend it. Perhaps it would be asking too much of you to try, especially now, as we find ourselves pressed for time. But it may give you chance to understand the depth of my feelings better for you to know that, though born in Ireland, I grew up in this very South, not one hundred and fifty miles from where we now find ourselves."

Captain Beam had just started to stand when the major's revelation caused him to fall back into his chair, disbelief flooding his face. "You, sir? Raised below the Mason-Dixon Line? How could that be? The 33rd Mass…"

"I escaped the dismal situation in which I found myself and made my way to New York, and then to Boston. I had hoped to find the salvation of relations there; I did not."

"I beg your pardon, sir, but I still do not understand…"

"Perhaps you will in time, Zack. Bear with me, if you can find patience in your heart. You know me to be an obedient officer and a professional military man, always ready to follow orders from my superiors. My impetus is personal; that is all I have wished to convey to you. Shortly you may understand more fully, especially if our scouting reports are true," the major said as both men rose from their seats, readying themselves for presentation to the men gathered outside.

"How so, sir?" the captain asked, fastening his belt and adjusting his saber and scabbard.

"Our foragers and scouts report we are on a road that will take us to a large plantation, the Endicott plantation by name, in half a days march. It was this information that caused me to alter our intended route of southeast to one of due east, at least until I could verify that report. I have done so. These reports are accurate; we will be there just at sunset."

Zack was confused by the estimate in the major's timing. It was just past dawn now and the regiment should be able to arrive at the plantation, if it was where they were told, much sooner. "Why dusk, sir? Our troops are in good shape and order, able to travel well and quickly. Noon should do it for us," he assured the major.

"In an unfettered march with no delays, you would be correct, Zack. But we will most certainly be deterred, perhaps often, between here and the plantation."

"Stopping, sir? May I enquire as to what our delays will be attributed to, as you seem to anticipate them now?"

The major looked sternly into the captain's face, breathed deeply and expelled his explanation with his breath. "Our contribution to the willful destruction of the South and of the people who occupy this miserable Hell."

"Sir?"

"I have been given direct orders from General Sherman himself to lay waste to and destroy whatever and whomever we encounter in our path to Savannah, as have all the brigade and battalion commanders involved in this march."

Captain Beam's face began to contort with incredulousness and he was about to address the statement when O'Sullivan continued. "This march to the sea is less a campaign than it is a demonstration of Northern might, as I have so stated. It is meant to be the final segment of what has been termed 'The Anaconda Plan', the Lincoln administration's plan to starve the South into submission, to break the will of the southern populace. The Union has thus far successfully blockaded the sea ports and inland rivers and waterways, and the effect has begun to turn the tide of the war in favor of the North. We have stopped even medical supplies from reaching the Confederate Army and the people of the southern states as well. The people of the South bleed and the flow shall not be stemmed."

"But sir, they are civilians that we will encounter this day.

In the eyes of a merciful God, do our actions speak well of us, in a kind and just light?"

"Captain, these civilians are the very secesh you have just spoken of with vehement bitterness! Those we may encounter this day are the backbone of these States, the Confederacy itself, its very heart and soul. Still that beating heart, free that rebellious soul and our mission is successful; the Union remains intact. And that *is* the ultimate goal, is it not?"

Captain Beam stopped his preparation and stood in the middle of the tent, visibly stunned. In the battles and campaigns of the last three years, the 14th Corps of Regulars had gone against the South's finest troops. The fighting was fierce and bloody, with many casualties inflicted on either side. That was war, the war all had enlisted to fight. But, thus far, the waging of war had always been against military units, not the civilians Major O'Sullivan was expecting to encounter during the day's march. The 14th Corps had not participated in any of the wholesale and wanton destruction that was rumored to have been perpetrated on cities in states such as Tennessee, Mississippi, and Alabama. Units that moved quickly like the 14th did not receive news on a timely basis, and much of it was the hearsay that happens among troops in the field, unreliable and baseless. The occasional whiff of information that had drifted past Captain Beam hinting at the intentional demolition of whole cities and civilian homes was dismissed quickly as being unlikely or impossible. This unit had been late for the occupation of Atlanta, but the city they saw on arrival was its own testament. He had persuaded himself that, surely, the destruction of cities the size of Meridian and Jackson, Mississippi, was beyond the ability and scope of even the

Union Army. The reports, official and unofficial, had told a different and ghastly story.

The Union troops that entered Meridian were unopposed by Confederate troops, the reports had stated. Nonetheless, those soldiers present boasted that there ensued wholesale looting, pillaging and raping by the Yankee army, and finally the burning and elimination of the entire city. Beam had dismissed in his mind as preposterous the assertion that, after the city lie in smoking ruin, unrecognizable as a once populated center, General Sherman himself had boasted in letter that "for five days, ten thousand of our men worked hard with a will, in that work of destruction, with axes, sledges, crowbars, clawbars and with fire…Meridian no longer exists." General Sherman was a good man, an honorable and capable officer of the Union Army. Beam had faith in the North's cause and in the men that led their effort to keep the Union intact. These tales of horror, in his mind at least, could not be true.

The look of disbelief was evident in Beam's face and Major O'Sullivan smiled slightly at the naivety at which it hinted. "Captain, are you not prepared to complete our victory in what may be our last concerted effort? I have thus far felt the comfort of safety with you riding by my side; knowing your valor and dedication were nigh has given me courage to fight at my best. Sherman is counting on us all, most especially on the will of his officers, to make this sweep to the sea a success. The Union needs your dedication to cause now as much as ever."

"I find it difficult to believe that a good and honorable general officer such as Sherman would condone such action against an unarmed populace," Captain Beam replied sadly as they neared the tent's opening.

The major turned to Beam and said, "Captain, two years ago I was aide-de-camp to the honorable General Sherman, and as such was privy to much of his post. I often read his letters aloud to him whilst he attended to other pressing matters. Therefore I feel I know the man as well as any other soldier in the field could or does. In '62 he wrote to his wife that his purpose in the war would be "the extermination, not of the soldiers alone, that is the least of the trouble, but of the people of the South."

Beam stared blankly into the major's face. "He stated that, sir, to his own wife? I can only wonder what the dear wife of an honorable officer must have thought as she read such lines, most likely in the placid and peaceful parlor of their home," he said, the sadness evident in his voice.

"Oh, I can tell you verbatim, Zachary. The general shared her response with me, as it impressed him, and I myself was so taken with her reply, I invoked it to my heart where it remains as a testament to the dedication to our cause that permeates our homeland. The loving and gentle Mrs. Sherman wrote back to her husband that her wish was for, and I quote, "a war of extermination, and that all Southerners would be driven like swine into the sea. May we carry fire and sword into their states, till not one habitation is left standing."

The devastating source of these words rooted Captain Beam motionless. In that instant, the war, and what it meant, had suddenly and irreversibly changed for him. He felt sickened knowing he was about to embark on what may amount to a rolling slaughter of civilian men, women and children. That realization drained the color from his face and Major O'Sullivan saw the obvious change as he extinguished

111

the lantern and the light from the rising sun illuminated the interior of the tent.

Both men stood at the flap of the tent, ready to emerge into the cold morning air, and history; the major was certain of it. This was an effort that would turn the war in favor of the North, and the anticipation of it was now coursing through him like adrenaline. He turned to the captain, eyed him up and down quickly in a brief inspection, and smiled encouragingly as he put his gloved hands on the captain's shoulders. "Zack," he said, cocking his head slightly and looking into the captain's eyes, eyes that had been staring blankly at the ground until now. "Zack, the Nation, nay, the entire world, will remember us for all eternity if we are successful in this endeavor."

Captain Beam looked back into the major's eyes and replied with a faraway voice, a voice that he did not recognize as his own. "It is that very prospect that causes the bile to rise now to the back of my throat, sir. I am a sworn and faithful officer of the Union Army of the United States, as are you, and I will die in my attempt to keep this nation as one. But in truth to you, sir, the thought of this day and what it most assuredly may bring sickens me and frightens me so as to cause me weakness."

"Zachary, we are giants; giants in time and of this history we are about to set in motion."

"Giants, sir?" Beam replied. "Major, do you recall your Shakespeare?" he asked.

"Ah, the immortal bard! His words remain fresh in my mind, more so than most scholars of literature! You see captain, unbeknownst to you and most, it was not until I was nineteen years of age did I learn to read and write; the 'situation' on which I have briefly touched having, in its cruelty, kept me from it. But I ravenously devoured the books I could obtain once my mind was opened to the magic of the written word. Why do you ask?"

"I am drawn at this time to recall 'Measure for Measure', act two, scene two, line one hundred and seven: 'Oh, it is excellent to have a giant's strength; but it is tyrannous to use it like a giant'."

Major O'Sullivan lowered his eyes to the ground momentarily in acknowledgement, then smiled slightly as he responded, "And the genius that was Shakespeare told us in Hamlet that 'There are more things in Heaven and Earth, Horatio, than are dreamt of in your philosophy'. One, five, one sixty-six. Lead out, captain," he said as he motioned toward the tent flap.

***

The two men emerged into the graying morning and a blast of frigid air as the sergeant major, caught by surprise at their abrupt appearance, quickly shouted to the company leaders to bring their troops to attention. Men hurriedly scuffled back into formation and extinguished their pipes and cigars. Hands were taken out of pockets to once again secure the freezing gunmetal of the rifles. O'Sullivan gave the order to Captain Beam, who in turn readied the company commanders, and on down the line until the order was given, bringing the coughing, tattered assembly to attention. The major commanded the troops "at ease" and instructed the sergeant major to have men strike his tent and pack it on one of the

many supply wagons. "And have them make haste, sergeant
major, we move out momentarily. I should like to address the
troops at this time with the Order of March and our objective
for the day."

"Yes sir!" The sergeant major responded, and barked
orders to several troops near him. The men set about the task
and brought the folded tent to a wagon in just under two
minutes. Two sergeants aided the captain and major onto their
mounts. Major O'Sullivan wheeled his horse and slowly rode
in front of the ranks of shivering soldiers until he was centered
and felt he was visible to the entire Regiment. The coughing
gradually subsided and he began giving the orders he had
carefully chosen for the day's march.

"Today," he said as he pointed to the narrow dirt road that
led from the enormous pasture in which they had bivouacked
the night before, "we travel down that small road to the
beginning of victory... and into history itself. We have been
charged by General Sherman to secure his left flank on a march
that will take us to the city of Savannah by approximately
Christmas day. The capture of the city is to be the general's gift
to the President. And the 14th Corp is going to tie the ribbon on
that gift!"

A cheer went up from the shivering troops as they took the
opportunity to cough, wipe their running noses on their sleeves,
and shift their weight from foot to foot, trying to get the blood
circulating from their knees down.

"We expect minimal contact with local troops; frays,
skirmishes and affairs being the likely extent, if that. The Gray
'trash' we have chased thus far seemed to have abandoned their
cause for the safety and warmth of the deep woods and caves,

such as vermin are likely to do when pursued."

Laughter erupted and quickly subsided as the major continued to ride slowly back and forth in front of the ranks. They were starting to fully awaken now, becoming accustomed again to the cold air of the overcast morning. The prospect of a relatively safe march would make the harsh weather somewhat easier to deal with. Captain Beam was leaning off to one side of his horse, conspicuously vomiting onto the ground and the side of his leg and mount. The troops close enough to see and hear it paid it little mind. Men at war often threw up for many different reasons: spoiled food, bad water, pre-battle anxiety, or in the case of officers, drinking brandy early in the morning on an empty stomach. No one thought much about it. None could know, but there was another reason that tore at Beam's insides this gray November morning.

"'Uncle Billy' has given orders to 'destroy at discretion' this day, and on through to the city of Savannah. Put simply, men: we burn what we find standing; we shoot what we find walking!" Another coughing shout arose from the troops.

"The Order of March will be this day, and remain until circumstances warrant change: scouts and foragers at the front, as usual, followed by the artillery, two companies foot troops, mounted troops, the remaining foot troops, then supply wagons and livestock. Commanders, ready your troops to move on momentary command. Scouts and foragers deploy and report back to column as you are able."

Orders were shouted down the line and whole masses of men and animals began to shift around to comply with the stated order of procession. Foragers and scouts rode off down the dirt road and would explore paths and side roads they would encounter to see where they led and what was on them, and report back to O'Sullivan and his officers. Beam sat dully on his horse, colorless and blank, kicking it to fall in where he knew he was expected. He took up his customary position just to the back of Major O'Sullivan. The great mass of men and animals began to slowly move like a huge, waking serpent, sluggishly reconstructing itself a section at a time; whole columns of men and wagons and horses stopping, waiting, starting to move again so their positions aligned as ordered. Waning, wispy smoke from hundreds of doused cook fires floated thinly into the gray sky as the last of 14th Corps left the trampled field.

The smoke would quickly drift away; the remnants of the fires and refuse would gradually melt back into the earth. The legacy they would commence this day would remain forever.

CHAPTER 12

The Endicott Plantation – Dusk, November 18, 1864

Haim! Jep! Where you two at? Git on down here to this kitchin! Y'all gon' wish the Yankees *do* git ya, ifn' I hafta lay into bof' y'all!" Letitia called out at the kitchen doorway toward the big room beyond. The house servants scurried in and out of the kitchen, eyes wide with worry, carrying foodstuffs and utensils out the back door and loading them in carts and wagons.

Word had passed along from town to town and plantation to plantation about the Union troops plundering the valuables and supplies of the homes and stores they came across in their march to the sea. Nothing of importance or value was safe from the marauding troops unless it was well-hidden in advance. Even then, the 'bummers', the convicts and professional thieves the Union purposely enlisted, had a knack for guessing where the choice items were concealed. It was, after all, what they had done as civilians. Slaves were told by their owners to hide the goods all around the plantations, even to use their own quarters to conceal the things the Yankees might take for their own or wantonly destroy. The field hands had been enlisted to help in moving and hiding the bulky goods such as chests of clothes, choice furniture, and the heavy hams and jars of preserves. For some, such as Haim and Jep, this was their first look inside the "Big House," and Letitia found them both staring at the paintings and decorations in the large dining room beside the kitchen. "Where you bof' been?" she yelled at them, coming up behind them and grabbing them both by their necks. "Them Blue Coats is mos' comin' down the road and you fools is busyin' yourselfs lookin' at white folk on the wall wearin' fancy git-ups!" She pushed them toward the kitchen and pointed to the pantry. "See all them jars? Git to movin' them into those crates yonder and git 'em onto the wagon out back! Sadai already got Mas'tuhs' silver and china loaded on, and don' be breakin' nothin' or I'll whup yo' two hides my *own* self!"

Haim and Jep were too terrified to speak back or do anything but obey Letitia's commands. No female slave of the Endicott plantation would dare stand up to Letitia, and very few of the men would try.

***

Cornell Endicott, the owner of the plantation, had once measured out six feet and marked it on the frame of the back door to the Big House. The male slaves all had taken turns measuring themselves, vying for the title of "Biggest Buck" of the plantation, as Cornell proudly phrased it. Bill, a recently purchased slave from Atlanta, topped the mark, plus a finger's width. At the insistence of the other female slaves, Letitia one

118

day strode reluctantly up onto the porch and put her back to the sill, passing the mark with a generous hand-width to spare. And even though from that day on they all knew how tall she was, none of them could begin to guess her weight.

Endicott, several years earlier, had ordered her to let a visiting livestock trader lift her to estimate how heavy she might really be. The man needed her full cooperation to get under her sufficiently to lift her off her feet, and Letitia had to be commanded twice to extend that cooperation to him. "Three thirty, three forty pound, I'll wager hard cash," was his estimate. Endicott, shaking his head, was in disbelief until the man, exhausted and rubbing his lower back, assured him, "Sir, with all due respect, I need to remind you I do this as part of my livelihood and my success in business is dependent upon my accuracy." Whatever her weight and height, everyone on the plantation knew of her enormous strength.

When Letitia was a younger woman laboring for Endicott as a common field hand, she had one day put down her hoe in the field and went to relieve herself down by the river, a short distance away. While there, she heard the braying of a mule that had gotten helplessly stuck in the thick mud of the adjacent marsh. It was the yearling mule for which a slave had been beaten for stealing and eating. Letitia had hiked up her dress, waded into the mud far enough to grab the mule by the head, and pulled him by the jaw and ears to his freedom. The animal was lame from having been immobilized for such a long period of time and could not walk on its own, so she lifted it onto her shoulders and walked the mile and a half back to the Big House where she deposited it in the front yard. Master Endicott was summoned to the door and was amazed to see the mule he was certain had ended up on a spit somewhere on a distant part of his property.

"Mas'tuh, I found yo' mule you beat 'Ol Dan for, you thinkin' he skinned it an' et it. When I git through wif my chores, kin I go tell'em you ain't mad at him no mo'? I know he'd be mos' overjoy'd to hear it."

Master Endicott rocked back on his heels and grinned at the enormous, muddy woman in front of him. He had owned her for most of his adult life. Now somewhere in her forties, she had always been obedient, if perhaps a bit defiant; a tireless worker and a good breeder, producing strong children, two of which he still owned. Malcolm and Theo, Letitia's grown sons, were two of the plantations best workers. Walking to the edge of the immaculate broad porch, he stood at the top of the stairs and said, "Letitia, you go on and get yourself cleaned up and come 'round the back when you do. It wouldn't do for the new 'house mistress' to be tracking dirt into the house she's overseeing, now would it?"

House mistress! Letitia was shocked at the words, as were all the slaves present. It was a position of honor to a plantation slave, something that had to be worked up to. Even the wretched have their rank, and house mistress was the pinnacle for a female slave. She would make sure everything that went on within the house went smoothly; making sure the house was clean, running well, and to the master's liking. All the other house servants would answer to her and her word was final, only able to be superseded by that of the master. For the saving of a mule, she had just been promoted to the equivalent of a general manager of a small, luxury hotel.

Cornell Endicott knew exactly what he was doing,

bringing Letitia to work in the Big House when he did. He knew she had the respect of almost all his slaves and could, if necessary, extract it from those who would not give it willingly. He had watched her more than she knew. The passing of his wife several years before had left a hole in the daily routine of the house, not to mention his personal life, and even though his wife had made few decisions in the house of importance other than artistic decor and acquisitions, or concocting the lists for social gatherings and parties, Cornell Endicott had realized he needed a strong woman to raise his two daughters, Abigail and Nicollete.

Nicollete, now eight years of age and frail, had barely known her mother. Lilly Endicott had been born and raised in London, and the move to the rural southern United States was a sacrifice she had made for the love of Cornell, who himself had come from British wealth and to America with his family as a teen and fell in love with the wildness of the South. Lilly had never warmed to her life in "The Colonies" and never completely overcame her homesickness for London. Some said it was this ongoing longing to go back that eventually killed her; the local doctor attributed it to complications of a longstanding pernicious anemia that was never correctly diagnosed. The death of her mother only confused the very young Nicollete; it devastated ten-year-old Abigail.

Distraught for weeks, Abigail felt abandoned and cheated by the loss of her mother, and no consoling by her father or the house servants was effective in bringing her out of the depression that seemed to be worsening. It was at that time that Master Endicott had brought Letitia into the Big House, and, totally by accident, a love that rarely happens between two people, any two people, formed to work a miracle.

***

Thirteen years prior, Letitia had given birth to her only girl, a beautiful baby she had named Neesie. A healthy, happy infant, Letitia was proud of this child, the last she had hopes of ever bearing. Neesie became Letitia's reason for living, raising her like a mother who had only had sons would do. She spoiled her when she could, seeing to it that her little girl was always warm enough and well-fed. Then, as so often happened in plantation life, Cornell Endicott had economic reason to sell the five-year-old. A good offer was made by an owner in Charleston for a sound, young female from strong stock, and Cornell found the offer hard to resist. Females were hard to sell, especially young and unproven. He had all the field hands he could gather at the time surround Letitia when he announced the news to her; he knew they would all be needed to restrain her if she reacted as badly as she might.

Letitia stood outside her cabin in the broiling Georgia sun, surrounded by a dozen slaves that both feared and respected her, holding her head high with dignity at the devastating news. Tears streamed down her broad face as she watched her only daughter struggling and screaming in the grasp of the overseer from Charleston who would transport her far away forever. She stoically looked at the faces of the other slaves collectively and said to them all, in a trembling voice, "Don' nobody need be scared; y'all don' gots ta fear me. Mas'tuh, kin I say goodbye to my baby?"

Cornell Endicott nodded to the overseer to let Neesie go

and the child ran desperately to her mother, crying and trying to disappear into the folds of the big woman's dress. Letitia squatted down and, trying to be strong, willed her voice to be quiet and soothing for her little girl.

"Chile', you gots ta go away now; there ain't nothin' me or you nor nobody can do 'bout it 'cept Mas'tuh, and he seein' fit now that you leave here. Wherever you git to, whatever happens fo' you, you jus' gots ta always remember that yo' Momma loves you, more than anythin', hear? An' I'll always be knowin' you loves me too." She stood slowly and looked down at the panicking child and said, "Now you go git on to Charleston an' make yo Momma proud doin' what they want." The overseer took the child, hysterical and struggling, and carried her to the buckboard, saying a few final words to Cornell and disappearing down the road away from the plantation. The slaves, some openly weeping, turned to go back to their respective labors. Letitia, head lowered in silent grief, turned and walked into her cabin. She decided again, for the second time in her life, to hate Cornell Endicott to the end of days with every fiber of her being.

But time has its own way of softening hate for some people, and fate sometimes introduces a factor that transforms one overriding emotion into another. And that factor, for Letitia, was Abigail Endicott.

***

Abigail had expressed fear of Letitia the times in her past when she had seen her. "Papa, she's so big, she frightens me, and Nicollete too!" But her father had always laughed at her and told her she and her sister had nothing to fear from the huge woman that could work circles around most of his bucks. He favored her, he told Abigail, and felt that one day before long she would oversee the house. And one day, he told her, Letitia's size and strength might just be needed to protect his precious girls.

The day that Letitia assumed her role as house mistress, she and Abigail met face-to-face for the first time, and life played the curious hand it does ever so rarely: the small girl of ten looked up at the enormous slave woman and Letitia looked back down at her; and a bond was instantly formed, a bond that would grow rapidly into a deep and abiding love between a high-bred white girl and a black woman that belonged to her father and would eventually belong to her, also. Abigail's depression disappeared almost overnight as she and Letitia became inseparable. With the exception of the color of their skin, they appeared to all, for all intents and purposes, as mother and daughter. Although Letitia was fond of Nicollete also, and treated her with gentleness and care, her relationship with "MizAbby," as she called her, was special by far. Cornell Endicott's oldest daughter rapidly became the light of her life.

***

Cornell Endicott rushed into the kitchen, his face solemn and grave. "Letitia, have the boys…"

"The boys been loadin' everythin' you done tol' me to have 'em move out the house, suh. You gots anymo' goods an' valables that's got to go, tell me now an' I'll have 'em fetched up!"

"A rider arrived just minutes ago and said a large column

of Union soldiers was making its way toward us along the Chatoosee Road. Unless they veer for some reason, they'll be here before nightfall, and it frightens me to think of the consequences. I've posted Jonas out at the boundary of the property and he has relayed the fact that the foragers have been spotted and that they saw him also. Oh Letitia, this terrifies me, I swear it; I fear for this house and the safety of my children. I've heard that between here and Atlanta, the only structures left standing are the chimneys of the burned houses!"

"Cain't do much to save this ol' house, suh, but ain't nothin' gon' happen to those two chid'rens as long as Letitia's takin' breaf.' You ain't gots ta worry 'bout that," she assured Endicott. "I'll cripple the Yankee that touches them girls."

"Thank you, Letitia, for your help. I'd be near to panic at this moment without you," Cornell told her.

"You ain't real far from it *now*, suh, ifn you don' mind I says so! You jus' go on an' take care of what business you needs to, Letitia gon' see to it this 'ol house gits cleared out. Would you fetch up Missy Abigail and Miss Nicollete fo' me so's I kin have 'em near me an' I don't gotsta worry where they is? Thank you, suh," she said as she whirled to check a load of goods from the pantry and more furniture from the upstairs bedroom. Cornell left to locate the girls and send them down to Letitia.

"Mary! Bill! Y'all take the bigges' buckets you kin find an' git on out to the big pump an' fill 'em as full as you kin carry back! Y'all hear me? An' hurry, won't be long it be freezin' up!" Bill and Mary appeared from around the corner and acknowledged her command.

"Yas'm, 'Titia, you want them big buckets we use on the

125

horses an' mules?"

"If they the bigges' we got, then they's the ones ta use, now git, and git back right quick; Mas'tuh say the Yankees comin' up purty quick-like!"

Bill and Mary looked at each other with fear and anxiety, not understanding the true nature of the situation at hand, but fully aware something big was going to happen soon. "Yankees gon' git us ifn they see us?" Bill asked Letitia.

"Yankees got no need o' your useless self, yours neither, Mary, now go git that water!" Letitia whirled and commanded the two, watching them fly out the back door into the darkness before she could finish. The sound of her name being called by familiar young voices spun her again toward the kitchen entrance to see Abigail and Nicollete running to her, fear spread across their faces. Letitia caught them both in her arms and lifted them off the floor, squeezing them and attempting to make light of the impending situation.

"'Titia, what's going to happen…"

"Now, don' neither one o' you chid'rens fret 'bout nothin'. Ain't nothin but some robbin' Yankees comin' to snatch some livestock and such 'for they move on to somewheres else. Nothin' else gon' happen, hear?" Letitia assured them. "You stay wif Letitia no matter what be goin' on."

"Will they damage our house?" Abigail asked her. "Will they harm us? Will you protect us? Will…"

An explosion a short distance from the front of the house cut short Abigail's troubled question and caused the sisters and the other females in the kitchen to shriek. "Letitia! They're here! It's the Yankees!" Nicollete screamed and started to cry

126

as the slaves began to run in panic out the back door of the kitchen in terror. Shouting and rifle fire grew louder and the huge woman drew her two charges close to her, not knowing what to expect next.

"They in the front yard! The Yankees be out in the front yard and they's more comin' up the road!" shouted a male slave, running terrified through the kitchen and out the back door. Within a few seconds he backed into the kitchen again, now with a musket pointing at him and several blue-coated soldiers scurrying through the door to secure the kitchen. They swore and shouted at the people in the kitchen to hurry into the room beyond, pushing those that didn't move fast enough as they herded them through the doors through the dining room and into the huge receiving area.

Major O'Sullivan drew his 1860 Army revolver as he passed through the front door and strode with authority into the middle of the huge atrium, spinning to look at the slaves being shoved and pushed by his company of troops to line the walls. More and more soldiers rushed in from the cold darkness of the outside until the room was close to full, slaves clutching each other in fear along the walls, soldiers forming a circle inside with rifles and revolvers pointing out at them, shaking off the cold of the night. O'Sullivan continued to rotate slowly, looking sternly over the sights of his sidearm at the servants and field hands huddled in the light of the enormous crystal chandelier hanging in the middle of the room and the many candles that lit the ornate tables scattered here and there. "I have no quarrel with the servants and slaves of this manor and property," he told them in a loud, clear voice. "But my ambivalence will not stand the test of threat to my person or any member of my company. Take arms against us, resist what you are ordered, and I will personally free your miserable souls myself."

The servants stood frozen, their eyes opened wide in fright. The number of Yankees and the guns pointing at them and the terror and confusion kept them all too petrified to take more than a shallow breath. Major O'Sullivan ordered a dozen troops to search the upstairs rooms for more occupants and valuables and looked around again, his gaze settling on the only white females in the room.

"Are you the children of the master of this house? *Speak! I'm asking you a question!*" he shouted at the sisters. Abigail and Nicollete nodded silently, burying themselves into Letitia's sides as she held them closer. "And where is he? *Tell me where he is hiding! Be quick about it, I am not a patient man, I assure you!*" he yelled in a threatening tone. Letitia glared at him as he shouted at the girls by her side. The major's questioning was interrupted by the sounds of soldiers struggling with a man, cursing him as they pulled and pushed him down the winding stairway and into the atrium to stand in front their commanding officer.

"Look what we found hiding upstairs, major! I'll wager he owns this big ol' house! I'll bet it's him, the owner!" one of the troopers said laughing and shoving the red-faced man toward the center of the room. The soldiers gave O'Sullivan room so that the man could stand in front of him face-to-face.

"Are you the master of this house? Is your name Endicott?" he asked, his eyes narrowing as he stared. Cornell Endicott's eyes avoided meeting the major's for several seconds, but he knew eventually an answer would have to be given. In his reluctance to reply, he offered a token nod. O'Sullivan motioned to the two young girls off to the side, now both crying in fear. "Are these two your daughters? Are they also Endicotts?" he asked.

The apprehension on Cornell Endicott's face turned to anger and he lurched forward at the major, only to be pulled back by two soldiers and held more securely. "If you harm them I'll…"

"You'll do nothing this evening, Master Endicott, but perish, as will your family, I assure you, but not before you answer one final question of mine," Major O'Sullivan interjected in a calm, conversational manner now that he had answers to his questions.

Letitia glowered at the sound of the threat to the two girls she now held even closer and the commotion and noise in the room eased noticeably from his words. "My last relevant inquiry to you, sir, would be: do you have relations in the Carolinas? Hardeeville of the South Carolina, to be precise?" Cornell Endicott lowered his eyes and averted his stare, forcing O'Sullivan to duck his head in order to look up into the plantation owner's face and make eye contact. "I have just stated, for the sake of your negroes and now for you, I am not a patient man and what little of it I possess has all but departed from me; I ask but this one last time," the major hissed through clenched teeth. "Do you have a relative proximate to the town of Hardeeville that masters a plantation there?"

Endicott remained silent and stared at his daughters who now squirmed and cried, afraid for their father and themselves. In one flowing motion, Major O'Sullivan stood erect and deftly flipped his sidearm in the air, grabbing it by the barrel with his right hand, and swung it with great force to land the butt on the left side of Endicott's face. The power of the blow spun the old man's head violently to his right, spewing blood and teeth across the face and chest of the soldier holding him on the right. Abigail and Nicollete screamed again and broke free of Letitia's grasp to run toward their father, the quick, rough hands of soldiers intercepting them before they could reach him. Letitia moved to take them back, only to be stopped by the barrels and bayonets of several rifles. "Move over next to the wall with the others, nigra," a sergeant commanded her, prodding her from the back with his musket. The big woman moved reluctantly to the wall while keeping her eyes glued to the sisters, being received and pulled closer by her two sons, both of whom silently wished the violence and presence of the Yankees would soon be over. Neither had any inkling of the accuracy of their hopes.

Cornell's knees buckled from the blow and only the strength of three troopers kept him standing, the semi-conscious plantation owner now barely supporting his own weight. The entire left side of his face was now turning a yellowish purple and his left eye swelled shut in the few seconds it took for the soldiers to prop him back to a standing position. The misalignment of his lower jaw allowed the blood to pour from his mouth and down the front of his ruffled linen shirt, creating a pattern of spattered crimson. What resistance the frightened father of the two girls had moments ago was now rapidly draining out of him with his blood and saliva.

"It is an unfortunate course you have chosen, Master Endicott," the major said, looking at the dazed man in front of him. "Master Endicott," he repeated again, exploring the sound as though it had hidden meaning to him. "The title sounds strange to my ear, not having been forced to mutter it for so many years. Let me venture an answer to my own question. I am guessing the gentleman of whom I inquire, a Bertram Endicott, to be your... brother; would I be correct, sir?" A soldier pulled up Endicott's drooping head by the hair in order for him to look O'Sullivan in the face. On the edge of unconsciousness, Cornell managed a nod to the affirmative.

"So, the illustrious Bertram Endicott of the South Carolina is indeed your brother! Good sir, it is cold this night, and that does indeed parallel the nature of the world in which we live. You will, yourself and your family, this very evening perish from this cruel world simply for the sins of your brother. Ah, the unfairness of life! I have tasted it! And so will you."

The girls screamed again and Letitia started toward them until Malcolm and Theo moved to grab her and tug her back against the wall, needing a concerted effort to do so. "Momma, no! Git back!" Malcolm half-whispered while putting up his hand to the guard that came at them ready to fire. "She good, suh! She be good! Don't want no trouble; don't hurts her, suh, please! We gots her!" he said, putting himself in front of the big woman whose eyes flashed defiantly at the soldier and then back at O'Sullivan. Two more sergeants entered the room from the darkness beyond the front door, followed by Captain Beam, and all three slowed to a stop to listen to the major as he spoke to Endicott and the room.

"But first, a story, an explanation of sorts is due, wouldn't you think? Perhaps a delightful tale of a boy forced to live a miserable hell on earth for no other reason than for being Irish!" O'Sullivan said, the mock politeness in his voice now slipping to reveal an angry tone. "The beginning is always a good place to start, so therefore: my tale begins in Ireland when I was five years of age. The potato crop having failed, my father decided rather than starve to death in the land we loved, he would take us to a new life in America. We would start again and life would be grand!" the major proclaimed to the room full of soldiers and slaves and the master who was slipping in and out of consciousness. "Passage required money, and we had none; my father arranged for a period of indentured servitude for us: he, my mother, my sister Colleen and me. A few years shining some master's brass and silver and we would be free to take our place among the prospering citizens of this blossoming land!" he said, stopping his pacing to turn sharply and glare into Cornell Endicott's swollen face, his tone becoming sharp and high-pitched. "Well I assure you, Master Endicott, that fate, and quite soon enough your brother, had something far different in store for us!"

The slaves against the walls suddenly settled into an uneasy quiet, looking at and listening to this strange Yankee in the center of the room, and the soldiers guarding them turned their heads away from their captives to listen to the story unfolding from the mouth of the commanding officer they so admired.

"We 'obligated' were rounded up in the night, taken to a ship wharfed remotely in Dublin harbor and thrown into the dark hold below deck. They chained us neck, hands and feet, and laid us on rough planking head to foot. The stench below was overwhelming; choking. We could not stand nor stretch out completely, and upon putting to sea, the rolling of the seas and lack of food soon sickened us all. For the next eight weeks we lay in each other's vomit and excrement; I in my family's, they in mine, unable to escape it. Sometime in the fourth or fifth week of voyage, I became aware my sister had died. She was two years my senior, but weaker than I. And so weakened were my parents to the extent they had not the energy nor tears to even weep for her! At five years, I knew little of death; not even enough to pray for the blissful release of my own. But I would learn that in the years that followed!" O'Sullivan began again to pace in the small area he occupied in front of Endicott, and his demeanor grew more agitated as he recounted his story. The room full of soldiers and slaves grew even more attentive.

"Days passed before the crew culled the dead from among us breathing corpses. I watched helplessly through my delirium as they pulled Colleen up through the hatch by her hair to summarily throw her overboard with their waste and the rest of our dead. To the captain and crew, they were one and the same; we were only Irish. We arrived in Charleston only to be dragged half-alive from out of the hold and herded onto the dock like tethered animals. The horrified faces of the people there informed us of our condition and those faces are forever burned into my memory! We must have appeared to them like living dead; colorless, emaciated, covered with infected sores and our filth.

We three went on the block several times that day, but failed to sell due to our condition, until a plantation owner by the name of Bertram Endicott offered and purchased all three of us for five dollars gold. Three human lives whose one collective sin was to be born poor Irish! *Bought for five dollars gold!*" O'Sullivan screamed into the face of Cornell Endicott then turned to his right to grab the musket from a soldier's hands, rearing back and swinging it in rage with all his strength into Endicott's left leg just above the knee. The soldiers winced as the leg buckled backward with an audible snap, sending the man sprawling onto his face, roaring in pain. The slaves and servants came immediately awake from the mesmerizing horror of O'Sullivan's tale, men crying out and women screaming at the swift and brutal move and its result. Abigail and Nicollete exploded into hysteria, struggling with their captors in order to run to their father. Additional hands came from behind to secure them where they were and muffle their shrieks of panic. Cornell lay on his stomach, unable to reach back to the leg that now twisted backward from the breaking of his femur, and blood and enamel blew onto the wood floor from his mouth with each huffing, labored breath.

Major O'Sullivan bent to examine the man's state of consciousness and looked up to inform the soldier nearest him, "Corporal, I charge you with keeping this man lucid, if only for several more minutes. Should he leave us, either in death or unconsciousness, I will see to it that you accompany him where he goes! Understood?" The soldier bent to grab the hair of the old man and raised his head to shake him.

"Yes sir!" the private shouted back, turning his rapt attention to the agonizing man on the floor. "Stay awake, you bastard! Wake up!" the trooper yelled, repeatedly kicking the groaning man in his ribs only to make him groan louder with each blow.

"Stay with us, Master Endicott, I have but a bit more with which to enlighten you and I wouldn't want you to miss my recollection of my life, as it were, on your brother's lovely plantation!" O'Sullivan paced again and struggled to regain his forced, mocking inflection.

"We were fed, watered and doused with lye, then literally thrown in the back of a wagon for the journey to Hardeeville; all the while my mother becoming less responsive and most feverish. Upon our arrival she was too weak to stand on her own. I helped my father carry her into the excuse of a cabin we were given and laid her in the one filthy bed therein, we there attempting to ease her fever with tepid water-soaked rags." Major O'Sullivan's breathing was getting deeper as he spoke and his face now began to redden in color. "Sometime in the night..." he said through his teeth, his jaw tightening, "your brother's two overseers came to our cabin..." He stopped to collect himself and it was obvious what he had to say next was difficult for him to express. Tears were forming at the corners of his eyes. Except for the fading sound of boisterous looters moving to distant rooms upstairs, the atrium was now almost totally silent. The adult women, most averting their eyes out of fear and habit, turned to the major and stared at this man of story with widening and tearing eyes, each of them knowing exactly what he would say next.

"They came to our cabin... and one would hold my father and me at gun point... while they took turns raping my mother repeatedly!" the major shouted down through his teeth at the groaning 'lord' of the house. "She was so weakened with fever she could not even struggle!" he said, standing directly in front of Endicott. "Her eyes rolled back in her head, her mouth opened... but there was no sound; no scream..." he managed to say, his voice breaking. O'Sullivan dropped suddenly to his knees and, taking Endicott's head in his hands, pulled it up forcefully to look into the man's glazed eye, making certain he could hear the rage and anger in his voice that was now pouring forth from a heart and memory that had contained it for so many years. *"I was but five years old! I didn't even know what they were doing to her!"* he screamed. O'Sullivan dropped Endicott's head back to the floor into the pool of coagulating blood and slowly rose again, raising his head and straightening his uniform, taking several deep breaths to attempt to regain his composure before continuing.

"When they had gone, my father wept profusely over her, and I for him, fearful, not fully understanding what had happened. I only saw his grief, that giving rise to my own. My mother died early the next morning and we buried her in a shallow grave in the small cemetery where the Negroes buried their own. From that day on, our life under your brother was a living hell! My father and I were given the most vile and dangerous of tasks. We were expendable; a Negroe's life was not. Four years later my father was given the task of dynamiting stumps and rock from one of Endicott's fields. He feigned difficulty with a fuse to persuade the two overseers to come to his assistance. When they were sufficiently close, he lit the charge, killing himself and one overseer, leaving the other severely injured, but alive and writhing in great pain. I ran to what remained of the only family I had left in the world and was horrified at what I saw. I was only nine, but such a hardened nine I had become! I then turned quickly to the injured overseer and, taking the Bowie knife he kept at his belt, I began to hack and slash at his face and eyes with all the fury I possessed before he could die, wanting with all my soul to see the reaction before he succumbed, and I tore at him so until the field slaves pulled me from him. That night your brother,

Bertram Endicott himself, whipped me unconscious and to near death.

"My next four years were that of a kept animal, such was Master Endicott's hatred for me. He chained me to an oak tree within sight of the back of his grand manor house and would watch me in satisfaction from time to time there where I sat at the end of a tether like a cur dog in the open, year-round, in the blazing heat of summer and the bitter cold of winter. His animals faired better than I. Compared to my lot, the Negroes seemed to me to live almost as royalty! In my fifteenth year, I think there about, an older slave named Topa came to me in the night with a key he had secured at great risk to his own life. He could have escaped on his own, but dared the chance to release me as well, pitying my dire misfortune and misery under your brother. He soon departed from me to pursue a course to Ohio and I made my way to the coast and, in time, with perseverance and much luck, I arrived barely alive in Boston. I fell in with countrymen who took me in despite their meager condition. Seeing my absolute destitution, they realized how much further it was possible for them to sink. I gave them a perverted sort of hope. I viewed the military as a tunnel of light and enlisted in '60; the rest of this tale you see before you."

Servants around the great room shot furtive glances at each other in disbelief, unable to fathom this recounting of a white man so beset upon and brutally treated by another white. All had felt the occasional sting of an Endicott caning in their lives, and some even the pain of an overseer's whip from time to time for the sin of being slow or producing light bags of cotton from the field. They were black, and white masters had the right to treat their blacks in such a manner; that was understood. But this profound cruelty to another white was foreign to them, beyond their comprehension, as was even the concept of white slavery. They would wonder more about it later. The man in the center of the room growing more volatile by the minute was the situation that bore watching now.

O'Sullivan stopped his pacing and spoke down to the back of the plantation owner whose awareness was now dancing back and forth along the murky edge of bliss. The corporal looked up at the major's face and renewed his attempt at keeping Cornell among the conscious. "I began this soliloquy by promising your death and I mean to keep that promise," the major said calmly. "But first, before I send you to hell, there is one last sight I intend for you to behold among the living: that of witnessing what I did at the age of five!" The major turned to a soldier close to him and said, with casual manner, "Sergeant, allow any men wanting to partake of these 'belles of the south' to do so, with my compliments. In fifteen minutes, be prepared to fall in for march; we are to regroup with the other companies southeast of this county in three days and consolidate our flank. We have more stops to make along our way."

The sergeant's face gradually brightened to a wide grin. "Yes sir!" he responded, turning to the soldiers surrounding him. "You heard the major; anybody wantin' any of these wenches better be gettin' to it; we ain't got much time!" Abigail's face distorted in horror and she screamed as soldiers on both sides of her grabbed at her arms to pull her back and up onto the large wooden table under the chandelier, sweeping off the heavy crystal vase that held a large winter bouquet and sending it crashing to the floor. Letitia's eyes opened wide in anger as she attempted once again to go to her MizAbby, bellowing *"No!,"* and she was again secured from behind by her sons. The two called out for help this time, their combined strength and weight being no match for their mother's rage.

"Rem! Andrew! Haim! Hep us! Jebel!" Theo blurted, wrestling his mother to the floor while Malcolm wrapped his arms around the woman's tree-sized legs. Haim and Rem rose to rush to the growing pile of bodies, both of them locking eyes with the soldiers guarding them as they went, raising their hands to show they were of no threat. The soldiers eyed the growing commotion among the slaves with dwindling concern, starting now to look back at the young girl lying on her back, thrashing and struggling against the strong gripping hands that held her on the table. Troopers were beginning to lay their muskets on the floor and loosen their belts as raucous laughter and shouting grew louder in the room. O'Sullivan bent again to Endicott to make certain he was still conscious. "I want this to be the last thing you experience in this pampered world you and your brother have created for yourselves, Master Endicott. I want you to carry this image with you to your death as you go, as I have carried it in life for twenty years! My deepest apologies to you and yours, sir, but a vicarious vengeance is all I am assured of at present!" Standing again, he glanced unfazed at the knot of men working to tear the clothing from Abigail and motioned to his sergeant major to approach. "Gather all the likely Negro males and prepare them to depart with the column. In the event they refuse to fight for us, they shall not remain to fight against us," he said, looking up across the room into Captain Beam's face, now filled with disgust. As O'Sullivan started toward him, Beam made a deliberate about-

face and disappeared quickly out of the front door into the dark. Stopping, O'Sullivan turned again to the sergeant major for one more command. "When they have finished," he said, motioning toward the table and the screaming Abigail, "torch the house, and be thorough; I want no trace, no memory of this manor to remain. Leave those who cannot flee. All but her; put her on my horse, whatever they leave of her."

The sergeant major looked puzzled, staring at the major and back at the growing assault behind them. "Sir?" he asked.

O'Sullivan's eyes turned icy as he put on his gloves against the cold of the outside. "I've not yet finished with this Endicott bitch," he said and strode to the door.

Female servants had joined the fracas to subdue Letitia and the weight of the pile of four men and three women could barely keep her massive frame from rising off the floor to rush to save her Abigail. Nicollete, screaming in terror, had attempted to run, but weathered hands had snatched her back, and she quickly disappeared into a sea of filthy blue uniforms, her cries becoming muffled by the soldiers' shouts of obscenities and laughter. Soon it was difficult to locate the small girl at all under the crush of O'Sullivan's men. And in short time, somewhere between the onslaught of penetrations and the vicious kicks and blows to her frail body from men who realized time would not permit their turn at her, an innocent and gentle Nicollete Endicott slipped away to the dark and soothing sanctuary of the dead.

Abigail's assailants also knew time was not on their side this cold evening and if they were to partake of her, they would have to do it quickly. A knife was produced to cut away the stubborn bodice, slicing the skin on her chest and stomach

140

along with it in a jagged, perforating pattern. Blood poured from the wound while the undeterred troopers pushed back her petticoats and pulled her undergarments from her kicking legs. Two soldiers each held a leg and spread them, pulling her to the edge of the table for access. "Step on up an' drop 'em, boys!" a soldier yelled with a laugh, standing between her legs and looking back over his shoulder. "We ain't got time to go by rank!" He leered down at her as he undid his belt and smiled at her as he spoke, revealing a grin of missing front teeth. The smile stretched a white scar that ran from the corner of his mouth to his left ear lobe so tightly that it made it seem as though his cheek would split in half. "Shuck damn, girly-gal!" he said, looking down at her and back at the men surrounding the table. "I ain't seen as purty a thing as you since we left Atlanta!" Brass belt buckles clunked with dull metallic thuds as they hit the wooden floor and filthy long johns were tangled down around their ankles as several men lined up behind one another in front of Abigail, her head now rolling from side to side as she screamed. A man at her head grabbed her thick brown hair with both hands and pulled tight, slamming her head tight against the table to keep it still.

"Somebody shut this wailing whore up!" a soldier shouted, becoming annoyed at the shrill sound. Taking a dirty bandanna from his pocket, another man replied, "I got somethin' right here oughta do it," he said, wadding it into a ball and stuffing it in the girl's mouth. By the time the next man was on her, Abigail had managed to work the rag out of her mouth and began to scream again. The trooper standing by her head, now angry at her resistance, let go of her hair and pulled his revolver from its holster and stood over her. "Let's see the harlot spit this out!" he said, shoving the barrel into her mouth, pushing it deep to lodge the muzzle against the back of her throat. Abigail's eyes bulged and the panic of gagging and choking took precedence over the ordeal of rape. Her face turning a deep red, she fought against the restraining hands now just to breathe. The eyes rolling back in her head told the men she was close to losing consciousness.

"Don't kill her. Major says he wants her alive for some damn reason. We best git, anyway, they're gettin' ready for us outside," a sergeant said to the remaining men now dressing again. "Sorry boys! If you didn't get none tonight, there'll be more a'comin' right soon at the next stop!" he said as they laughingly retreated from the girl who, now unrestrained, rolled from the table and dropped to the floor in a heap, gagging and vomiting. Abigail lay curled up in her blood, naked to the waist, struggling to take a deep breath. As she lapsed into unconsciousness, soldiers immediately lifted her and dragged her toward the door where an impatient Major O'Sullivan stood just past the porch, waiting by his horse. The remaining troops had secured firebrands and were accomplishing the major's other order with as much relish as they did the rape. Soldiers pointed their rifles at the younger field hands and ordered them outside. The muzzle of a musket barrel stared Malcolm in the face as he laid his full weight on his mother. "Git up, buck! You're gonna fight for the Union! How you like that, boy?" a soldier told him, grinning down into Malcolm's shocked face. Malcolm rose slowly into the muzzle while Letitia continued to scream from the bottom of the human pile. "Stay down, Momma," he told her, putting up his hands and offering no resistance as he joined the other chosen male slaves.

"How 'bout these others?" a trooper asked, pointing to the men still restraining Letitia.

"Too old; look at 'em. They ain't of no use, won't stand the march. We got the good 'uns. Come on, let's git 'em on out and git this place to burnin' like the major ordered," he said, pushing the confused and frightened field hands before them.

Torches were taken to the upstairs rooms and all curtains and flammable materials on both floors were ignited while the slaves and servants not involved with securing Letitia or chosen for conscription began to panic and race for the doors. Theo, now concerned with their safety, spoke to the other slaves in a warning tone. "We gots ta keep hold onto Momma, but we gots ta git out the house, they done set it a-fire! Momma, yo'cain't go chasen' after MizAbby, she gone, they gots her; you comin' wif us out the back do' and we all be gittin' outa here 'fore we burn or they shoot us!"

The men and women holding Letitia cautiously let her rise and gain her footing then began to push her with great effort toward the kitchen and the back door. She gradually moved backward, pushing against their full efforts, looking over their heads as long as possible toward the atrium and the front door where her Abigail had disappeared. Once outside, they pushed and pulled her to the safety of the darkness that was now meeting a growing orange light from the engulfing mansion.

Cornell Endicott lay still on the floor, his labored breathing making a heavy wheezing that was quickly becoming lost to the sounds of fleeing slaves and the growing crackle of fire around him. He moved his head slightly to attempt to focus his remaining useful eye and locate his younger daughter. The lengthening flames of the room illuminated a crumpled shape he could only identify by the torn clothing that partially covered it. He attempted to mouth the name of his dear Nicollete, wanting to speak it one more time before the now roaring fire consumed the room and them both. "Nih…cleh," he mumbled through the swelling and the blood, as tears ran from the eye that was now closing, signaling the beginning of his passage to the Garden where he knew she would be waiting for him, smiling and innocent as always.

***

"Load her across my saddle, private," the Major said, impatiently looking around at the status of his troops and the whereabouts of his missing captain. The fire from the house was starting to brighten the immediate area, aiding in the recognition of his company of freezing men.

"You want her lashed down, sir? Don't know if I'd bother if I were you. She don't look so good, bleedin' and all. I don't reckon she's gonna make it," the trooper said, eyeing the unconscious Abigail with disdain. "She ain't gonna be no good to you."

"*I'll* decide that, soldier! Now fall in with the column and leave this wench to me!" he barked back to the man. The private saluted in fear and melted away into the darkness while the major mounted his horse and looked down at the bleeding girl. "Before I've finished with you, Miss Endicott, you'll wish you had departed this world as easily as my mother!" he hissed as he rode away from the huge structure behind him, now fully engulfed in monumental flames. The house whined and groaned as flames rose into the freezing air of the night. The silhouettes of slaves could be seen running back and forth in front of the toppling manor, they all the while yelling and screaming in panic.

O'Sullivan trotted fifty yards from the inferno then stopped to turn and admire the first of many mansions and common homes destined to be so destroyed on the march to Savannah. Flames from the barns and outbuildings scattered around the property were beginning to grow and the frigid night air was becoming alive with the roaring of fires and the yelling of unseen slaves moving about in the dark. The snorting sound of a horse caused him to whip around, drawing his revolver as he turned toward it. Captain Beam sat five yards from him, slumped on his mount, illuminated in the glow of the now enormous pyre of the plantation house. "Captain Beam, where have you been?" the major asked in relief, lowering his sidearm. The flames from the house lit the sky and the solemn face of the captain as he dejectedly slouched on his horse.

"I chose the cold and dark to what I witnessed inside," he replied.

"I need you to assemble…" O'Sullivan began to say, looking off to his right to where the dim shape of the company was waiting for specific orders to move out and in what direction.

"I'm going home," Beam interrupted in the middle of the major's sentence.

"You're what?" O'Sullivan asked, not fully understanding the statement. "Do you mean *deserting*? You would desert our cause? The Union? Your commission? Captain, I…"

"This evening I bore tragic witness to the Union Army's

downward spiral into a shameful abyss from which I feel it will not escape. I am withdrawing from this madness before I too am swallowed up in the depravity of it." His eyes lost focus as he thought back through the campaigns and battles that were in his mind and memory, they righteous and just. "I... I look back now on my expectations..." In a dry tone, Major O'Sullivan cut the captain off in mid-sentence.

"Expectations, Zack? 'Oft expectation fails and most oft there where most it promises; and oft it hits where hope is coldest, and despair most fits'," the Major said calmly, cocking his head to look at his captain for reply. "All is indeed well that ends well."

Beam's face turned angry and his words bitter and loud. "Your poetic irony is not lost on me, major, but this," he said as he pointed to the conflagration behind his company commander, "this course of action for us, the Army, the Union, cannot end well! *You are not Helena, I am not a king, and this is not some goddamned play acted out upon a stage! This is real!"*

"'All the world's a stage', captain, and that," he said, pointing to the inferno, "is policy."

"That is murder!" Beam screamed back over the roar of the flames. *"And that,"* he said, trembling, pointing to the young girl lying near death over the major's saddle, *"is sick and twisted vengeance!"*

Beam slowly sat back in his saddle again and looked pensively toward the fire. "The honor is gone from this, drained from it like the blood from a fallen warrior. I am going back to my farm... and sanity."

"If you ride off, I'll shoot you myself, captain, do you hear

146

me?" O'Sullivan yelled and raised his revolver once more at him as the captain whirled his horse to ride north.

Beam stopped at the warning and turned back toward the major, his stare fixed and resigned. "Then end my part in this cruel'st play, if this be the best of acts," he said, pointing to the fire. O'Sullivan kept the gun trained on him as he absorbed the words. "Search not for the quote, major," Beam said, preparing to turn again from the madness he loathed. "It is not 'the Bard'; it is Beam." He turned and rode, melting into the darkness of Ocoosa County.

O'Sullivan's hand trembled, wanting to pull the trigger and do what he felt he was fully justified to do, but images of past battles flooded his memory and his deep belief that he still drew breath because of Zachary Beam caused him to reluctantly lower his gun in frustration and bitterness. ***"Goddamn you, Beam!"*** he shouted into the darkness. *"Goddamn the South!"* he said in a quieter voice, looking at the burning house. *"And goddamn the Endicotts, all of you!"* he hissed at the girl draped in front of him, taking her hair in his gloved hand and lifting her head and weight back across his saddle, letting her freezing body slide from the horse to the ground. He looked down with hatred and disgust at the young girl now at the brink of death from bleeding and the cold, her shape not quite identifiable as human in the semi-light of the fire. "Perhaps I shall see you and your family in Hell when this is over," he said, firing a shot down at her as his horse danced uneasily on the frozen dirt road. "Perhaps we'll all have another lovely visit such as we did this night!"

Major Trevor Sean O'Sullivan of the 33rd Massachusetts holstered his revolver and galloped into the dark to take command of his freezing troops and push on in the cold of night to the next plantation on their march to Savannah and infamy.

CHAPTER 13

"izAbby! MizAbby!" Letitia yelled in a loud whisper as the horse disappeared down the road.

"Stay here, Momma, he ain't gone far 'nuf yet," Theo cautioned her. "Stay put jus' yet, they all be gone right quick. They freezin' jus' like us!" he said, shivering from the cold alongside his mother in the thick brown tangle of bare wisteria bushes by the side of the road.

Letitia stared at the body in the road, looking for any sign of life. "Lawd, she ain't movin', boy; I gots ta git her 'fore she dies, ifn she ain't awready dead now!" she said, creeping out to the edge of the road still bathed in the orange glow of tall flames. She crawled to the body, looking down at this girl she loved so dearly as tears flowed down her broad face at what she saw. Abigail's upper body was covered in dark, freezing blood, the skin on her chest and stomach showing the intermittent slicing from the knife wounds. The petticoats and dress she wore were soaked with her blood, but as Letitia scooped up the girl into her strong arms, she could detect her still barely breathing. "Theo! She alive! She takin' breaf'!" she yelled her joyous whisper to the bushes. Letitia looked around and made her way keeping as low as she could to the roadside, carrying the girl in her arms as easily as she would a doll. "Boy, we gots ta git her outa here, go somewheres she gonna be safe. Might be mo' Yankees a-comin'; we don't know. Cain't take her to our cabin, that too close to here, too easy for Yankees to find if they be lookin' for us."

"Where we gonna go, Momma? Ain't none of us safe right now, I don' reckon. Them Yankees crazy! They all full 'o hate like them gray soldiers! Ain't nothin' right about this; ain't *nothin*!" Theo said, shaking his head in confusion. "They done took Malcolm, too. What they gonna do with the nigras they took? They gon' kill 'em? They gon' kill Malcolm?"

"Ain't gon' kill 'em, I don't 'spect; they'd a done that in the house ifn they wanted to. Malcolm a good boy, a smart boy. He slip 'em if he git the chance. Me and you gon' take MizAbby to the shanty."

Theo looked up from Abigail's body into his mother's face with surprise. "The shanty, Momma? Fo' true? You still remembers how to git to it?" he asked his mother while she tearfully pushed the girl's blood-soaked hair from her face and tried to cover her as best she could against the bitterness of the night air. The huge heart in Letitia's chest was beating fast while at the same time breaking for this girl, this broken, bleeding daughter of a dead slave owner she hated; this now-orphaned white girl that had, against all logic, become her reason to live.

"Ain't been to it in a spell, but a body don' never rightly forgit the way to where they was born!" she tearfully replied. "You go git to our cabin; fetch all the clothin' and blankets you kin gather up. Anythin' else you kin grab too, and bring my mule tail and darnin' needle. I gots ta sew this chile' up so she don't bleed to death! Hear me, boy? Now go, git! Kin you find yo' way to the shanty?"

Theo nodded. "I reckon I kin when the sun come up. I'll find y'all."

Theo disappeared into the darkness and Letitia rose with her precious cargo cradled in her arms, looking around in caution as she edged out onto the road of frozen ruts and icing holes to travel down it's length to the cut that would take her off the plantation proper along a barely recognizable path that led to a small, hidden cabin known only to the slaves. The light from the burning house was fading on her back just as the full moon was freeing itself from the clouds and she had no trouble identifying the oak tree that served as the turning point southeast away from the road. From here on it would be mostly a matter of feeling her way though dense woods by way of sheer memory, weaving in and out of thick forest devoid of the guiding moonlight; six miles almost all of which she would travel in near total darkness, groping for remembered signs that told her which way to turn and when. The 'trace', as it was called amongst the blacks, stayed overgrown from little travel, keeping it unnoticed by the unaware whites of the county. The shanty was intentionally difficult to find, and the lives of many slaves had depended upon that fact over the years.

***

Letitia's arms ached from carrying her MizAbby. Twice she had tripped on unseen obstacles in the black underbrush and twice she had barely caught herself to keep from falling on the girl. The occasional stop she permitted herself allowed a breathing spell for her, but mainly served as a check to see if this white girl, so obviously near death, was still breathing. Her feet were numb and frozen, but they felt the path begin to slant downward through the dark woods and tangle, the winding hint of descending trail leading down to an open clearing of natural grassy field on the side of a steep hill. The clearing appeared gray in the moonlight, giving her some illumination by which to see, and Letitia knew the shanty she sought was just beyond it. The door had no latch and Letitia nudged it open and stood in the dark of the doorway. "Anybody in here? Don't mean no harm," she announced, hoping to find no one inside to frighten.

No answer came back and she walked in, shuffling the dark floor to keep from tripping as she made her way to where the one small bunk had been so many years before, the one on which her mother had given birth to her. Letitia felt with one hand for the bed and could tell pine boughs and straw were there under what seemed to be a blanket. She lay Abigail down in the blackness of the cabin and searched the closest wall for the flint and steel that had always been hidden there. Suddenly, she realized how cold she was and hurried outside to look for tinder. A small bowl lay near the door and she bent to pull dead grass from the ground outside where the field began and, putting it in the bowl and striking flint with steel, created a small kindling blaze. She brought the small flame back inside and could see firewood by the tiny fireplace on one wall. It was time to build a real fire and tend to this freezing girl, still hovering near death. Letitia covered her with the remnants of what had once been a horse blanket and did what she could do to comfort her. Abigail had not awakened during the walk to the cabin and still showed no signs of response, and Letitia knew this was not good. The lacerations had begun to thaw and the bleeding had started again, but not nearly as bad as before. She sat down on the floor beside the bed and seeing there was nothing more she could do for the girl, she leaned against the bed and fell asleep.

CHAPTER 14

The sun was already up and Letitia woke to the realization she was cold. The fire from the night before had long burned itself out and she turned quickly to see if MizAbby was still breathing. Though the child had not moved in the night, her chest was rising and falling slowly, and Letitia smiled at the welcome sight. "Oh, MizAbby, stay wif' me now; stay wif' me, baby girl," she said, examining her again for the bullet hole that should be obvious. "Lawd, there ain't even no hole *in* you, MizAbby!" she exclaimed to the unconscious girl, looking her over again and again for bleeding. "That Yankee man missed you all t'gether! Don' know how that can be, but he sho' 'nuf did! 'Magin that!" she continued, smiling at Abigail, whose purplish color indicated her need for more heat. Letitia went outside for more tinder and looked up to see Theo entering the sloping field from the forest above, making his way down to the shanty, a bundle of belongings slung over his shoulder. Though Theo was a large man himself, Letitia picked him up off the ground when they met and hugged her oldest boy, glad he was safe.

"Anybody see you, boy?" she asked him, looking back

over her shoulder for anyone who may have followed him.

"No, Momma. Nigras was too busy runnin' back to they cabins to fetch belongin's like me," he told her, turning to show her the full sack that draped over his back. "Mos' still screamin' and gatherin' things to leave on out to somewheres."

"Go where? Where them nigras think they be goin to?" Letitia asked, surprised at Theo's words.

"Don' know. Momma. All the cabins still standin'. I seen ol' Mose, and he say long as the Yankees lef' his cabin standin', he's stayin' put; some others too. Noah one of 'em, and Mamie, she stayin'. Fact, it was ol' Mose tol' me what to look for to git me here."

"Give me my needle and tail; I gots ta sew on this chile' 'for she wake up," Letitia said, heading back into the cabin to relight the fireplace in order to ward off the frigid morning. Theo withdrew a blanket from the sack to lay over Abigail, then began extracting the possessions he was able to recover from the slave quarters he could not know they would never see again. Letitia threaded the needle with hair from her mule tail and began to close the split on Abigail's chest and stomach. The unconscious girl responded by groaning and moving her head as if having a bad dream and Letitia saw it as a good sign. With the wounds closed, she covered the girl again with blankets, then turned back to Theo. "Fetch more wood for the fire, then see can you find some thistle up in the field; it don' matter if it be brown or dead-lookin' from the winter, jus' git down to the root an' bring me some. I'll make a poultice for them cuts and some tea for to make her feel better when she wake up."

"What we gonna do fo' food, Momma? Mas'tuh smoke

house an' stores all burned up or taken off by Yankees," Theo said.

"We hunt an' scrounge for roots an' things, jus' like we always done in lean winters, I s'pose; we git by. Gotsta keep this girl livin', that bein' the big thing in this cold," Letitia told him, looking back over her shoulder to the bed. Her eyes opened wide to see Abigail now laying awake, tearing eyes staring up at the dark crude rafters of the cabin, her face twisted in frozen anguish. She had awakened from her sleep only to continue back at the point of horror she had left the night before.

CHAPTER 15

You doin' good, MizAbby, you is! That stitchin' I done took to you real good," Letitia said, looking down at the expressionless Abigail. She was barely accepting the root tea Letitia had been brewing for her the last few days and the little food she would eat was not nearly enough to sustain her, much less build any strength.. "Chile, yo' gots ta eat! Ol' Letitia love you, you knows that, ain't no doubt, but I cain't be liftin' you up an' takin' you out to the necessary fo'ever. Theo been gone three day down across the Chatoosee lookin' to see what the Yankees done lef' over there, maybe find some food fo' us and all; he ain't gon' always be here to hep. You gon' hafta be gittin' up and gittin'…" Letitia saw Abigail slowly turn her head to look at the door of the cabin and stare silently. The shanty filled with added light and Letitia turned to see Theo standing in the doorway holding the body of a black man in his arms, tears rolling down his face "Momma… Malcolm dead, Momma," he said and looked down at the brother he held.

Letitia rose from the floor next to the bed and walked toward him slowly, in shock. "Boy?" she asked, needing to know more.

"Nigras on the other side of the Chatoos' tol' me the Yankees come through there like they done Mas'tuhs plantation and burned up everythin'. Took all the young bucks too. Some got away in the dark; Malcolm one of 'em. Soldiers on horses took off an' run 'em down, what they could, an' shot 'em. Mas'tuh Rummels nigras tol' me where Malcolm body be layin'; he mos' made it back to the river 'fore they catched him an' shot him. Mas'tuh Rummels house burned down too; nigras sayin' all the properties be gone now from the Yankees."

Tears flowed down Letitia's face as she took Malcolm's face in her big hands, and her lip quivered as she spoke. "Take yo' brother out aways from the shanty and dig what hole you kin. The dirt too hard to carve out much, I knows, but do what you kin. Fetch stones from the field an' cover him good; don' want no critters carryin' my boy off," she said, sniffing back her tears. "Put him where I can keep a eye on him."

***

Theo put the last of the stones he had gathered on top of Malcolm's makeshift grave while Letitia stood motionless, staring at yet another of her children lost to her. Walking to stand next to her, Theo wiped the red dirt from his hands on his pant legs and both stood silently, looking down at the collection of stones. The cold wind was intermittent and gusty for the dell, and the sky was bright with a high, gray overcast. Both remained silent until Theo spoke first. "You gon' say 'words', Momma? I don' know what to say on bodies, 'cept Malcolm was my brother an' I'll miss him," Theo said, his voice quivering.

Letitia heaved a big, shuddering sigh and thought a moment. "Malcolm was a good boy, hard workin' boy; never caused nobody no trouble. He deserved…"

"Momma!" Theo interrupted, pointing to the shanty where Abigail stood leaning unsteadily in the doorway, looking out at the two, obviously wanting to make her way to where they were. Letitia turned to run to her, gathering her petticoats up in her hands as she went lumbering back to the cabin. Wrapping her arm around the girl, she slowly guided her the thirty yards to the grave and held her up, steadying her by her side.

"Malcolm dead, MizAbby, you know? How you be feelin'?" she asked her, not sure how long she had been conscious of the situation. Abigail, pale and clearly in pain, nodded her head and stared down at the rocks without expression.

"The Lord is my Shepard," she began slowly and quietly, coughing and clearing her throat, still sore and horse from the gun barrel. "I shall not want; he maketh me to lie down in green pastures…" she continued while Letitia and Theo traded glances between themselves and the grave. All was silent in the dell save for Abigail's weak and raspy voice mixing with the occasional gust of cold wind that swirled through the tall dead grass.

CHAPTER 16

Abigail sat on the bed with a blanket wrapped around her, a look of concern and puzzlement on her face. "'Titia, I think there's something wrong with me. I mean, something must not be right," she said while Letitia stoked more wood in the small fireplace, her back to the girl. She knew almost without a doubt what worried the young girl, and it worried her too. Letitia knew her MizAbby as well as the girl knew herself, and she was well-aware that the young woman had not had a period in the almost two and a half months since that terrible night. The morning sickness, Letitia had hoped, was simply an adjustment to the basic food they had to rely on, scrounged and hunted as best they could. But now the situation was becoming obvious to her, and it was time, she supposed, to explain the matter to this unsuspecting white girl who shivered slightly on the bed, a look of innocent curiosity on her face. Letitia left the fire, walked the few steps to the bed and sat down next to it, taking Abigail's hands in hers, her own dwarfing the small white fingers she held with genuine love. "Letitia guessin' you mean yo' 'crimson rider' ain't stopped by to see you in a while, that what botherin' you chile'? That what you think be wrong?" she asked.

"Yes, that and I can't keep down the food you and Theo give me. I'm really thankful for it, I really am, but..."

"Baby girl," Letitia stopped her, attempting to choose the right words to explain to her cherished MizAbby what was going to take place in the months to come and how it would culminate. "They's changes happenin' to you right now, an' it got to do wif' what happened that evil night back when. Now, I knows we don' talk 'bout it much 'cause it scare you still, an' rightly so. But the truth be, when them Yankee mens... took on you the way they done... well... it seem purty sure now one of 'em lef' a baby up inside you."

Fear flooded Abigail's face in confused disbelief and she looked into Letitia's for another answer, anything but what she was hearing. "A baby?" she screamed, bursting into tears and covering her face with the blanket in horror and shame. "No! No!" she sobbed loudly. "I don't want a baby! I can't be a momma!" she said through her tears. "How...how can that be?"

Letitia looked around the cabin, searching for some better way to explain, some "good" words to comfort the girl she so loved and tell her that all would be alright. Theo sat propped up against the door sill repairing the handle on the water bucket, also in realization of the predicament, looking down at his task with an insular deliberateness. Abigail scurried off the crude bed to slide down beside the immense woman on the floor for comfort, tucking in under her massive arm where she had always felt safe and troubles had not dared stay very long. Perhaps, she thought, Letitia could make this baby go away too. "Can you do anything, 'Titia? Can you stop it? Please do something if you can! I don't want a baby! It comes out down there, doesn't it? It will hurt! I…I don't want to hurt down there ever again!" she cried into the woman's huge breast.

Letitia cradled her head and kissed her hair, patting her on the back and consoling as much as she could, having already accepted the fact that Abigail would most likely give birth sometime in the "searin' month," August, barring anything unforeseen. "Ain't much nobody kin do now, chile'. Ever now an' agin' somthin' happen to keep babies from comin' full on, but mos' times they be born jus' like I reckon they s'pose ta be. All we kin do is keep you healthy… an' wait on it."

"I can't! I can't do it! I can't bear the thought of a baby from… from one of those… men…" her voice trailing off, her mind succumbing back to the memory of the night of the rape and so much violence and death. "Whenever I think about what they did to me, what happened… oh, Momma, you just don't know! You can't imagine what it was like…" Abigail ceased talking and collapsed into uncontrolled sobbing, burying her head into Letitia's shoulder, the big woman now wrapping both arms around her tightly as the crying intensified and shook them both. The girl had called her Momma. In the darkest moment of a dark hour, she had verbally acknowledged the black woman as her surrogate mother and Letitia bit her trembling lips at this acceptance that touched her very soul. She turned her head to look through the door, past Theo, out over the grassy field to the grave of Abigail's half-brother Malcolm, forcing back not only tears for Abigail's expression of her love, but for painful memories of her own past she had forgotten lie dormant within her.

"I know, I know, baby girl. It was a terrible thing they

done to you, a terrible thing. No girl should hafta bear somethin' like that in they life, no how. Ol' Letitia jus cain't 'magin what that mus' bin like fo' you," she said, gently patting Abigail's hair "My po' baby. Jus' go 'head an' cry, chile'; let it out." Her gaze finally drifted back and she caught Theo's knowing eyes meeting her own, wide with anticipation and expectation at what she would say next to the girl she cradled so tightly. He looked at his mother then down at the girl and stared intently back into her eyes again, waiting. Letitia slowly shook her head "no," then lowered her face to bury it in Abigail's long, curly hair, stroking it with heartfelt tenderness as she had done countless times before.

CHAPTER 17

The rising sun was still well down behind the tree tops at the far upper edge of the dell, but it was light enough for Theo to discern the movement of something making its way down through the high grass toward the shanty. "Momma, look like they might be somebody comin' down the dell, I cain't rightly tell!" he shouted back into the cabin door.

Letitia, bent over at the fireplace, stood erect and spun toward the daylight making its way into the dark interior. She hurried to stand in the doorway, instinctively refraining from rushing outside and exposing her presence to whoever might be approaching. Scanning the top of the hollow, she quickly located the quirky movement that Theo had locked his eyes on. A fast visual arc around the meadow top for other possible movement reassured her for the moment that this visitor seemed to be alone. What looked like the head of a man, a white man, would appear over the top of the grass for a few seconds then disappear, only to reappear again closer to them.

"It's a white man, Momma! Oh no! What we gon' do?" Theo asked, the panic evident in his voice.

Her gaze still fixed, Letitia studied the bobbing head and odd movement. "Sumpin' wrong here, boy. He look like he crawlin' or even mos' tumblin', like. We best stay put here, see what he do, where he go." Standing just feet in front of the cabin, Letitia and her son braced and stood ready to defend themselves and the shanty against this unknown intruder. Fifteen feet away from them up the sloping hollow, an obviously injured white man slowly pulled himself out of the grass and painfully rolled to a half-seated position, cursing and rubbing his right leg.

"Ho the cabin!" he shouted to them between his swearing. "Don't mean no harm, I'm alone. Can you help me? I'm hurt bad. *Oh, sumbitch, my leg,"* he groaned as his head tilted back in obvious pain.

"What wrong wif yo' leg?" Theo asked, a small confidence growing in his voice.

"Goddamn horse up and died on me, *up and damn died*! I was on the road up yonder above the field here… Aw, *Jesus!…* and she just fell with me on her; no warnin'. She buckled down and rolled on me! This leg was just gittin' to heal up from a hurt I got a while back, and now that swayback nag done gone an' broke it again, I reckon. Oh *damn*, it hurts!" The man cradled his knee as best he could and rocked back and forth in pain. "You got water I kin have? I'm powerful thirsty!" Letitia stared at him for several seconds, studying him, his story and his speech.

"You a Yankee, ain't you?" she asked, unmoved by his predicament and apparent suffering. "What you doin' here? Yankees come through here some time back and lit out after they done tore up ever-thing and killed lotsa the white folk.

What you be doin' in these parts?"

The man attempted to stand but the pain it caused made him think better of it and he rolled and rubbed as he tried to ease his pain and talk at the same time. His misery and frustration were evident in his voice. "I'se with 'Uncle Billy' and his Army when we came through here back 'afore Christmas sometime. I was scoutin' on ahead of 'em when some damn bush-whacker shot me in the leg from outa nowhere! Bullet shattered my leg bone an' I fell in a ditch; stayed there for days, so I lost 'em all. They were headed to Savannah; prob'ly gonna tear it up too, like they did Atlanta, I reckon. A family that saw things diff'rent from the rest of you took me in and there I stayed a-healin' till somebody found 'em out and burned down the house. I took off to runnin' north on that nag up yonder, she dropped dead as I said, an' here I be. Hey, boy, you gonna fetch that water or not?"

Theo stood staring and listening to this desperate and injured man, a fitting example of the Union Army that utterly destroyed the way of life he and all the people of Ocoosa County had known. A sense of defiance and power had gradually grown within him as the man had told his story and he made no attempt to move to help him. Letitia and Theo looked at each other in silent agreement and Theo turned to the man to speak. "Ain't gon' be no water fo' you. No nothin' else neither, I don't reckon. Go, git on outa here; crawl on back the way you came. Jus' git out, Yankee."

The man grew angry and his voice became loud and shrill at this refusal of aid. **"Goddamn you, uppity nigra!** You damn colored are all the same! The Union come through here tryin' ta help you, and you don't **want** it! Well I'll tell you somethin' boy, somethin you don't rightly know, I'm willin' to wager. It don't matter now! The war's over! North won; Lee give up his troops an' ever'body went home, 'cept the dead an' me, I reckon. Hell, Lincoln's dead too; somebody kill't 'im. All this," he motioned around him, pointing back to the direction from where he had come, "all this war wasn't for you, none of you 'colored'! Lincoln didn't care a tinker's damn about you nigras from what talk I heard. He done set you all free so's to cause as much ruckus as he could in these here rebel states; figured you'd all run off, leavin' your owners to fend for themselves with crops an' chores an' all. Thought that would put a quick end to all this fussin'. But yer all so damn dumb, you **stayed put**! What's wrong with all a ya? Are ya stupid?" The veins in his neck were standing out as he sat in the red clay and weeds yelling at them with all his remaining strength and anger. The frustration and pain of this wounded man caused his body to shake and tremble as he spat his words out at this huge black woman and her son poised defiantly in front of him. *"Yer free! Yer Master's gone; chains is gone! Go on, git outa here! I am! I'm goin'! I'm gittin' myself back to Pennsylvania ifn' I got ta crawl there!"* This Union soldier, broken, starving and lost, would never see his home again.

Abigail's curiosity had finally gotten the better of her acquired caution and she poked her head around the corner of the doorway in order to see this man that was causing such a loud commotion. She stood in the doorway, motionless in fear and bewilderment that a white man had found the dell, and she watched him as he screamed at Letitia and Theo. The man's attention was drawn away by this pregnant young girl with long dark hair and his ranting ceased as he gawked back at her

167

in surprise. "What's that white girl doin' here? Why you got a white girl with you? You alright, girly-gal?" Abigail's breath stopped in her throat at the words and her face twisted in horror.

Pain from the soldier's injured leg suddenly gripped him again and a toothless grimace of agony filled his face. A scar that ran from the corner of his mouth to his ear threatened to crack his weathered cheek in half. Abigail retreated back a step and burst into panicking tears as her voice came back to her enough to shout to Letitia and Theo. *"It's him! He's one of them who hurt me, who did this to me! I know he's one, I remember him!"* she screamed as she held her swollen stomach with one hand and covered her mouth with the other.

The man's face dissolved into a look of fear and confusion and Letitia turned from looking back at Abigail to glare at him with rage. *"I didn't do nothin' to this girl; she must be crazy with fever or somethin'! I don't even know her!"* he shouted as Letitia strode the short distance toward him. He attempted to slide back away from her advancement but made no progress. He kicked at this approaching giant with his good leg as she effortlessly knocked it out of her way with her arm, spinning him slightly in the dirt. As his hands went down to brace himself from falling backwards, Letitia's huge left hand caught him firmly in the throat. She held him fast in an iron grip of hatred.

"You was there that night? You done this to my baby? You one of 'em done this? I'm gon' kill you here where you sit, boy!" she bellowed with all the anger she possessed.

"Momma!" Theo shouted at her and began to approach as Abigail screamed and cried in the doorway of the shanty.

168

Without looking around, Letitia motioned back to her son with her free hand while she spoke down into the face of this doomed man she held in a grip of death. *"Git back, boy! I'm gon' kill this Yankee done this to my chile'! I'm gon' choke the breaf' right out his damn body!"*

The soldier's eyes bulged and watered as his face turned red then purple. He grabbed at her arm with both hands to wrest her hand away and break her hold, but to no avail. No sound escaped from his mouth that now drooled and attempted one last time to speak. Letitia looked directly at him as she tightened her grip and watched the eyes roll back in his head. She steadied her weight with her left hand as she pushed him onto his back and eased herself down to her knees by his left side, all the while maintaining her grip on his throat. As she felt him start to go limp, a last surge of self-preservation suddenly tightened his entire body in a final effort to save himself. With his arms flailing at her arm and face in a last dying panic, she turned to her right and freed a heavy stone partially buried in the red clay. Raising it up over her head, she allowed the rage she suppressed at her helplessness that terrible night to flow through her, and the power she sensed in her right hand, the control that had never before been permissible in her life, felt good to her. *"You done wrong to my baby! You an' yo' mens heaped a evil on her she don' deserve!"* The man's struggling was slowing and his straining eyes looked directly at the stone she held over him. He knew, in a brief moment, it would end his life.

Letitia brought the rock down with all her strength and fury and the soldier's eyes followed it as it slammed into his face with the sound of a splitting melon. His struggling arms fell to the ground and his legs twitched and jerked as Letitia threw the stone off to the side, examining the distorted concave bowl of flesh and bone that had moments ago been a face and was now filling rapidly with blood. Breathing heavily, and with much effort, she brought herself up to her feet and stood staring silently down at what she had done, sickened yet satiated, fighting a brief instant of remorse to allow a righteousness to reign forth.

Theo approached from the rear and came around to her front to push her away from the body still spasming in death throes. He put his hands on his mother's chest and looked back at the body with morbid fascination for long seconds. "You killed him Momma; oh Lawd, you done killed a white man!" He pushed her back and Letitia retreated only because she allowed it, looking over Theo's shoulder at the dead man on the ground as she stepped backward.

"I sent a deb'il back to Hell is what I done," she said in a defiant tone while she kept her eyes focused on the Yankee. ***"Ain't gon' be nobody harmin' Letitia's chid'rens never agin', you hear me Yankee? Don' pass on me yet, you hear me? No body ever be takin' my babies from me agin'! Not never no mo'!"*** Her nostrils were flaring in her rage as Theo moved her back to the front of the shanty.

"You done killed a man, Momma; a white man! What all we gonna do wif' him?" Theo asked her, glancing back to a body he knew, despite the circumstance, would be a death warrant for them both if ever found out by the whites of Ocoosa County. "We kin bury him! That's what we do! I kin go 'round back and dig him a hole, won't *nobody*…"

"Don't want that trash buried here!" Letitia said as she

170

pushed up against Theo again in order to spit over his shoulder toward the body that now seemed so small and harmless. "You tump an' tote him down to the Big Chatoos. Be sure ain't nobody seeing you, and you ease him in by where the rocks is, by the bend. Water quick an' fast there; by the time he wash up down river, nobody be the wiser where he come from. Git to it, or I'll tear him up wif' my own hands, hear?" She whirled suddenly as she thought of Abigail and ran to stand in the doorway, quickly scanning the tiny interior for her MizAbby. Peering into the darkness of the cabin she saw the girl huddled on the floor in the far corner, trembling and staring blankly at the crude plank wall. Letitia crossed the short distance and bent to touch the girl's shoulder, hoping to give some amount of reassurance, wanting to console and comfort this light of her life. Unresponsive and silent, Abigail continued to stare without acknowledging the woman's presence, grabbing at her shins again and again to bring her knees closer to her chest to keep her retreat from that night as tight and complete as possible. Quietly, Letitia slowly eased herself down to sit on the floor at arm's length from the girl, gently, lovingly resting one hand on the girl's knee, bowing her head in silent reflection as she remembered how this bare corner of a sparse shanty could provide such strange asylum to a young pregnant girl devastated by the memory of rape.

CHAPTER 18

August 17, 1865

Theo! Cut strips from my ol' petticoat and lay 'em close to me! An' move the lantern closer so's I kin see!" Letitia commanded, less alarmed than her voice suggested.

Theo, more nervous than his mother, did what he was told and waited for her to tell him he could wait outside. "Y'all gonna be needin' me anymo', Momma? I be right outside the do' ifn you be needin' me."

"Go on, boy, but don't wander; I might be needin' somethin' else, maybe water," Letitia told him as she held Abigail's hand and looked down into her face of fear and pain. "MizAbby, now you jus' do what ol' Letitia tell you an' this thing gon' go good an' it be over wif right quick. You push when I tells you to push, an' push hard, like you use ta push back when you was a little girl an' got all seized up inside an' had trouble goin' to the 'necessary', remember?" she told her, attempting to get her mind off the pain at hand. Abigail nodded as she grimaced, trusting the slave woman's knowledge of what was happening to her. "We jus' kin wait. Is all we kin do. Letitia keep checkin' fo' the head an' when I sees it, you does jus what I tells you, hear?" she reiterated and wiped the sweat from the frightened teen's head. "You gon' do jus fine!"

Theo sat with his back against the cabin wall just outside the door, the light from the one lantern weakly shining through the window above his shoulder. The warm night, the summer sounds of the crickets and frogs breaking the silence of the dell, lulled him off to sleep, only to be awakened a short time later by the screaming of a sixteen-year-old girl and the wailing of a newborn baby.

"Look, MizAbby, yo' gots yo' self a girl, a baby girl!" Letitia said, smiling down at Abigail, the squirming infant in her big hands. She tied off the cord, cutting it with the pairing knife Theo had brought from their quarters nine months before, and showed the infant to Abigail, still breathing hard and relieved the ordeal was over. Abigail stared blankly at the baby she had given birth to just minutes before and slowly turned her head to the wall while her breathing slowed to normal, uninterested in looking at it, much less holding it. "Don' you wants ta hold it, baby girl? You gots yo'*own* 'baby girl' now!" Letitia said, trying her best to be cheerful. Hopefully, she thought, Abigail would take to the child more when she had rested and the infant needed to be fed. And she would have to feed this baby; no one else for many miles around could do it for her. Theo stood in the door, looking in on the awaited event that had just happened, and saw concern in his mother's eyes as she looked at him then back at the new mother now turned completely toward the wall, with the baby quietly laying swaddled beside her.

***

The following day, despite Letitia's best efforts, Abigail had still refused to hold the child or even look at it. The baby's crying made it evident it was hungry and would have to be fed soon by someone. Letitia decided to work with Abigail some more, coaxing her, reasoning with her to at least try to feed it even if she felt she didn't want it, at least until someone could be found to wet nurse. As night fell and the hungry baby cried itself to sleep, Letitia and Theo drifted off as well, leaving a very wide-awake Abigail to silently glower at this infant she was quickly growing to despise, her eyes narrowing and her teeth clenching in hate. Her breathing became faster and deeper as she scowled over at it, knowing that somehow, when the opportunity arose, she would find a way to send it back where she believed deep in her heart it had come from.

CHAPTER 19

D awn was breaking and the shanty awoke to the weak squalling of a baby in distress. Letitia could see that Abigail had not made any attempt to feed it and she knew something had to be done. Quietly, she motioned Theo outside and both proceeded down the slope in back of the cabin to obey nature's first call of the day. Finishing, they approached each other from their respective areas and Letitia told her son what had to be done.

"Boy, that baby gon' die 'less we find somebody gon' nurse it, and that's fo' true!" she said, looking back at the shanty forty yards from them. "You hightail back to the plantation, see if that Creole woman still be there; Marie. She was wet nursin', maybe she still there an' doin' it. Fetch her back here no matter what! Tell her she *gots* ta come! Now git!" Theo started up the hill and reaching the cabin, turned to walk to it and stopped, spinning quickly to yell to his mother. Letitia had begun to walk back up the hill, thinking as she went for a solution to the problem at hand, when Theo's voice made her look up.

"Momma, git up here quick! Miz Abigail gots the baby

and the knife!" he yelled, turning to carefully approach the young mother who was struggling in pain up the hill into the grassy field holding her squalling infant in one hand by one of it's arms and the paring knife in the other. Letitia's mass was a blessing in many circumstances but not in trying to move it uphill very quickly. She struggled up the slope to fall in line behind Theo and Abigail, who stumbled just ahead of him swinging the screaming baby as if it weren't a living thing.

"MizAbby! What you gon' do, chile? Don' hurt yo' baby, you hear Letitia talkin' to you? Don' you be hurtin' it!" she yelled at the girl who turned at the words to brandish the short knife at them both. Seeing the knife, Letitia recoiled in horror, immediately feeling a betrayal deep within her, a sorrow as painful as if the knife had actually slashed her. Her 'baby girl', a child that she treasured more than her own life, had threatened her.

"What we gon' *do*, Momma?" Theo asked, his eyes wide with fear and confusion. "Look at her face, Momma! It don't look like Miz Abigail!" he said, as the girl turned to them once again, glaring with a wide-eyed hatred on her face. Letitia saw the face and realized something was happening beyond her understanding, past what she was seeing. She stood rooted, not knowing what to do next, when Abigail stopped her purposeful uphill movement and, letting her baby fall from her grasp, dropped to her knees, twisting back toward the frozen mother and son to glare at them again, her eyes narrowed and determined. *Momma sent that devil-man that hurt me back to Hell with a stone. I'll send this thing back the same way!*

She dropped the knife by her side, grabbed a stone from the ground in front of her and raised it above her head in a swift motion, looking down at the howling baby in front of her, eyes tightly shut, its tiny arms and legs churning the air in panic. *"Get back to Hell and your father!"* Abigail growled in a loud, guttural voice neither Letitia nor Theo recognized. The rock came down as she finished her words, striking the helpless girl in the face, the squalling ceasing immediately.

Letitia and Theo stood paralyzed, helpless at the sight, frozen and weak in their shock. The grimace of hate rapidly melted from Abigail's face and turned to horror at what lay in front of her and she covered her face with her hands, convulsing in tears. Reaching down with her right hand, she picked up the knife and held it to her stomach, raised her face to the sky and screamed **"No!"**

Theo was becoming unstuck from his trance of horrific disbelief and moved toward her to stop her just as Letitia finally brought herself to speak. *"No, Abigail, don't! MizAbby, don't!"* she yelled, moving toward her. Theo ran to the girl from behind, and only feet from her tripped on something unseen in the tall grass, his fall and momentum carrying him into the back of Abigail and toppling her forward. Letitia reached her and grabbed her by the hair to pull her back and take the knife, only to find the handle protruding from her stomach, blood beginning to boil from the wound. *"Oh no! Oh no, not my baby girl! Not my MizAbby!"* she cried out in grief and panic, tears flooding her face. She knelt over the girl and looked down at her, feeling truly helpless for only the second time in her life. Abigail's eyes rolled back in her head and she tried to speak, but Letitia put her hand to her mouth and hushed her. "Don' try to talk, baby girl, jus' be quiet, now. Letitia gon' git you back inside an' git some help!" she told her, picking her up in her arms and getting assistance from a recovering Theo. Laying her down back inside the shanty, Letitia surveyed the situation and made a quick decision. "Boy, git into town, Watsonville, an' git that doctor what birthed Nicollete and fetch him here. It the only'st chance MizAbby gots to live! Do what yo' gots ta to git him here! *Jus' git him!*"

"You wants ta bring another white man down in here, Momma?" Theo asked, looking back and forth at his mother and Abigail.

Grabbing him by the front of his shirt with one big hand and pointing to the bed with the other, Letitia bellowed, *"That's my MizAbby layin' there, the life ebbin' out her wif' her blood! I bring Satan his own self here ifn it save her! Now git to doin' what I tol' you, boy! Git!"*

Theo broke from her grasp and disappeared out the doorway and Letitia spun to sit down by the bed, looking intently into Abigail's face for some sign of hope that this would all turn out alright. An overwhelming feeling of dread told her deep down in her soul that, in the end, it would not.

CHAPTER 20

The snorting of horses and the sound of voices awakened Letitia and the morning light through the opened door blinded her slightly as she adjusted her vision to see Theo and a tall, well-dressed white man standing just inside the cabin.

"I'm Doctor Fale, ma'am. You're Letitia, I know. I recognize you from the Endicott Plantation," he said, approaching the bed to look sadly down at the dead girl lying still in front of him. "And this was Abigail Endicott. I recognize her also. I had assumed these past several months that she had perished in the carnage last November and was shocked at the story your son here told me. I agreed to come in case he was right."

Letitia looked up in surprise at his words and turned to look at Abigail, realizing suddenly that the hand she had been holding through the night was now cold. Tears began and flowed and streamed down her face as she gently pried the girl's fingers from her own and put the arm by the girl's side. She rose to her knees and turned to bury her face in the blood-soaked dress, releasing the rest of her grief. Dr. Fale gently took her by her broad shoulders and helped her up and off to the side in order to examine this girl he had known almost since her birth. His appraisal of the situation took only a matter of seconds and he turned to Theo and his weeping mother. "The story your son told me seems to be accurate, from what I can see here," he said. "You know of no reason she did these things to herself and her baby?"

Letitia wiped at her eyes with the edge of her tattered dress and spoke through her tears. "She done had her baby a couple days back an' wanted nuffin' to do wif' it, I 'spose on account it was from one o' them Yankees that raped on her. I figger'd at first it was jus' the blue feelin' women sometime gits after they has a baby; they feelin' all mixed up inside an' all fo' such a while. Then she jus' up an' took it out in the grass and bashed it in the head wif' a rock." Justified or not, Letitia was not comfortable with telling a white man, seemingly kind enough in appearance, that she had killed a white Yankee in a similar manner just months before. "An' she done this a' fore she went," Letitia told him, pointing to the floor. There by the bed, having been scratched into the floor with what could have been a paring knife, were the words "Hells babee." "Don' know my letters; what it say, suh?" Letitia asked the man looking down at the words and shaking his head.

Dr. Fale heaved a sigh and looked at the two, saying, "Abigail obviously thought that the Devil was responsible for this child and I assume that is what made her do this. May I see the baby?"

"I wrapped it in some cloth I was keepin' to patch MizAbby's dress," Letitia told him. "I put her outside in a bucket I tied up to a branch so's nothin' would git her. She out here," she said, leading the two men out to a tree close to the shack. Fale took the bucket down and looked in, the sight clearly repulsing him. Placing the bucket on the ground, he took a deep breath and turned to the two.

"There remains nothing left to do but bury these two. I'll help you if you'd like. I feel I owe it to the Endicotts to give at least one of them a proper burial. They were friends of mine. There was nothing left of her father or her sister to inter," he said.

"Kin we lay 'em to rest over there by my other boy?" Letitia asked him.

"Of course. Theo told me of his story. The Yankees did indeed cause such widespread pain and despair with their coming and going. I've seen with my own eyes their toll on this county. If you've been here the entire time, you should know that all the plantations were destroyed."

"Ever' one?" Theo asked, his eyes wide now in disbelief.

"All of them," Dr. Fale responded. "I won't begin to tell you the horror I have seen and worse that I have heard. Shall we start? We have much work to do." The three gathered pieces of board and some sharp rocks to begin digging as best they could into the grassy turf next to Malcolm's grave. By the end of the afternoon, two mounds of rock lay prominently in the green grass of the dell. Dr. Fale, his white shirt stained red from dirt and sweat, looked down at the two mounds and said, "If you'll provide me some flat board, I'll make markers for them. I'll carve their names in them; your boy's too," he said. Theo went behind the shanty for smooth planking and he and his mother watched in fascination as the doctor used his penknife to carve the names into the wood. Tapping them in

181

with a stone, the doctor rolled down his sleeves and put his coat on, walking back to his two horses. After a few preparations, he mounted and looked down at the two. "I am indeed sorry for your losses and your grief. You loved your boy, I'm sure. And I know you did indeed love Miss Endicott. I had seen that with my own eyes on my visits to their plantation. And ma'am, you should know this: she most certainly loved you back, more than you shall ever know. She did, in fact, most lovingly think of you as her mother. I know that as fact."

Letitia bit her quivering lower lip and tears began again as Dr. Fale turned his horses to ride up through the grassy field and back to Watsonville.

***

Theo came into the cabin just after sunrise to find his mother gathering the few things that could be considered belongings and placing them in a blanket.

"What you doin', Momma? Is you goin' somewheres?" he asked.

"*We* goin' somewheres, boy; we leavin'," she replied, her voice filled with determination.

"Leavin' where to?" Theo asked, falling in to help her gather articles around the shack.

"Leavin' to 'I don' knows where'; we jus' be gittin' out o' this dell and sayin' our goodbyes," she said.

"Goodbyes?" he asked again, confused by what she was saying. She turned to him and looked him in the eyes.

"Boy, we needs to say goodbye to those three souls reposin' in this here field; goodbye to this shanty, goodbye to this whol' land. We needs to just head out, north maybe. You gots any other ideas where to?

"Theo," she said, taking his face in her hands, "there ain't nothin left here no mo'. We gots go somewheres and live what us two gots lefta life. Don' you reckon?" she asked.

Theo smiled slightly at her words and looking down, absorbing her words, nodded his head in agreement. They put the last of their things in the blanket and looked around in the shanty one last time. "I hopes no body ever has need to stay here no more; no *real* need. I hopes all that change some day," she said to him.

Walking out into the rising sun just now poking over the trees of the forest, they made their way to the graves one last time and after staring for several seconds, Letitia turned to begin the journey up and out of the dell. Theo was surprised at her quickness and was left standing at the mounds, looking up to see her walking away. "You ain't even gon' tarry to cry over 'em one more time, Momma?" he asked her.

She turned back to him and stopped, shaking her head. "Boy, this ol' woman all cried out; I feels like I got no mo' tears to give. Me an' you gon' find some place we can smile agin'! My ol' heart been breakin' over an' over so long now, I done fo'got what feelin' good *feel* like," she said, and turned again to walk as Theo caught her, both of them making their way up through the field of green grass and into the forest of fern and tangle, following the trace as it wound upward to emerge onto an ascending dirt road bathed in the bright Georgia sun; a dusty, switchback ribbon of rust-red clay that just happened to lead north, and, perhaps, to another life.

CHAPTER 21

Saturday, September 16, 1995

*L*ucas McClain? What kind of FUCKED UP place is *this?!"* Loretta yelled at Luke as he made his way up the walkway to the steps of her porch. Looking up, he froze in his tracks. Mouth open, he looked right then left, searching for someone else she might be talking to, a 'Lucas' there other than himself. His wide eyes focused on the irate woman standing at the top of the steps and he cautiously spoke.

"Loretta? Are you alright? What's the matter?" he asked her. "Am I in trouble?"

"No, Lucas, I mean Luke; I'm sorry, I'm just so damned upset I can't think straight, that's all," she said as he approached the steps with apprehension. "Come on in," she told him as she turned to walk back into the screened porch. Luke cautiously followed her and stopped when she took the map she was holding and spread it on the table. Two cups of coffee were already there, one for him, he assumed.

"I've been just so upset since I got this Thursday, I don't know what to do," she said as she pointed down at the map.

"You been here a long time, I know you must have heard about all this. You tell me what's going on, will you?"

Luke looked down at the map and was mildly relieved that Loretta's anger didn't have anything to do with him after all. "I see you got your map; from Tom, I assume. So what's got you so worked up?" he asked, looking the map over with a cursory inspection. He knew this county like the back of his hand; what lay on the table in front of him was like looking in the mirror to him. He had, at one time or another, delivered mail to just about every area he was looking at. This was Ocoosa County, *his* county, the roads and fields etched in his memory like his name.

"This…and this," Loretta responded as she pointed out the notations she had become so familiar with in the last two days. "Do you know what's up with these? I've been asking some questions since I got this map, and I'm not very damn happy with the things I've been finding out, with the answers I've been getting."

Luke examined the blue additions to the map and nodded as his face assumed a somber look. "Yeah; yeah, I remember these. Let me ask you something. Who have you talked to about these?" he asked, reaching down for a coffee cup he still figured was for him.

"The people I work with, for starters; they told me a lot to begin with. Then I went and talked to Wendell Stimson, the old general practitioner here in town. You know him, right? Didn't you do work for him?" she asked.

"Oh, yeah, Doctor Stimson, of course; I did all the 'froufrou' trim on his house for him. He was my doctor until he retired a few years back. I think he was everybody's doctor around here off and on, at one time or another in their lives," Luke said as he took a seat at the table and continued to study the map and drink his coffee. "Oh, this *is* for me, right? Sorry, I should have asked, I guess. I just assumed…"

"Yes, it's yours," Loretta tersely replied as she paced back and forth by the table, glancing down at the map as she spoke. "Do you want to hear what Doctor Stimson told me? You're not going to believe this, but those babies…"

"Were murdered by their mothers? Is that what he told you?" Luke asked, cutting her off in mid-sentence.

Loretta stopped her pacing and slid into the other chair at the table, staring at Luke. Peach hopped up on the table in front of her and remained all of a half-second before Loretta grabbed her and dropped her to the floor, never taking her eyes off Luke. "You know about these murders? Does everybody know about these but me?"

"Loretta, yes, the people around here read the papers, you know. So do I when I get the chance to sit down and do it. I remember especially when these two happened; the people of Watsonville were shocked. This is a small county. Things like that aren't supposed to happen here."

"My point exactly, Luke! That's what's got me so damned pissed off," she shot back at him. Maybe now, Loretta thought, she had someone sitting in front of her to whom she could explain why this whole thing was so upsetting to her. "Look, I go see the guy you tell me to see. I get this map. I get back to the clinic, I see these neat little markings about gruesome little murders and start asking some questions. Well, that opens up a goddamn can of worms, let me tell you! The information they have at the clinic leads to more sources of information that tell me things are way worse than I had imagined! Then, to top it off, Doctor Stimson tells me I may want to go talk to Gerald Martin about these deaths. What in the hell is *that* old man's problem?" Luke tried his best to suppress a smile when she mentioned Gerald Martin's name. He knew any humor at this point would not be taken very well.

"So, you got to meet Gerald, did you? I guess I don't have to ask you how that went. He is eccentric, to say the least. Frankly, I think it's him that's driving away his business, not the competition. All he does is bitch anymore, you know what I mean?"

"Sure do," replied Loretta. "I try to ask straightforward questions about what he knew concerning this and he starts spouting ghost stories, like he's trying to scare me off or something."

"Ghost stories?" Luke asked, looking up with subdued interest from his coffee at the mention of the word. "What did Gerald have to say about ghosts?" he asked, trying to sound nonchalant. Though he tried to mask it, Loretta could sense Luke's sudden interest and tried her best to recall the tirade Gerald Martin allowed himself at her expense the day before.

"Well, he informs me that even more babies than I had been led to believe have died and that he and his father have a theory that these deaths have all occurred because of some idiotic 'bad things' that happened here a long time ago. That's about the gist of it. Said 'this county is carrying a burden', or some nonsense like that."

Luke's eyes were looking at the map but they were unfocused. Something Loretta had said took him from the present and put his mind wandering into the past, his and the county's. "The 'Burden'," he intoned, looking back up at Loretta.

Loretta looked back at him and reacted in disbelief. "Oh, Luke, *please*! What 'burden'? You don't believe in this ghost crap, do you? Is that what you're telling me? Damn it, what's wrong with you country people? *People* killed these kids and then killed themselves, and for whatever reason they did it, it was for a real reason, a flesh and blood reason, a mentally deranged reason. Can't you see that?"

For all the common sense Loretta was making, Luke couldn't help looking at her as though she had just insulted him and the county in which he grew up; couldn't help looking at her suddenly as the outsider she, in fact, was. At the risk of sounding like an ignorant, superstitious redneck he felt he should say something about the 'presence' that had always permeated this county, the one whose existence the locals had, powerless after so many years, just taken for granted. "Loretta..." He stopped to choose his words, making sure what he was about to say was comprehensible and taken the way he intended it. "Loretta, you're an intelligent woman. That's plain to see. And it tells me a lot about your heart to see you so upset about these babies and all. But if you'll look at the facts, I mean really examine what you know at this point, and also stop to consider how much you probably *don't* know, I think you'll see that something more is going on here."

"Something more like what?" she asked him.

Luke rose from his chair, took a couple of steps, then turned around to face Loretta, putting his hands in his pockets. He had the appearance and demeanor of a trial lawyer about to start to argue a long, difficult defense. "Okay, first tell me what you know so far; what you've been told about this. Let's go from there."

Loretta searched her memory to try to organize her information into some sort of chronological order. "Well, okay, I got this map from Tom at the courthouse, took it to the clinic, saw the writings, got some input on the '89 deaths from the staff, mostly because the woman and the infant were patients there. Len Harkness said, to the best of his knowledge, the Shilke woman was fine prenatal, was well-adjusted, looking forward to having the baby. She, for some reason, shot herself and I had assumed at the time she had shot the baby too, but I later found out from Doctor Stimson she crushed its head!"

Luke stood in the middle of the floor and calmly nodded his head.

Loretta could plainly see his placid attitude concerning these details and asked, "How can you be so casual about this? Doesn't that one specific fact bother you? *She crushed her infant's goddamn head!"*

"Go on," Luke told her in a low, controlled voice.

"Then I went to talk to Wendell Stimson about the '87 deaths because they were his patients and I thought he might have some additional information my clinic didn't. Oh, he did alright! My people had told me they thought the woman was crazy to begin with, but he said it wasn't so; said she was a perfectly well-adjusted young woman waiting to have her baby. And then this 'well-adjusted' woman puts five bullets into her husband's chest, drags her baby out into the yard and purposefully crushes its head too! Then kills herself!"

"Let me ask you something. Did either one of the women leave a note or any writing anywhere indicating any reason why they were doing what they were doing?" Luke asked her in a continued calmness.

Loretta immediately thought of the mutilation of the Duncan baby, but hesitated to fully reveal the extent of that information she had assumed had been given to her in confidence. "There was some 'writing' on the Duncan baby that may have meant something," she answered in a cautious tone, measuring her words.

"I'm sure it did mean something," Luke said with a hollow voice. "It wasn't written with a marker, either, was it?"

Loretta's eyes opened wide. "How do you know that? *Luke, tell me how you know that!* Doctor Stimson said that wasn't released to the public!"

Luke turned to stare out the screen door and chose his next words with care. It was time to inform this Atlanta native of Ocoosa County's sporadic, inexplicable history of an especially gruesome form of infanticide. "Because it's happened before, Loretta," he told her at the end of a big sigh as he turned to face her. "The mother in '87 just happened to leave the writing on the baby, as horrible as that is, I know. Some have and some haven't. Most likely the mother in '89 left a note somewhere else, saying something about 'the Devil' or 'Death' or 'Evil'. Is that what the writing on the '87 child said? Do you know?"

Loretta looked up at him with unblinking eyes, barely able to form her words. "The Duncan infant had the word 'Evil' carved into its back with scissors." Tears started to well in her eyes and threatened to spill over from confusion and panic. "Luke, for God's sakes, tell me what's going on around here with these people, please!" she pleaded in desperation, her voice cracking.

Luke walked slowly back to the table and took his seat again, with a look of attempted explanation now on his face. "Hon, these baby killings have gone on around here for a long, long time, I'm sorry to say; way before I was born, even. I remember my dad even saying once, when I was only a young boy, that this county seemed to be trying to set some kind of record for baby deaths. I didn't know what he meant then, I was young; he said I'd know when I got older, like he knew then it was going to keep going on. Used to call the rural parts of this county 'Deadland' in a half-joking way, and this baby thing was what *that* was about. I didn't want to say nothin' to ya 'bout it earlier. When they were reported in the papers, and I suppose most of them were, they always seemed to fit the same pattern: mother has a baby, and within a week or so goes violently crazy and kills the infant, usually herself and maybe the husband if he's around. I remember one instance that happened around '62 or so, that woman killed everybody that was home at the time: herself, the newborn, her husband and his two kids from a former marriage. Shot 'em all."

"Except the infant, right?" asked Loretta, trying to establish an emerging heinous pattern that was bouncing back and forth in her analytical brain.

"Yeah, except the infant. She crushed its head."

Loretta felt sick in the pit of her stomach. "Luke, don't people around here wonder what's going on? I mean, if these murders have been happening for so long, hasn't someone just decided, 'damn it, I'm going to find out why in hell this is happening here' and done something to stop it?"

"Loretta, *of course* people here want it to stop; we want to find out why it happens, but the problem is, it happens on such an irregular basis, no one can predict it. There are a lot of fairly new residents in this county, like yourself, and to you and them this is something terrible and shocking…"

"You're telling me it isn't shocking to the old time residents?" Loretta asked him, incredulous.

"YES! We think it's terrible when these things happen, Loretta! But the sad thing is… we've come to expect it. Don't know why it happens, can't predict when it will, but we all know it will. It's just a matter of time. Hell, we even have some couples leave the county to have their babies somewhere else so it won't happen to them. Look at it this way: how many thousands of babies are born in this county over time and nothing happens? Everything's fine, things go the way they should, kid grows up healthy and life goes on, just like anywhere else. But every so often… we get this," Luke said as he motioned to the areas in blue on the map. "And we really don't have a logical reason why. That's where people like Gerald and his father step up and offer their spiritual explanations; 'the Burden'."

"What's this 'Burden'?"

"According to Gerald and his father, and that's where he got it from, his father, bad things, 'evil' things happened in this county long, long ago; they don't offer a 'who' or 'what'. And from time to time the residents pay for that evil. And it appears they pay for it by killing their newborn babies. Just seems like a high price to forfeit for something you were never even involved in, you know?"

Loretta had been listening to Luke intently, and at the same time, her ingrained need to formulate patterns was firing up and kicking in, starting to subconsciously sort and organize the information she had been told thus far. One pertinent question came to mind that had not yet been touched on.

"Luke," she spoke slowly, shaping her question as she asked it. "The places these things happened: these two places, for instance, these are way out." She pointed to the locations and then looked at him. "Are all the locations of these past deaths, are they all as remote as these?"

He looked at the map and thought for a moment. "Well yeah, most are, sort of, anyway. None of the deaths that I remember, or have heard of, happened right in town, any town, not just Watsonville; all were pretty much out in the country, out at least a little ways. That's why my dad called the remote places 'Deadland', like I said. Why?"

"I wonder if that means anything; seems like it would have to, somehow. I mean, why always so remote? One other thing, and this might be important, so think: have any of these things occurred at the same location, place, the same address, by any chance?"

A bulb suddenly seemed to illuminate Luke's memory. "In fact, yes, now that you mention it. I know of two that supposedly happened at the same place: the one around '77 happened on Pebble Stretch Road, 406 to be exact; I've delivered mail there many times. And from what I've been told, a very similar murder of an infant happened there in the thirties. They had to be the same address; when I delivered mail there prior to '77, there weren't but five houses on the road then. In '36, I'm sure there weren't that many. It's got to be the same place."

"Is that out in the country too?" she asked.

"Very much so, why?"

"Were there others? Others that occurred at the same locations? This is important, Luke. Think!"

"I can't say for sure, but I remember growing up a lot of the old-timers used to say that the house on Rabba Road at the Sheltoee cross road was a bad place; that more than one strange death had happened there in the past. Told us kids to stay clear of it."

"Baby deaths?"

"From what I personally remember, I know it happened at least once there for sure," replied Luke.

"When? How long ago?" Loretta demanded.

"'75; I remember because my mother knew her mother. Naomi Brown was the girl's name. Pretty girl; eighteen, maybe nineteen. Same thing; killed her baby, then herself."

"And did she crush the child's skull too, like the others?"

Luke responded, sounding almost defeated when he realized what he had to admit to Loretta. "Yeah… she stabbed herself with a kitchen knife… after she smashed the baby's head with a brick out in their backyard."

"That's it, we need to go, come on!" she announced, as she bent to slide off her slippers and reached for her light hiking boots.

"What? Where are you going? What do you mean, 'we'?"

"'We're' going somewhere we can get some answers to some of these questions I, and all of you in this county, have. Luke, don't you see? As bizarre as these murders are, the chance of them happening at the same place accidentally would be so slim as to be almost impossible! That tells me something *is* going on here, whether its spirits or 'something in the land' like Gerald Martin says or whatever. That one fact, coupled with the murder pattern and the notes or references to evil shows me there's a pattern to this that we have to uncover to solve this thing. There's a link here we're not getting."

"Solve it? Us? Loretta, I've got a truck full of soffit and fascia board! I've got work to do for you today, remember? I'm no detective, I'm a carpenter!"

"Uh-huh, I can just hear Jesus saying that to the disciples in the Garden: 'I'm no Messiah, I'm a carpenter'!" Today I want you be a detective for me, not a handyman, okay? Luke, this is important to me, and it should be important to you!"

"Okay, okay," he gave in. "Where are we going?"

"To the UGA library; we're going to Athens."

"Athens? What about the stuff in my truck? It's full; I'll have to unload it first."

"Come on, we'll put it around back of the house. It'll be alright, don't you think? I'll help you unload it. I'll pay you for your time, if you want me to, but I want you to come with me and help me. Let me lock up; finish your coffee." Luke finished the last tepid gulp left in the cup and set it on the porch table. They quickly unloaded the wood and soffit and placed it around the back of the house, covering it with a tarp. "Think it'll be okay here for the day?' Loretta asked.

Luke nodded his head in reply. "Oh yeah, no one will bother with it. Folks around here might be baby killers but they're pretty honest." As soon as this poor attempt at black humor passed his lips, he immediately wished he could have taken it back. Loretta flashed him an icy glare. "Sorry. Let me clean off the seat and we'll get going," Luke offered, trying to get her mind off his insensitive joke.

Loretta took her place on the seat among a collection of

odd tools and papers, many of which had been pushed off the seat onto the floor. Luke's truck was at least as bad inside as it appeared outside. "You sure this thing will make it? Want me to bring the map in case we break down?" making her own attempt at some insensitive humor.

"Yes-it-will-thank-you-very-much! And no, we don't need your map!" he replied, trying not to let her know he knew what she was doing. She was sharp. He liked her sense of humor. He had already added it to the growing list of things he liked about this little Atlanta woman.

They wheeled down Main and caught the on-ramp for highway 441 to Athens, got on and Luke ran a little faster than he normally would have just to show "Viper Babe" she had misjudged his truck. This time, Loretta knew what *he* was doing. "Wow. Eighty. How's it do on the track?" she asked him, a wry grin on her face.

"Now that's enough, young lady!" Luke proclaimed, pretending to be more irritated than he was. "This truck is going to get you to Athens, quick and safe, so you can find out what you want to know, and then it's gonna get you back home again the same way, alright? Now, no more about my truck, hear?"

Loretta reluctantly allowed her grin to fill her face and said, "I know, I'm just kidding, you know that. It obviously must be pretty reliable. I haven't heard you talk about breaking down anywhere. And look at that; eighty-five! Damn!" she said, pointing to the speedometer.

"Now…"

"Okay! I know! I'm kidding again! I really do want to thank you for coming with me, though. I could have gone myself, I guess, but I just felt I wanted you there, you know, you knowing so much about the county and all." *Not to mention the fact I'm starting to like being around you as often as possible.*

"Yeah, it's okay, I don't mind. I'm glad to help, seeing it means this much to you." *Not to mention the fact I'm starting to like being around you as often as possible.*

As the truck rolled toward Athens, Luke pointed out to Loretta various points of local interest that could be seen from the highway: what was new, how long it had been there, what had been there before. He really was an expert on Ocoosa County. "What makes you think you're going to find any answers in the 'Bulldog' library?" he asked.

"The girl that I replaced at the clinic, Rosemary, had gone to the University of Georgia for her degree, and had done a genealogy project for her family not too long ago. She said the library had a wonderful new program that had a database of most of the old newspapers printed in the state in the last hundred years of so. I'm thinking we can use that database to look for articles that tell of these killings. It's worth a try."

"I'll have to let you do that, I don't know a damn thing about computers," Luke told her, shaking his head.

"That's okay, you can help with collecting what we find and sorting it, kind of a computer gofer. Can you handle that?" she asked, smiling.

"Yes, I suppose so," he replied, the sarcasm evident in his voice.

As the truck got farther from Watsonville, Loretta began to notice the mild, constant sensation she had gotten used to while in town was ebbing again, becoming conspicuous by its absence. *There, it's gone again! What is it with this thing? This might be a good time to mention it to him, maybe find out if there's a good reason for it… no, on second thought, I don't want him to think I'm weird, not right now. Never mind. Later.*

After long seconds of an awkward silence, Luke glanced over to her and asked, "You really are a 'kid' person aren't you? I mean, with all this concern, you'd have to be, I reckon."

Loretta absentmindedly stared out the window, thinking about his question. "Always and forever," she replied, her answer pleasing her, making her smile. "I really do love kids; always have. Even though I don't have any of my own, I still love them, all of them." Loretta tried to sum it up for Luke, and herself, this passion she had for babies and children. "I don't know, you look into a baby's eyes and you see such promise, so much future. I guess that's it, the hope you hold in each one of them. And you, what do you really like? Anything get to you? What do you hold as sacred, if anything?"

"Dogs. I guess I'd have to say dogs."

"Yeah? Dogs?" she asked as her memory immediately flashed back to the conversation at her table the day they met, where the mention of dogs in his past quickly reduced Luke to an emotional, fidgeting wreck. *I wonder if now is the time he can talk about it,* she thought, not wanting a repeat of what happened before. "Luke," she said with caution, "if it's going to be too tough on you to go into, I understand, really, but…"

"My uncle John raised American Fox Hounds," Luke blurted out, cutting off her inquiry in mid-sentence. His stare was fixed a mile down the highway and Loretta's sideway glance could see his jaw tightening slightly, as was his grip on the wheel. "It's like a really big Beagle with long legs, in case you don't know. He never had less than sixty at a time, but never more than ninety-nine. Said that one hundred was bad luck; I don't know. He kept them all in one great big pen; all of 'em. Now that many dogs, especially all together, forces you to accept a certain reality about animals, in this case dogs. If one got sick or the least bit injured or weak, the others would sense it, and by morning of the next day, it'd be dead."

"How? Why?" Loretta asked, slightly horrified. She was, after all, a city girl.

"They'd kill it; sometimes tear it up if they had all night, 'specially if it was a full moon. You could hear 'em sometimes. A big pack like that, they live a certain way, like men in prison, I guess. The weak just don't survive. Anyway, my uncle would come out the next morning and find a dog dead and he'd go into an absolute raging fit, like he couldn't anticipate it happening or somethin'. He kept a hoe handle by the gate to break up fights, and when he saw a dead dog, he'd go into the pen with that hoe handle and start swinging at the dogs, thrashing and beating any that were too slow to get out of his way. He would continue until they were all howling in terror and he was too exhausted to do it anymore. He had his first heart attack doing that. I hoped he'd die. I was ten when that happened."

"Oh my God!" Loretta exclaimed, shocked at the cruelty she was hearing. "How could he do such a horrible thing to defenseless animals?"

"'Cause my uncle John was an ignorant son of a bitch, that's why," Luke said through clenched teeth. "Of course, he'd make me go in afterward and pick up what was left of the dead one."

"Oh Luke, I'm so sorry; that must have been terrible for you!" Loretta said, putting herself in his position as best she could imagine.

"Not as bad as the look on the faces of the rest of the pack. They'd pile up in the corners of the pen, thinking I was going to do the same thing to them. I've never been able to get that look out of my mind; seventy, eighty dogs; that look of sheer terror and fear they all had. I hated him for that; I always will."

"I... Luke, I'm so sorry I brought it up, I..."

Without taking his eyes off the highway, Luke loosened his grip on the steering wheel and reached over to pat Loretta on the knee, reassuring her he was alright. His hand was pale white from gripping the wheel. "No, it's okay sometimes I can handle it better than others. Right now, I'm okay with it. And since I am, there's something else..."

"What? What else happened?" she asked, not really sure she wanted to hear more. *Maybe he needs to tell me, since he's talking about it. Okay Loretta, just get ready*, she thought.

"That many dogs together, there's always litters being born. It can't be helped. When Uncle John would see puppies, he'd start counting adult heads as best he could. If he thought the pack could stand the added count, he'd look the pups over and let the strongest ones live. If he was close to ninety-nine, he made me go in, take them from their mother and dispose of them. They'd only be a few days to a week old."

"Dispose of them? You mean he made you kill them? Oh Luke!" Loretta said, covering her mouth, her eyes welling up. "How old were you when he made you do that?"

"I started doing it when I was about eight or so, and did it till I was maybe fifteen."

"I can't believe he was so cruel he made a little boy…"

"I'd load the pups in a basket I kept just for that," Luke continued, wanting to get this all out while he thought he could. "He had a .22 Colt Woodsman pistol that he'd hand me as I was about to go, and a box of shells. I drove the farm truck, even back when I was eight and nine, I just had to stand up to drive it, I was so small. I'd load the basket in the seat next to me and put my hand in to feel each one when I could take my right hand away from driving. I thought… I thought they should feel the touch of at least one human attempting to be kind to them. There was a special spot on the other side of my uncle's property I'd take them to."

Now Loretta could see Luke starting to show his signs he was close to losing his composure completely. Brink signs, she called them. Luke's were very obvious and he was showing all of them now. "Luke, don't…"

Luke had a white-knuckle grip on the wheel now; his stare rigidly fixed straight ahead, his breathing becoming pronounced and deeper. He was fighting back old tears with all he had. "I'd let them out of their basket," he continued, "let them stumble around, blind as they still were. It was still a little bit of freedom, you know?" His eyes were filling and his voice was starting to break. "I dug the hole while they wandered around; they couldn't go far. Then I'd take each one…" Tears were running down his cheek now and he was having difficulty getting out the rest of what he wanted to say. He was keeping a stoic face as best he could, but the repeated tightening of his stomach muscles told her he was close to losing it altogether. Loretta was crying too, and wanted him to stop for his own sake, but she knew he had to finish for it, too. "Then I'd take each one," he repeated, trying to get the words out, "and... and I'd nuzzle each one for a few seconds or so..." he said, his top lip quivering, "because... because that was the only affection they would ever have." He blinked rapidly, trying to rein in his tears, but they had gotten too much out of control by then. "Then I'd put each one flat on the ground on its stomach and put one quick bullet through the back of its head; they never felt it. It was over without any pain," he said, his breathing getting calmer, his control retreating back from the edge. "I'd bury them there and drive back to my uncle's. Between the age of eight and fifteen, I guess I took care of maybe a thousand pups that way."

Loretta had a look of deep sorrow covering her face and she wept openly at the nature of his story; but mostly for him, for what this memory did to him. She reached over and touched his arm, and without looking, he brought his left hand over to pat hers, silently saying "thanks." A recovering minute passed and Loretta turned to Luke to ask, "You really are a dog person, aren't you?" rephrasing what he had asked her about children.

Luke smiled and realized what she was doing and tried to recall her reply. "Always and forever," he said, pleased with himself he could mimic her and truthfully say so. "Even though much of my past with them is a painful one, I love dogs. Someday I'll have one or two of my own again. Hounds are different from other dogs. Once you look into a hound's face, you're hooked; least I was, anyway. They call it a 'pleading' look. It's in the eyes. They all have it, all hounds. It grabs you right off. I just want to see those faces looking back at me 'not scared', that's all.

"You will, I'm sure you will," Loretta said, touching his arm again. She stared at the side of his face as long as it took for her to fall a bit more for this man she barely knew.

CHAPTER 22

The UGA parking lot was half-full as they found a parking place farther away than they wanted. "Must be because of early assignments already; I remember those days," Loretta said as they passed the columns and walked through the tall doors. As they walked up to the desk, a young man was busy putting books back in a cart and stopped what he was doing as they stood in front of him waiting for help.

"Can I help you? You look a little lost!" he said smiling.

"Yes. I hope so, anyway. Neither of us is familiar with the library here, but actually we're looking for something specific. We're interested in seeing if we can access old articles from Georgia newspapers, and a friend of mine told me that you have a program here that makes it a lot easier than looking through copy after copy. Do you know what I'm talking about?"

"Sure do. What you want is the Georgia Historical Archive Program, affectionately known as 'the GHAP' by those of us who've spent time compiling it!"

Loretta was appreciative, both of the existence of the

program and his knowledge of it. "It sounds like a wonderful tool for research."

"It is, and it's really an ongoing labor of love for us in the History Department. See, several years ago, the Georgia Historical Society got together with the State Historical Archive Department and decided the best way to preserve the history of the state was to gather all the records, books, papers and anything else that was of historical merit and just do it the old-fashioned way: go through it page by page and record as much as they could by area and category."

Luke spoke up and said, "I'm not much of a scholar, but wouldn't something like that take forever?"

"Ten years ago or so, yes, you're right, it would have. But that's where the wonderful world of computers comes in, *and* the incentive the State Board of Education came up with! Through grants and some unexpected sizable endowments, they devised an 'Applied Historical Contribution' fund for state colleges and universities to encourage participation on a voluntary basis. Those people are smart, they knew what they were doing. The fund provides for computer equipment, stipends, limited scholarships and credits in the history field toward graduation for anyone who wants to put in the time and tedium going through these old documents and articles, copying them and cataloging them. They've provided a very stringent procedure to follow that's kind of a pain, but it makes it all very uniform and workable. I've earned three credits so far just for what I've done."

Loretta was impressed. "Wow, that's amazing! That's just what we want. Can you point us to it?"

"Sure can. Turn around and look down between those

book stacks right there. See the door down there? Room 301. It's usually jammed by now on a Saturday, but y'all got here early enough, I guess. All you do is go to GHAP on the desktop, follow the prompts and it should take you to your area of interest. The program's far from done, may never really be, but you won't believe how much info it contains at this point. Need any help, get me or one of the staff, we'll help you figure it out!"

"Thanks, you've been a big help," Loretta said warmly as she and Luke turned to walk down the gray carpet toward the room. "This sounds like exactly what we need. If the answers aren't in this program, we may never find them," she told him as they opened the room and looked at the computer that just might unravel this horrible mystery.

Luke pulled up a chair next to Loretta as she began the program. It was all pretty much meaningless to him what she was doing, choosing this, 'getting out' of that, but strangely, it had his interest just the same.

"Okay," she said, looking intently at the screen and the menus it was presenting to her. "Georgia, yeah. Archives, History, N.E. Georgia, Ocoosa County, okay; we're where we want to start."

"How can you... do that so fast?" Luke asked, watching her type and keeping her eyes glued to the screen.

She turned to him, and with a matter-of-fact tone, asked, "How can you nail sixty Simplex in sixty seconds?"

Her reply bewildered Luke for an instant as he thought about it. "I can't!" he told her.

"Huh," she huffed in mock indignity, as she looked back at the screen. "Don't ever refer to yourself as a roofer around

206

me!"

Still bewildered and a bit insulted, Luke replied, "Alright, I *won't!*"

Loretta directed her attention back to the program. "Okay, we have Ocoosa County. Now we want to know about deaths, but just baby deaths," she said as she selected again from the menu categories. "Here. 'Deaths', 'infant', 'Ocoosa County'." A solid page of names came up instantly and showed itself to be the first one of eighty-nine. "Whoa, no, that's not what we want!" Loretta said, looking at what must be a listing of all the infants that had died in the county for any reason over many years.

"Wouldn't we want 'infant murders', 'infant homicides'?" Luke asked, trying to be helpful.

"Uh-huh, right; there you go, you're getting the hang of this! See? Computers aren't hard, it's all logical procedure; like framing a house, you know?"

He nodded in agreement, mostly to appease her. "Yeah."

Loretta typed in the specificity they wanted and narrowed the search even further. "Ocoosa County, infant homicides, blunt trauma, all dates, chronological order by date," she said out loud as she typed in the words, hoping to bring the search down to exactly what they were there to find. She hit enter and in less than a second, twenty-one names appeared in a neat column. Loretta and Luke both stared at the screen for long seconds, their mouths open in shock, their eyes unblinking from the implications of what was before them. "Oh my God!" Loretta managed before slowly bringing her hand up to her mouth.

"Jesus Christ!" Luke said lowly. "Look at all of 'em! I

never knew there were that many! There's one, two...there's twenty-one of them, all died from blows to the head."

Loretta breathed deeply, trying to maintain her composure, letting her medical training in nomenclature take over to distract her from the morbidity of this discovery. "Blunt trauma, that's what we looked up, not 'blows to the head'; forensically, there's a difference. Blows could be from a hand, a fist. If it's classified as blunt trauma, it almost always ultimately means an implement was used," she told him. "Like a rock."

"Yeah," he echoed with resignation, "...like a rock."

She moved the mouse to each name, and the 'pointing hand' appeared at each one. "See that?" she asked him. "That means there's more information filed on each one." Loretta clicked on the first name listed and the screen displayed the typed copy of a newspaper article dated June 1, 1878.

"1878? It goes back that far? *Jesus!"* Luke said as the article appeared.

"At least that far, and this program may not be complete in this area yet. I hope to God it is. Twenty-one babies are way too many to die like that," Loretta said, shaking her head. "Okay, it says: 'Ocoosa Infant Found Murdered- Frederick Douglass Tyree, infant, was found murdered at his residence on Chatoosee Road, the home being built on the former site of the Endicott plantation where the baby's mother and father had labored as slaves up to the end of the War. The baby was unearthed by neighbors who had questioned the parents on the whereabouts of their newborn after not having seen it since shortly after the birth of such. The infant's head had been found to be crushed, as if in a (sic) accident. Noah Tyree,

208

father, said his wife had acted strangely after the birth of Fredrick, their eighth child, the first born in the cabin they had themselves erected on the site of the destroyed plantation house. Mr. Tyree claimed his wife, Mamie, was responsible for the demise of their son Fredrick, having taken the child from its bed during the night, apparently using a rock to kill the infant a short distance from their cabin. Authorities have arrested Mamie Tyree and may pursue criminal charges against the father at a later date. He is for now being left to care for his remaining children'."

Loretta looked back up at Luke for a verification of what she had just read. "See that? The same pattern! It started that long ago! What in hell is making this happen?"

"See what the next one says," Luke said, pointing to the second name listed on the screen.

Loretta clicked on the name and a recounted article similar to the previous one filled the screen.

"October twelve, 1890- A five day old infant female, unnamed, was killed by one or both of her parents on Rabba Road..."

"There!" Luke said, excitedly pointing at the screen. "That's the house I told you about, the one at Rabba and the Sheltoee Cross Road! I know it's the same house! So the old-timers were right; another death did happen there. Naomi Brown wasn't the only woman to kill her baby at that location."

"Same location, maybe not the same structure," replied Loretta, "but that's close enough for me to see this isn't just coincidental. Let's read the rest of this one."

"...sometime during the last two or three days, according

to investigators, Sheriff Marcus Renfro among them. The bodies of the mother, father and infant were found accidentally by a relative, a Miss Ellen Mayfield of Athens. Roland Ullman, the father, was found shot to death in the barn at the said location, and his wife, Jenny, died of what appeared a self-inflicted rifle shot to her head. The infant, according to Sheriff Renfro, appeared to have been killed by a heavy object having struck its head, seeming to have been purposefully done. A letter was recovered in the home by the visiting relative which, according to Sheriff Renfro, indicated that the murders were intentionally committed by the wife, Jenny Ullman."

"I'd bet a good paycheck that note said something about 'evil' or the 'devil' or something similar," Luke said.

"I wouldn't take that bet," Loretta said. "I think you're absolutely right. Let's go on to the next one. I'm going to click back to each of these before we leave and copy them all, but let's bring up some more and see if we can see an obvious pattern."

"Hell, Hon, I'm no Colombo, and I can see it *now*!" Luke told her.

"September 28th, 1893 - Mother, Anne Stevens, baby unnamed/name unknown, seven to ten days old, occurred junction of Bear Run and Thomasville road... " Loretta recounted out loud as she scanned the article for pertinent points.

"I know it! I know just where that is, and its way out of town!" Luke broke in.

"...mother taken away from the scene screaming about Satan, baby's head crushed."

Loretta clicked on the next name, saw an almost carbon

copy of the last incident, and continued down the list through the years. "1905, Mother, Agatha Ring, baby, male, Jacob, head crushed with field stone, father; Mason Ring stabbed to death, Pebble Stretch Road. 1910, Pearle Ferguson, baby unnamed/name unknown, dead from head trauma, Colman Crossing, near Big Ocoosa River..."

"I think we've seen enough so far as to easily determine that these all happened with a pattern that almost anyone could recognize," Loretta turned to tell Luke.

"All we had to do was look," Luke replied in a somber tone.

"Yeah, but I can't blame you or anyone else in Ocoosa for not seeing the pattern, not without a comprehensive program like this. This really saved the day. God bless these kids and the time they put into this thing," Loretta said, shaking her head in subdued awe. "This has made the difference between maybe solving this thing or having it remain a mystery forever."

"What do we do now, Hon?" Luke asked, unsure of what would come next in a computer search.

"Well, I'm going to go back to each one and print the clipping copy; that's where the body of info is that we need to piece the whole thing together. Then, I'm going to the ladies room. I've got to go *bad*! I've been holding it 'cause I couldn't break away from what was coming up on the screen. *Now*, here's what I want you to do while I'm gone: go back to each of these names and use the mouse, this thingy I've been using, and put it on each name and click. You'll get the same clipping we're going to copy. See in the upper left hand corner where it says related articles? Point to it, and if there's anything there, the arrow will turn into the pointing hand; if not, it will stay an arrow. Okay?"

"Then what?' Luke asked, staring at the screen with a frown, all this becoming more complicated to him by the second.

"If the hand comes up, click, go up here," she said, taking his hand on the mouse and guiding it around the pad, moving the mouse to the appropriate place. "Go to 'select all' and point to 'print' up here and it will all print out in the order it is on the screen. Just remember to keep putting paper in the tray. Okay? Got it? You can do this."

Luke, still frowning, slowly shook his head from side to side, showing his confusion.

"Loretta, I don't know. I've never sat in front of one of these things before, what if I break it?"

"You can't break it unless you throw it, and even if you're tempted to, please don't!"

"I'm a simple man, you know that, I make my living with my hands!" he insisted in a growing panic.

"That's good, 'cause that's exactly what I want you to use, your hand, to move this mouse where it needs to go and do what I told you so we can get out of here, get home and solve this thing!" she said as she did a little dance in front of him and the copies of the clippings were filling the tray. "I'll be right back!" she said as she exited the room and walked quickly away, looking right and left for a sign for the restrooms.

Luke surveyed the screen and the keyboard back and forth for a nervous minute. *I wish she'd have had the time to write that all down, dammit. Well here goes,* he thought as he pointed to the first name and clicked. As the entries were selected one by one, some had attachments to print and some did not, as

Loretta had told him to expect. Luke noticed that the more recent murders had more related articles to print than the earlier deaths. *I guess that kind of makes sense*, he thought to himself.

As the sheets of paper flapped into the tray, he took them one at a time and placed them in order to coincide with chronology of the main clippings, briefly eyeing each one as he flipped them over on their face. One related item caught his eye immediately: a copy of a clipping pertaining to a name he and every Ocoosa County native knew well. *Huh, ol' Norman; I'll be damned. Wonder how involved he got in any of these? Let's see*, he thought as he scanned the short article looking for specifics. *What? I always heard moonshiners caught up with him! Huh! How 'bout that?*

Loretta appeared from around a corner, a look of great relief on her face. "How'd you do? You ready to start programming now?" she asked, admittedly having some fun with him at his expense.

"Real funny!" he replied as he tapped the sheaf of paper on the desk to get the stacks neat and uniform. "I think I did this right, take a look and see," he said as he pointed to the two stacks in front of him. "This is the stack of the main articles of clippings that you printed and this," he said as he pointed to the other stack with evident pride, "is the one I did of related clippings and things. Want to check them?"

Loretta flipped through his stack and nodded with admiration. "Not bad for a computer novice. Think you want to start taking classes?" she asked, knowing what his reaction would be.

"Hell no!" he replied, rising from the chair and stretching. "If we're done here, I'm going to go find the men's room before we take off. I'll meet you at the truck, okay?"

"Men's room is down that way, turn left at the wall and on down to the end, then right. Thanks for your help, and thanks for coming with me. I really think we can solve this thing with these and some luck," she told him, giving him a heartfelt smile.

"No problem. I'll meet you outside in a minute," he said, returning the smile with one that more than matched her obvious sincerity.

CHAPTER 23

Pulling onto the loop, Luke accelerated for 441 and home. It was still early in the day, noon, and even though he had done none of his planned carpentry work, he felt nonetheless that he had accomplished something. He smiled to himself as Loretta sat next to him examining the copies she held in her hands, copies of news clippings she hoped held the answer to this evidently century-old mystery, one that made her start to choke up every time she thought of all those babies. She sat cross-legged on the bench seat, sifting through the stack of papers that Luke had copied during her potty break, when a name on one caught her eye and caused her to practically choke as she tried to speak. "Hey! Holy shit, that's *me!*" Loretta said as she stared wide-eyed at the article, scanning it quickly for a confirmation of the name. "This is my name, I think. It *has* to be! But how…" she declared as she turned to Luke and back at the copy of the clipping she held in her hand.

What's you?" Luke asked with a combination of puzzlement and irritation, not being able to take his eyes off the road long enough right then to confirm what exactly she held or what it said. "What are you talking about, 'that's you'?" Luke could now see from the several short glances he had managed that Loretta was holding a copy of one of the related articles that had printed out while she was in the rest room. "What's you, what's that one about?"

"It's about a sheriff that lived here a long time ago, a Sheriff Norman Tomms! This is an article about him being found dead back in...let's see...May of 1926!"

"Yeah, I saw that when it printed out. So? What's that got to do with you? Norman Tomms was a Sheriff back in the '20's, real famous in Ocoosa County. So what?"

"Tomms!" Loretta exclaimed to him. "Tomms is my maiden name! It was my father's last name!"

"Tomms? Yeah? That ain't a real common name," Luke offered, surprise mixed with curiosity now evident in his voice. "What was your daddy's name?"

"Lester. Lester Tomms; why?"

Luke kept his eyes on the road as a broad smile came to his face. "What? I'll be damned, you Lester Tomms' young 'un? Hell, I *knew* your daddy!" he said, almost bragging. "That was a long time ago, before he had you! You'll be happy to know you're holding an article about your granddaddy! I'll be damned!"

"You did!? You knew my dad? Really?" Loretta asked, spinning sideways on the bench seat to face Luke. The excitement flushed her face and made it difficult for her to decide what to say, what to ask next. This was big; really big. This was taking her breath away. She could feel herself starting to hyperventilate. Loretta knew she had to calm down. Taking deliberate deep breaths, she licked her lips and swallowed hard, choosing her next words. "I can't believe this! Where do I start? How did you know him? When? Was he from here? Tell me! What was he like? What…"

"Calm down, now!" Luke said, as he laughed at her and reached over to slap her on her thigh as though she were a child he was trying to control. "Take it easy! Yeah, I knew him a long time ago. Not very well, he was older than I was by about twenty years, maybe, but I saw him around town a lot before he left. Yeah, he was from here."

"Oh, God, I've got so many questions I want to ask! I just can't *believe* this!" Loretta blurted out, trying to mentally organize some sort of order of importance for her thousand questions. "Was he tall? Short, like me? Was he a nice guy?"

Luke laughed again, shaking his head at this woman who had suddenly transformed into an inquisitive little girl that wouldn't shut up. "Loretta, you've got to calm down, girl! You're gonna to have a conniption right here in this truck if you don't stop!" He laughed once again and took his eyes off the road long enough to study her well, seeing a radiance in her face that was new to him. He was quickly beginning to understand what this revelation meant to her, and he felt glad to see she was able to be this happy about something for a change. "I'll tell you what I do remember, but like I said, I didn't know him well at all, only in passing. We said hi and nodded when we passed in the street."

"What was he like?" she asked, still wide-eyed, propping her elbow on the back of the seat, settling in to listen to whatever Luke might have remembered about this man who had always been a mystery, one she had given up on trying to solve a long time ago.

"Well, like I'm saying, we'd only pass in the street once in a while and sort of acknowledge each other, like people do in a small town, you know? My daddy and uncle both knew him pretty well. He had done some work for them somehow in the past, but I don't remember what. He was just an average guy, plain-looking and about five foot nine or so. Didn't stand out in a crowd or anything. Wish I could tell you different, I really do," Luke said, silently kicking himself as the last of his words escaped his mouth that he didn't have the quickness or imagination to have made up some sort of interesting past for her father when he had just had the chance. In his effort to be honest with her, he had blown the opportunity to lift her spirits. It was too late to go back and try; she was too smart not to know what he would be up to.

"Oh," Loretta replied, visually disappointed there wasn't more to hear.

"Now this ol' boy here, now he's a different story altogether," Luke said, reaching over to tap on the article Loretta was still holding in her lap, seeing an opportunity to redeem himself with the shining history of her grandfather.

"Who, Sheriff Tomms, my grandfather?" Loretta asked with a surprised curiosity. "What about him? He was a sheriff, huh?"

"What *about* him? He was just a genuine, goddamn legend in Ocoosa County, that's all!" Luke said, nodding his head with authority. "Whatever your daddy lacked in notoriety, your grandfather more than made up for it. The stories I grew up with about that man paint him as the best damn lawman in the East in his time."

"He was famous? Really?"

"Sure was. They say he was a big man; imposing. Made a real impact on people physically. I've always thought he must have looked a lot like John Wayne. That's the way I picture him. I don't recall ever seeing a real photo of him, though. Kinda strange, I always thought."

"Whoa!" Loretta exclaimed with a quiet awe. "I can't believe it! What made him so famous?"

"He had the reputation of not putting up with much from anybody, for one thing. He was a just and fair officer of the law, but he enforced that law in this county with an iron fist, supposedly. He tended to go in shooting and ask questions later, if at all."

"How'd he get to be a legend? Did he do something real special?"

"Well, there was one incident that I remember hearing about a lot when I was a kid that has always stuck in my mind, most other people's too, I would guess."

"What? Tell me!" Loretta begged Luke, as a little girl would to her father for a bedtime fairytale. She continued to sit sideways facing Luke, her legs crossed on the torn bench seat, eyes wide open and staring with anticipation.

"As the story goes, as I've been told anyway, there was a particular situation in the early '20's that established his reputation for good in this county and all of Georgia for that matter. Happened over in Engstrom one summer."

"What happened? Wait! Now, is this 'bullshit' or is this true? Don't make things up, now, this is important to me, Luke!" Loretta insisted, frowning at him with concern.

"No! This is the way I heard it happened, really!" he countered, slightly surprised at her language. "What happened

219

was there was this farm boy over near Engstrom that got to be around eighteen or so and got bored with life on the farm. Believe me, I know how *that* can happen! He was a big boy, huge, like a football player, I picture him. They called him 'Bull' 'cause he was so big. So Bull leaves town and the state and goes to some city up north, Chicago I think it was, and gets involved with some crime gang or something; enforcing, acting as muscle, you know? Pretty soon, he's got his own gang started, a dozen or so guys maybe, and he's making money and a reputation, too. He gets big to the point he's got to lay low for a while, so he takes a half dozen of his boys and comes back to Engstrom for a little vacation; the 'prodigal son' coming back to his roots to show the locals how big and successful he'd become. Sounds like a bad time gettin' ready to happen, don't it?"

"*Damn*, it does!" Loretta said, unconsciously biting a nail, something she rarely did unless totally preoccupied with the emotion of a moment. Luke picked up where he had left off.

"They stayed at the one small hotel in town, since there was a problem with his folks not wanting anything to do with him anymore. They all fished and stuff for a few days but they got bored real quick, even Bull. I guess you can't go home again, like they say."

Loretta nodded. "I'm still not sure that's true, though. My verdict is still out on that one," she said.

"Well, it was true for Bull, it seems. They got ready to leave town and decided they'd make a little easy money before they left."

Loretta was staring so intensely by now she was forgetting to blink and swallow. She finally managed both and blurted,

"Did they rob someone, burglarize some place, what?"

"Bigger, *way* bigger," Luke replied. "On their way out of town, they parked their cars in front of the Engstrom hardware store and busted in with guns drawn. Bull must not have planned on ever coming back, so he didn't care none. They took everybody in the store hostage, tied up the store clerk and started taking the money and everything else of value they could carry."

"This is where my grandpa comes in, huh? I can tell!" Loretta said, grinning with the giddiness of a child.

"Oh yeah, and *how* he comes in!" Luke replied. "Somebody ran and got Sheriff Tomms and told him what was going on. He pulls up, parks in the middle of the street, gets out and strides right up to that front door. Now, he was famous for carrying two pearl-handled .45's and never being hesitant about pulling them. Okay now, you got to listen up here, this is where the story gets good!" Luke said, nodding his head, smiling in self-satisfaction.

"Shit! Tell me, c'mon, what happened? What'd he do?" Loretta blurted, her impatience overtaking her.

Luke looked over at her and frowned, pretending indignation at her language. He looked back at the highway and continued. "It has been told through the years, over and over again, that at that point Sheriff Norman Tomms drew both of his guns, kicked open the front door of that hardware store and just waded on in, guns blazing!

"Guns blazing at *what*?" Loretta asked in excited confusion. "He just walked in and started *shooting*? At what? He didn't even know for sure what was going on inside! Wouldn't a sheriff be afraid of shooting innocent people?"

"Well, I *have* heard that when it was all over, a few of the town folk inside were bloodied some, but not bad. What happened next is from the accounting of the clerk, mostly. He was tied up sitting on the floor against the shelves in the back of the store, helpless. He had to sit there and watch everything. His account, and that of the hostages, tells some kinda story that went on in that store."

"Shit, Luke, tell me what happened! Will you finish the story?"

"Stop saying 'shit' so much," Luke admonished her.

"Okay, okay," Loretta agreed, not letting the rebuke dampen her excitement, "finish the goddamn story, will you?"

Luke chuckled at her and continued. "They say Sheriff Tomms just walked in, whirling and twirling, firing both guns all around the store, hitting gang members one by one."

"Now *that's* bullshit! I can't believe that!" Loretta countered. "C'mon, Luke! That's just unbelievable! How did he know where they were? How the hell could he avoid killing any of the hostages, or getting shot himself?"

"Don't know, Hon, 'wasn't there," Luke replied, shrugging his shoulders. "All I know is what I've been told, and what I've heard is that when the smoke cleared, and there was a lot of lead flying back and forth in there, all the bad guys were laying dead; Bull too."

"But how…?"

"How'd he know where they all were, right? That's a logical question; one I asked too. Supposedly, the sheriff knew the layout of the inside of the store like his own house; he had been in there so many times in his life. He just figured going in where they'd have to be, I guess. And, evidently, he was an excellent shot with both hands. Must have been, to have killed the gang and none of the hostages. Just like the Phantom!"

"Who?"

Luke gave her a sideways glance and remembered her age. "Never mind," he sighed.

Loretta was incredulous, again left in her unblinking state. "How... how long was this supposed to have taken?"

"Storekeeper swore for years it was all over in sixty seconds."

Loretta's stare had been fixed on the side of Luke's head for the entire story. Now her gaze shifted back down the highway in front of them, reflecting her puzzled shock. "I can't... I mean, I just..."

"I know, I know," Luke said, agreeing with her about the fantastic details that constituted the legend of Norman Tomms that had circulated in the county for almost three-quarters of a century. "But listen to what the storekeeper said happened next; this is the part that kills me. According to him, the sheriff walked up to him, cut his hands loose, bent down and pointed his finger in his face and told him: 'First, you go get the coroner; second, you get some help in here and clean this mess up. When you're done with that, you hightail it over to my office and tell me just what in *hell* went on to make me have to come down here and do all this!'"

"He was that... insensitive? That blunt?" Loretta asked.

"He was that cut and dried, they say. No nonsense. And that's the incident that launched your granddaddy to fame forever in Ocoosa County. Pretty cool, huh?" Luke asked as he smiled and looked over at her.

Loretta sat motionless and stared out the windshield at the

road before them. The sign for the exit to Watsonville was coming up. She kept staring straight ahead as tears began running down her cheeks. "Why are you crying?" Luke asked, shooting several short, confused glances at her.

"*Because*, damn it!" Loretta replied in a raised voice, irritated that Luke, a typical man, did not immediately understand. She twisted quickly to punch Luke on the arm then resumed her highway stare. The emotions from the revelations of the last twenty minutes were finally bubbling over.

"Because!" she repeated, "half an hour ago before I saw this," she said, shaking the copied article she still held in her hands, "I only had half a past! Now…" she said, looking down through her tears, "I have so much more; a whole other side I never knew." It felt odd, this sense of connection that was creeping into her as she sat in a truck barreling down a highway back toward a town she now knew her grandfather had ruled with an uncompromising hand seventy years before. Her tears started again at the realization of what she was verbalizing to herself and this fifty-year-old handyman sitting next to her. "You got any Kleenex in this damn truck?" she asked Luke, leaning forward to attempt to open his glove box, not waiting for a reply.

"Yeah, there's napkins in there I got at Zaxbey's last night. Go ahead, pop that, it'll open." Loretta hit the door with the side of her fist and it flew open, throwing napkins all over the truck floor. Picking up a handful, she wiped her eyes, avoiding giving Luke the opportunity to look at her full in the face. Somehow, being strong in front of this man was important to her, though she wasn't sure why. She could cry in empathy for his hurting; that was okay. Her own personal weaknesses were something she wanted to shield for the time being. She sniffed strongly several times to clear her stuffy nose and as she did her eyes began to dry. She lifted her chin slightly as a strange feeling of belonging gradually came over her. Loretta began to gently sway side to side with a growing contentment as her tears were becoming a memory. An easy smile was working its way onto her face as a sense of pride began to take hold of her.

"My granddaddy. A sheriff!" She turned toward Luke who, taking the off-ramp for Watsonville, was smiling and nodding also for the importance of this discovery for her. She could feel her mystery sensation beginning again in the pit of her stomach, adding to her sense of well-being. Loretta turned again to look at the road ahead and, still smiling, proclaimed to Luke, the windshield and the entire county, "My granddaddy! John Wayne! *Damn!*"

CHAPTER 24

May 8, 1926

S heriff Dumpy" the children called him behind his back, though they had enough respect for his position not to let him hear it. But he knew, nonetheless. Sheriff Norman Tomms was a quiet man, and uncomfortably shy at times. Five feet four, portly and balding, a round face with wire-rim glasses; easily mistaken for a bookkeeper, a clerk in an office. His clothes never fit him right and that had always secretly bothered him; a personal vanity he would not admit. And because of it, being photographed was to him an embarrassment to be avoided at all costs. His appearance always made him seem a bit... 'undone'. His lack of visual impact contributed to the general feeling that, early on in his first term of Ocoosa County Sheriff, even the constituents that elected him quietly voiced concern as to whether this unlikely man could achieve and maintain the respect necessary for conducting his appointed duties. This concern was quietly laid to rest along with the body of one Edgar "Bull" Brzynski three summers before in the small town of Engstrom.

Mr. Brzynski was 260 pounds of jealous young man, struggling in his rookie year of professional football at the Cleveland Bulldogs training camp. Bull had felt the necessity to abruptly leave camp one August day and return to his hometown of Engstrom due to the compelling rumor he had heard whispered among his teammates that his wife of seven months was keeping company with a farm equipment salesman from Macon. Engstrom was a small town and there was little trouble locating the salesman at the town hardware store. He confronted the man, accusations were made, a scuffle ensued. Bull grabbed the man and kept him held in a half nelson. Then he drew a knife and held it to the man's throat. This was the beginning of the event that would fill a humid August day and convince those skeptical residents of Ocoosa County that Sheriff Norman Tomms had been, after all, a sound choice.

"Never seen the likes of it, before or since," was the catch-phrase of the county for years when the topic came up, and it did with frequency. The story echoed off the barbershop walls almost daily for years to come. And like a weed inadvertently nourished on a regular basis over time, it would, of course, grow.

***

Sheriff Tomms was reached by runner somewhere in Watsonville and informed of the drastic situation. Arriving quickly, he got out of his car and made his way politely through the hardware store door. Patrons had gathered inside the store but kept their distance from the entangled pair standing against the back wall. The crowd parted when Sheriff

Tomms entered the store. All talk ceased. Norman stood calmly at the front of the crowd and, facing Bull and his hostage, asked the crowd behind him, without turning around, "Please, for your own safety, please, will you all go outside? I'm asking y'all, please."

A few complied, but most stayed. It was August. It was hot. This was a small town where nothing much happened. "Let's see what Sheriff Dumpy's gonna do with this here," was the palpable thought that hung thick in the humid air. Tensions, morbid curiosities, were high.

The sheriff took a seat in a chair in the middle of the floor and spent the next sixty-three sweltering minutes reminding Bull that he had known him since he was a little boy, had watched his first football game, gone fishing with his father, had eaten supper with his family, and pleading calmly that Bull really didn't want to do this to the man he was holding. Bull continued sputtering obscenities and threatening the salesman's life. "He's a goner, sheriff, he's a goddamn goner! He's had at my Jenny, an' I'm gonna kill him for it! I *got* to, you know that!" Bull screamed. Then his eyes began sending clues to Sheriff Tomms that time might be running out for this terrified Macon man.

Norman had noticed that the rapid darting of Bull's eyes was getting more and more frequent and the darting coincided with agitated and threatening movement. The blade that he held to the man's throat was getting increasingly active, and now starting to draw a noticeable trickle of blood.

It was as if a timer had gone off in the sheriff's head. He had been calm in his approach with Bull and outwardly remained that way; but there was an almost tangible internal change, a quiet intensity that was suddenly focused on resolving this standoff. His knack for detecting subtle nuance in behavior was telling him this situation needed to end *now*. Norman glanced down at his watch, and with a measured reluctance looked at the floor to his right, and then, with resolve, down to his left, as though the solution to this nightmare was written there. He looked up at Bull's face, breathed an audible sigh, then quickly, with marked determination, rose from the chair and closed the distance between himself and the pair, stopping four feet from them in the silence of the store. His eyes never left Bull's.

"Forgive me, Edgar," he said. The words were hushed, calm, prayer-like.

Fluidly, unhesitatingly, he drew his .45 semi-automatic and, pointing it at Bull's face, pulled the trigger once, shooting him directly through the bridge of his nose. Bull's wide eyes disappeared in a red mist and his bulk collapsed in a heap where he had been standing just a second before. Sheriff Tomms did not see the body of a grown, homicidal man lying in front of him. What he saw was an eight-year-old who had once told him with the enthusiasm of a little boy that more than anything in the world he wanted to be a football player when he grew up.

The salesman screamed in terror, and covered with blood and brains, ran hysterically through the stunned crowd out into the street, scrambling into his car and driving away from Engstrom forever. Norman's glasses and crisp white shirt were flecked with pink.

When the ringing of that single discharge had faded, the store was dead silent and remained so for several seconds.

Norman broke that silence and said, in his reserved, almost embarrassed manner, "Will someone go fetch Doctor Meadows for me please? I..." He stopped talking until he could control the noticeable trembling in his voice. *So this is what killing a man does to you,* he thought as he began to fight a sweeping nausea that joined his trembling. He sat back down in the chair he had occupied during his failed negotiations, took off his glasses and closed his eyes, massaging the bridge of his nose with his middle finger and thumb. "I... have paperwork to do now and... I need to... change my shirt, too, I guess."

Those that witnessed the events that day were more than willing to inform the other residents of Ocoosa County at the drop of a hat that, yes; Sheriff Norman Tomms could do the job they had elected him to do.

CHAPTER 25

Sheriff Tomms walked through the door of his office and was greeted by his secretary, May Harper, standing with a man he vaguely recognized. "Sheriff Tomms, this is Jepthy Searcy. He's stopping by to register a statement of concern about his neighbors, the Rainey's, wasn't it? Tell the sheriff here what you told me, Jepthy." They shook hands, Norman shyly, and the gaunt, amiable young man in baggy, faded overalls began his story.

"Well, ya know, sheriff, it prob'ly ain't really nothin' to be alarmed at, but why I'm here is that my wife went over to visit with the Rainey woman, on account a she's just had baby an' all. She had it just a week, ten days ago I reckon, and the midwife that delivered it for her told us she had a girl, named it Grace after her grandma, bless-her-heart, and they was all okay."

"And has something happened to make you think they're not okay now?" asked Norman, with mild interest in his voice.

"See, they're four miles south of us on Big Shoals Road, and with tendin' to crops and all, we ain't done much visiting. So my wife, Effie, made it a plan to ride over there an' carry them some food an' all, but when she got there, she got to figurin' somethin' wasn't right."

"Did she find something that made her think things weren't right? Did she see something?"

"She come back all upset and told me how their front door was wide open an' that nobody hollered back when she hailed them. She thought they mighta been out back doin' whatever an' not a-heard her, so she proceeded 'round the back of the house to fetch 'em."

"And what happened then?" Sheriff Tomms asked, his curiosity now coming gradually to life.

"She got to the backyard and didn't see nobody, but when she looked at the back of the house, she seen the screen door was 'most broken off, hangin' from a hinge. Then she got really scared, 'specially when she smelled the smell."

"What smell was that, Jepthy? What did she say it smelled like?"

Jepthy suddenly got serious. He leaned forward toward the sheriff for emphasis. "Like death, sheriff. She come home and told me it smelled like somethin' dead was just over the fence in the pasture; powerful dead. She come home all upset an' wanted me to go tell somebody, so I drove in here to let y'all know. Didn't know who else to tell."

Sheriff Tomms nodded his head and said, "Thanks for making the drive in, Jepthy. I know it's a real journey from out there. You go home and tell your wife not to worry, I'm going out there right now to take a look, see if I can find anything wrong. I'll get back with you with what I find. You did well, son."

A sheepish grin lit Jepthy's face as he shook the sheriff's

hand. "Hell, sheriff, I been wantin' to meet you for a while anyway, you bein' a famous lawman an' all."

"Famous? Jepthy, I'm not…"

"You know what I mean; that shootout you had with that big football player fella in Engstrom a few years back. Everybody still talks about that. That must have took a whole lotta brav'ry, facin' down somethin' like that!"

Norman's eyes turned away as his memory darted back to the image of an eight-year-old boy lying faceless in a pool of blood. Looking back at Jepthy, his eyes burned into the young man's as he said, "No. That took something a lot different." Sheriff Tomms turned without another word and walked out to his car.

**

Norman never warmed to the image he had created for himself that August afternoon. *A sheriff shouldn't have to be a gunslinger, not most of the time anyway,* he thought, as his car bumped and rattled along the ruts and the dust of Big Shoals Road. *A man in law enforcement should be calm, observant, methodical; that's how crimes are solved, not with guns blazing unless the situation can't be resolved any other way.*

The sheriff pulled off the dirt road and followed a rutted drive for several hundred yards through a field that ended at the Rainey house. He got out, stood, and looked around; a general observation. "Always look at the first thing first," he was fond of saying. A huge granite rock, half the size of his car, lay off to the right side of the empty front yard. It looked out of place jutting up among the weeds and gravel scattered in the expanse.

He took note of it, what his viewpoint would allow him to see, and walked up onto the porch and paused again. He looked around. Nothing seemed wrong here.

The inside of the house was more disconcerting. He called for the Raineys but the house was silent. Chairs and tables had been overturned, as though at least two people had been struggling inside from the parlor to the kitchen and out through the back door. He moved slowly and deliberately, making mental notes on what was obviously out of place, being careful not to touch anything unnecessarily. There were occasional drops of blood apparent here and there leading through the kitchen. Standing in the back doorway, he examined the screen door. *Someone went through this quickly with all their weight. They wanted outside fast*, he thought.

The view from the back steps was that of a small, fenced backyard of red Georgia clay and weeds. A vegetable garden of collards and mustard greens occupied the back left corner and a sizeable oak tree to the right with a worn, wooden swing hanging from a lower branch. Beyond that was a pasture, perhaps eight to ten acres, a solid sea of waist-high grass, ready to be harvested for livestock feed. The boundaries of the pasture were outlined with trees in the distance. With the sun shining, a cloudless blue sky, and a gentle breeze blowing from the field onto his face, Norman felt that being here in this place, now, could have been a lovely experience on a fine Georgia day in May - except for the faint yet unmistakable odor of decomposing flesh mixing somewhere out in the distance with sun-drenched grass. He drew a heavy sigh. It brought him back to the realization that this was not a social visit. This was a *real* visit.

Sheriff Tomms walked to the back of the yard and stopped. He turned around to face the house and mentally followed an imaginary path from the back door, through the yard, to the open gate where he stood. *If someone ran hard enough to break that door, most likely they'd run all the way through the yard, through this gate, and keep on going straight out into that pasture*, he thought. *People running fast like that will usually keep on a straight path if they can, especially if they're panicked.* Rough gravel lined the sides of the narrow path that ended at the high grass and he picked up a big handful of it, putting it in his pocket. He waded into the tall grass perhaps ten or so feet, stopped, then began to systematically throw the stones he had just gathered from his left to his right, ten to fifteen yards out from where he stood, eight stones to the semi-circle. When the arc was completed, he walked another ten feet straight ahead and repeated the process. The stench was getting stronger.

On the fourth stage of this methodical foray, one of his stones caused a pair of buzzards to burst up out of the grass and take flight. *Whatever it is that's dead, it's right there*, he told himself. Making his way through the tall grass toward the spot from where the birds flew, he stopped and listened. *Flies*, he thought. *A lot of flies.* A half dozen more steps and Sheriff Tomms could distinguish brightly colored cloth down low in the grass. The smell of death was now overwhelming. Two more steps and he was able to confirm the shape of a body that appeared to be a fully clothed female lying facedown. Though they had never been introduced in life, Norman felt sure he was now meeting Mildred Rainey. He stopped again, looking around like a cat on the move. He began to slowly walk in a large circle around the corpse, stopping every three or so steps to look at it again. Norman suspected that if someone's footprints had made a path to or from the body, the path might show as a pattern in the grass. The circle finally brought him even with the lower extremities and such a path took shape, but small and irregular, nothing made by a human. Bite marks were apparent on what remained of the exposed calves, with small chunks of flesh missing in some areas. *This path was made by small animals, eating on her a little at a time. Obviously too small to drag her off and small enough not to have been able to disturb her much at all,* he thought. Tomms concluded that this person had died in the position in which he was now finding her.

He approached the body and looked down, surveying the immediate area it occupied. An object was visible in the grass by her right side; a rock, a small boulder almost too big to be easily carried by a woman of this small stature. And he was willing to bet it was, indeed, carried there by someone. *A rock like this does not belong in a pasture that gets harvested. Not good for the machinery,* he told himself. Norman spent several long minutes studying the body; how it was dressed, how much of the body was covered, the position. Through the mercy of nasal fatigue, he had finally become tolerant of the stench.

Something about the position of the corpse puzzled him: the body was stretched out straight, face buried straight down in the grass, but the arms were tucked under the body, as if she died falling over holding something close to her chest. "Oh, Jesus, no," he mumbled out loud. Against his personal policies of investigative procedure, he bent down and attempted to roll the body over on its side. The terrible suspicion he had needed to be proven or dismissed right then. He mentally estimated the body had been here from six to seven days, judging by the amount of decomposition. It was rigid and stuck to the grass beneath it. *Leaking fluids would do that*, he thought. *And blood.* "Please don't be, please don't be," he muttered out loud.

With effort, the body pried away from the grass and stiffly rolled onto its side, then over onto its back. Sheriff Tomms had prayed silently that his suspicion would be wrong, but the horrid truth he was afraid he would find was there at his feet: the woman's arms were clutching the body of an infant, a girl, and it was immediately obvious that the baby's head had been crushed by a heavy object, perhaps a rock. *Oh Grace, I'm so sorry,* he thought to himself. He glanced again at the boulder in the grass and could see a brown stain on one side of it. *With no rain in the past week, that's a blood stain,* he thought.

Though the woman's eyes had dried up, he could still determine they had rolled back in her head. A wide, ragged gash was visible in her neck, and a large area of brown dried blood covered the front of her dress from her throat down. A knife was now visible in the grass her body had covered. *That's probably what cut her throat and killed her,* he concluded. *But who did this?*

A barely visible piece of folded paper peeked over the edge of her dress's front pocket. Norman squatted down to gingerly remove it. Somehow it had escaped the cascade of blood that covered Mildred's entire front. Unfolded, it revealed a neatly written letter which, though brief, explained Mildred's state of mind sometime prior to the baby's and her death:

ARTHUR H. HEATH

This must be done. The child, though beautiful, is evil, from Hell itself I feel. God forgive me what I know I must do.

The sheriff read the note again and again, trying to absorb the thinking of the woman that wrote it and perhaps get an idea of how long before the murder it was written. *This was written thoughtfully, on a flat surface and with care,* he thought. *The ink is too even to have been written otherwise. This was not scratched out in haste by a frantic woman headed out her door in a rush to kill her baby. It is a female's handwriting, most likely Mildred's. That should be easy to confirm by comparison with past stationary. The woman who wrote this letter was very frightened of something and had decided beforehand to do what she did. But she obviously regretted having to do it. And before she did it, she had decided she couldn't go on living after she had. She may have been the one that brought the knife here.* The knife, he now noticed, was covered with a solid brown stain, an indication to him it had stayed in the bleeding wound rather than having been taken away after the cut was made. Her right hand was heavily stained as well. *My God,* Norman thought as the implausible conclusion became evident to him, *she cut her own throat! For whatever reason she felt she had to, she crushed her baby's head with this stone then took her own life with the only implement she probably had to do it with. But why use the stone on the baby when she could have used the knife?*

Sheriff Tomms took several deep breaths and composed himself. He felt fortunate he was alone so that no one could

238

watch his reaction to what he was uncovering. Incidents such as this can cause a person to doubt oneself. The ability to do a sheriff's job objectively was a motivating source of pride for him and something such as this was a tragic but true test of his resolve. Norman had always hated tests. Tests were not in his nature. Tests revealed things one might prefer to conceal, such as insecurities and shortcomings. He stood looking down in silence for long minutes, as the enormity of the scene slowly crept into his reality.

Instinctively, he took one last scan of the scene and turned to walk back to his car. Taking string and a small square of cardboard from his trunk, he fashioned a crude but effective police sign and strung it across the drive in front of the house. "Do not cross. Crime scene. By order of Sheriff Norman Tomms, Ocoosa County." It wasn't much of a deterrent, but he knew it would keep the honest people honest. Besides, no one would have much cause to come way out here unless they had a reason.

Ambling back toward his car again, he stopped to pull out his notebook from his back pocket. Details and thoughts in a case like this could sometimes be hard to remember and sort out when writing out reports, although some, like those today, tended to stick in ones mind forever. That was the downside to criminal investigation; crime can create some memorable images that can be difficult to erase. There were always reports, and this case was going to require a lengthy one. Norman was going to have to recall all of this in detail, possibly over a lengthy period of time.

As he wrote, his attention was subconsciously being drawn once again to the big granite boulder in the front yard.

The fact that it was there, obtrusive and decidedly out of place, was weighing on the back of his mind despite what he had just uncovered out in the field. "Well, last things last, that's the other part of it," he said softly under his breath as he stood looking at the stone. Big. Granite. *Almost like a... like a monument*, he thought.

Norman walked his slow circle around the stone, the tall grass and weeds all but hiding the bottom of it. He parted the grass and searched the base of the rock and the far side revealed something he could not have expected: imbedded in the stone's face was what appeared to be a metal plaque, tarnished with age, bearing time-obscured lettering.

Working with his pocket knife, he removed the rough corrosion, and some brisk rubbing with his handkerchief started to reveal an inscription, well-done in its time, crafted with care by someone who felt this spot was worthy of permanent recognition:

THIS MARKS THE LOCATION
OF THE FORMER LOWNDES PLANTATION
BUILT 1804 A.D. DESTROYED BY WILLIAM
TECUMSEH SHERMAN AND THE ARMY OF
THE UNION THE 19TH DAY OF NOVEMBER
1864

Sheriff Tomms reached out and gently touched the tarnished piece of bronze in awe, momentarily forgetting the revulsion he felt just a few short minutes before in the pasture. He rose and turned, facing the house once more, humbled by the huge slice of time he had loosened with the blade of his knife. This had once been a wondrous place, a place of history, and it had existed, with its humanity and struggles and stories, right where he was now standing. The sense of humility was overwhelming, much as the odor of death had been, and he surveyed the land again, this time not to see what was there now, but to imagine what had stood there sixty-two years before.

CHAPTER 26

Driving back to Watsonville, Sheriff Tomms decided to issue an all points bulletin for Virgil Rainey, the husband of the slain woman, but mostly as a procedural formality. Of course, he wanted to talk to the man, find out what he knew, if anything, about what happened. But Norman had a strong suspicion that the husband was ultimately not responsible for the murders. He found himself becoming uncomfortably bothered by an awakening memory of a past case and a nagging feeling that came with it.

Six years before, in 1920, he recalled there had been another case of infanticide, a newborn also murdered by its mother. In that case, the mother, a Nettie Racine, was alive, but was so distraught, what she could testify about her actions was unintelligible to the point of being useless, mostly psychotic babbling. Ultimately, she ended up being declared insane at the time of the murder, at least, so there was never a trial. A panel committed her to the Andrea Jeffers Institute for the Insane in Albany, where he assumed she remained. She was young, eighteen or so, had no husband or immediate family that anyone could manage to contact, and it was reported a friend had stayed with her toward the end of her pregnancy. She delivered the baby there in her home with the help of the friend, a friend whose identity was never discovered. What was bothering Sheriff Tomms was his recollection of her wild ramblings about 'evil' and 'child of death' and the like, eerily similar to the note he was bringing back to the station with him. And another fact, one that he, for some reason in his investigative mind, felt might eventually prove to be significant: It, too, had occurred on the purported site of an antebellum plantation. The older locals had long believed that the Jenkins Plantation had been located at the junction of Bear Run Road and Thomasville Road, but without an eye witness left from that period who could say for a fact, it was just a local belief. There were no physical remains to give reason to believe so, no marker such as he had just found, no real evidence at all, but Norman's intuition for patterns and behavior were crying out to him that where the dead Racine infant had been found six years ago was exactly where that plantation had stood. Added to what he had just discovered, that would be too coincidental for his mind to accept.

The hair on the back of his neck started to rise and his stomach, despite all he had seen that afternoon, now began to feel queasy as he dredged up one more fact of that past homicide. Norman remembered the four-day-old Racine baby killed in 1920 also died from blunt trauma to its head.

CHAPTER 27

T hen you know where it is? Yes sir, then turn right and… yes sir, six, maybe seven hundred yards. You'll see my string and probably the county medical examiner, he should still be there. If he is, please tell him I did disturb the body, but only to roll it onto its side, looking for the infant. Yes, sir, I'm in the process of finishing it up now. Yes sir, thanks. If you need me, call. Thank you, sir, you too. Good bye." State authorities having been notified, and the medical examiner already there, Norman had a long report to complete. And pieces of a puzzle he wasn't sure he *wanted* to complete. He needed to pay a visit to Randolph Martin.

***

"Randy" Martin knew the county and knew more than most about Civil War history in Georgia, especially Sherman's March to the Sea. The war was his passion. At only twenty-six, he had searched out the Confederate veterans still living in Georgia to sit and listen to them as patiently as though he were an eighty-year-old Rebel soldier himself. Though carrying the scars and handicaps of a terrible and vicious war, the old men never passed up a chance to tell a listener, young or old, just how and where they lost that arm or leg or eye. Randolph Martin, Watsonville pharmacist, could recite their details as well as they could.

***

"Howdy, Randy. Are you busy? Can I come in?"

Randolph looked surprised to see Norman standing in his doorway. "Sure, Norman, come in, please. Is anything wrong?"

"Yes, something's wrong, but not with you, though I think you can help me. That's why I stopped by."

"Me? Does it have something to do with the pharmacy? Come on, let's go into the study." The two walked the short distance down the hallway to a small room off to the left and entered, continuing their conversation as they stood inside.

"No," chuckled Norman, beginning again, "not your work. The War."

"Big war? '14-18?" Randolph asked.

"Blue-Gray," Norman said.

"Well, I should be able to help with that, if anyone can. What do you need to know?" Norman had his attention now.

"First off, did you know the Raineys, out on Big Shoals Road?"

"Not really," said Randolph, "except to fill some prescription for…"

"Mildred," said Norman, filling in Randy's memory.

"Right, Mildred, and … Vincent?"

"Virgil."

"Yes, right, Virgil. Is she sick, Mildred?" Randolph asked with concern. "What do you mean, *did* I know them?"

"No, she's not sick, I'm afraid; she's dead."

"Oh, my God, no! What happened? She was pregnant, wasn't she? Last I knew…"

"I can't really say much, the investigation's just underway," Norman said, wishing he could divulge more to an old and trusted friend. "Yes, she was, but she had the baby last week, and… the baby's dead also."

"No! Oh, no!" Randolph groaned as he dropped into one of the chairs at the small table next to him, a look of astonishment and grief contorting his face. Looking up at Norman, his eyes were misty, and it bothered Norman to think he had just reduced his friend to this state, out of the blue.

"Randy, I can't really say much more, but in time you'll know the whole story."

"Is… um… Virgil, is he… okay?" Randolph asked, his voice filled with trepidation, not really sure he wanted to be told.

"Yes, I assume he's okay, but I don't know for sure. He wasn't there and I've got an APB out on him. I need to talk to him."

"Jesus, Norman, do you think he…?"

"Look," Norman said with some reluctance, "against my law enforcement judgment, I'll tell you this because you're my friend and I think I can trust you to keep this confidential. Mildred and the baby are dead… alright, they've been murdered, maybe a murder-suicide… but it doesn't seem at this point that the husband did it. It just doesn't seem so to me. But as I've said, I still have to talk with him, if and when he's found. He certainly needs to be told if he doesn't already know"

Randolph sat motionless, staring up at the sheriff, still unable to fully fathom what he was being told. It was time for Sheriff Tomms to start asking the questions he came there to ask, if for no other reason now than to get Randolph's mind off the deaths.

"Randy, what I need from you now is information about this county and the Union's march to Savannah. That was the biggest involvement in Georgia during the war, wasn't it, I would guess?"

Randolph sat back slowly and allowed the academic question to dull his concern for the dead woman and her infant.

"Well, not with our troops, no. There were battles that involved tens of thousands of men, on both sides. But as far as devastation and destruction, Sherman's March was the worst thing this state has ever seen. Ever." Randolph was sitting up now, alert and preoccupied with his area of expertise, and Norman was encouraged to see him shifting away from the murders.

"Yes, that's what I'd always heard. Tell me this: were there many plantations destroyed?" Norman asked pointedly.

Randolph's wealth of knowledge and his enthusiasm for sharing it always came with some degree of animation. He seemed to have absorbed that from the old veterans; it was ingrained in their stories.

"Are you serious? Norman, the Union Army destroyed everything they came upon from Atlanta to Savannah. Military, civilian, homes, churches, rail lines, livestock, crops, people, entire towns. Everything. They left as little standing as they could. Anything in their path that escaped their torches or guns was only because they didn't have time to destroy it or they just didn't see it. Period. And you've got to remember, it was winter. The people left alive had nothing. Many of the poorer folk died from exposure.

"In fact," Randolph leaned to one side in the chair, propping his elbow on the table and crossing his legs to get comfortable, "there have been papers and documents, letters and telegraph messages discovered in the last fifty years or so that show strong evidence that an official policy of the North was to target civilians. Can you imagine that?" Randolph asked the sheriff, himself incredulous with the facts he claimed existed.

Norman looked stunned. "No, I can't. That doesn't seem possible. Are you sure?" he asked. "Why?"

"There's enough written evidence to prove it for a fact. And do you know who was almost certain to have instigated that policy, the *official* policy, the one that was in place from the outset of the war? Lincoln himself!"

"What?" Norman asked in disbelief. "Randy, Lincoln was a great man, a great president. That's incomprehensible..."

"But it seems certain to be true. Look, Lincoln absolutely hated the idea of state's rights. His idea of government, the *only* government for this country, was an all-powerful, centralized federal government, and he seemed to have decided from near the beginning of the war that if he shattered the South, 'broke their back', destroyed the day-to-day workings of the people of the South and not just the Confederate Army, that his victory would be swift and complete. He needed a short war, a quick victory to ensure his reelection. Lincoln actually rewarded his generals for destroying towns and cities in the southern states. He wanted to teach the South a lesson that they'd remember for a long time. Secessionism wasn't just treason to Lincoln. It was *worse* than treason. It was the ultimate crime against his precious Union."

"I never knew it was that bad," said Norman, lost in the implications that Randolph's facts suggested.

"'Lot of people don't. Don't feel bad," said Randolph. "I suppose even if you were there and lived through it, time has a way of softening the edges of things, erasing the details, like water does to stone, you know? And I'm sure the average soldier, North or South, never really had the big picture of what was going on, what exactly they were fighting for. It all came down to day-to-day survival. But I feel like the truth needs to be remembered and spoken, or put forth somehow from time to time; maybe etched in stone or bronze so people can read it now and then and remember what the truth really is, with all its hard edges, the edges that cut through the haze of time."

'Bronze'. Norman quickly came back to the present. He needed to get back to the questions at hand. "What about the plantations in Ocoosa County? You say they were all destroyed?" Norman asked.

"Every single one," Randolph said in a sad, matter-of-fact manner. "All eight of the big plantation houses in this county and all the property belonging to them, all burned to the ground. The Yankees wanted to erase them from memory. And they did it with a remarkable swiftness."

"Randolph, here is what I need to know, what I came here to find out: do you, or does anyone you know of left around here, know exactly where those plantations were located? All

249

eight that you know of?" There was an intensity in the sheriff's eyes Randolph had not seen very often.

"Well, look, it's been, let's see, uh… sixty-two years since they were destroyed, all eight in this county in a matter of three or so days. Everything burned completely, totally; the Union soldiers saw to that. Hell, they were enjoying themselves. No Rebel troops to speak of anywhere in the area to give them trouble. It was a field day. No foundations of any structure were left; most had none to speak of anyway, and as time passed, as things got overgrown, it would seem the lands were claimed then sold and then cleared again, and settled all over like nothing had ever been there. The land has a way of doing that; watching, it seems, what we humans do, then fixing it back again. I really believe that; the earth is so neutral. People forget. They go on with their daily lives. Houses got built again on those lands, homes that are most likely standing now, and being lived in too, I imagine."

May was a warm month in 1926, but Norman felt a cold chill pass through him. It settled in the pit of his stomach. "Being lived in," he repeated in a far-off monotone. He was staring into Randolph's eyes while his mind was sweeping down Ocoosa roads, headlong into the deep forests and open fields. "Being lived in."

"Are you okay, Norman?" asked Randolph, concern cocking his head. "All the color just left your face!"

Sheriff Tomms looked his friend directly in the eyes for several long seconds. "Randy… do you know where they were?"

The tone in Norman's voice was one that Randolph Martin had heard but a few times in all the years he had known him. This was Sheriff Norman Tomms talking, not his old friend. He stared back at the sheriff in acknowledgement of the obvious seriousness of the matter at hand. His eyes broke the hold of the sheriff's and looked over at a large bookcase against his wall. He looked back at Norman and said with his own gravity, "I have something that does. I'll get it for you."

Randolph left his chair with the reluctance of a man charged to complete a task he wished he did not have to perform. He crossed the room, stopping in front of his enormous bookcase, and quickly surveyed the top shelves, his eyes coming to rest on a book smaller than most. Plucking it from among the others, he stared down at it, and Norman could tell his friend was making up his mind as to whether or not to release custody of something important to him. The pharmacist walked the distance back to the table, still obviously uneasy with his decision, and laid the book in front of Norman for his inspection. He tapped the cover and backed away.

Norman's eyes studied the worn, leather-bound volume, then rose to meet Randolph's. "What is this, Randy?" he asked.

"A journal. A handwritten journal."

"Where'd it come from?"

"Do you remember Fred Runner?" Randolph asked.

Norman searched his mental directory, barely smiling as he associated the name in the banks of time. "Fred... Freddy. Yeah."

"He gave me this," said Randolph, "along with some of his other things in '18, before he shipped out to France. Baseball mitt, some clothes, books; personal stuff like that he'd rather leave with a friend than with his folks. They were angry with him for volunteering, so he wasn't getting along well with them at the time anyway. He said he wanted to leave the things, 'just in case'."

"And he didn't come back, I remember very well," said Norman. "I liked Freddy. I missed seeing him around."

"Died of influenza soon after he arrived in Europe, remember? I don't think he ever got to pick up a rifle," Randolph said. "His folks were devastated, naturally, not just because their only son died, but the fact they weren't speaking when he left made it all the worse. They never got to say goodbye. They felt they couldn't stay here after that and up and moved to Ohio or somewhere up that way soon after they were notified."

"I recall them leaving. It was quick; they didn't say much. So, what's in this?" Norman asked, fingering the old book.

"What you want to know...and more. It will tell you where the plantations in Ocoosa were and what went on in them during November of '64. It's the 'what went on in them' that I've never shared with anyone else till now, Norman. I wish you didn't feel you had to read this; I wouldn't be giving it to you now if you didn't think it was necessary. It only amounts to several pages, but when I read it the first time, I couldn't get through it all, it upset me that much. It was horrible what happened to those people."

Norman was starting to almost feel apprehensive of what he was holding; now gingerly touching it. He respected Randolph's opinion, and if this little journal was as upsetting as he was being told, then he trusted its contents must be very graphic indeed. "Who wrote this? Do you think, knowing what you know, that it's true?"

"The first two pages are missing; you can see where they

were torn out. So if they contained any actual indication as to who wrote it, well, they're gone. But when you read it, it becomes obvious that it was written by a doctor; that'll be evident," Randolph said, trying to be of as much help to his friend as possible. "And that gives me a clue as to whom I think may have written it."

"Who?"

"Fred Runner's grandfather, on his mother's side, was a Doctor Norton Fale. There are references in the book where the author says he treated injured people, and he uses medical terms; says something about returning to his practice, too. Norton Fale would have a good knowledge of Ocoosa County, and the person who wrote this obviously did. My bet is that Doctor Norton Fale wrote this. It must have been a horrible chore for him or anyone. Maybe he felt it was his duty, or a responsibility or something. He states that he delivered many of the children that were killed, so it must have been Fale. He probably had known most all of those people."

Norman was curious. "Did he see all this, all that he wrote about, happen himself? How could he do that? The plantations had to be spread out, right? He would have had to be riding with the Yankees to actually witness much of what happened himself."

"Of course. No, I don't think he saw any of what he wrote about happen firsthand," Randolph said. "Most all of it seems to be recounted from testimony from the slaves that were present when the Yankees came through and who witnessed with their own eyes what went on. And you have to remember, these are Yankee soldiers the slaves are talking about here, soldiers they had been waiting for, their 'saviors', their

253

'deliverers'. The events they claim to have seen must have scared them to death," Randolph said, shaking his head. "Norman, this is really rough reading, I have to warn you. It may be only a little more than several pages long, but... I'd rather you left it here and forgot about it unless you really think you need it. Before I read it, I could not have imagined such cruelty. I guess I've always been a little naïve. It was a Pandora's Box for me; I don't want it to be that for you."

"Thanks for your concern. You're a good friend, Randy; the best I've got. Can I borrow it for a while? I'd like to read it anyway. I *need* to read it."

Norman stood, shook Randolph Martin's hand, and picked up his hat and the small, worn journal. He walked through the darkening room and out into the hall, turning right to the front door and opened it. Only then did he realize it had been raining for some time, and quite hard. Randolph saw the rain and looked around for something in which to place the journal for protection. He walked back to a small table in the study and lifted the edge of a doily that draped over the side and pulled a cigar tin from a shelf. The tin was brightly colored, the top showing a mustard colored banner with the word "Havana" scrolled across it in black. Under it was an abbreviated scene of a beach with palm trees and a blue-green ocean in the background. A dark, beautiful woman with long curly black hair dressed in a white blouse and multicolored ruffled skirt held a cigar in one hand and beckoned invitingly with the other. The sides of the tin were decorated with similar scenes, colorful snippets of an idyllic Cuban life. Randolph opened the tin and put the book in, sealing the top securely. "That'll keep it dry. Hubert Anderson brought this back for my father from

Cuba in '98. Thought he'd like them. Dad smoked the cigars the first week." he said, handing the tin to Norman.

Norman put on his hat and thanked Randolph once again.

"Thanks, I'll take good care of this. I'll have it back in a couple of days, if that's alright."

Norman walked out onto the porch and assessed the rain. He tucked the tin under his arm for protection and jogged the short distance to his car.

Randolph leaned against his door frame. His face was void of expression and his body sagged like that of a man defeated. And when he spoke to Norman one last time, the voice was that of someone whose energy and emotion had been used up; drained. "Norman..." he hesitated. "Norman... I realize you need to know these things for a good reason, a 'crime' reason, but you'll wish you never read what you've got there," Randolph said, shouting to be heard over the rain, pointing to the book. "You're going to regret learning about things you're never going to be able to forget. If it will help you solve a murder case, well... I hope Mildred Rainey and her baby are worth it."

Sheriff Tomms' face was being pelted by a harder rain now as he stood by his car, looking at Randolph on the porch. He was barely able to see the hollowness in his friend's eyes from the distance in the rain. Norman looked at his friend and wondered exactly what he was saying, but did not reply. He got in his car and drove away in the pouring rain.

CHAPTER 28

There was no one at the sheriff's office when Norman pulled up in front. Through the rain, which was increasing in intensity by the minute, he could see May had left a few of the lights on for him. She was thoughtful like that, and with the absence of a deputy for the time being, it was good to have someone in the office with him that thought the same way he did. He made his way the short distance to the front door and let himself in, somehow avoiding becoming thoroughly soaked. Once inside, he hung his hat and gun belt on the hat rack just inside the door. Retrieving a towel from the other side of the room, he returned to wipe down his pistol. The original issue walnut grip on the right side had a bottom corner broken off up to the lower screw and water tended to collect there on the frame, causing rust. *Gotta get a new one of those someday.* He placed the cigar tin on the corner of his desk and searched his desk drawer for the forms he would need to file the report on the murders he had discovered earlier that day. Sometimes this was the hard part, the paperwork that followed any action he took in the conduction of his sworn duty. But as he sat gathering the forms he was looking for, he knew the most difficult part this time was behind him: that part he had found lying out in a pasture on Big Shoals Road, stiff and covered in dried blood.

Before he started the paperwork, Norman opened the top desk drawer, reached toward the back and pulled out a small leather bag intricately decorated with fine beadwork and a row of tiny, delicate feathers that hung from the bottom edge. He kneaded it gently between both hands and softly muttered a line of Creek dialect, quietly singing the words he recited in the silence of his office. He repeated it in English, the translation almost exact and, he thought, just as beautiful on the tongue:

"My spirit will float upon the flower-wind;
It knows no death.
It will dance around you in the air,
Singing the 'forever song.'"

He smiled, kissed the beading, and returned the bag to the back of the drawer from where he had taken it. The short, private ritual reminded him he should phone his Hazel and tell her he was going to be late getting home.

The phone was a relatively new luxury for the police station in Watsonville. The fact that it was a 'new-fangled blessing' was becoming more and more apparent as each day passed. It gave him comfort as he heard the rain pelting the windows that he could inform his wife that he was safe and going to be late without sending someone way out of town to his house to give her the message in person. Norman walked over to the phone on the wall and cranked the handle to get Bertha, the town operator. "Bert, hello, it's Norman. Fine, little wet. Uh-huh, roads are getting worse, watch out when you go home. Okay. Would you ring Hazel for me? Thanks." The phone rang the Tomms' two rings at his house and his wife Hazel picked it up quickly as if she had been waiting for the call.

"Hi Hon, it's me. Yes, bad connection; must be the rain. Oh yeah, it's pouring here too. Any leaks? Did you look out on the porch? Good. Okay, this is what... alright... is it important? Should I come home now? Well, okay, then just remember what it is and we'll talk about it when I get there, okay? Are you sure? Here's what I've got to do before I leave tonight: I've got to get reports started on a double murder I discovered today. Yeah, well, for privacy's sake, I don't want to say too much on the phone, but I'll tell you the details when I get home. It's bad. Then I've got to go over the requisitions that May started for me and authorize them so they can go to Atlanta tomorrow. Uh-huh. Yes, that's really all I've got to do. Maybe the rain will let up by then too. I saw Randy this afternoon... he's good. I had questions I thought he could help me with. He was, very; okay then, I'll see you when I'm done. Love you too, sweetie; goodbye." The sheriff hung up the phone and walked back to his desk. He took a sheet of blank paper and jotted down his suspicions as to the similarities between the Racine case of '20 and the Rainey discovery of the morning, and the similarities between both of them and the possible locations of past Ocoosa County plantations. One of those locations was confirmed, the other he now highly suspected. There had been infant deaths prior to these, none of which he had investigated as an officer of the law. The reporting had been sketchy and the sensationalism of the crimes had quickly subsided. But the nature of the crimes had bothered Norman at the time and still did. His psychological makeup always pushed him to look for patterns and habits.

I wonder if these past murders fit the same pattern as these last two? he thought. *If I can determine where these plantations had been, my guess is that these murders took place on the old sites. But why? Maybe this journal's got some answers.* Norman put his note aside and opened the colorful tin. The rain was coming down harder and he could hear heavy sheets of it hitting the side of his office in waves. *This just might be where I ought to stay for the time being*, he thought. *So I might as well get this thing read.*

Taking the journal out of the tin, he examined it again, carefully looking it over as the important piece of literature it was. He adjusted his desk lamp, took his magnifying glass from his top drawer in case he needed it, and settled in to read this small leather book that frightened Randolph so badly and just might add the missing piece to the puzzle he knew needed to be solved for the sake of this county.

***

Six riveting, frozen minutes passed before Norman was conscious of blinking or taking what might be construed as a full breath. The only two things that had moved in that horrible space of time, those minutes he wished now he could take back, were his fingers turning page after ghastly page, and his eyes, incredulously deciphering each of the handwritten sheets as they took in the details of the horrors Randolph had warned him about. *In the depths of the soul God has given me,* he thought... *I cannot comprehend how people can do this to one another*. Taking off his glasses, he slowly propped his elbows on his desk, letting his face sink into both hands. He took a deep, ragged breath and let it all the way out in disgust for his own species. At that moment, for the first time in his life, he was ashamed of being human. Norman knew he was very close to breaking down; this short, shy little man, sitting motionless in the glow of his desk lamp except for a trembling he did not like; by himself in an office being tormented by torrents of hard, gusting rain. For the first time that he could recall, he felt alone, vulnerable, afraid; and the dark and the weather were not helping. It frightened him in that stark moment to realize he lived in a world where the things he had just read could happen; did happen. He had been an officer of the law long enough to have seen his share of the dark side of people; it was part of the job. But this, coupled with what he had discovered earlier at the Rainey house, took away his very breath, chipped heavily at his faith and his hope. It was too much for one day for one man.

I wish to God there had been an easier way to find out I was on the right track; I didn't need to know all this, he thought as he slowly moved to add to his page of notes. He jotted down the confirmation of his suspicions and put a big asterisk next to it to give it priority for investigative order. He folded the paper and put it in the bottom of the tin, then placed the journal with it, keeping the two together for reference. *I've got to get that back to Randy as soon as I can; he needs to put it away and never take it out again. No one should have to read something like that in their life. I should have listened to him. But at least now I suspect it wasn't their fault; not really.*

Norman replaced the lid and his eyes lingered a moment on the mocha woman on the cover, offering with one hand and inviting with the other. *How tempting*, he thought. *Run away to a Paradise where mothers don't bludgeon their babies to death and everyone loves each other.* He managed the slightest chuckle and shook his head. *We are who we are.* Mentally exhausted and spiritually fatigued, he arranged the work on his desk for the morning, deciding it was time to head home. The requisitions would just have to wait. He put the tin in his bottom desk drawer to keep anyone from getting curious. This was not something he wanted anyone to stumble upon. The rain was letting up and now was a good time to make a break for his car. Norman put on his hat and gun belt and shut off the lights, locking the door behind him in the continuing drizzle and got into his car. It was late and the streets of Watsonville were deserted.

***

The paved roads of Watsonville ended quickly and Norman found himself struggling with the dirt roads that had turned to muddy quagmires from the heavy rain. A haze was hanging in the night air and his tires were continually getting caught in the deep ruts of the clay roads. *Times like this I wished we didn't live so far out*, he thought as he negotiated the curves of the narrow country road that would lead to another and then another and eventually to his house.

The treacherous condition of the road presented a paradox for Norman; if he tried to drive too fast in the thick mud, the car would careen uncontrollably from one side of the road to the other, sliding dangerously; too slow and he could feel it bogging down. *Last thing I want to do is get stuck out here tonight*, he thought. *Man, this is the worse I've seen it in a long time.*

At six and a half miles from town, the dirt road took an abrupt ninety degree turn to the right, necessary because of a natural rock formation in the land. The road would, further on, make a long looping left curve to end at a "T" in the road where he would continue on for another four miles before coming to his last turn toward home.

Norman slowed his car to make the turn but could feel the tires starting to sink into the red clay of the narrowed road. Instinctively, he accelerated to gain speed, trying to avoid stopping altogether, and his wheels spun as the car coasted helplessly into the turn. The tires bottomed out suddenly, hitting the layer of gravel placed under the clay on the road to aid in conditions such as this, and Sheriff Tomms' vehicle propelled forward, sliding sideways into the turn, first to the right. He turned the wheel hard to the left, attempting to straighten the car through the turn. The thickness of the mud caused him to overcompensate and the car to spin wildly to the left, the front left wheel striking a low, solid birm of rock that formed the left shoulder. The car spun and catapulted over the narrow grassy ledge, rolling over and over down the steep embankment thirty feet below the level of the dark, muddy road. The vehicle came to a stop on its side between the bottom of the slope and the watery base of the tall trees that surrounded the rock formation, the headlights shining brightly down the concealed wash. Sheriff Tomms, ejected in the roll, lay unconscious, propped up almost in a sitting position against a small boulder, water and ferns all around him.

The beam of the headlights gradually dimmed to darkness in the settling night haze of that remote stretch of Ocoosa County road, along with the life that belonged to the man that would eventually be acclaimed as its most famous sheriff.

The search that was organized early the next morning had little trouble locating the wreckage; the ruts in the road telling the rescue party the likely story of how and why it happened. The large hematoma on the left side of Norman Tomms' head told them the rest of the story. It was later to be concluded by the medical examiner, and thought by those at the scene who recovered his body, that Sheriff Norman Tomms had died passively and peacefully sometime during the night, much in the same manner he had attempted to live his life.

CHAPTER 29

The procession of cars carrying law enforcement officials and citizens from as far away as Brunswick and Moultrie stretched from one end of Watsonville to the other, heading slowly to the small cemetery just south of the town boundary.

The afternoon was sunny and warm, contradicting the event that was bringing tears to the eyes of grown men; men who had known and respected this balding, reserved little man, this shy public servant that had gone about his appointed duties as conscientiously as he knew how. A short, pudgy man who would never know the admiration being demonstrated on this small, obscure Georgia hilltop.

Norman, had he known, would have been embarrassed by it all.

A warming breeze steadily blew across the gently swelling hilltop and Hazel Tomms, dressed in somber black, managed to weakly smile through her veil with politeness and a willed pleasantry as she greeted scores of strangers to accept their condolences. Her conduct and demeanor had always paralleled that of her husband; today would be no different.

Randolph Martin was just another face in a crowd that strained the boundaries of the small, rural cemetery. His position near the back of the black-attired throng was sufficient, he felt. He could hear the words being spoken by the minister well enough, and the grave itself was something he would see on a fairly regular basis in the future. Norman would like the occasional visitor, he was sure.

While the preacher spoke, Randolph's attention was casually drawn off to the crest of another hill perhaps two hundred yards to the right of where he and the diverse congregation of mourners stood. There on the grassy knob, in bright sunshine, stood two men, one wearing what was most certainly the finest coat he possessed, arms by his side and standing rigid in respect. His black, broad-brimmed reservation hat sat tall and straight on his head. The other man, wearing traditional dress, slowly danced and shuffled and spun in place next to him, alternately bending to scoop red dirt from the ground and raising his face and hand to the blue sky, offering the dust he held to the wind, letting it drift away to join the spirit of Norman Tomms on its journey to the afterlife. Randolph watched the two with curiosity for a minute or so, knowing it was as close as the two dared come to the collection of white people that crowded the cemetery. He turned back to see what he could of the ceremony in front of him and, looking back once again to the sun-drenched knob, saw they were gone.

As the line of mourners eventually thinned and parked cars began to pull away one by one from the low, simple fence that surrounded the hilltop, two figures Hazel knew well slowly, respectfully, approached from out of the corner of her eye. Randolph was the first to walk up and take Hazel's hands

265

in his. Looking at her with deep sadness through his own watery eyes, he cleared his throat to make his voice strong and sure, but his words trembled out at her despite his effort.

"Hazel... oh, Hazel, what... what can I say?" he stammered, the sympathy evident and genuine in his voice.

"Randy, you were Norman's best friend, you know that and so do I. You needn't say a thing, dear. No doubt he thought his life enriched with someone like you in it; that's all that needs be said. It's all that counts now. Thank you for coming," she replied with her typical kindness.

"If there's anything you need, anything..."

"Thank you, Randy. If there is, you know I'll call. Thank you," she interrupted, not wanting him to continue on with what she knew he would go on to say. It was unnecessary.

Randolph turned to go before his tears got the better of him and acknowledged the approach of May Harper with a subdued nod as he passed her. She repeated Randolph's cautious, sympathetic advance and came to stand in front of Hazel. The two women stood facing each other through black veils, openly weeping as their eyes met, alone now in this hilltop cemetery, standing in a balmy breeze they both knew Norman would have loved. They collapsed into a sobbing embrace, heads on each other's shoulders, consoling each other's loss of a man they both knew so well and would dearly miss. May pulled away first, lifting her veil to dab at her eyes and said, "I am so truly sorry for you, dear. Other than you yourself, most likely no one else knows what a loss this is more than me. Norman loved you dearly; I can tell you that. I saw it in him every day I worked for him. I'm sure you know it; he wasn't the kind that would be afraid to hide that."

Hazel nodded, summoning up her weak smile again. "I know he did. Thank you, May. He thought the world of you, too," she replied. "He told me so many times. We probably knew him better than any two people in this world. When he was at his best, he was so wonderful," she said, managing a broader smile.

"And when he was at his worst, which was rare, he was still so damned good!" May responded, trying to make the conversation lighter.

The smile Hazel had forced quickly faded as her eyes left May's and her face began to quiver. "He would have been a wonderful father to the child I'm carrying," she managed to say, before her grief overtook her again and she collapsed once more into a shocked May Harper.

May pushed Hazel back enough to look her in the face and asked her, "Hazel, did Norman know? He never said... I didn't..."

"Norman didn't know," Hazel said through her flowing tears, her sobs making it difficult for her to speak. "I spoke to him by phone... the night he... he died. I told him I had something important to tell him. He was preoccupied with his work, but he offered to come home then if I wanted him to. I needed to tell him in person; I wanted to see his face. So I told him to finish what he was doing and I'd tell him when he got home. He never knew. He never will. Oh May, what will I do? What will happen now?" she asked as she looked through her tears into May's face.

"The people in this town will never let the child of Norman Tomms want for anything; don't you worry about that, dear," May said as she put her arm around Hazel's shoulder and started walking slowly down the hill with her. "I'll see to it."

Hazel spoke again as she walked, lifting up the veil that clung tightly to her face from the gentle wind they were walking into. "The one thing Norman's child will need the most is Norman for a father, and that's one thing the town or you can't give," she said to May, as a deputy from Pike acting as chauffeur opened the door to a long black automobile for Hazel.

He helped her in and shut the door. May stood by the side of the car as Hazel opened the window. Both women were tired of crying but the tears remained just the same. "Thank you," Hazel weakly told her.

"Anything you need, anything," May replied as the car began to roll down the narrow, rutted road back toward Watsonville.

CHAPTER 30

P ercy Granville was technically considered a public
servant, though there was not much public-minded
about him. A petty man, consumed with his social and
professional standing, it was evident to most Watsonville
inhabitants that knew him that Percy's main concern was how
he was perceived by his superiors. Watsonville had a very short
social ladder, but Percy was determined to climb what there
was of it.

County clerk in May of '26 was not a complicated post;
consisting of recording things, mostly. Records of land
transactions and ownership, marriages and the occasional
divorce; all things of a legal nature needed to be duly noted and
recorded. But keeping track of the legalities of Watsonville and
the surrounding smaller towns was not a very time-consuming
job for Percy. Besides, he was too busy grooming himself for
bigger things, better things. Local politics was a means to an
end for him. Being in the right place at the right time was what
Percy excelled at, and he prided himself on showing whoever
was at whatever function that Percy Granville was the man
they needed to fill that next higher and better paying job they

were looking to staff. It made no matter to him what it might be.

The Watsonville Mayor had charged Percy with the task of collecting and disposing of Norman Tomms' personal effects. An interim sheriff was going to take over from another county, and the Watsonville politicians wanted the office to be presentable and ready. May had gotten in touch with Hazel, asking what of Norman's effects would be of value to her. "His service pistol and his badge would be the only things I can think of I would really want," she had told May. "I can't think of much else there would be that would make me think of him. I want to remember those things about his career, they were important to him. The personal things, well, I've got those here, and I've got the memories in my heart." May had attempted to do the job of cleaning out Norman's desk, but could not bring herself to do it, becoming weepy and having to stop and sit down every time she began. The mayor understood and therefore gave the task to Percy. Taking care of "someone's junk," as he put it, was beneath him, he thought, and fortunately, this was the Saturday he watched his nephew Dewey.

***

Rumor had it that Dewey DePaul's father had abandoned him and his mother, having run off with another woman three years ago when Dewey turned twelve, convinced the local doctor's prognosis for the boy was correct; though Dewey, now fifteen, would age physically in a normal manner, he would always be "six, maybe seven" years old mentally. "Can't abide by a woman that's a bad breeder," Mr. DePaul was heard to say later on while staring down into a glass of beer. "T'aint none of it *my* fault!" Marrying a bearded woman from Valdosta that headlined in a carnival side show and bore him three perfect sons years later, he felt his conviction was vindicated, his philosophy sound, and his life complete.

'Dum-Dum Dewey' the boy's peers would taunt him, and it often drove the hurt and confused child to anger and even violence, thereby necessitating a constant, watchful eye on his whereabouts and activity. Putting him to work in the sheriff's office would accomplish two things for his Uncle Percy: take care of boxing the odds and ends in the desk, thereby freeing him up to attend a local fund-raiser a few blocks away; and give Dewey something to occupy his hands and the simple mind that guided them.

"Now Dewey, listen to me," Percy told the boy, alternating between looks in the mirror to check his appearance and glances down at the boy who was sitting in the sheriff's desk chair, looking around the office in child-like awe. "I have somewhere to go for just a while, but while Uncle Percy is gone, I have a job for you to do, an important job that has to be done just right, do you understand? Dewey, are you listening to me?" Dewey turned his attention back to his uncle and nodded with a blank expression. All that occupied the young man's mind was the fact his uncle had told him that the job he had for him to do today would involve hammering nails into a wooden box.

Dewey loved to hammer things, loved to use tools, any tools, even when he didn't know what they were. He could never understand why his mother, why everyone, wanted to

271

take them away from him whenever he picked them up. Today would be different, and he was looking forward to doing whatever Uncle Percy wanted him to do, as long as he could use a hammer on something. "See the desk you're at? I want you to take everything out of it and put it all in this crate here," Percy told his nephew, pointing to the wooden box at his feet. "Try to be neat, make it look pretty and it will all fit, okay?"

"Okay. Then when I'm done, do I get to hammer nails in it? You said I could hammer something."

"Yes, you can hammer the lid on it, use these nails," Percy responded, pointing to a box of nails on the floor, the exasperation starting to show in his voice. It was important he arrive at the function on time and his nephew was going to cause him to be late. He turned to continue talking into a mirror, checking his tie once again and noticing the red shaving rash that always crept out from his collar when he got hot enough to sweat. "And do a neat job with that, too. My friend Will is going to be here in a little while. Do you remember him? He's going to paint some letters on the box so we know what's in it." Dewey's eyes lit up at the sound of the word 'paint'.

"Can I paint too? Will he let me paint too?"

"I'm sure he will. Now, I've got to go now Dewey. Can I trust you to do what I told you? It's important!"

"Uh-huh, I'll do good, Uncle Percy, I will," the boy assured his uncle as he watched him go out the door. Dewey opened the bottom drawer and rummaged through it, seeing mostly papers and odd forms and letters. His young eyes then came across a colorful metal box, a beautiful box, unlike anything he had ever seen.

"Wow," he thought, holding the tin in his hands, trying to remove the tight lid. "This is swell! I wonder what it's for."

Try as he may, Dewey could not pry the lid off and after thirty seconds of struggling and failing, lost interest altogether in wanting to see the contents, and settled for looking at the wonderful images on the outside of it. His arrested mind quickly grew bored with the pictures and he placed the tin in one corner of the bottom of the crate, clumsily dumping the remaining contents of each drawer in on top of the last until the desk was empty. "Now I get to do hammerin'!" he said out loud, a big grin on his face as he reached for the claw hammer at his feet and the box of nails his uncle had left. Dewey's enthusiasm for using tools far outweighed his skill, and the majority of the nails were left sticking up, only partially hammered in. He could tell this wasn't quite right, it certainly didn't look right, and his child's logic concluded that a lot of bad ones would hold as good as a few good ones, so he kept on nailing.

"Hey, Dew, watcha buildin' there?" Will asked as he entered the sheriff's office, a small bucket of black paint in one hand and a brush and stencils in the other. He put them down on the floor and rested his hands on his hips, surveying the wooden pincushion in front of him and the boy beaming with pride responsible for it. "That's some job you did. Figure you got enough nails in it?" he asked, smiling at the boy and the comical waste of nails. "Must be most of the box stickin' up out of that crate top. Reckon it'll stay closed, do ya?

"Uh-huh, sure do! Can I help you paint now? My Uncle Percy said if I asked you, you might let me paint some too. I like to paint, Will! Can I?"

"Well, seein' as how it looks like you got nailin' pretty much down pat," Will said, trying not to laugh out loud at his own humor, "I'll hold the stencils on the box and I'll let you swab paint over 'em. How's that sound?"

"Okay, I can do that!" Dewey said, his face flushed with excitement.

The stenciling done, the paint dried, it was time to put the crate in the storage room in back of the office. Dewey and Will walked the box of Sheriff Norman Tomms' effects to the makeshift wooden shelves at the back of the small, dark room and put it on the second shelf, waist-high. Will shook the dirt from his hands and Dewey copied him, shaking as long as Will shook, stopping when Will stopped. "What's in that ol' box in there?" Will asked him as they shut and locked the door.

"Uncle Percy said it was just junk; stuff somebody didn't need no more or somethin'," he replied.

"Stuff that belonged to Sheriff Tomms, I reckon, but that's good enough for me. I figger your uncle wants me to stay watchin' you till he's back. So, ya want a ice cream? How's that sound to ya, Dew?"

"Yeah!" Dewey replied as they turned to casually saunter the short distance down the block to Martin's Apothecary.

CHAPTER 31

July 23, 1935
12:17 P.M.

T here are days when the uncertainties bother me more than others," Hazel Tomms admitted as she reached for the pitcher of tea now sweating like she and her guest. The July afternoon heat had a way of draining enthusiasm for doing anything but sitting and enjoying the rare company she received. "Would you care for more?"

"That would be wonderful, dear," said Tildie Martin as she held her glass closer to her hostess. No air seemed to be moving and she noticed the tiny beads of perspiration on her arm as she stretched it out to Hazel. "I'm so glad now that I rode on out here with Randolph. He and Gerald are headed to the Riggin's farm, did I say that? Old Man Riggins needs liniment for his hip where that new horse of his kicked him. Myself, I can't imagine such pain! So, we can sit and visit until they get back! It's been a while since we done that together."

"I'd like nothing more! I get some visitors out here, but not much real company, you know?"

"Who do you talk to when you need to? You must get so terribly lonely out here! Lester is just a boy…"

"And that's part of the problem," Hazel broke in. "It's not his fault, of course, he's just a boy doing what boys do, but growing up without a father is hard on a soul. I never knew just how difficult it was going to be on us both, I guess. As I say, some days I'm more at ease with it than others."

Tildie nodded her head in understanding, mentally thinking what a challenge her son Gerald could be at times, even with a father to help raise him. He had been a fussy infant from the start, and despite the wives-tale warning her father had proclaimed, ("cranky little, cantankerous big"), she was confident her little boy would eventually grow out of his 'hard to please' stage. She had also often thought, in the nine years that had passed since Norman's death, how fortunate she was living close in to what Watsonville had to offer and how difficult things must be at times for the widow and son of Ocoosa County's most famous lawman. "Dear, have you ever thought of moving closer to town? I realize Norman loved the seclusion you have here, but things are different now for you. You have other considerations to take into account; there's your safety…"

"Oh, Tildie, no one is going to bother us out here! I'm completely safe here. Look at it the way I do: the Indians and the wolves are long-gone. I'm too far out for drunks to wander by and pester me. And Lord knows any would-be robber worth his salt in these parts has got to be aware I don't have any money! I've got Lester at night, he can shoot if he needs to, I taught him that. And people come by most every day with the washing I take in. But mostly, this is the house Norman and I

276

built. It's the house where we had…" Hazel ceased speaking immediately, hoping her silence would halt the tears she was so close to crying over her choice of words. Tildie knew the mistake as soon as Hazel spoke it and reached to grab for her arm in consolation. Their hands fumbled until they found each other's. "…I had Lester. I love this house. Not a day goes by that I don't feel good, strong memories of my dear husband here somehow. Try to understand when I say that I'm afraid that if we left, I might lose that forever. And I don't think I could bear that." Helpless to stop them, Hazel's tears began to flow freely and now Tildie was powerless to control her own. Their hands tightly squeezed each other's over the pitcher of tea in mutual support and both allowed themselves the opportunity and freedom to weep openly.

A minute passed and Hazel looked up to the porch rafters and sighed deeply, blinking away the tears she was tired of crying. "As I said, some days are better than others," she said, laughing slightly.

"You don't have to be alone to feel that way. We all do from time to time," Tildie said as she wiped her tears and her beaded brow with the small napkin she held on her lap. "Some days I worry about things more than other times, pretty near like yourself, I imagine."

Hazel frowned a look of concern that was genuine and also served as a way to stop dwelling on her own hardships. "Is something wrong, especially?"

Since Hazel had asked, Tildie stared off to the side to attempt to formulate a measured answer. "Not so much wrong as bothersome," she answered, trying to downplay the seriousness of what she perceived as a manageable situation.

"It's Randolph, actually Randolph and Gerald; the time they spend together out and about."

"You should be thankful they have each other. They seem to get along so well, the boy and Randy; he's two now, right? What do you see wrong?"

"Almost three, and yes, he's his father's pride and joy. Randolph loves the boy to no end; wants to have more children, but the doctor warned me…"

"Yes, I remember; you poor dear! And nothing can be done? No medicine, no operation?" Hazel asked, all the while shaking her head in empathy.

"No medicine and no procedure without great risk. Besides, I'd have to go to Atlanta or farther to have anything done, and we couldn't afford that anyway. What has me concerned…" Tildie said slowly, "is Randolph's interest… no, to be honest, his fascination with these baby murders that happen here abouts."

"Oh," Hazel expelled the word in a grunt, shaking her head in disgust at the mention of Ocoosa's 'burden', the occasional horror that had become all to convenient to brush under the rug of everyday life until it reared it's head again from time to time. "Honestly, Tildie, how long is this thing going to go on? Do you think it will ever stop? What on earth is *wrong* with some of these young mothers in this county?"

"I don't know, my dear, I'm ill to think of it and sick near to death when I've heard it's happened again. I just don't know. But Randolph dwells on it like he has some understandin' of it nobody else knows, and that just isn't comfortable to me. And I just don't want him tellin' Gerald all about it, scarin' the boy needless-like; you see my point dear?

This 'burden' is powerful hard enough for grown people to tolerate, much less a child of three! Now, please don't misunderstand me, Randolph loves his boy, it's plain as day he does, and he spends most of his free time with him, which isn't all that much now-a-days," Tildie continued between sips of tea, trying to paint a fair picture of her husband. "They drive out of town and walk in the woods; Randolph has always loved the forest, you know. He claims they play games like hide and seek, they look for animals and tracks and such..." Tildie hesitated as though she were unsure whether to continue with what she wanted to say. "But I do suspect he's talkin to Gerald about these babies."

"What on earth do you mean?" Hazel asked, her eyes opening wide. "Why do you think that?"

Tildie let out a sharp sigh as she decided to finish what she felt she had to discuss with at least someone. "Well... I was talking to Bertha Miller?"

"Bertha, yes, uh-huh," Hazel confirmed her familiarity with the person of topic.

"...and she told me Monday week ago she was picking wild raspberries with her son and his cousin out off Rabba Road and she claims she saw Randolph and Gerald off a short ways from the old Brightman house, just standin there..."

Hazel gave her a blank stare and asked apprehensively, "Standin' there doin' *what*?"

"Lookin' at the house. Just watchin it and eyein' it for the longest time, Bertha said. Said Randolph would squat and talk to the boy; point at the house and talk more."

The name was familiar and Hazel searched her memory for a connection. "The old Brightman house, isn't that where one of…"

"Yes! One of them babies was murdered some years back! I'm just kinda concerned; you see my worry, dear?" Tildie felt she had made her case to her old friend and decided to leave it where it was.

Hazel nodded deep in thought. "I often wonder what kind of a daddy Norman would have made to Lester," Hazel offered wistfully, taking a drink of tea. "Good I 'spect. I think I knew him well enough to be most sure of that."

"Oh, he'd have been a fine father to the boy, no doubt in my mind, least-ways," Tildie agreed, sitting forward in her chair as Norman's name came up again. "Speaking of Norman, this just crossed my mind; do you remember Randolph asking you about a small brown journal he claims he lent Norman years ago?

Hazel focused her eyes on nothing particular as she searched her memory. "Yes, yes in fact I do remember that, I recall that was shortly after Norman passed. I take it he hasn't found it yet? He's still looking for it? Is it important?"

"Yes he is, but you know, it's strange, he seems more concerned about knowing where it is than he does gettin' it back again. He claims there's a big difference between the two. I don't know."

"Well land's sakes, after all this time…no, it hasn't shown up 'round here," Hazel said, shaking her head in minor apology.

"Oh well, I'm sure it will turn up somewhere, my dear, if it's meant to be, I guess. You know how things… *Oh my*! Do you feel that? That breeze? How lovely! And in the middle of this heat!" Tildie remarked in surprise as a dry, gentle wind suddenly blew onto the porch from somewhere out in the field. "And what a delightful fragrance! Is that honeysuckle, or what is that, Hazel? What do you have out here that's blooming? That's jasmine, isn't it?"

Hazel's head lifted erect and a knowing smile overtook her face as the breeze caressed it, the sweet smell wafting around the two of them. She rose from her seat to walk slowly to the edge of the porch. Folding her arms across her stomach, she gazed out at the broad field that served as a borderless backyard to her home. It shimmered green and motionless in the bright sun that shone directly overhead, while on the porch, her cotton dress and the curtains that hung in the open windows gently flapped and fluttered in the swirling wind. Still looking out at the land in front of her, she spoke back to Tildie. "This happens two, maybe three times a year; no predicting it. Anytime of year it 'wants' to. Always dry and comfortable and sweet-smelling. I like to think it's my Norman come to call on me, to say 'hello', you know? I take the breeze as his kiss on my face. And when this happens, I... well, there's just no way I can feel sad or wanting, it makes me feel so good inside; so light. It feels like a deep, easy tingling inside me," she said, closing her eyes and savoring the experience she longed for. "I'm glad you could be here while it happened."

Tildie had risen to join her friend and took her place by her side, putting her arm around her shoulder and leaning her head over to touch Hazel's. "That's a wonderful thought, dear. Hold onto it," she said, turning to look at her and smiling. Hazel responded by putting her own arm around Tildie's waist and the two stood in easy silence as the comforting, fragrant breeze began to wane and fade, the languid heat returning to suggest to the women that they do nothing in particular but enjoy each other's company and the moment.

Indifferent, unmoved, the land looked on in shimmering serenity.

CHAPTER 32

L uke pulled in behind the Camry and shut off the engine, silently thanking the truck for getting them to Athens and back without incident. The engine sputtered and shook for several seconds before finally dying, prompting Loretta to stare at him in an attempt to make a silent comment. Luke knew what would be coming and purposely avoided her eyes. He had pushed the truck harder than usual trying to prove what it could do to his skeptical passenger, and the poor engine was simply trying to register a complaint. Loretta hopped out, papers in hand, and asked Luke from across the hood, "You hungry? I'm starved. I'll fix some sandwiches, that okay?"

"Yeah, thanks. It just occurred to me it's lunchtime, I could use something. I'll go 'round the back and just check on the tarp."

"I'll open the back door for you, come in that way," Loretta yelled to him as she climbed the steps and located her key.

The tarp and material for the job he intended to do for her that morning were fine and he climbed the back steps and entered Loretta's kitchen. It was the first time he had actually been in her house rather than the porch and it looked just as he thought it might: feminine colors and décor; cat ornaments scattered here and there. He could see a dining room through the kitchen doorway and saw Loretta had set the papers they had just collected on the large table there.

"I've got sliced ham and turkey, canned chicken, peanut butter and jam, you name it. Which do you want?" she asked.

"Little of each on the same sandwich if that's okay," he answered.

"*All of them?*" Loretta asked in mild disgust.

Luke stood in the middle of the kitchen in an exaggerated pose, hands on his belt buckle, and proclaimed, "It's a 'country' thing, ma'am. You wouldn't understand!"

Loretta fell back against the counter covering her mouth in laughter at this posturing. "White or rye? This is *disgusting!*" she asked him, still laughing.

"Whatever you're having will be fine," he said calmly, smiling himself now at her and his ability to make her lighten up for just a few seconds. *She needs more of that. Her smile can flat light up a room.*

Luke took it upon himself to sit down at the incredibly small dinette that stood next to her kitchen window and wondered if the spindly metal chair would support him. He eased himself down slowly and let his weight test it. It held.

Loretta set down two plates of sandwiches and a pitcher of iced tea and plopped down confidently in the chair opposite him, quickly arranging things on the tiny tabletop to make sure they were just right. He watched her, mentally shaking his head at her actions. *Why do women bother doing that?* he wondered.

"See those two stacks of paper in there? The ones we just

got? That's our raw data," she told him as she nodded toward the dining room table and took a bite of her sandwich.

"Why do they call it 'raw' data? As opposed to…cooked?

"No," she answered, momentarily searching for an example Luke could grasp. "Okay, see these things I used to make the sandwiches? Bread, mayonnaise, ham, turkey? Those things could be raw data, kind of, for an end result, in this case the sandwich. Putting it all together makes it 'analyzed' or 'processed' data, see?"

"So when are we gonna 'cook' our data?" he asked her, showing her he preferred his definition better than hers.

"Soon as we're done with lunch," she told him.

They finished and Loretta put the dishes in the sink, poured two more glasses of tea for them and walked him into the small dining room.

"This table should do. It's the biggest work area I have, it's going to have to," she said as she took the main stack of articles and began to spread them out in order on the tabletop. Luke told her that the pages he printed out were roughly in chronological order with the murder clippings.

"Good, we'll match them up and staple them to the main articles so we'll have all the data pertaining to each one together. Now…" Loretta looked down on the array of raw data that she hoped would contain the answer to why these heinous crimes had been happening for so long in this quiet little county. "Alright, let's start with the first thing first, that's the way I like to do things," she said as she paced in front to the table, now almost completely covered with paper. "What do we know from these right now?"

"Well, let's see," Luke said, sitting in a chair at the table, looking at the papers and recalling the information they saw on the library screen. "We know, according to what we've read, these murders have been going on since at least as far back as 1878. A woman crushed her infant's head with a rock then, and that seems to be the pattern that we're seeing in all the cases that came later. It's been mothers that have done it, sometimes killing themselves and their husbands too, depending on the situation at the time, I suppose."

"One thing interesting that's come up with the first one is that I never realized this happened with a black mother. This..." Luke scanned the first accounting for the name, "Mamie Tyree and her husband had been slaves, so I assume they were black."

"That's good," Loretta said, nodding at Luke's accumulation of facts so far. "Slaves in the South were black. Duh! What do you think about the fact that the rest of the Tyree kids weren't touched? The clipping said she only killed the infant that was born in that cabin. Think that's important? Or did they just make note of it because it was just... a fact?"

"Don't know," Luke replied, obviously deep in thought with the collection of facts that was only getting bigger and more uniform in nature as they proceeded. "And I'm wondering now if it means anything that the Tyree residence was on the site of a plantation. Endicott was a big plantation owner in these parts before the Civil War, from what people around here have said, but I never knew exactly where the place had been. Now I'm pretty sure I do."

Loretta picked up sheet after sheet, rapidly scanning each for similarities and differences. "Here, look: 'Pearle Ferguson, 1910, May 20th, body of week old infant discovered'. Seems husband panicked, tried to help her by burying the infant in the woods. Someone's hunting dog dug it up and the story broke from there when the husband, Jeremy Ferguson, broke too."

"Hey look," Luke said, scanning for locations among the clippings. "Here's a total of four so far that have occurred at the Rabba Road location! The older cases don't give an actual address, but the '62 and '75 cases do: 6 Rabba Road. That's the house I was talking about! *Four* murders there!"

Loretta slid into the seat beside him and started looking for addresses also.

"This seems to be where we should start, looking for matching locations. Before we get going, you want to stop for a spell and take another short break? I'm a little draggy. I'll make some 'bat poop' coffee!"

"Yeah, coffee'd be fine. I'm going to keep going, though, 'shoot till I win', you know? I'm on a roll here," Luke said as he turned to examine another page. Loretta stood in back of him and observed him for several seconds, glad he was as enthused with this quest now as she was. She smiled to herself and walked into the kitchen to make the coffee.

Placing the two black cups of coffee on a tray along with Luke's cream, she looked around for napkins as she heard Luke call to her.

"Hey, Loretta, come here! You're not gonna believe this!" he said as she arrived next to him with the tray.

In front of Luke on the table were eight stacks of papers, laid out side by side. "I went through all the main articles and sorted them by location. Hon, all these murders, all the ones we have any printouts about, all happened in only eight locations! Twenty-one baby deaths; eight locations! Now, what's *that*

287

mean?"

Loretta stared at the eight stacks as she automatically put the tray down on the table. She was stunned by the sight of the eight piles. This *did* mean something. This thing had something to do with the places where it was happening. She continued to stare as her mind began to race, trying to form a pattern, attempting to see the similarities, compare the differences. She flipped through the top papers on each of the stacks, looking for a place to start.

"Okay, okay, the Tyree baby, killed in 1878, in a cabin built on the site of an old plantation on Chatoosee Road. In 1918, a 'Virginia Holiman' also killed her baby at the then address of 1470 Chatoosee Road. Think they're the same place?" she asked Luke.

Luke thought as he stroked his chin. "You know, they just might be. The 1470 address was a general address back then, almost an 'area', really. I know where that address would be, and it's remote, which fits the pattern that I see forming for all these locations."

Loretta picked up the second stack and went from front to back, scanning for any stated addresses. "I don't even have to look for the crime or the method used in the death of the babies now; that has stayed almost identical through all these so far. What I want to find now are the locations and the number of deaths that happened at each," she said. "Here: 'Mildred Rainey, daughter Grace, 146 Big Shoals Road, 1926'. 'Edna Mahaffee, child name and sex unrecorded, 146 Big Shoals Road, 1951'."

"That's the one my father was referring to when he said to me the county was trying to set some record with these deaths!

I was about five years old!" Luke said in an excited tone, glad that his memory was accurate enough to corroborate these findings.

"And," Loretta continued, picking up where she left off, "'Diane Joseph, son Michael-John, 146 *Big Shoals Road*, 1984'! Infant approximately one week old, 'head crushed', naturally. I'm afraid I'm getting way too damn casual about that fact."

Luke picked up the next batch of papers and repeated Loretta's process as he had before she had entered the room with the coffee. "These are all at the junction of Bear Run Road and Thomasville Road, number fourteen; there's very little doubt it's all the same address. Ain't ever been more than two or three houses at that intersection. And yeah, it's out in the country too. 'Stevens, 1893; Racine, 1920; Pratt, 1950, all there at Fourteen Thomasville Road. *Wow!*"

Patterns. Similarities. Differences. They were adding up fast. And yet, there were things that still puzzled Loretta.

"Okay, why the long stretch of time between these events? That's got me wondering now," she said as she picked up one stack only to set it back down to examine another.

"Long time between what?" Luke asked her, rummaging back and forth between three of the collections. "There was one in '50, one in '51 and another in '54; how much closer together do you *want?*"

"No, no, that's not what I mean. *They* all happened at different locations, as bad as that is, I know. But what I mean is, why so long between these murders at the *same* locations? Here, look…"

She picked up a stack of four clippings along with the

related articles, and looking through them quickly, she located the dates of each.

"Here: all these seemed to have happened at 406 Pebble Stretch Road: 1905, 1936, 1954...the fifties were a bad time for this, weren't they? And the last in '77. Let's see, that's..." Loretta took a pencil and began to figure the difference in years between the events at the address. "That's... thirty-one years between the first and second... eighteen between the second and third... and... twenty-three years from the one in '54 till the one in '77," she said as she looked up at Luke with a perplexed look on her face. "Why so much space in between if this, seemingly, is bound to happen, for whatever reason, at these locations?" She looked back down at the other gathered sets and surmised, "They all seem to be happening about the same way: periods of time go by at each house before these things occur again. Why?"

"Different people," Luke offered. "You got to figure, after something like this happens, the mother is either dead from suicide, gone completely bonkers and is put away, the husband either kills her and winds up who knows where, or he dies in the whole nasty process. Then I guess someone else moves in."

Loretta's eyes flashed at the last part. *"Someone else moves in!* Right! That's it," she chirped. *"They're* gone and someone else moves in to live there for..."

"...For a spell until it happens again in the same house," Luke spoke up. He stared unfocused at the floor for a second while continuing his thought process. Then, in a flash of deductive enlightenment Loretta would later praise as brilliant, Luke somehow hit upon a crucial fact that thus far had not occurred to her.

"But it doesn't necessarily happen to the people that move in next just because they're there," he said as it came to him.

"And why not?"

Luke spoke slowly as if his speech and thoughts were one process. "The clippings only give the ages of some of these mothers, and almost all that are noted are young, obviously childbearing age. They've just had a kid and always had it within a week to ten or so days of the murders, we know that so far as fact." His face was almost glowing as he stated the next fact he was realizing himself as he mouthed it. "*But the people who live there in between these murders might not be of childbearing age! They might not bear a child while they live there!*"

Loretta was stunned as Luke's logic sunk in and took hold, allowing her own reasoning to take over and expound. "And the child being born, either right there in the house or while the family was living there and took it back there from the hospital, seems to be the big factor! *Those* are the children that are singled out and murdered so violently, not the other kids! But why?"

"Dunno," Luke said, pondering the question, "but it does seem, from what we've read, that the other deaths are 'beside the fact', you know? They, either the husband or other kids or both, die from time to time because they interfere, or because they're just plain 'there at the time.' That's the take *I'm* getting."

"Uh-huh, I think you may be right. The collateral deaths are 'opportune' or *necessary* to perform the intended killing and that's the baby that's just been born there or brought there newborn. I don't think the mothers really wanted to kill anyone

291

else but the infant, and maybe themselves because they've done it," Loretta said, sitting on the edge of the table with her arms folded.

Luke was finishing his coffee while petting Peach and sat back in his chair. "I did look at the attached papers to see if there was anything in them to shed much more light on this, and there really isn't. It's just mostly added info as to what people thought who knew them, what the investigators found, and whatnot. We already know most of that from the main articles."

The clipping about Norman Tomms, Loretta's grandfather, came to mind again. She wanted to reread it thoroughly to see if it contained anything pertinent to any of these murders. "Let me see the article again about my grandfather," she asked Luke. "Do you remember which stack it's attached to?"

"This one, the Pebble Stretch Road pile," he said, picking it up and handing it to her. "If you're going to read it, read it to me, too. I want to hear what ol' Norman had to do with investigating any of these, if he did." Loretta flipped the other papers out of the way and began to read.

"May 9th, 1926 - Ocoosa County Sheriff Found Dead - Sheriff Norman Tomms was found dead at the base of Marshman Rock early this morning from what seems the result of a late night vehicular accident. Sheriff Tomms appeared to be driving to his home when tragedy struck him. No foul play is indicated at this time. Investigators who have reviewed the scene are attributing the crash to the heavy rains last night. Tire tracks in the road suggest that Sheriff Tomms lost control of his automobile on the muddy road, which then rolled down into the

292

deep ditch at the base of Marshman Rock, ejecting him and resulting in his death sometime during the night.

"Narrowly elected sheriff in 1919, Sheriff Tomms was well-liked in Ocoosa County. He leaves behind a wife, Hazel, and many county residents who counted him a close friend. Funeral arrangements will be announced in this paper shortly."

"Huh," Luke said, his mind awash with the stories of the sheriff that he had heard all his life. "That sure doesn't seem the way a man like him would go, you know? I had always heard that moonshiners ambushed him on that road; that the town folk found him and his car the next morning all shot up, full of holes. Guess that puts an end to *that* story."

Loretta stared at the article, the wheels turning quickly once again, trying to add things up, tie things together, make things fit a logical pattern. "This article was dated May 9, making the day they're talking about, the night he died, May the 8th, right? If that's the case," she said, flipping back to the 1926 death clipping, "then this murder, an infant girl named Grace Rainey killed by her mother, one Mildred Rainey, might well have been investigated by my grandfather." Loretta quickly reread the article detailing the incidents that happened at 146 Big Shoals Road. Her eyes widened as she neared the end of the article.

"Damn it! I didn't see this the first time! Here it is right here, what I'm figuring: 'Sheriff Norman Tomms, recently deceased Sheriff of Ocoosa County, had made the initial discovery of the bodies the same day of his fatal accident. He had also been instrumental in the investigation of a similar homicide which occurred in 1920 at 14 Thomasville Road, where an infant was determined to have been fatally beaten about the head by its mother, Nettie Racine. *Sheriff Tomms stated to the Press at time of the investigation that it was his belief that the location of the murder was somehow significant to the case,"* Loretta said excitedly as she emphasized the last sentence. "Luke! He was onto it back then! If he thought that, then he had to have a reason. Something at those crime scenes must have strongly suggested to him that the two were too similar to be coincidental, just like we've felt from the start."

"*You've* felt; I been kind of late to catch on," Luke said, half-smiling.

"But you're seeing it now though, right? It's becoming more obvious as we go along: the locations of these murders are the key. They, for some reason, are the cause."

"Loretta, how can a 'place' make you want to take the baby you just had out into the yard and pound its head to mush?" Luke challenged her, cocking his head as he looked to her for a plausible answer to his stark question, a question that was just too neat, blunt, and concise.

Loretta stood in front of him with her arms tightly folded, looked him in the eyes and asked, with a marked insinuation in her tone, "I don't know. How about your 'Burden'?"

The faraway look quickly returned to Luke's eyes as he pondered that possibility, the one he had just been beginning to dismiss. It seemed to him it was time to seriously consider it once again.

The city girl from Atlanta was getting riled once more and she was not as able to control it as well as she would have liked. *Shit or get off the pot, country boy.* "**Y'all have told one another around cook fires in hushed fuckin' tones for Goddamn-ever that 'bad things' happened in this county a** *long time ago to cause this shit to happen! Now, do you believe that, or don't you?"* she yelled into his face, bending down to him in the chair from which he wished so desperately to escape.

Luke wanted to be mad. He wanted to jump up and react, if only because Loretta was who she was, an outsider, someone who hadn't had the time to appreciate what the people of Ocoosa had grown up with; a newcomer that only recently had experienced the inevitable horror and dismay the longtime residents knew they would, from time to time, wake up to in their morning papers. She had caught him trying to escape his own web of superstition, and now he had no choice but to sit there, tied up in the silk of reason she was rapidly spinning.

"I guess... I don't know..." he tried to reply. He didn't know what to say to her.

Loretta's anger deflated as quickly as it blew up. She pulled out a chair and sat down in it, facing Luke, and propped her elbow on the table as Peach jumped up and found her hand. Stroking the cat calmed her and she began to speak in a much more controlled voice. "Luke, I'm sorry, I apologize, really. I've never been a superstitious person; not at all. Ghost stories have always made me laugh 'cause I don't believe in spirits," she said, smiling now. "But what this is all pointing to is showing me that... somehow, what you people here have believed all these years may have some real basis to it. There's not much else that can explain all this," she said, motioning to the collection of papers. "I don't know what else to believe right now."

"Me either," Luke said in a low, defeated monotone. "Looks like I'm back to square one."

She looked down at the Norman Tomms paper and gave it a longer thought. They sat in their own respective, contemplative silences for perhaps thirty seconds, a short span of time that seemed like minutes, when Loretta finally spoke, asking, "Tell me, if a sheriff investigated a murder, he'd have made out a report of some kind, wouldn't he?" she asked, looking back up at Luke. He abandoned his pensive pout to answer her.

"Well, yeah, he'd have to sit down and file an official report that would go to the state. Where are you going with this, may I ask?" he said, his doldrums receding.

Loretta continued petting Peach as she thought and talked. "My grandfather - God that sounds strange coming from my mouth - was at the scene of the Rainey murder, correct?"

"From what we've gathered from these papers, it seems that's the last major thing he would have done as sheriff," Luke acknowledged.

"Then if it was, and he made out a report, it stands to reason that that report exists, at least somewhere."

"Whoa, girl," Luke said as he rose to stretch and move around. "You're talking seventy years here. That paperwork is long gone; has been. Lotta polywogs have grown to frogs since 1926!"

"Yeah, you're right. But it seems certain from this timeframe that the sheriff died the night of the same day this woman and her baby were discovered, let's presume by him. If he investigated the scene, and did in fact make a report, then he may not have had a chance to file it with the state; it may never have left his office!"

"How's that going to help us?" Luke asked. "We're still

talking seventy years. That old sheriff's office was torn down long ago."

"Because if he died suddenly like that, all of his 'stuff', all his papers and things would be left there, and what would they do with all that?" Loretta asked, getting more enthused with her own line of thinking. Standing now, she started to pace around the table, taking quick reassuring glances at the paperwork she was positive held the answer to this mystery of 'why'. If only they could decipher it. Something deep inside her was sure her grandfather could still help, seventy years after his untimely death. And it somehow felt warm and light and comforting.

"It might have all been, well, 'dispersed', I guess you'd have to say, *if* they had the time to do it proper. Or, it may have been as simple as putting it all in a box and getting rid of it somehow."

"Or storing it!" Loretta said, spinning to look at Luke, her eyes wide with excitement at the possibility that her grandfather's belongings might just still exist somewhere in Watsonville, covered with dust, holding the key to all this. "I know it's a long shot, but I'm thinking a sheriff's effects would be something the local authorities would want to keep, at least for a while; something they could refer back to if they needed. And I admit this is an even BIGGER long shot, but if that's the case, then his effects could very well still be stored around here somewhere. But where? Where would YOU think?"

Luke was seated again at the table, taking his turn petting Peach. and pondered the question. "Like I said, the old office has been gone for a long time. I'm not sure they would have ever stored stuff like that there anyway. But you know who might know at least something about this sort of thing now?

Tom Billingham!" he offered as Peach sat in front of him making audible purring sounds.

"Yeah, Tom!" Loretta half shouted, her enthusiasm making her animated and even slightly giddy. "Let's call him and ask!"

"Loretta, its Saturday afternoon. I've got his numbers from when I did work for him, but he's not going to want to help us on a weekend; he's a government employee!"

"So were you at one time and *you* worked Saturdays! Call him, please! I just have to know; get this out of my system, anyway!"

"Okay, I'll give him a ring. He might know about official storage of papers and documents and things. That will at least tell us, *you*, if this is a track we should follow or give up on. Where's your phone?"

Loretta reached over to a small table and handed the phone to Luke. He looked through at least a dozen small pieces of paper, one at a time, which had clogged his wallet for months, setting some off to the side to throw away. A small card appeared in order with two numbers on it and the name 'Tom B.' under them. "This is it. Let me give it a try."

Luke dialed the first number on the card, and as the phone rung on the other end, he said out loud, "Damn it, this is his office number. I'm sure he's not going to be there on a Saturday." He let it ring three times and was about to hang up and try Tom's home phone when someone picked up on the other end. "Tom! You're there! I'm surprised. This is Luke McLain, how you doing?" Loretta pumped her fist in the air in triumph, happy that Tom Billingham was exactly where she had hoped he'd be.

"So what are you doing there on a Saturday? Oh, yeah. Weekend work is a pain, but sometimes... uh-huh, I remember Saturdays! Had to work them all my life! Tom I need a favor, if you can: do you recall that little lady I sent you last week sometime for a map? Yeah, Loretta... uh-huh, the nurse..." Luke glanced over at Loretta and held his look for seconds while listening to Tom on the other end. Loretta could tell the conversation was about her. "Yeah, who wouldn't?" Luke said into the receiver as he grinned slightly, while a barely detectable flush came to his face. Loretta's face straightened to stunned puzzlement, her head cocking a bit, her mind guessing what the comment on the other end might have been. Whatever it was, she liked Luke's response. The suspected flattery, suggestive as it might have been, made her feel good in the depths of her femininity.

Luke chuckled into the phone. "Uh-huh; Tom what we want to know is if the county, actually Watsonville too, I guess, has a place where it stores old official records and papers and the like? Yeah? Are you going to be there for a bit? Can we come down? Good, we'll be there directly.

"He says come on down and tell him what we're after; he'll try to help us as much as he can," Luke said, hanging up the phone. "Seems he wants to help *us* with what we need," he added with a wry smile on his face. "You must have impressed him the day you two met. What did you *say* to that boy? He's dopey as *hell* about you!"

Now it was Loretta's turn to blush, but she took the discomfort of being on the spot as she had learned to, sitting and smiling and accepting it.

CHAPTER 33

Loretta locked up for the second time and they piled into Luke's truck once more to make the three minute trip to the courthouse. Luke looked up to the sky as he got in his truck and casually noticed the sunny sky of the morning was turning cloudy, and fast. Low, black-bottomed clouds were creeping quickly in from the Northwest, and the air was beginning to feel different. *Huh; odd they're coming that way this time of year. Air is feeling moister, too*, he thought as they wheeled toward the center of Watsonville. Not having listened to the radio at all that day, Luke and Loretta were unaware of the line of violent thunderstorms that was approaching toward Atlanta, even as they were now making their way toward Tom and the courthouse. Early morning tornados had been reported in the Knoxville area and had sporadically touched down from the Smokies down into the upper northwest corner of Georgia. Atlanta had been warned of severe weather and precautions were being taken as far to the east as Augusta. Several inches of rain had fallen in the North Georgia mountains and flooding was becoming a problem in many areas. But the weather in Watsonville was still pleasant enough not to over-shadow the zeal Loretta was feeling as they pulled up to the courthouse and saw one vehicle parked in the lot. It had to be Tom's.

Tom Billingham greeted them both outside, coming out just as they pulled up and were getting out. "How you been?" he asked them both and 'hellos' were made all around. "I've just locked up, getting ready to head out when we're done. So, just what is it you think I can help you with?' he asked, locating his car keys in the bottom of his pocket and glancing at Loretta for opportune long seconds.

"Loretta and I, well, mostly her, are trying to track down some information about these baby murders that happen in this county from time to time," Luke began, trying to present their request as cohesively as he could.

"Yeah, terrible thing to have happen in a quaint little locale like this," he responded, his face showing an appropriate concern.

"My thinking, exactly," Loretta said.

Luke continued with their request. "We located some paperwork today at the UGA library that tells us more about them than we knew, and we also found out that this little lady here is the granddaughter of Norman Tomms, a big time sheriff of this county back in the 20's."

"Wow, so you never knew that before today?" Tom asked, a big grin on his face. "Congratulations!"

"Thanks," Loretta replied, again feeling a sense of family pride that felt so odd to her.

"Loretta seems to think that her grandfather had some information about these deaths that could be of use to us now. She also thinks that, somehow, his paperwork from that time might still exist and be stored away someplace around here.

Now, you being the county clerk and all, what do *you* think? If in fact it does exist, where might it be?"

Tom thought for several seconds, lost in concentration. There were a lot of facets to their questions and concerns, and just as many to the answers he had available to give them. "Records, papers and the like of officials like that are usually sent up to state level if they're applicable or pertinent to anything current or ongoing. Reports or paperwork pertaining to a homicide would most definitely have been sent on up to Atlanta at the time."

"We don't think my grandfather had time to actually file them to be forwarded, if he had time to complete them at all," Loretta tried to explain. "He died accidentally the day he discovered one of these murders. Tom, I just have this... this feeling that what he found out the day he died is still around here, packed away with God knows what else he may have left behind. We're asking you if you can help us find it. *If* it exists, where do you think we should be looking?

"You know," Tom stated again, taking more time to think. "Even if we could locate his official effects and paperwork - I hate to sound like a typical government worker here - but those would be official government property; the state agency that he worked for at the time would retain ownership and jurisdiction over them. I don't think I could let you have them if we *could* find them. Do you see the position I'm in? I really would like to help with this, but..."

"Maybe not, Tom," Luke spoke up, assuming a bearing that neither Loretta nor Tom was aware this simple handyman had to offer. A much different Luke McClain than either of them recognized materialized before them, and began to speak.

"You see, technically, legally, there is a statute of limitations on official documents, local, state or federal, that runs out twelve years after they are documented and/or filed. The 'Freedom of Information' act guarantees the public the right of access to such documents. The only exceptions that I'm aware of are those pertaining to national security, and I think we can safely assume these documents we're after do not deal with those issues."

Loretta and Tom both stared at Luke, listening to his soliloquy with open mouths.

"*If* such a collection of material was to be located, certainly the statute would have run out on anything that might be contained therein, and this young lady beside me, being the rightful heir to her grandfather's effects, would have complete and total legal right to take possession of them forthwith, post haste, and... whatever." Luke stopped talking and saw them both looking at him in their individual states of shock. *"What?"* he asked. Caught, he knew they wanted an explanation. "Okay, so I like to watch 'Law and Order' when I can; it's my favorite show!" he acknowledged, feeling a bit embarrassed by their stares.

"Wow!" Tom said, smiling and shaking his head in mild disbelief. "You know, you're right, actually! Tell you what, if this fine young lady can provide proof she's the granddaughter of this Sheriff Tomms, if we can locate his things, I guess you can have them. How's that?"

Loretta was grinning at Luke from ear to ear, impressed more than ever with this man who had originally showed up on her doorstep to fix some soffits. "Way to go, boy!" she said as she popped him on the chest with both hands, congratulating him on his legal discourse. "That was damned amazing. And impressive!"

"You *do* have some proof, don't you?" asked Luke. "I'd hate to have pulled a speech like that out of my butt for nothing!" he said, giving a laugh to ease his own discomfort.

The clouds overhead were thickening and growing darker by the minute as Loretta dug into her purse for some identification. No one seemed to notice the heaviness of the sky, the anticipation taking priority for the moment. "Here," she said as she handed Tom an old driver's license. "That's got my maiden name on it, 'Tomms', see?"

"This is nine years old; expired," Tom commented. "How come you still have this?"

Loretta suddenly was the one feeling embarrassed, and shyly admitted to them both, "I hated my picture on it and I told them I lost this one so I could get another."

Both Tom and Luke looked down at her as though she had admitted to a minor crime. Their stern looks broke as they looked at each other, Luke admitting first with a laugh, "I've done that!"

Tom responded with his own chuckle, agreeing, "Me too!"

The laughter subsiding, Luke turned back to Tom and asked, "So Tom, you got any idea where we might begin to look?"

Tom thought and replied, "Well, as I'm sure you know, the old sheriff's office was torn down years ago. I heard it used to be across the street where the bakery is," he said, pointing to the little shop one hundred feet from them. Loretta stared at the shop, trying to imagine a man who resembled John Wayne walking out into the hot Georgia summer sun, surveying all that he could see, just waiting for trouble to happen. "It had a storage area in the back that was full from what I've been told. Instead of going through the expense of building a new facility, the City decided to long-term lease an existing building they thought would do the job for the foreseeable future. It's worked out…"

Loretta's eyes widened as her stomach jumped. She felt like something had taken hold of her and was keeping her paralyzed, flooding her with a soothing feeling of well-being. She forced herself to speak and blurt out a question, interrupting Tom in mid-sentence.

"Is it at the corner of Gilmore and Garden? That building?" she asked, her breathing getting faster, her eyes burning into Tom's, frantic for his answer. "918 Garden?"

Tom was only able to answer slowly as he looked at her, amazement at her knowledge of the location. "Yes, yes it is. That's *exactly* where it is."

Luke and Tom both stared incredulously at her and then at each other. Luke was the first to shake off his shock at her question and said, "I've asked you this before, but I guess I have to ask again: And you would know that… how?"

Loretta was now able to move and found she couldn't stop moving. Pacing and animated, she replied, "I don't know; I don't know how I know. But it's there! I know it as sure as I'm standing here! My grandfather's things are there!"

"I'll take my truck, Tom, if you want to meet us there. I know where it is," Luke said as he and Loretta headed for his truck. "Seems like you do, too," he commented to Loretta, now sitting back in the passenger seat, her eyes focused out through the windshield toward the intersection and the feeling that had mystified her for the last three months.

"Let's go, Luke. C'mon, push this thing," she said to him, her determination evident in everything about her.

CHAPTER 34

Tom was getting out of his car as Luke's truck arrived and parked in the street in front of the pale yellow building. Loretta hopped out and could immediately feel her sensation intensifying, becoming a pulsing, wave-like hum within her as she approached the building to stand in front of it. She surveyed the front of the structure, as if looking for a way to get in before Tom had a chance to get his keys out. "C'mon Tom, open it, quick, please!" she said, her building frenzy starting to worry Luke.

"Hon, you're gonna have that conniption yet unless you ease off some. Try to calm down, okay? We'll get in there directly; give the man a chance to open it up," Luke advised her, knowing her well enough by now to know it would do no good to try to talk her down.

As Tom tried a series of keys with no success, he commented to the pair, "On my way over here, I realized there's no power on in the place. The City keeps it off unless we know we need access to it. That was the one drawback to leasing this place; the wiring was old and a little dangerous. Keeping the power off most of the time is a safety precaution.

It's Saturday and there's no one to turn it on." Luke stepped back to his truck and retrieved a flashlight from under the seat, returning just as Tom found the right key and unlocked the padlock on the front door on the left of the building front. They entered a small, dusty office barely lit by the light of a tiny semblance of a window high on the right wall. An open door at the back of the room obviously led to the darkened storage area. Loretta was right in back of Tom as they entered, practically pushing him out of the way.

"Easy now, Loretta, it's dark and there are a lot of things lying around you could trip on. This place is hazardous enough with the lights on; it's really bad now," Tom tried to warn her as she passed him to head into the dimness of the room beyond.

"Loretta, wait!" Luke shouted to her as she disappeared momentarily into the dark of the next room. Luke turned on his flashlight as the two men passed through the doorway into what seemed a cavernous dungeon of a room, dimly illuminated by skylights which littered the high ceiling at regular intervals, all encrusted with algae from many years of neglect. Their intermittent light cast an eerie green glow in the large room; better than total darkness, but not nearly bright enough to locate something whose shape, and even existence, was of question. Luke's flashlight threw a hazy beam on Loretta's back as she stood ten feet in front of them, staring into the green soup of light toward the back of the black room. Amorphous shapes were strewn about the floor, some covered with tarps, some barely recognizable as road barriers, parts of long-forgotten floats used in parades of the past, old signs from days gone by of streets that were now just memories. "Loretta, stay right there and let us help!" Luke chided her, trying to

keep her from hurting herself in the darkness. "We'll use the flashlight to help you look if you'll just wait a minute!"

Without turning around or answering, Loretta started to make her way to the back of the room like a programmed machine, shoving objects out of the way she could move, climbing over the ones she couldn't, her eyes locked straight ahead.

"Ms. Carmichael! Please don't do that! You're not even supposed to be in here! If you get hurt..." Tom realized Loretta was not listening to him and looked at Luke as he continued. "There's the issue of liability, you understand. The City could be sued if you hurt yourselves. And there's the fact that this is municipal property in here..."

Loretta had climbed atop a large lump of unknown material covered with tarp in the middle of the room and stood motionless, bathed in the murky green of a sky light. Her eyes were focused on a back wall that was, in effect, a massive shelving unit of wood stretching from wall to wall, floor to ceiling. Whatever lay underneath the tarp she was standing on was shifting and tipping, causing her to adjust her balance to keep from falling, but she recovered to stand rigidly still, almost at attention, her gaze transfixed on the shelves barely visible thirty feet in front of her. Luke held his light on her and watched while she slowly, stiffly raised her right arm to point to the highest row of shelves on the back wall. She remained pointing as she turned her head to speak to the two men who were watching this eerie spectacle amid the mold and dirt and the green, dusty air of the room. Luke's flashlight illuminated Loretta's face and he could see the glazed, faraway look in her eyes; a look that sent a chill up his spine.

"It's there," she said, turning back to look at the wall of darkness, a peaceful smile taking over her face. "My grandfather's things are there."

The flashlight's beam left Loretta and shot past her to the wall beyond, wandering around the shelves of unknown objects that were piled and stacked on them until it stopped on a wooden crate high on the top shelf. Though covered with years of dust and dirt, black stenciled lettering was barely legible. Loretta read aloud what was written on the box as Luke's light cut through the dust and dark: "Norman Tomms, Ocoosa County Sheriff."

The warmth that was flooding through her lit her face as she stared lovingly at the crate. *All this time... it wasn't just a feeling... it was a beacon. I'm here, Grandpa.*

CHAPTER 35

L ook out for the nails!" Luke warned Tom as they made their way through the mildewed obstacle course of the storeroom. "I ain't never seen a nail job like this before! Who sealed this up, a retard?" he complained, grunting and backing his way out of the front room with the crate and out onto the street where big rain drops were starting to fall. Loretta watched intently as the men loaded the dusty crate into the back of Luke's truck.

"You two going to be able to get this thing out wherever you're taking it?" asked Tom, trying now to keep the rain from hitting him in the face.

Luke nodded, also squinting from the rain, throwing a tarp over the box and turning to shake Tom's hand. "Thanks, Tom, I owe you one. Looks like we got some weather moving through. I'm gonna get her home, let her explore this thing," he said, having to almost shout, motioning to the crate. "Hope we didn't trash things too much in there!"

"Who'd be able to tell?" he replied with a grin of resignation as he waved and turned to get into his car and out of the ever increasing rain.

Loretta climbed into her seat, took some of the napkins that were still on the floor board and wiped the moisture from her face. She handed some to Luke as he got in and cranked the engine and pulled away down the street. He turned his head to look at her as she twisted sideways to check the box through the back window of the cab, making sure it was secure. "How did you know?" he asked her as he wiped his forehead and under his eyes. She looked back at him and realized he needed an explanation. Hell, he deserved one, anyone would. She knew she wouldn't have the box in the back of a truck headed back to her house if it wasn't for this man sitting next to her. She owed him a lot, more than the explanation she was having difficulty forming to satisfy even herself.

"Luke, I don't know for sure, really I don't. But ever since I've been here in town, for three months now, something's been tugging at me, pulling on me, especially at that intersection back there. I know this sounds crazy, it does even to me, but I think somehow that crate back there is what brought me here from Atlanta, what made me feel so good when I was here that one time years ago," she said, glancing back at the tarp that was now wet with rain. "I just never said anything to anyone about it. I figured y'all would think I was nuts. And this smacks of 'spirits', and you how I feel about that."

"Well, I sure as hell don't understand what's goin' on, but something must be; look at you. You look like one of them girls that seen a vision at that pool in France or something," he said, making note of the radiance still on her face.

Loretta laughed. "You mean the grotto in Lourdes? Do I really?" she asked as she looked at herself in his rearview mirror. "No I don't!" she said, checking her face as best she could. "I just look happy, that's all. And I am," she told him, giving him a genuine smile of appreciation. "Thank you, Luke."

"Glad to oblige, Hon" he said. "Now, let's get this thing back to your house before the bottom falls out of the sky… and it," he added as he looked at the quickly darkening sky and the heavy drops making his visibility harder by the minute. "I'm kind of curious myself to see what old Norman Tomms might have had lying around." The truck turned the corner onto Bessemer Court and Loretta's house came into view.

CHAPTER 36

The rain was quickly soaking both of them as they threw the tarp back and took hold of the crate. Luke warned her about the nails as he had with Tom. "They're all rusted to hell, too; that makes 'em even worse. Let's get this up on your porch and then we can decide what we want to do with it."

"Okay," she shouted through the rain as they both hurried with the box, now covered with runny dirt, toward her porch steps.

Setting it on the porch table, Loretta ran to get towels for them both and they dried what they could of themselves as they eyed this artifact that had such a hold on Loretta. Peach wandered onto the porch and eyed the box, contemplating a jump up to give it a more thorough cat inspection. Loretta caught her before she could leap. "No, baby, don't get up there, it's full of nails. You'll get hurt."

"You got a claw hammer?" asked Luke, giving his hair a last toweling.

"Of course!" Loretta answered, smiling.

"And do you think you can…"

"Make some bat-poop coffee?" she asked before he could finish his question. "I was just thinking the same thing!"

"Yeah," he replied with a smile back at her. "I'm hooked! See what you've done?"

"I'll get some started and the hammer, but don't start to open it without me, I want to be there," she told him from the kitchen.

"I won't," he replied, walking around the table, eying this sturdy square crate from the distant past. "This is your thing. I'll leave the big discoveries all to you."

"Let's bring it in on the dining room table, the light's better in here. Besides, with this rain, I can hardly hear myself think out there," she yelled back at him. Loretta put down several layers of newspaper on her table and they both attempted to wipe as much moisture as they could from the box before they brought it into the house. They eyed the box as they sipped their coffee and planned the best way to open it.

"A good-sized screwdriver will help as a crowbar. You got one?" he asked, taking a long swallow of his coffee.

"Uh-huh," she said as she went to get it.

She returned with just the right sized tool he had wanted and Luke said, "Alright, what I'm going to do is try to slip the end of this screwdriver under the lip of this lid and tap all the way around the edge before I try to pry the whole thing off. It's so old, I just don't want the thing to fall apart all over your floor."

"Whatever you think is best. I just want to get inside it," Loretta said, her anticipation growing. As Luke tapped and pried, it was obvious to her that this man was at his best with a tool in his hand. There was an ease, a sureness in what he was doing, as simple as it might be. Her admiration for him was steadily growing, and she felt it all too well. It confused her, but another feeling was taking precedence at the moment.

Constructed with a bracing on its surface, the top remained in one piece as Luke hoped it would and, working with his fingers, he loosened the cover and lifted it off gently, looking for a place to put it. Covered with half-hammered rusty nails, he hesitated to place it on the floor because of Peach. He made the short walk out to the porch and placed the cover outside, propped up against the side of the steps, nails inward, as the rain pelted his back.

"Oh! Uhhhh!" Loretta cried out from the dining room. Luke spun as he heard her and ran back in to her, confused and alarmed. He saw her standing in front of the crate, holding herself, her arms clutching her body as she stepped back away from the box. He grabbed her by the shoulders and turned her to him, looking her up and down.

"What happened? What's the matter?" he asked, his face a concerned frown.

"Something came out of the box!" Loretta said as she looked down at the crate and then up at Luke.

Luke continued to instinctively hold her, and looked quickly around on the floor for anything; a roach, a rat. "Where did it go?" he asked her, still scanning the floor for a glimpse of whatever it was that caused Loretta to cry out in such a panic.

"Through me!" she told him, the glow that had been on her face now mixed with surprise. "My God, Luke, it felt like a warm breeze flowing right through me! I could feel it! It smelled like... like flowers! It still does!" she said, staring at

the box and sniffing the air. "I've smelled that before somewhere... but how...?"

"Flowers?" Luke asked her, confusion on his face. "Loretta, that's *mildew* you're smelling! Look at it in there!" he said as he brought her closer to the crate in order to look down in it. "See all that black on the papers? That's mold and mildew! It stinks!"

Loretta approached the box and put her hands on the edges and peered down into it, a tender look on her face. "No, it's wonderful. This was all his, all this," she said with affection. She reached in and began taking out the papers one by one, oblivious to the mold that coated the contents. Luke stood by, cringing as Loretta touched the dank forms and memos, laying them on top of each other on the table at the base of the box. She handled them delicately, forming neat piles of like papers and looking briefly at each one.

It was obvious to Luke that the contents of the box were dumped in, put there by someone in a hurry, or a person who didn't care as to the task they were performing. He watched as the papers came out, treated like valuable documents by this woman who had needed so desperately to find a tangible part of her unknown past. *I guess this all means a lot to her, stinkin' or not.* Loretta uncovered down to a depth where objects were starting to appear. Pens, pencils, rulers were forming a layer unlike what she had just removed. She stopped to examine them. "This all came from a top desk drawer. These are things you use off and on all day to do clerical work, paperwork," she said, her hand sweeping over it. Luke noticed something odd among the paper clips and pencils and his curiosity got the better of him. He reached in and extracted what appeared to have been at one time in the past a small leather bag, the bead work covering one side of it now wearing a film of green. Feathers, long shrunken and paled by time and moisture, hung evenly from the bottom edge.

"I'll be damned, looks like your granddaddy might have been an Indian, or part, anyway," he said, holding the bag with two fingers, handing the damp object to an eager Loretta.

"Why do you say that? What is this?" as she examined it curiously.

"It's a medicine bag," Luke told her. "Indians would make one and put things they considered sacred or precious to them in it and carry it with them; gave them strength. They'd pray on it too, kind of like Catholics and their rosary beads."

"I want to see in it, see what my grandfather thought was precious to him!" she said to Luke with excitement. "Let me open it!"

"Go ahead, it's yours," Luke told her.

Loretta struggled with the tight, slimy drawstring, finally loosening it enough to shake out the bag's contents. What appeared to be a tooth with serious decay on one surface, a lock of hair, clipped finger nails and a small gold ring spilled out onto the newspaper covering the table. "What is this stuff?" she asked, checking with her finger to ensure she had emptied everything out of the bag. "I thought it was supposed to be valuable."

Luke took the ring and wiped the mold from the surface of it, revealing an intricately engraved surface with the initials "HT" cut into the top. His discovery brought a smile to his weathered face. "This is something your granddad considered very valuable to him, and you will too, I reckon," he told

318

Loretta, handing it to her. "This ring belonged to your grandmother, see the initials? 'HT'; that was Hazel Tomms, his wife."

Loretta looked at the ring as though she were gazing at a Faberge egg. "This was my grandmother's? Oh, Luke this means so much to me! You don't know!" She examined it through misty eyes, rubbing it with her fingers in order to see all the detail. As dirty as it remained, she slipped it on her ring finger, examining how it looked, and turned her attention back to the hair and fingernails.

"Why this stuff? What did *it* mean?" she asked, confused.

"Indians felt if you had possession of things like these, it would keep the soul of that person closer to you when you were separated. Funny, but I can't picture the Norman Tomms I remember hearing about being like this, but there it is," Luke said, shaking his head.

"I'm beginning to think my grandfather was a sweet, wonderful man that people didn't know as well as they thought they did," Loretta said, looking again at the ring and back down to a green-tinged collection of artifacts in front of her. "My father must have been a lucky man, having him as a dad."

Luke had walked back to get his coffee cup, draining the last few warm swallows, and thought about Loretta's last comment while sauntering back to her and the box. In the back of his mind, there was something wrong the timing between Lester and his illustrious father. "I've been thinking about that some," Luke said as he scratched his head. "Tell me, do you know when your daddy was born? How old he was when he had you?"

Loretta thought for just a second. "Well, I know he was

twelve years older than my mom, exactly; to the day."

"Really?" asked Luke. "Huh, that doesn't happen very often."

"Yeah, it had something to do with how they met; they were both celebrating their birthdays at parties at the same restaurant in Doraville and met for the first time that night. Love at first sight, and the circumstances, I guess. That was in '59. My mom was born December 16, 1938; I know that plain as day, I had to fill out so many forms for her when she was hospitalized with cancer. So that would have my father being born..." Loretta tried to figure it quickly in her head.

"He'd have been born December 16, 1926; now, subtract nine months from that, and..."

Loretta let the math play back and forth in her mind for several seconds, and the fact finally struck her. "He was born seven months after my grandfather died!"

"That's what I've kinda been thinking: your daddy, Lester, never knew *his* father either. And Norman Tomms never knew his son. If you think about it, if the timing was just right, Norman may never have known he was even going to *be* a daddy; it's a real possibility, that close and all. That would tend to explain something else, though," Luke offered.

"What?" Loretta asked.

"How it was possible for Lester to walk away from you like he did. In his own mind, he might have thought if he could get along without a father, then maybe you could too. It's 'wrong' thinking, I know, but there's a lot of wrong thinking men out there."

"And women, too," a somber Loretta added, motioning to the papers they had collected from the library earlier in the day.

She approached Luke with a body language that would have told even the most unobservant man that she was in need of a hug right then and there. Luke extended his arm out and Loretta smoothly docked with his side, feeling as though she had always belonged there. She put her arm around his back and they both looked down into the box, now practically empty of its discolored contents. "Most of these papers we've gotten out of here so far tell us nothing we're really after," Loretta said. "I've been scanning them for anything useful to us, and most are blank, just blank forms and memos; no reports or anything relevant to these cases. Maybe he didn't live long enough to even do it." The disappointment in her voice was evident.

Luke started to gingerly poke around the last layers of papers and shook his head. "I was hoping I might spy those two pearl-handled .45's in here, but I guess... hey, what's that?" he said, catching a glimpse of color in a bottom corner of the crate. Removing the papers on top of it, he uncovered what appeared to be a metal cigar box; brightly colored with a banner proclaiming "Havana" and a pretty Spanish-looking girl evidently wanting him to come and smoke her cigars. "Hey, take a look at this; seems your granddaddy was a smoker! This here is a cigar box! Way to go, Norman!" Luke proclaimed, hoping to draw a connection between a vice it appeared he and her grandfather shared.

Loretta knew exactly where he was going with this and gave him a sideways, knowing glance. "They didn't know any better back then. You do!" she said sarcastically. Luke shook the box and could tell it contained something, something heavier than cigars. He tried to pry off the cover but the moisture of seventy years had sealed it tight, rusting it in place.

Turning to Loretta, he picked up the screwdriver and motioned to her with a twisting motion, asking silently if he had her permission to pry it open with the tool. "I just don't want to scratch it up, it's so pretty. Is it okay?" he asked.

"Go for it. It's no good unless we can open it. What do you think's in it?"

"Hard to tell, Hon," Luke answered, working the screwdriver gradually around the edges, making a bit of progress with each pass. The lid finally separated on one side and lifted off completely, revealing a relatively rust-free interior. Inside, free of mold and mildew, were a small, brown book and a single folded piece of paper. "Huh, its not cigars; it's an old book and a sheet of paper," Loretta said. She slipped the paper out from under the small, leather-bound book and unfolded it to see what might make it special enough to have warranted being intentionally sealed up separate from the rest of the effects. Her eyes widened as they traveled down the page, taking in the writing she knew immediately must be that of her grandfather.

"Luke!" she exclaimed, absently walking around as she read. "This is *it*! This is what we wanted! Look, read this!"

Luke stood close to her as they both read the words and writing of Sheriff Norman Tomms silently to themselves. "See?" Loretta finally spoke, "See what he says here?" she pointed out to Luke. "His investigation of the Rainey murder that day! I knew it!" She read the short but revealing list out loud, too excited to keep quiet now that she had in her hands what she somehow knew was the key to the mystery of the deaths.

"--Investigated murder-suicide of Mildred Rainey and daughter Grace on Big Shoals Road this A.M.

--Husband Virgil not entirely ruled out as perpetrator.

--House on Big Shoals Road former site of Lowndes Plantation (SIGNIFICANT???)

--Murder and method of Grace Rainey identical to Racine infanticide of 1920 at Bear Run and Thomasville

--Infants killed in like manner both crimes-heads crushed with rock/stone (WHY?)

--Note found on Rainey woman similar in substance to testimony of Nettie Racine (mother) in '20--Both cite that infants were "Evil" (????)

--Location of Racine murder may have been site of Jenkins Plantation (COINCIDENCE???)

--Saw Randolph for information on War--got journal—*ASSUMPIONS ABOUT LOCATIONS CORRECT—return journal to Apoth. as soon as poss."

Loretta looked up at Luke with astonishment. "It's all here! He saw the connection between the murders of '20 and '26; both women killing their babies, using the same method, a method he couldn't understand, like us. And he discovered that at least the one was on the site of an antebellum plantation and he strongly suspected that the other killing took place at another one! We know from these clipping copies the Tyree case of 1878 happened at the site where an Endicott plantation once was. And look," she said, pointing to the last entry on the page, "remember, he's indicating that the locations of these murders is a significant factor, just like *we* think!"

"And from what he wrote there, it seems whatever he read in the journal he mentions, and I assume this book is the journal he's talking about, is what made him think so," Luke said, taking the journal out of Loretta's hand. "It also appears he's talking about the source of this book being Randolph Martin, if 'apoth.' means apothecary. That would be 'drug store', wouldn't it?"

"Yeah, that's what they used to call drug stores in the old days, you're right. Who's *Randolph* Martin?" Loretta asked as her eyes went back and forth between the journal and Luke's face.

"Gerald's father. He was the pharmacist in Watsonville before Gerald took over for him years ago. The Martins have owned that store since the twenties. Looks like you've got some reading to do, Hon," Luke said as he lifted the empty crate from the table and walked it the short distance to the porch. It was only then did he start to realize how much harder the rain had become.

Loretta was clearing the papers from the table and Luke was approaching her as the lights dimmed from not too distant lightning. "Looks like we're in for it tonight," he told her as he winced from the cracking thunder that shook Loretta's small house. Heavy storms had always bothered Luke, only because

324

they brought such thunder and lightning. He didn't fear them; it was more a jittery uneasiness, a reaction he had acquired from having to work out in them growing up on the farm. And delivering mail during a Georgia downpour out on desolate country roads had always been one of the postal challenges he could have done without. But he had gotten through them all; he'd get through this one also. "You start to check that out and see what it says about all this, and I'm going to use your bathroom if you don't mind. Where is it?" he asked, looking down the short hallway that was off to his left.

"Right down there, first door on the right, switch is on the left. Put the seat up please!" Loretta called to him, half-serious, as he started over to the hallway.

"Uh-huh," he called back without turning, shaking his head as he walked away.

Loretta sat at the table and inspected this small leather book, carefully looking it over as the important thing it must be for her grandfather to have put it away in such a secure manner.

CHAPTER 37

The sound of the flushing toilet was being drowned out by the rain pounding against the side of Loretta's house. Successive flashes of lightning and the accompanying thunder made it seem the neighborhood was under attack by well-placed artillery and Luke winced as he washed his hands and looked at himself in the mirror. *Damn, how long has this day been? I hope everything at the house is shut up and tied down. This only seems to be getting worse by the minute,* he thought as he reached for the miniscule lavender guest towel, practically useless due of its size. He chuckled to himself as he replaced it on the rack and was reaching to open the door when Loretta burst through, her eyes huge and her left hand covering her mouth. The force and surprise knocked him back against the towel rack on the wall in back of the door, and the quick glance he could manage told him she was in deep distress, getting ready to vomit.

"What's wrong? Loretta, what happened?" he asked her as she grabbed him by the shirt with her right hand and pushed him backward out of the door, quickly closing it in his face. "Are you alright? What's wrong?" he called through the door, putting his head close to it in order to hear over the rain. He thought he could hear the tell-tale sound of her vomiting into the toilet, and he waited until it stopped before he repeated his question. "Are you okay? Loretta? *Loretta*!" Luke shouted, listening closely for a reply.

"Yes," came a weak voice, the echoing hollowness of it telling Luke she was talking into the toilet while she answered him. "I'll be... I'm sick... just go..." Loretta stopped talking as she began to throw up again. The rain seemed to be getting louder and a long, drawn out rolling of thunder forced his ear closer to the door. "Just go... just sit down... and give me a... a while... the book," she said, her words echoing in the bowl. He heard it flush again and stepped back from the door, looking out of the hallway into the dining room. The lights dimmed again as a brilliant flash lit the darkness outside, then resumed its shining on the open book lying on the table. Luke walked out and stared down at it. *Is this what happened?* he wondered. He turned his attention toward the bathroom door, then in front of him at this small, leather volume of yellowed pages, as he took a seat in the chair Loretta had occupied only minutes before. And he began to read.

only the chimneys remaining, standing amid stark remains of charred wood, as though they the occasional sentry on roads I did at one time know well and travel with lightest heart; now, having suffered such profound destruction, so unfamiliar to my eyes.

It had always been, hitherto, a quite pleasant country, and the inhabitants of town and plantation most agreeable and courteous; they now being but memories of the fairest kind and I find my soul greatly forlorned at the eternal loss of all.

Being of such proximity to Atlanta on the Union march, the Endicott plantation on the Chatoosee Road had the dread misfortune of being the first to feel the wrath of Sherman's Army on the 18th of November, the year of our Lord 1864.

The Endicott's did all perish; Cornell Endicott and youngest daughter Nicollete dying in the pyre of the plantation house according to the Negroes that bore witness to these dread events; and Abigail, the eldest of the two Endicott daughters, being raped by Yankees and shot to death by a Union officer; though her remains being unavailable for my distraught and concerned inspection.

It was at this charred ruin of a grand home that I came to the medical assistance of one 'Jebel', a field hand, who had been fairly burned attempting to retrieve the bodies of Cornell Endicott and his daughter from the conflagration. Though in great distrust of me, owing to, undoubtedly, what he had witnessed, he did with some persuasion allow me to debride his burned flesh and bandage as best I could his injuries. Upon my assurances as to his recovery, he did indeed demonstrate a marked and heartfelt gratitude.

The Donahue plantation on Colman Crossing on the Big Ocoosa River lay next in the path of these barbaric troops, seemingly led by Satan himself, due, I say here, to the heinousness of the actions that were to become so typical of them.

A surviving female slave there, a 'Carrie', reported to me the most hideous of affairs, tales of degradation and depravity that were to be repeated throughout my heartrending journey.

Carrie recounted to me that Beatrice, wife of Col. Laurence Donahue, Master of the plantation, attempted to flee the house in order to divert the troops from the whereabouts of her ill husband who had been hidden in the nearby smoke house by his faithful servants. A mounted officer used his saber, he pursuing at full gallop, to behead the escaping Mrs. Donahue whilst she ran. He allegedly attached her severed head to his saddle horn by the hair as a trophy for having taken it with but a single sword stroke.

Son Beauregard and daughter Priss faired no better, as the troops, tying him to the staircase of the Manor, practiced their bayoneting on him and he quickly surrendered his brief life to the Almighty.

Priss, but seventeen years of age, was with child; she being the fair and loving wife of Captain Oliphant Samuels, he of the Confederacy and absent to war. Carrie relayed to me, through her constant tears, that Priss was held that day securely by several of the men as the infant, so innocent in the womb! was cut by knife from the same to be kicked about the floor in glee by the barbarian troops. 'One less bastard Rebel' was the phrase Carrie recalled the men telling her Mistress to her stunned face before she, too, quickly succumbed to the comforting netherworld of death.

Master Donahue, being large of girth as a result of age and many debilitating ailments, was unable to escape the smokehouse as the troops, upon seeking to loot the same of meats, discovered his whereabouts.

Three female slaves there present did testify to me their Master was bound hand and foot, the soldiers lifting him, with great effort, and hanging him through his chin by a ham hook, leaving him to twist and buck in an extreme agony of the worst sort. The nature of his impaling rendering him unable to utter but squeals and grunts, the perpetrators laughing amongst themselves how the sounds resembled that of a large hog, finding the image quite fitting.

Upon the departure of these troops, the slaves attempted in dire vain to release their Master from his misery, his great weight preventing them from successfully lifting him from the hook. A slave present there, a 'Daisy' related how the three could but sit and weep as Master Donahue's struggles eventually slowed to stillness, and his merciful passing.

All structures available and evident to the Union troops were set ablaze, their column then proceeding to the plantation of Macarthur and Dorothy Mabry, he of the Carolina Mabry's; located at the Hickem Ferry and Peach Orchard Roads.

A similar experience awaited these two, they having been dearest friends of mine, as they were beaten and bludgeoned to near death for refusal to disclose the whereabouts of their valuables. A house servant stated that, as the pair lay dying from their injuries, the soldiers, with aid of turpentine, set ablaze the couples' two year old daughter Julianne, she a cherub of God that I had myself delivered unto His earth, and hurriedly placed bets amongst themselves, wagering as to the distance the child would travel before its demise. The servant present said he did believe the Mabry's were still conscious so as to have witnessed this; the sight and sound being their last in this Earthly life.

Again, the plantation house and all outbuildings were put to the torch as the soldiers moved on to continue their wanton destruction of this county.

The Lowndes plantation on Big Shoals Road was set upon similarly as the others; Andrew, the owner, I can only gather from what I have been told, being forced to witness the rape of his wife, Martha, and their daughter Lorna, the latter showing then with child. They too, in finality, did perish in the flames of the home they loved so well.

A full dozen negroes witnessed the demise of their owners, Benjamin and Anna Rummels, they of 'Moss Wind', a plantation of great expanse at the Sheltoee and Rabba Roads, both being thrown to their deaths from their balcony to the ground below.

This may have been an unknown blessing for the two, as the subsequent treatment of their four daughters, as has been so tearfully relayed to me, would have been more than mortal parents should be asked to bear.

Robin, six; LaDonna, seven; and Angelique, eight, were repeatedly and with extreme malice raped by, what appeared to the witnesses, the majority of the invading company to the point of their merciful losses of consciousness.

As was the practice of the Union in their treatment of our civilian countryside, the troops were directed to poison the wells with the carcasses of slaughtered mules or livestock. In a variation of this, for the sole purpose of the cruelest of sport, the three children were carried to the well and thrown therein; the betting in this circumstance consisting of whether or not the freezing water at the bottom would wake the three to the point of awareness so as to elicit screams before they drown. A Negress, Clara, watching in horror unseen from the bushes, informed me that, indeed, those that wagered the children would wake walked away the richer.

Elizabeth Rummels, eighteen, tall, fair of face and full eight months with child, did herself also suffer to have her unborn violently cut away from her, she succumbing rapidly in that most despicable process.

The fire and smoke caused by the burning of this great property blackened the sky for a full day.

It became a labor of dread for me to leave the devastation of one plantation with the knowledge that the discoveries awaiting me at the next would but add to my troubled heart.

I had delivered into the world many of the children whose dire ends I learned of through the veils of tears I observed among the remaining slaves and servants who, in many cases, attempted valiantly to aid their Masters and Mistresses after the fact. The bravery and dedication to their owners demonstrated by these people came as no less than a great surprise to me.

The Jenkins house at Bear Run and Thomasville Road; the Pope Mansion on Old Hunter's Road; and the Sweet Plantation, it belonging to my sister Margaret and her husband Marshall, all have perished likewise to the others afore mentioned herein; the Masters of the homes suffering the most cruel and miserable of deaths, all; the females present, regardless of age or condition, perishing from or shortly after the brutality of rape. All the former plantations, having been etched in my clearest memory of kinder times, I will always remember as great homes of both grandeur and gracious warmth.

I am, and shall remain, in the darkest sorrow at the loss of my only sister, Margaret, and I pray God to open Heaven to her and her loving husband. They both having been earthly treasures, they will be, I have utmost faith, welcomed assets at His right hand. It is my great fear that I, and Ocoosa County, shall not again see the likes of them.

I am greatly distraught and deeply saddened to now realize the devastation and depravity an advancing Army brings with it, and the destruction it leaves upon passing.

I have returned home to Watsonville, and my practice, a different father to my children, a changed husband to my wife; I embrace them with warmth more often now, and impart to them with greater frequency my heartfelt love for them, in word and deed.

And I return a different servant to my God; with greater questions and, admittedly, a diminished faith in His unknowable plan for us, His faithful and obedient.

I impatiently look to Him, beseeching a Divine explanation as to the reason for what has happened here to us, His faithful, the people of this county; good, God-fearing people, all. Forever, I feel, I shall stand amazed at the breadth of destruction I have seen, and I admit I fall dismally short in failure in my attempt to understand the hatred that has caused it.

I sincerely wish to state here that I hope not again in what remains of my humble life I am His witness to the horror I beheld in that journey to places I did once know; to the ignominious demise of those I had counted as friends.

CHAPTER 38

L uke looked down at the last of the words and slowly closed the journal. His thoughts wandered, but not far.

He was a child of the twentieth century, and as such had witnessed the heinous acts men had committed against each other with great regularity during most of his life, brought into his living room by virtue of the miracle of global communication and an ever-widening media intoxicated with its own power of sensationalism. Hitler in Nazi Germany; Stalinist Russia; Pol Pot in Cambodia; The Hutus of Rwanda and the Serbs in Bosnia and Croatia. The list was long and would be added to as long as men are willing to band together in hatred for other men. Luke long ago had begun to dismiss the images the evening news was intent on showing him of slaughter in places so far removed from his life. The constant exposure to violence brings a callousness, an insidious acceptance of it, and he had become just another casual viewer who shook his head in resignation and changed the channel, looking for something else to watch that left no memory or aftertaste. But these handwritten words had touched him, had incensed him and sickened him like no visual images of far-off death and strife ever had. These were *his* people, residents of *his* county, *his* state; people who may have been related to him somehow. This touched home, and 'home' made all the difference.

Luke was unaware how long he had remained in his trance. He turned back toward the hallway to see Loretta sitting on a chair against the far dining room wall, her clasped hands between her knees, staring blankly at the floor in front of her.

"How long have…"

"Not long," she answered him in a weakened voice.

"You going to be okay?" he asked her, his voice as soothing as he could make it.

"Yeah…eventually," she replied. "That took everything out of me. How can that have happened?" she asked him, directing her eyes toward the journal in front of him.

"How much of this…"

"Some… enough."

Luke sat back in the chair and looked down at the book as he searched for an answer to Loretta's question. He sighed deeply at the simple truth that would be the basis of his reply. "People don't see eye to eye, somebody gets the upper hand, and things go way farther than they should. That's the short answer, anyway. This…" he said, holding the journal in his hands, "this…" Luke could not formulate the words he needed to comment on the small leather volume he held. He shook his head in disgust at it and set it back down on the table. Turning back to Loretta, he let his eyes examine her for several seconds before he spoke. "I think you're right, about the places," he told her, having to raise his voice over the sound of the rain.

"Huh? Why?" she asked him, her attention bringing her back to life.

"Whoever this is," Luke said as he motioned toward the book, "wrote this right soon after it all happened. He was at all those places, all eight of 'em, and the locations he gives for them correspond pretty near exactly with the addresses and locations of the murders we found in the clippings. So you and your grandfather were right; it seems to be the places themselves doing it."

Loretta's eyes widened and wandered around the room as the implications rapidly piled up in her mind. She rose from the chair and walked slowly toward Luke and the book, stopping by his side, her hand on the back of his chair.

"My grandfather figured it out from his investigations and this journal. And you think this came from Gerald's father?"

"I'm pretty positive," Luke said as he nodded his head.

"Then I guess maybe what Gerald told me at his store makes sense now," Loretta said.

"What exactly did he say?" Luke asked her.

"Gerald quoted something he said his father had told him a long time ago. It was something like 'the land remembers what bad things happen on it' or something like that. And I guess now maybe it 'holds' it when it was something this bad," she said, pointing to the journal.

"The 'Burden,'" Luke said, a hint of justification in his voice, as he rose from his chair and walked to the window to watch the sheets of rain illuminated in the street light in front of the house.

"'The Burden,'" Loretta repeated, a sad resignation in her words, sitting down in the chair Luke had just vacated. "Now we know it's true."

Luke winced as a brilliant flash of lightning exploded close by, followed immediately by an ear-splitting roar of thunder. "Goddamn!" he muttered to himself.

Loretta was staring at the journal, contemplating the horror it contained, when the bright flash of lightning lit the edge of it with white light long enough for her to notice an irregularity in the last pages. It appeared at least one or more pages toward the end of the small book had the corners folded, dog-eared, marking them for a reason. Curious, she picked up the journal and began to flip through blank pages to the back. Luke turned as she was opening the book and called out to her. "Loretta, no! Don't ..."

She raised her hand to him, assuring him that it was okay; going back over the inhuman atrocities was not her intention. She found the folded corners and opened to the last several pages of the book, praying silently they would not contain more of the graphic descriptions that had so quickly and thoroughly nauseated her. Quickly scanning the words written there, she called to Luke. "Luke, listen to this. This was written by the same person who wrote the rest of this, the first part. This must have been written as a kind of epilogue, later on. And it gives another date, too: August 25, 1865."

Luke walked over and stood behind her as they both read silently to themselves the last entry Norton Fale had chosen to include as an afterthought in his journal of sorrow.

The 25th of August, 1865- I record these words herewith as the chronicle of a heartbreaking journey from which I have recently returned, it having taken me to a place hitherto unknown by me, and I am quite certain, no other white person of this county.

A man of color, a former slave of the Endicott Plantation, did call upon me before break of day, the 21st; and he, fearful of his reception by me and mine, did hurriedly and with dire panic bid me to accompany him to a location some distance from Watsonville proper.

He informed me that my skills were urgently required in the aid of one Abigail Endicott, the eldest daughter of Cornell Endicott, she being the daughter believed by me to have been fatally wounded by a Union soldier in the massacres perpetrated in this county just nine months prior.

After refreshing this troubled man with food and drink, we did travel by horse to this remotest part of the county, it being located within a neglected area of woodland between the boundaries of the former Endicott and Mabry plantations. Barely so sizeable to warrant the term 'trail', the path, leading to the well concealed cabin that was our destination, was known as 'Nathan's Trace' by the slaves of the area, only they knowing of its whereabouts or much less existence; it being named after the past Negro emancipator of this area of Georgia. The secluded cabin there located bore the name, amongst the colored, of 'the Shanty in the Dell', it being situated in a small hillside clearing evidently heretofore unseen by any white person of matter.

It was there in said cabin I was to find, much to my renewed anguish, the body of Abigail Endicott, she evidently having expired several hours prior to our arrival, due to a knife wound to her abdomen. She was attended there by her nanny, a slave woman by the name of Letitia, who, it was obvious and quite evident to me, was bereft with uncommon grief at the passing of this fair Endicott child.

338

The tale imparted to me by this most morose servant was one of stunning and sad revelation, as it seems that the Endicott daughter had been spirited to this place at the time of the destruction of the Plantations and nursed to health by her servant and the servant's son, one 'Theo', the same that traveled to fetch me, from wounds she suffered at the hands of the Union Army.

Subsequently, I was told, Abigail had given birth to an infant daughter only two days prior to her death, it being the product of brutal rape having been perpetrated upon her by the same soldiers responsible for the deaths of her father, Cornell; and dear sister, Nicollete.

Letitia informed me, with her son Theo verifying her recounting, that Abigail had refused to care for or nurse the infant and did indeed, just before incurring her own fatal injury, remove the child from the cabin in a crazed and belligerent way, and crush the infant's head with a stone she drew from the field in proximity to the cabin. Held at bay by knife point, Letitia and Theo could but watch in their horror at this terrible occurrence. The infant body I examined did indeed fit the description of events they sadly imparted to me.

Suicidal in her remorse for her crime, Miss Endicott attempted to take her own life with the knife, and to the great misfortune of all, was subsequently fatally injured by such in Theo's effort to disarm her. This is indeed a woeful tale, the veracity of which I do not doubt, considering the evidence I did myself witness there.

Before departing, I aided the two in preparing a proper grave for mother and child, fashioning two crude but sufficient markers; one for the Endicott girl and baby, buried together so as to meet the Almighty, at least, as mother and daughter; and a marker for the grave of another of Letitia's sons, he succumbing to a Yankee ball some months prior. It was with a heavy heart I bade the two farewell and did, once again with pensive sadness, make my way back to Watsonville.

***

Loretta closed the book and looked up at Luke, her eyes wide now with a sudden understanding. "That's it! That's why these babies have all been killed the same way, with a rock! With the mothers going unexplainably crazy within a week or so of the birth and crushing the child's head with a stone!"

"Like they were possessed or something? By her?" Luke asked.

"I have never in my life believed in that sort of thing, like I said, but, yeah, this is what it seems like to me: it's as if the spirit of this Abigail has somehow inhabited these plantation sites and is taking her revenge for what happened to her, and she's incited the spirits of the other females who were brutalized and died there at those places; stirred them up, too; made them angry about dying the way they all did. And, in their vengeance for what happened to them, *they're not allowing any new life to grow there!* Jesus, I can't believe what I'm saying here, this sounds so totally off-the-wall," Loretta said shaking her head.

"Hon, I hate to say it, and I hate to have to believe it too, but I think you're absolutely right! What you just said pretty much explains what's been going on here for over a hundred years," Luke told her.

"Exactly a hundred and thirty years, if you count Abigail Endicott as the first," Loretta said sadly, gently laying the book back on the table and slowly walking to the window to check on the rain for no good reason except to take her mind off the scope of what she had just realized.

Luke slid back down into the chair and handled the book

340

as he thought about something that caught his attention in this last entry.

"You know, the man who wrote this, the author, mentioned a 'Nathan's Trace'. I haven't heard it called that since I was little," he said in a loud voice, trying to be heard over the unrelenting rain.

"Who was Nathan? Was he somebody?" Loretta called back without looking away from the torrent outside, allowing herself to at least momentarily be distracted by something other than death.

"'Nathan' was Nathan Freebody, a slave that was freed when his owner passed away; he was 'willed' free. Story has it that he took it upon himself to emancipate as many other slaves as he could by stealing them and getting them up north. Kind of an 'Underground Railroad' set-up, you know?"

"What happened to him?" Loretta asked, still looking out her window.

"Oh, they finally caught him and hanged him," Luke said in a matter-of-fact tone, "some years before the war. But it took a while to catch him; they never knew how he traveled back and forth. That's why this author was so surprised to be where he was taken; no white man had been there. It was just a small foot path known only to the slaves, and they kept it a secret among themselves so as to protect Nathan's coming and going. And you know, now that I've read this, I'm thinking that ol' Nathan may have lived in that 'shanty' this guy talked about. He must have, no one could ever locate where he stayed. And from what this says, it seems the other slaves used the place as kind of a hideout from time to time. I'll be damned, I'll bet that's it!" Luke said, proud of himself for solving another of

Ocoosa County's long-standing mysteries.

Loretta would always claim she never knew exactly why, but something Luke had said worked into her mind and needed further clarification. As she was about to turn to him, her vision suddenly faded to a surreal scene she did not recognize in a place that was not her home; a slow motion depiction of hair, heavy hanks of curly brown hair, falling silently to a salon floor to lie there still with a cold finality; a "deadness" that somehow signaled to her very core the terrible end of something she could not immediately interpret or understand. The sound of an infant crying somewhere in the background created an increasingly loud and ominous undercurrent. Her vision slowly panned up to the head from which the hair had come and it turned toward her, revealing a pale face with scattered freckles that looked easily at her, showing a comfortable smile. Loretta saw the simple and trusting eyes of blue turn black and empty like those of a doll.

Recovering with a shake and gasp back to the reality of the rain and wind, she turned from the window, and facing Luke with a gnawing apprehension, asked, "You said you haven't heard the path referred to as 'Nathan's Trace' for a long time. What do they call it now?"

As she asked the question, she felt a coldness washing over her she could not comprehend but only fear.

"It's not a 'path' anymore; it's a dirt road way out in the sticks. Now its 'Black Nate Road'," he told her.

CHAPTER 39

The words entered Loretta's brain and sped down a thousand threads of neurons, looking for the place in her memory with which they could stop and align, giving a meaningful association to the name. In just under two seconds, they found it.

Loretta froze and for seconds was unable to utter any sound as her face distorted into one of wide-eyed panic. Her hand rose to cover her mouth. *"Oh Jesus, Luke, no!"* she said as the words finally worked their way out of her in a horrified cry.

"What?" he shouted at her, her alarm startling him.

"Black Nate Road!" she screamed at him as he rushed to her to grab her by the shoulders and control her. "Black Nate Road is where the Hyder's live, Danielle and Bo!" Luke's face showed he wasn't grasping the significance of what she was saying. "Luke, they just had a baby ten days ago! They're home there with it now! We have to do something! That baby is either dead or will be!" she said, looking around in fear, trying to break his hold and go somewhere, do something.

Luke reached the phone in a matter of steps, grabbing it to

dial 911. Loretta stood close by him and looked up at his face with controlled panic, watching it to follow the conversation he may have.

"Watsonville 911, what is your emergency?"

"Karen? This is Luke, Luke McClain," he said, relieved the reply came so fast.

"Luke, what's wrong? Are you alright?" she said, recognizing his voice.

"Karen, yeah, I'm okay. Look, I'm at 1121 Bess..."

"1121 Bessemer Court, I've got it on my screen in front of me; what's the emergency, Luke? Take it easy, calm down."

Luke let the loud crackle of lightning in the line die before he attempted to speak. "Karen, the woman here with me, Loretta Carmichael, and I have good reason to believe a baby is in real danger right now out on Black Nate Road. We think it may even be dead by now, and if not, it could be real soon."

"Why do you think that? Have you been there? Have you seen it?"

"It's a long story; we don't have time for it now. No, we haven't seen it. Is Lamar there? Can he go out there now and take a look?" Luke asked, the urgency evident in his voice.

"Luke, Lamar just responded to a multi-vehicle accident out on 77 at the Oglethorpe County line. It's a bad one; Sheriff Gaines from Oglethorpe is working it with him. Highway patrol is there, several emergency vehicles from both counties. I don't know how long he'll be tied up there. We don't have a deputy yet either, so there's no one else to respond. Let me see..." as she looked at her screen at her county map. "Black Nate Road is on the other side of the county from where he is right now..."

"Yeah, I know," Luke confirmed, cursing to himself, his look of frustration plain to Loretta. She knew he was getting bad news from the person on the other end.

"…so he couldn't arrive out there any sooner than an hour even if he left right now, maybe longer in this storm."

"Okay Karen, here's what I want you do for me: contact Lamar, tell him what I told you and tell him to *please* get out to Black Nate Road as soon as he can; number… do you know the address?" he turned and asked Loretta.

"Number 13… *Shit!*..13…1330! That's it!" Loretta said, surprised that it was still in her memory bank. Some people get muddled during emergencies. Loretta was just the opposite; she was a nurse.

"1330; tell the Sheriff to look for the sixth mailbox on the right side of the road; yeah, and tell him there used to be a Bulldog 'G' decal on the side of it. It may still be there. Tell him to turn down that drive. And send whatever ambulance might be available too, okay? Thanks, Karen. Bye."

Luke put down the phone and turned to Loretta to fill her in on what was going to happen and why it would take so long. As he began to speak, another bolt of lightning made him squint in anticipation of the inevitable booming of thunder. He took her by the shoulders once again to emphasize what he wanted to tell her and to be able to manage her in case she didn't like what he had just been told.

"Hon, Sheriff Franklin's office said he can't be there any sooner than an hour; there's a bad…"

Loretta's arms flew up to break Luke's grip on her shoulders, grabbing the front of his shirt with both hands, pulling him off balance and close to her. Luke could see her eyes narrow and her jaw tighten in the uneven light from the storm outside. "Your country ass better listen to me *right now*, Lucas! There's a baby out there in this shit and it's in *big trouble*! If I have to go myself, I will; you just tell me how to get there! But with you or without you, *I'm going*!"

'*Lucas*'. *Oh Christ*. "You'll never find it..."

"***Then take me there, goddamn it!***!" she screamed as she let go of him and pushed back away, keeping her eyes locked on his. She began to quiver as the fire in her died quickly and changed to a helpless pleading. "Luke," she said, her eyes full of impending tears, "Danielle Hyder told me they moved into a double wide at 1330 Black Nate Road, and it was down in a hollow. Don't you see? 'Dell' is another name for 'hollow'! It's the same place, Luke; it's where the shanty was! It's where Abigail Endicott killed her baby, the first baby that died that way, and if we don't get out there, Danielle is going to kill hers the same way too, if she hasn't already. You know she will! *Please*!"

Luke studied the face of this little Atlanta woman and swung his head to briefly survey the continuing downpour. Glancing back at her again, he spun and strode to the table, grabbed his keys and turned to her. A flash of lightning lit his silhouette for a second as he stood motionless, facing her in the dimming lamp light.

"Let's go," he said.

CHAPTER 40

Locking up was the last thing on Loretta's mind as she stood next to Luke in the porch doorway ready to dart down the steps to his truck. "Ready?" Luke asked, looking down at her.

"Yeah," she said as they broke and ran through the torrent to his truck, he getting in behind the wheel and reaching to unlock her door. They were both soaked despite the short run, and Loretta reached down and felt for whatever napkins might still be on the floor from the afternoon. Luke reached under his seat, searching for a few seconds to finally pull out a partially folded white towel. As he handed it to Loretta, she could plainly see a dark object fall to the seat from the folded cloth, bouncing heavily and sliding down next to Luke. The towel was rough from dried putty and partially stuck together, but it was better than the soaked napkins. She handed it to Luke and he dried his face and neck, dropping it to the seat as he turned the key to crank the truck. Loretta slid her hand over to the towel and used it to hide her search for the object she had seen fall to the seat. Her hand found the grip of the holstered gun that had already wedged itself down in the crack of the seat.

"Luke, what's this? Why do you have this?" she asked as she picked it up and held it for examination. Luke had his head turned, looking in his side mirrors in order to back out of the drive, and turned back toward her voice long enough to see what she held and take it from her, depositing it once more on the seat beside him.

"It's a .38. I keep it under here just in case," he said as he finished backing and put the truck in drive. He started slowly down the street, trying to adjust his vision to the wretched visibility.

"Can we put it away? It makes me nervous sitting out up here," she said. Luke didn't reply. It was hard enough to drive without having to argue about something he could easily take care of without a fuss. He reached over and hit the glove box with his fist, grabbed the gun and dropped it in among the papers and napkins, keeping his eyes on what he could see of the street the entire time. "Thanks," she said.

"Uh-huh," he replied. This wasn't the time or the place to protest or attempt to explain. He knew her well enough by now to know it probably wouldn't do any good anyway. Making their way through the flooding streets to the town limits, Loretta asked him about the mailboxes.

"How did you know how many there would be on that road? And what the Hyder mailbox would have on it?"

"Because I've delivered mail there many times in the past. On a rural route, that's pretty much all you ever see, the mailboxes," he replied, peering into the wall of rain in front of him. "I've never seen most of the houses on that road; they're all set back in the woods, down drives. And in the case of 1330, down in a hollow."

"Do you think you can find it when we get there? With all this rain?"

"I think so; *if* we get there, that's going to be the trick. I'm having a real hard time seeing in this," Luke told her, leaning forward over the wheel to squint through the windshield.

"Please, hurry, Luke. I know this is rough going, but that baby…"

"Loretta," Luke cut her off, the exasperation plain in his voice. "I can only go so fast in this. I can't see more than twenty feet and my damn wipers aren't going fast enough to clear the windshield!" He reached over to pat her thigh, noticing then just how soaked she was. "Hang on, Hon. I'll get us there somehow." The truck swung off the paved road they had been on and mushed into the clay and gravel of Colman Crossing Road, the dirt road that would take them to Black Nate Road and the hollow. Luke felt the immediate change in the way his truck handled and it wasn't for the better. As much as he had had to fight the flooded paved streets, plowing through this mud for miles was going to be treacherous. *If only I could see where the hell I'm going*, he thought, wanting to keep his apprehensions to himself. The truck alternately fishtailed and glided, losing traction in the mud even at the low speed he was driving, and it gave an unsettling feeling to them both. Luke negotiated the sharp turns by letting the truck glide into them as he let off the gas, accelerating again as it evened out back into the straight-aways. Where the narrow dirt road straightened, the best he could do was keep them in the middle of what he could see and maintain a steady speed.

"Here's Black Nate now," he said, coming out of a sharp right turn and pulling the wheel hard to the left to barely catch a side road with no visible sign. "That's a tough turn to find even in good weather," he told her as the truck started to descend down a gradual switchback of a dirt road, now a flowing river of mud and gravel. The occasional glimpse of a mailbox appeared on the right side of the truck and both Luke and Loretta mentally counted as they slid downhill into a tree-lined black oblivion illuminated only by the withering beams of Luke's headlights and the ever increasing lightning. After what seemed like miles, the vague shape of another mailbox grew larger on the right. "Is that five or six? Is it six?" Loretta yelled, the dim white shape becoming more defined as they approached. The outline of a red "G" was barely visible on the side. "Luke!" Loretta shouted as the image clarified in the headlights.

"I see it! That's it!" Luke replied, turning the wheel hard to catch the hidden driveway he remembered from his past. The truck fishtailed to the left and slid sideways into the mud until the wheels picked up enough traction to propel it forward again down the steep drive. Lightning flashed and the two could see they were being dumped into a descending, meandering blackness. Blurred by the driving rain, Luke could only use his instincts to guess exactly where the drive was under his truck, which was now sliding and coasting on its own into an abyss. He strained to see through his windshield, but the silver curtain of rain made everything in front of him look the same. "*I can't see SHIT!*" he yelled in exasperation and fear to Loretta, who was bracing herself from sliding to the floor by putting her feet on the dash board and pushing back hard against the seat.

"There!" Loretta shouted, pointing through the veil of driving rain to the left where the border of trees fell away from

350

the drive. The dim form of a trailer started to materialize at the far left edge of the headlight's beam.

Luke looked in the direction she pointed and automatically pulled the steering wheel in the same direction, taking the truck off what he still assumed was the drive, and toward the only recognizable object they had see since leaving Black Nate Road. "Hang on!" he shouted as the truck dipped and bumped onto the unevenness of what constituted the large, sloping front yard of the property. Small scrub oaks were becoming more concentrated on the muddy slope as the truck careened downhill and it was all Luke could do to swerve and glide past them with so little control of his vehicle. The beams from his headlights bounced around wildly, illuminating bare trees then nothing and back again, supplemented every few seconds by brilliant lightning that, incredibly, seemed to be getting brighter and more frequent. Stepping on the brake with all his strength, Luke slowed the truck, sliding to a mushy stop with the headlights pointing at the trailer a hundred feet or so from them down the hill. The beams from his lights and the lightning were all that were lighting the otherwise dark scene, and the two sat for seconds pondering their next move. "Looks like nobody's here. No lights," he said, staring through the rain-obscured windshield.

"I haven't seen any lights for the last few miles, anywhere. I think this whole area has lost power. I wouldn't be surprised, would you?" she asked him. "I mean, look at this storm!"

They both stared at what they could see by his lights and the almost rhythmical lightning. Luke turned to her and said, "It's up to you, Hon. What's our next move?"

"We've got to at least go down there and check, see if that

baby's okay, see if they're even in there," she told him.

Luke nodded with reluctance. "Yeah, we're here, we're wet. You might be right about this. Ready?"

They both exited the truck at the same time, running around to the front to stay in the beams from the headlights, joining hands to steady each other, squinting from the torrent that was hitting them full in the face. The rain and wind squalled around them, making their descent down the hill a slow, treacherous approach. The scrub oaks scattered every several feet were giving them something to brace themselves with and reaching one after another quickly became the goal which marked their progress. Loretta lost her footing between trees, and Luke's strength kept her from hitting the ground and sliding away from him. "Easy, girl!" he shouted to her as the trailer was getting closer. The filtering effect of the many oaks made the headlight's beams practically useless, shining only dimly now on the front of the trailer. A small wooden porch stood leading to the front door and Loretta was the first to see the shape of a man lying slumped against the right pillar on the top step. She left Luke and cautiously let herself slide down the rest of the slope into the yard in front of the trailer. Despite the rain, she thought she could see a pool of dark liquid running down the steps, disappearing into the splashing water in front of the short stairway of wood. A bolt of lightning told her the actual story. "Luke! It's Bo! I think he's bleeding bad!" she called back at him, turning to see him fifteen feet or so in back of her, his attention drawn to something moving to his left.

"LORETTA! IT'S HER!" he yelled, keeping his eyes on what looked to him to be an apparition, a ghost in a white, rain-soaked nightgown, steadily making its way up the hill past

them, following the beams of light up through the river of red mud and water.

Loretta turned from Bo instinctively and, slipping twice, made her way back to Luke who had also turned to parallel this figure back toward his truck. He reached for Loretta and took her hand to pull her toward him and another flash of lightning exploded close to them, identifying the figure to her as Danielle. *"It's her, it's Danielle!"* she yelled at the side of Luke's head. *"**DANIELLE! DANIELLE!**"* she screamed at the woman who was oblivious to their presence. Something in Danielle's left hand was glinting in the headlights and Luke could see in the next flash of lightning that she was carrying a large kitchen knife. He needed another bolt to confirm the nature of what dangled from her right hand. He realized what it was at the same time Loretta saw it and shouted to him. *"**Luke! She's got the baby! Oh Christ, she has the baby!**"* Loretta screamed as a wind-swept sheet of rain hit her in the face and partially filled her mouth.

Danielle held the infant by a leg, carrying it in the same manner a child would carelessly carry a lifeless doll. Luke kept moving uphill, slightly ahead of Loretta, keeping his eyes on Danielle as much as he could, fighting to keep his footing in the mud that hid the unevenness of the rocky yard. He gained enough distance to take up a stance in front of this possessed woman in an attempt to stop her progress toward his headlights. Loretta approached from the side to get close enough to be heard above the wind and rain and the almost constant booming thunder of the storm that was now right over them.

Danielle stopped walking and turned to the pair,

alternately brandishing the knife at each of them. Her face was twisted into a determined sneer that displayed her clenched teeth and her wide, lifeless eyes.

"Danielle, don't! It's not your fault! Don't hurt your baby!" Loretta yelled at the freckle-faced girl that stood before them, slashing through the rain with the knife, willing to kill them both for trying to halt her mission, a mandate from the past that she would never comprehend. *My God, she's not blinking! Her eyes are wide open even in this rain! How can that be?* Loretta thought. Through the howling of the wind, she could hear the wailing of the infant, and the conversation she had had with Dr. Stimson flashed through her mind. Her breathing quickened even more as she vowed to herself that what had happened to the other infants in the past was not going to happen here to this one.

Luke knew he had to act fast. He turned to run the thirty feet to his truck, heading into the lights to get the best possible view of the ground, now a wide cascading sheet of red mud and water. His clothes and boots were soaked, adding to his weight. His thighs and calves burned and refused to cooperate as he fought to free each step from the sucking mud in his leaden sprint to his vehicle. Reaching the passenger door, he grabbed at it to rescue himself and pulled his weight to the truck to open it. Using the edge of his hand to open the glove box, he recognized the feel of the holstered .38 and brought it to him, pushing at the snap to release the retaining strap on the worn holster. The years of sitting unused under his seat had rusted the snap and it refused to budge. *"Goddamn it!"* he yelled at the snap and himself, using all his hand strength to finally break the strap itself. Luke brought his torso out of the protection of the cab and looked back down the hill at Danielle, who still dangled her infant from one hand while swinging the huge kitchen knife at Loretta. Gun in hand, he slipped and slid back down the hill, staying in the beams of his truck lights until he stood within ten feet of Danielle. *"DANIELLE, LET HER GO!"* he shouted at her, trying to divert her attention from Loretta. *"PUT THE BABY DOWN, DANIELLE!"*

Suddenly, the maniacal girl that stood just feet from Loretta stopped swinging her knife and turned toward Luke, standing motionless in the torrential rain except for the movement of the infant she held. Her nightgown was a wet second skin, clinging to her own to give her a ghoulish gray appearance. Her unblinking doll-eyes stared at Luke for five long seconds, a look that frightened him to his core. *She's a goddamned ghost*, he thought. *She can't be real!* Danielle dropped the baby to the ground in front of her and Loretta made an instinctive move toward it to grab it. Danielle turned her head once more, snarling, breathing fast and hard now, the rain blowing out of her mouth with each breath. She swung the knife at Loretta once more then dropped down to her knees searching under the muddy water for something unseen. Within seconds, her hand emerged with a softball-sized rock and she simultaneously dropped the kitchen knife into the flowing mud, freeing her hand to flip her infant facedown in the deep, soft orange mud in front of her knees.

"DANIELLE, NO!" Loretta yelled with all her strength, vainly trying to get through to this young mother that was moments away from joining the legacy of so many others that had gone before her.

Luke stood incredulous, seven feet in front of Danielle and

the baby that was now suffocating in six inches of wet Georgia clay. The only option he had was becoming starkly clear to him as he raised his revolver to point it directly at her chest. *"STOP! DANIELLE, STOP!"* he screamed, watching her next move in terror. Danielle pressed her hand to the baby's back to keep it from sliding away from her in the mud and raised the rock over her head with the other. In horrified desperation, Loretta tried the only thing that came to her mind.

"ABIGAIL ENDICOTT, DON'T YOU HURT YOUR BABY!" she shouted in the angriest, most authoritative voice she could muster. Danielle froze and turned back toward her, and just for brief seconds, there in the truck headlights that were beginning to fade, Loretta could see the twisted grimace of Danielle's face soften, her eyes blinking in the rain. For an instant, there was a look of confusion on the freckled face of the girl with the rain-soaked, shoulder-length hair; kneeling in the mud of an extraordinary place, an ancient, neutral place that itself was helpless to let the people of Ocoosa County forget what had happened upon it 130 years before.

The brief interlude with reality passed as quickly as it occurred, and Danielle's face distorted once more into a maniacal sneer of hatred while she raised the rock high above her head. Luke shook, straining his eyes to clear them in the rain that made what he was seeing seem so surreal, so slow motion. The gun shook with him but he managed to keep the sights wandering around Danielle's chest.

Danielle opened her mouth to speak and the sound that emanated from it was loud and bellowing, raspy and deep. A brilliant streak of horizontal lightning lit the entire sky and shone down on the scene that would stay burned into their memories forever.

"*GET BACK TO…*"

Luke did not let her finish her sentence, did not let her complete what he and Loretta knew in their bones at that instant she was going to do to the suffocating infant whose struggling was starting to slow. He fired once, hitting her squarely in the chest, knocking her on her back, her lower legs folding back underneath her. Her eyes stared straight up into the black, raining sky, fluttering once again while she tried to speak. "My baby… my baby," her lips whispered, the words lost forever in the howl of the torrential rain. Loretta dove for the child, scooping it up from the mud, cradling it and turning it to the light to inspect its face. The baby's front was completely covered and no features could be seen beneath the thick mud that coated her face. Loretta used the edge of her hand to scrape away as much of the mud as she could, revealing a tiny face that still attempted to cry. *She's plugged*, she thought, letting the rain wash away even more of the red mud. *I've got to aspirate it.* Loretta placed her mouth over the infant's toothless, straining mouth and gently sucked until she could taste mud and water in her own. She spit it out and repeated the procedure on the baby's nose. Enough fluid came out so that the newborn began to sputter and hack, giving short, hiccupping cries that told Loretta that her resuscitation just may work.

She flipped the baby over onto its stomach and supported her chest, patting her back to release the last of the obstruction in her lungs and airway. A few seconds of gentle thumping and a weak but steady wail started pouring from the little mouth. A child's cry had never sounded better to Loretta.

Turning her over again, Loretta could see the tiny face straining to cry harder, its strength almost depleted. *Good girl; cry. Go ahead and cry as hard as you can, we're going to get you out of here and get you safe*, Loretta thought as she looked around her and then down at Danielle lying dead in the pouring rain. A fleeting pang of guilt and sadness passed through her for the young mother that never knew what happened or why, and now never would. Loretta clutched the infant to her cold, soaked chest, trying to preserve as much body heat as she could, and began plodding her way toward Luke, who had fallen to his knees and was now sitting back on his heels, motionless, the gun still cradled loosely in his hand as it sank into the mud by his leg.

Luke stared at the body of the young girl that just seconds ago was such a threatening menace; now so still and harmless. His trance was shutting out the wind and rain and lightning that now didn't exist for him. His eyes involuntarily blinked and batted, but he could not turn away from Danielle.

As Loretta reached him, lights began to filter through the trees at the top of the hill and a siren could be heard above the wind. An ambulance bounced its way down the driveway, now almost impassible from the flooding rain and eroding clay that had already flowed downhill. The vehicle pulled hard into the yard to follow the path Luke had taken and came to a stop just behind his truck. Two EMTs burst out of the cab into the swirling rain and made their treacherous way to Loretta and Luke.

"What's the situation here?" yelled the husky young man, his white uniform shirt already soaked and clinging to him.

Loretta held the baby to her chest with her left arm and

gestured to the pair with the other. "This woman is dead, I'm pretty sure; gunshot wound to the chest," she yelled back, pointing to Danielle. "There's a male down there on the porch hemorrhaging badly; multiple lacerations, I think. I don't know if he's still alive, I couldn't check him. I'm okay, he's okay," she said, pointing to Luke who had still not moved. "This infant is in trouble, though; dehydrated, malnourished, hypothermia. Might have airway problems too."

The female of the pair was pulling a gurney from the back of the rescue vehicle and slid it down the hill to join her partner. "Go take care of the guy. He's this girl's father. I've got her, I'm a nurse; peds. She's stable for now," Loretta told them.

They guided the gurney down the hill toward the trailer and Loretta turned back to Luke, holding the baby close to her again, letting the wailing muffle into her rain-soaked blouse. "Luke! Luke!" she called to him through the rain. Luke was sitting back now, his arms resting on his knees, still staring at the body of Danielle. He looked up expressionless at Loretta and stared blinking into her face. Loretta looked down at him and couldn't find words for him in that moment; couldn't say anything that would make a difference to him, that would make what happened better or alright. Luke let the rain hit him full in the face for half a minute, waiting for words from her that didn't come. Resigned to the silence, he turned back to the body and watched it, staring at it again as though it was his duty now to look over it, guard it somehow, keep it from disappearing into his imagination. *This is real,* he thought. *I did this. Oh God, I really did this and I can't take it back. Oh Jesus God.*

Loretta turned to watch the paramedics struggle up the hill with the gurney, pushing and pulling their desperate cargo toward the ambulance. Bo was strapped down, covered with a now soaked blanket. An oxygen mask covered his face and two IV bottles swung from steel rods at the head of the gurney. *That was damn quick. He's alive, but he must be bad,* she thought, her mind understanding the setup that approached her. "How is he?" she asked the petite blond medic, now completely rain-soaked also.

"Multiple lacerations; he's bad, real bad. Almost no vitals, but we're gonna work on him on the way, see what we can do," she yelled back, trying to be heard over the rain and wind.

"What about her?" Loretta asked them both, pointing at the body of Danielle, now surrounded by flowing mud that threatened to wash her down the hill. The male medic pulled a sheet from under the gurney and, after doing a quick check for vitals, attempted to cover the body with it, but the wind would not allow it to lay flat, flipping the bottom edge of it back up over the head and off.

"This is a crime scene now; she's dead. Someone has to stay with the body until the sheriff gets here," he said, getting down into Loretta's face to be heard. "Sheriff Franklin is on his way; dispatch notified us just before we turned down the drive. We can't wait though, we have to get him in stat. We might lose him anyway, he's most bled out. She did a number on him. Can you stay with them?" he asked, pointing over to Luke and the orange-spattered body.

Loretta looked at Luke and Danielle, then down at the baby in her arms. Luke could hear enough of the conversation through his haze of thought to understand the situation they and he were in. "Go, get her out of here, I'll be alright. Go. I'll wait for Lamar. It's all we can do. I'll be okay," he said, looking up at Loretta and gesturing toward the top of the hill, illuminated now and then by bolts of white lightning. The only thing the paramedics were sure of in this unconventional situation was that the man on their gurney and the baby had to get to more intensive and stabilizing treatment than they could provide there, and quickly. Accounting for the man sitting in the rain was not their responsibility.

The baby she held to her chest was rapidly weakening and Loretta knew it did not have much chance to live unless they started treating it *now*. She held it tightly as she bent to speak to Luke. "I can't stay! I've got to…"

"I know," he replied. "Always and forever," he said, looking up at the baby as he tried to manage a weak smile in the downpour. He held up his hand to her, and without saying a word, Loretta interlocked her fingers with his and managed what she could of a weak smile back at his understanding. She turned to follow the medics to the rear of the ambulance.

CHAPTER 41

Hand her to me," the rain-soaked young man said, taking the infant from Loretta and handing it to his female partner. He turned back and pulled Loretta up into the ambulance and closed the doors, quickly toweled his face dry. He simultaneously squatted to examine Bo's face and introduce himself, while at the same time pointing up to the female attendant who was wiping her glasses and assessing what to do next. "I'm Matt, this is Tina," he said, holding up his hand without looking, at the same time Tina was extending hers. Loretta briefly high-fived the two and scanned the logically arranged shelves of supplies for the things she felt she needed to save this baby that now lay on a towel-covered stainless steel shelf. Though she was a stranger to them, a team was established in a matter of seconds.

"Loretta," she answered back, asking for supplies in the same breath. "Blanket?"

"Bottom drawer, left," replied Tina, pointing. "It's going to be tight in here; if you don't see it, ask," she said. "Good to have you aboard."

"Got it," Loretta answered, grabbing the white, sterile

blanket from the drawer. She saw bandage scissors in a tray and used them to cut away the tiny shirt that at one time looked as though it may have been pink in color. The soggy mass of paper and plastic that had been a filthy, soiled diaper came loose with a tug and she threw them both in the corner out of the way, swaddling the baby to give it warmth. The infant continued to cry, but the sound was getting noticeably weaker as the minutes passed and Loretta knew every second now was critical.

"Tina, I'm not getting any pressure on this guy; pulse is weak and thready. He's in shock. Let's get his feet up, use those blankets," Matt said as he pulled another liter of Ringers from the cabinet. "I'm starting another unit of Lactated Ringers on him. Can you locate the last of these bleeders? If we can't stop those, he's gonna bleed out what we're pouring in."

Loretta subconsciously took in the chatter while tending to her own life-saving measures for this child in front of her, whom she knew was in its own grave danger. Wrapped for warmth, the color was beginning to brighten and "pink up" in the baby's face, and it gave Loretta encouragement, but she knew from her years of experience this infant was far from being out of the woods. It still needed IV fluids, and fast. "Pediatric IV kit?" she asked, not looking up.

Glancing over, Tina nodded toward the cabinets Loretta leaned against. "Drawer by your shoulder," she told her, going back to her task of stemming the flow of blood from the baby's father. "Christ, she really tore this guy up. If he does make it, he's going to have some permanent limitations; nerve involvement," she said, looking at the locations and depth of his wounds. "What the hell went on here, do you know?" she asked Loretta.

"Yeah, but it's a long story," Loretta replied. "When this is all over, remind me to tell you," she said as she prepared a bag of normal saline for her struggling patient. With the baby on its back, she slid it forward on the stainless tray until the little head dangled off the edge, supported by Loretta's hand, letting the weak but constant attempt to cry bring up a good vein in the neck. *That's where we're going in*, she thought as she readied the needle she hoped would be the lifeline to bringing this innocent newborn back from the brink on which she now teetered. Swabbing the neck with alcohol, Loretta was amazed at the amount of grime and dirt built up on the newborn's skin in the short time since it had been born. *She must not have even bathed this poor thing*, she thought. *Some of this is from tonight, but not all of it. As soon as it became something that wasn't real, something evil, it became a 'thing' that didn't have to be cared for. Jesus.*

Inserting the needle, Loretta adjusted the flow and checked the pulse and airway once more. Satisfied for the moment, she turned to Matt and Tina, still feverishly working on Bo. Two IV's of plasma expander, oxygen flowing full, tourniquet on the right arm and the other lacerations in the process of being controlled. "What do you think? Will he make it?" she asked, looking at the young welder that just ten days ago joked so easily about becoming a father.

"Hard to tell," Matt responded, an unsure cautiousness in his voice. "I just want to get him to Athens Regional before he goes down on us. He'd be flying out of here if the weather wasn't so bad, he's in that much trouble. We've got all the Ringers running now he can take, clamped what hemorrhaging we can. ER knows he's coming, they're ready for him. He needs whole blood and a clinical crash team. The sooner we can get out of here the better. I just want him as stable as we can get him before we go."

"Sounds good…" Loretta started to say when Tina cut her off.

"Loretta! Her color!" Tina said, pointing to the baby.

Loretta swung around to her tiny patient and saw the baby's color had gone from increasing pink to deepening blue in the matter of the several seconds she had listened to Matt. The little mouth was open and it was obvious the newborn was having difficulty breathing. "She's cyanotic! ***Goddamn it***, she's obstructed! I need a scope and bulb, stat!" she barked, keeping her eyes on the child's face while Tina slapped a pediatric laryngoscope into her outstretched hand and Matt placed a tiny rubber suction bulb in front of her. Loretta immediately judged the scope, even though sized for an infant, to be too large for her minute patient. And there was the possibility of pushing the obstruction further down if she couldn't locate it right away. Loretta felt something creeping into her psyche that she didn't like; something she had not as yet experienced in her fifteen years of nursing: panic.

Loretta had treated thousands of children in her career in pediatrics; children injured from accidents, battering parents; children debilitated by fast moving infections and slow growing cancer. The look in the eyes of each and every one of them staring up at her had touched her. It always had and she knew it should. The day she couldn't empathize with her patients was the day she knew she should walk away from her profession. But through them all, through all the cases that touched her heart, she had kept in control, had always remained professional and objective enough to do what she had to do. Yet all those years of getting down and tough when the situation called for it were draining from her as she looked down at this infant that had had no real chance to survive since shortly after its birth. Loretta fought the growing, frightening panic with everything she had. It was time to reach back.

Momma, help me! If you ever helped me before, do it now! She thought while discarding the blue bulb and digging out another IV kit. *I want this baby to live, Momma! I want it more than anything I can remember wanting. Can you hear me? Help me!* "Matt, pen light!" she ordered, the paramedic slapping the pen into her hand OR-style. *I'm squarin' my shoulders, Momma; I'm 'bowin' myself up like you said to. Just give me the strength not to break down, not now. Make me strong, Momma, please! Do it now!* Loretta took the bandage scissors and cut a 10-inch piece of clear plastic tubing from the IV kit, placing one end in her mouth. Shaking, she hyper-extended the infant's neck to fully access the airway, watching the baby struggle silently in front of her, the little face straining to breath and getting darker. She probed the tiny throat with the pencil-thin light and her finger, sliding the tube alongside it, looking for the foreign object that would, within a few more seconds, either kill this infant outright or render it mentally handicapped for the rest of its life from oxygen deprivation.

That's it! she thought, seeing the brown obstruction down by the larynx. Keeping her light on it, Loretta sucked gently and steadily on the tube, extracting a thin brown piece of leaf from the baby's throat. *That's it, that's all it was going to take to kill this poor little thing after all she's been through,* she thought, spitting the leaf and tube to the floor. She handed the light back to Matt and slumped back against the metal drawers, smiling in relief and clcsing her eyes to fight the tears she wanted to cry and thank her mother for helping her through one more crisis. *Thank you, Momma; I love you.*

Matt looked up from his last check of his patient and smiled. "Now *that* was slick! I don't remember seeing that in the book," he said.

"Not in it; not ours, anyway. A Special Forces medic showed me that; said he used it on a Kuwaiti boy..."

Just then the ambulance tilted to a dangerous angle and stopped just short of overturning. Tina jumped up from her squatting position in fear, bracing herself with the inner walls of the vehicle. Matt's eyes widened as he grabbed the gurney Bo was on and steadied it in pure reaction. Loretta clutched for the baby to keep it from tumbling off the steel shelf. "We're sliding! Time to go! Tina, get us out of here!" Matt yelled.

Tina turned carefully to climb into the driver's seat and put the vehicle in drive, giving it gas, but it was obvious by the feel that the tires were spinning uselessly in the mud. The angle became less precipitous as the ambulance righted itself, turning to face uphill, but the sea of mud it sat in was dragging it slowly downhill. "We're stuck, I can't go anywhere!" Tina shouted back at Matt.

"Take over back here, I'm trading places with you!" he said, standing while she crawled back to take his place at Bo's side.

"Can you get us out of here?" Loretta asked him, concerned for all of them but especially for the two patients that needed more care than the three of them could administer there. Time was getting extremely crucial for the survival of the baby and her father.

"I think! I do this on weekends for fun! I'm the mud boggin' champ of Ocoosa County!" he told the two women, a hint of a smile on his face. Matt slid into the driver's seat and buckled up. "Hang onto those two, this might be rough!" he shouted back over the sound of the rain which still hit the side of the ambulance with sporadic, violent blows. He let the vehicle roll back and cut the wheel hard to the left, allowing it to face parallel to the side of the hill. Applying just enough gas, he traveled across the hill as far as he dared, building up a steady speed. When the trees on the other side of the property got close enough, he pulled the wheel to the right and climbed the hill just enough to allow him to turn the opposite way and retrace his path, but just several feet higher. They bumped and shook as the ground gave way and rose, the mud bottoming out to rock for a ways then turning to deep red mush again. Two more severely tilted switchback passes in the yard, and Matt put them back at the spot where the ambulance and Luke's truck had left the uncertainty of the obscured driveway for the abyss of the sloping yard.

"Way to go!" Tina yelled, feeling the vehicle right itself on the flatter surface of the road. "Goddamn, Matt, I don't believe you did it!"

"Shit!" Loretta chimed in from the back, "I guess you weren't kidding!

"I am the King!" he said, a grin on his face, secretly exhaling in relief that the vehicle didn't roll over. He radioed their status to Athens Regional and started the bells and whistles as the headlights cut the rain and dark upward to the

main road all of them hoped now was still passable. Somewhere on the gravel road that wound upward toward more miles of country black top that would lead them back to Watsonville, their lights and siren would meet and pass those of Sheriff Franklin, heading downhill to find the sixth mailbox on the right, looking for a big Georgia "G."

***

Luke was still sitting in the mud and rain, motionless, staring at the body in front of him, when the growing wail of the siren blended with the receding squall of rain then gradually overpowered it. The headlight beams and emergency lights danced and played through the trees as the car made the treacherous drop down the long drive. Luke never looked up as the car came to a sliding stop close to his truck and two men bolted out into the storm at him. The squad car's kaleidoscope of lights now illuminated what he had done with his .38 just twenty short minutes ago, making it seem so unreal, so very much less serious than he and these two men in uniforms standing over him knew it was.

CHAPTER 42

September 27, 1995

L uke looked through the glass door of the courthouse as he held it open for Loretta and welcomed the sunlight he saw. It represented a freedom he never appreciated more than now. He passed her as they walked and veered to take a seat on the first bench he came to that lined the broad walkway to the street. He sat down with deliberation and bent to prop his elbows on his knees, rubbing his temples and staring blankly at the cement walk, contemplating the seriousness of what he had been through in the last ten days. Loretta took a seat next to him and remained quiet long enough to give Luke a chance to compose himself. She could see the stress in his face and searched for something supportive to say to him.

"Well, it looks like its over. From what I heard, I think you're done with the whole thing," she said, keeping her tone even and positive. "Is that what Rick said?"

"As far as the courts are concerned, I guess," he replied. "And don't think I don't count myself as being a lucky man.

I've come to realize in the last week or so just how bad this could have gone, believe me," he said, still massaging his forehead and temples, trying to rub away the tension of the last ten days.

"You *were* lucky Rick didn't have much of a case load. I can see where he played a big part in this turning out in your favor."

"Uh-huh, *damn* lucky that the guy who handled my divorce used to be one of the most successful defenders in Atlanta before he decided to go where the money is and handle divorces. His knowledge of criminal law is unbelievable! You know, something he said back when I was splitting with Betsy came back into my mind when Lamar seemed like he was going to go out of his way to nail me to the wall on this. Rick and I were having a conversation about law in general, and he made the statement: 'never mind the facts; show me the evidence.' All I can say is, *thank God* Thad Gaines responded to the scene with Lamar, because if you think about it, what else could they have thought when they got there?" Luke said, standing to turn to Loretta as though pleading his own case to her. His close brush with being charged with felony manslaughter was making him jittery now that it was all over. The relief was starting to show in his animation and Loretta watched him as he paced in front of her and gestured as he talked, staring away then looking down at her as he made his points to her and himself. *Well, at least this is positive fidgeting,* she thought as she watched him parading back and forth. *Talk to me, Marlboro Man. Let it all out, country boy.* "I mean, what would *you* have thought, what would *anyone* have thought, coming down that river of mud in a pouring rain,

371

finding me sitting in that red soup with a gun in my hand? Five feet away from a dead woman in a nightgown with a bullet hole in her chest and not another soul around to explain things?" he practically shouted at her, his eyes wide in near hysteria. "And of course, the knife I claimed she had was washing away down the hill in a muddy slurry, taking my justification with it!"

"Luke, take it easy," Loretta said, her voice purposefully calm. "You're right, it looked bad, you being there with Danielle dead and all. But your statements about the circumstances finally bore out with my and Bo's story of what happened. And you more than satisfied the 'two-step' rule in Georgia: you had to make a move back to the truck for the gun, then open the glove box, *then* take the gun out of the holster to use it! And you had to break the strap to do it; the damaged holster was there in the truck as evidence! Really, with all that, all you had to do was sit tight till we could corroborate your story and things would straighten out, just like they did."

Luke stopped pacing and squared his body in front of her, bending down into her face to make his next point.

"Sit tight? Hon, it's damn near *impossible* to sit tight with a .357 Magnum pointing in your face and a piss-ant sheriff like Lamar Franklin reading you your rights, shaking and screaming and spitting rain the whole time!"

Loretta grinned at his description of Lamar and used it to break the growing strain that was more than evident in Luke's voice. "'Piss-ant'! *That's* the term I've been searching for to describe Lamar!" she said with a lilting laugh. "Luke, I know it isn't funny, really. None of this was. But I've got this mental image of Lamar there shaking his gun..." Loretta burst out laughing, trying to stifle it out of respect for Luke and the seriousness of his predicament, but it was no use; she covered her mouth while tears of laughter ran down her face and she turned away from him. Luke's look of astonishment at her attitude quickly disintegrated into his own growing laugh as he joined her by recounting the sight that only ten days ago terrified him to his bones.

"Yeah," he said, his chuckle growing into full laughter, "Yeah, he was standing in front of me, hopping up and down like a one legged man at an ass-kickin' contest," he drawled, walking over to take a seat next to Loretta once again. The imagery made her laugh even louder.

"Oh, Jesus!" she said, keeping her mouth covered, hiding the saliva she was helpless to contain from the intensity of her reaction. She was becoming breathless. **"Luke, you gonna have to stop!"** she said, barely getting the words out.

Luke ran with the feeling, hardly able to speak himself through his growing hysterical laughter.

"Hon, you should've seen his eyes!" he managed to say, struggling for breath. "They were this big!" he told her, his hands forming a six inch circle at her.

Loretta rolled back, breathless, gasping for air in sporadic gulps, her face bright red. Unable to speak, she reached out to push Luke's shoulder to get him to stop. He was determined not to let this feeling fade. It was something they both needed, and at this point, he was helpless to stop it anyway.

"And Sheriff Gaines!" he squeaked, still seeking a long breath. "Thad was... Thad was trying to hold onto Lamar... to keep him..."

Luke's laughter was making it hard for him to continue,

and passersby had smiles on their faces from the two sitting on the courthouse bench in the sunshine convulsed in teary laughter.

"...To keep him from bouncing like a damned puppet and shooting me at the same time! 'Don't shoot him, Lamar! Don't shoot him'!"

Loretta knew she had to stop and breathe, but Luke's story was keeping her from having any success. She held him at arm's length while she rocked back and forth, shaking her head for him to stop. Gradually, necessarily, they eased back to a controlled state of giddiness, and Loretta reached into her purse for a tissue, offering one to Luke. She wiped the tears that had been streaming down her face as she coughed up the occasional reverberations of laughter.

"Oh God!" Loretta said, still chuckling and wiping her eyes and nose. "I haven't laughed like that for a long time."

"Not since *I've* known you," Luke said, still smiling at his own story as he continued to recover.

"You know who else saved my ass besides Thaddeus Gaines? Karen Moffat, the dispatcher," he said, nodding to himself as he stared at the sidewalk, thinking back to the night of the storm and the shooting.

"How so? What do you mean?" Loretta asked.

"Hell, Loretta, she knows Lamar Franklin; she works for him! She knows how that little 'wannabe' would react to a situation like we had there! All he's handled since he's been sheriff are a few bar fights and speeders through town! She's the one that requested Sheriff Gaines respond with Lamar. I found that out later. Black Nate Road is clearly Ocoosa County; he knew that. But he's seasoned enough to have known she wouldn't be requesting him to accompany Lamar unless something serious was up. Plus, he knows Lamar too! Yeah, I figure I owe both of them big time. I'm fixin' to tell them that, too."

"You owe the State Attorney's Office too, don't you think? I mean even with all our statements, and the actual facts of the situation, the evidence notwithstanding, he could have easily disregarded all that and recommended charges be brought and then there'd been a Grand Jury. If you think about all that, you really *are* a lucky man," Loretta told him, sitting next to him, playing with the balled-up tissue in her hand.

"Yeah, lucky except for one big thing," he said, getting somber again. "I killed somebody."

Loretta knew it was time for her to jump in and defend Luke against himself. She turned to face him as directly as she could, leaning down to look up into his down-turned face.

"Luke, if you've ever listened to me before, you need to listen right now; no right-thinking person wants to take another human being's life. That's a fact. I know it and you know it. You did what you absolutely had to do, there's no two ways about it. As much as I dislike guns, if it had been in my hand, I'd have done the same thing. We know now it wasn't Danielle's fault, what she was going to do. But because you did what you did, there's a baby that's still alive right now. *You* did that. *You* gave that child a chance to grow up and have a life! Yeah, go ahead and feel bad about Danielle. No one can blame you for that; hell, I know I would too. But you also need to let yourself feel good about that baby. You deserve to. You're a hero! You're *my* hero."

Luke looked her in the eyes, wanting to say thank you

more than he knew how. "How is she?" he asked. "What's the latest on her?" he went on, diverting the topic from himself.

"Doctor LaStazzi is volunteering his services and time, mostly because he's a good guy, but I think part of it has to do with me; my involvement in this whole thing. He maintains she wouldn't be alive now, wouldn't have had *any* chance to live if it wasn't for me," Loretta said demurely. "He says she seems to be doing remarkably well for a newborn that obviously wasn't fed or cared for properly in its first ten days of life. More tests will have to be done as she recovers, see if she's progressing mentally at a normal rate. We don't know yet if there was any extensive damage from the lack of oxygen there in the water and when she was choking. Bo is going to recover but might have some permanent disability from nerve damage from the deep knife wounds. Danielle severed his brachial arteries and nerve and some other stuff."

"He's exactly right. It mighta been me with the gun at the last second, but you're the one who got us there, revived the baby; hell, figured it all out to begin with. *You're* the real hero here," Luke told her, the admiration in his voice plain and sincere.

"I'd have never been able to do it without you," she said. "We make a pretty good team, huh?" she said, grinning at him with a well-deserved pride.

Luke extended his arm and Loretta slid closer to him on the bench as he put his arm around her shoulder. "I reckon," he replied. "You know, I've been thinking the last couple of days, there's something else we might ought to do as a pair; something I want you to come along with me on."

"What?"

"I got to figurin', that journal that your grandfather got from Gerald's father, Randolph; well, your grandfather wrote that he meant to return it. I know it rightfully belongs to you now, but I'm thinking maybe we ought to do just that, give it back to him."

"*Randolph Martin? He's still alive? I mean, when his name has come up, I just assumed he was...*" Loretta asked in shock.

"Yeah, but barely, last I heard. He's old and give out, paralyzed on one side and wheelchair bound. He's been mostly deaf for a long time and I know he doesn't see well, either. I don't think he can speak very good anymore, if at all. He's a mess. His wife Tildie, Gerald's mother, died many years back. Gerald moved in with him years ago when his father's health got bad to the point he couldn't live by himself. I reckon Randolph must be somewhere in his mid-nineties or so," Luke said.

"Gerald's not married?" Loretta asked.

"Nah, never been; let's face it, who'd have him?" Luke answered, chuckling slightly.

Loretta chuckled back, both at his answer and her own question. "Well, there *are* cranky women out there!" she said.

"So, are you with me on this? Will you do what your grandfather wanted?" Luke asked her.

"Sure; I don't want to read that dreadful thing again. Do we take it to him at his store?" Loretta asked.

"No," Luke told her, "I'd like to give it to his father directly if we can. So we'll run by his house and see if he's there."

"You think Gerald will be home during the day and not at

his drug store?"

"Might be; he's home as often as he's at his shop, taking care of his dad and all. It's fifty-fifty. We pass his house before we get to the store; we'll look for his car. Ready?"

Loretta nodded her head. "Yeah, okay. Let's go"

CHAPTER 43

T
here's his car; he's home," Luke said as they drove slowly in front of the Martin house. He made a u-turn and parked in front of the house on the street, sizing up the old structure. Loretta grabbed the tin as she got out and walked to meet Luke at the closed white gate. "Now, I don't know what mood Gerald is going to be in. You never do. Or if he'll even let us see his father, so don't be real disappointed if he runs us off," Luke told her.

"This was mostly your idea, so either way, it's alright with me. I'd like to see him get it back too, but if Gerald insists on being 'Gerald', I can walk away with no problem; I'll be okay," Loretta said. She looked up at the house and it occurred to her immediately that it looked like Gerald: shades of brown, old but kept up; well-done to begin with, which contributed to its longevity. They climbed the steps, passing between the two tapering pillars that framed the entrance to the open porch, and crossed the short distance of worn planking to the door, rang the bell and waited. Half a minute passed and the door opened slowly to a surprised Gerald Martin standing in the doorway inspecting the two with startled caution. Luke was the first to break the tense silence.

"Hello, Gerald, how are you?" he asked, trying to act as casual as he could.

"Hello Luke," Gerald replied as he looked back and forth at the two uninvited intruders on his porch. "How come you're not in jail? They let you out already? What do you two want?"

Looks like he's going to be 'Gerald', Loretta thought, mentally shaking her head.

Luke decided immediately that there was not much else to do but keep calm and try to explain to the old man what the situation was; how it stood. Perhaps telling him an abbreviated account of the last ten days would appease him enough so that he and Loretta could accomplish what they came there to do.

"Gerald," Luke said, exhaling a deep breath, "the short of it is, they never even brought manslaughter charges against me because this lady here, you do remember her, don't you?" he asked, wanting to make sure Gerald knew the characters involved in the story he was about to relate.

Gerald tilted back his head and inspected Loretta again through his glasses to check his memory, giving the appearance of a man who had just swallowed a bug. "Of course I do. Hello, missy," he said in his abrupt 'Martin' manner.

Jesus, Loretta thought as she replied with a deadpan expression, both in her voice and on her face. "Hello, Mr. Martin. How are you?" she said, flashing back to their first encounter.

Luke sensed her attitude and jumped in to continue his account of the last ten days. "Loretta, here, gave statements on my behalf, and so did the husband of the girl that died…"

"The one you shot? The one you killed?"

"Uh, yes, Gerald, the woman that was about to kill her baby, that's the one I'm talking about," Luke replied, resigned exasperation beginning to show in his voice. "Anyway, as I was trying to say, the situation that presented itself, and the accountings of what happened, and why, from all three people who were there convinced the authorities not to bring charges. So that's why I'm out walking around now."

Gerald crossed his arms and leaned into his next question, squinting at them both. "So why are you and missy here? What do you want?"

"Loretta is pretty much responsible for figuring out this whole thing; why the babies have been dying all these years. It all started with the map she came to you with to ask you about. Do you remember the map?"

"Luke, dammit, if you're going to stand here and test my memory all day, I've got other things I can be doing! Yes, I remember the damn map, now speak your peace!" Gerald said, clearly becoming irritated.

"No, Gerald, why we're here is we have something we found in our search for answers about these deaths and we're pretty sure it belongs to your father. We're here to give it back to him. We'd like to do it personally if you'll let us," Luke told him. Loretta held the tin in front of her without saying a word, presenting it to a startled Gerald. He stared down at the box intently and, by his expression, it was difficult for either of them to determine if he knew what she was holding in her hands, much less the significance of what it contained. Gerald slowly took the box from Loretta and shifted his stare back up to their faces. "Where did this come from?" he asked in a hushed, uncustomary monotone.

"That's an interesting twist to this thing. See, Loretta here…"

"I'm the granddaughter of Norman Tomms, Mr. Martin," Loretta interrupted. All five feet of this Atlanta woman stood tall on the porch of the Martin house as she verbally declared for the first time her connection to this town, its people, and its history. Her pride was more than evident. "I found that out while we were searching for clues. I didn't know until then. We discovered this with his things. There's a journal inside and a note that says he most likely got it from your father back in May of 1926, the day my grandfather died. Evidently they were friends. We're here to give this back to him, that's all."

Gerald hesitated, dropping his eyes from the pair standing in front of him to the colorful tin and back to them. He looked back over his shoulder into the house and back at their faces. "Alright. He may not be up to it now. He's not well, but I suppose you can try. I want you two to know right now this is against my better judgment, but seein' how you're here…" Gerald took a step back and held the screen door open, motioning them with his head to come in.

Loretta sensed something more than the mere acquiescence to their desire to restore a long lost article to Gerald's father. Something else was going on in the mind of this irascible man she cared little for, and his puzzling agreement to their wishes bore further studying. *"Okay, what's up with this? What's wrong with this picture? This means something to him."*

As if expecting them to follow, Gerald stepped in front of them and led them through the house without looking back to see if they were with him. The house smelled strongly of liniment and medicated powder as they traveled down a short hallway past a dining room off to the right and the entrance to what appeared to be a study on the left. Passing the doorway, Loretta hesitated just half a step, but it was long enough for her to look to her left to see a darkened room lit only by window light. Against one wall was a huge bookcase that looked out over the comfortable room containing a stuffed chair and an assortment of doily covered tables, one of them round with two wooden chairs. The walls of each room she saw in passing seemed to have at least several framed pictures of Confederate soldiers that broke up the expanses of old, strongly patterned wallpaper. Battle maps of famous Rebel victories and defeats hung sprinkled among old rifles and pistols secured to the walls. Her sense of pattern and nuance also absorbed the other decorations that lay about; the knickknacks, what they were, where they were placed. As she passed through the house, Loretta's eye took in the yellowing of what had been white, the fading of that which had once been colorful; the placement of the furniture, the delicacy of the doilies and the type and style of the picture frames on the tables and piano. *A woman lived here once,* she thought. *But it was a long time ago.*

The three came to stop at the entrance to a sunroom on the south side of the house. Gerald stood in the doorway as the two looked into the room beyond him. The long room occupied a back corner of the house, fully glassed to the ceiling on two sides, awash with bright afternoon sun. In the center of the room, an old, sweatered man slumped forward asleep in a wheelchair. Gerald turned to them and gave stern warning, his face a solid 'Martin' frown. "Now, my father is old, and not well! He's ninety-five and he's had two strokes! He's got palsy and cataracts, and he's almost totally deaf. Don't upset him and don't expect much from him!" Loretta and Luke acknowledged what Gerald said and the three proceeded into the room to stand in front of the small pale man. Gerald bent to place his hand on the old man's right arm and gently shook it. "Dad? Dad? You have company. There are people here to see you. Dad?" Gerald spoke in a mild, pleasant tone that surprised Loretta. This was a kinder Gerald Martin than she had seen thus far, and it pleased her to see he was capable of it, at least with someone.

Randolph Martin gradually stirred, waking from his dreams to the reverberations of his son's voice. His head slowly rose and his opaque eyes opened to stare straight ahead, unable to locate the sounds that were waking him. Gerald touched the old man's arm once more to give him a reference point and Randolph's face rose to the familiarity of the sound of Gerald's voice. "Dad, there are people here to see you," Gerald stated again, always unsure how much of what he said was getting through to his father. He motioned toward Loretta and Luke, and Randolph slowly turned his unfocused eyes their way. His right hand, unaffected by stroke, rested on the arm of the wheelchair and shook constantly with a noticeable palsy. Loretta bent down to put her face in front of him and spoke in a friendly manner, her pleasant tone of voice almost necessitating at least the slight smile she gave to him.

"Mr. Martin, my name is Loretta. My friend and I have come to see you! Is that alright?" she asked him, not sure if she was speaking loud enough to be heard. Randolph's shaking hand rose to find hers and Loretta took it to give it a gentle squeeze. It told her he was aware of them. "We have something that belongs to you. We want you to have it. Can you see it? Do you know what it is?" she asked, holding the tin in front of him. Randolph's eyes lowered away from her voice down to the tin and lingered for a few seconds. Loretta rested the box in his lap to steady it, allowing his eyes to focus on the brightly colored top. "Do you remember this? Did this belong to you a long time ago?" she asked as his hand dropped to the top of the tin to gingerly touch it. His fingers stroked it, lingering on the dark girl, and his gray eyes acquired a faint gleam. The three could see his face soften slightly as his hand played along the edges of the box. It seemed to them as though he recognized it.

"He knows what it is! It must have been his!" Loretta said, looking back and smiling at Luke and Gerald, the both of them nodding in acknowledgement of what she said. Bending down again into Randolph's face, she gently slid the tin out from under his hand and flipped the top of it off to reveal the journal inside. "And this belongs to you, too. Do you remember this, Mr. Martin?" Loretta was looking into his face as his gaze settled on the small brown book that lay in the tin. She watched his eyes struggle to take in what lie there in front of him and send the significance of it down the now convoluted paths into the dusty recesses of his memory.

His hand pulled away from the tin with surprising speed as if he had been burned, retracting it as though he didn't know what to do with it, where to put it. Randolph tightly shut his eyes and threw his head back in apparent pain, his lips pursed and trembling. The tin slid from his lap to the floor, spilling the journal as it hit the faded green shag carpet. Loretta instinctively bent to retrieve it while Gerald leaned to comfort his father.

"It's alright, Dad, it's alright," he said loudly, attempting to calm the old man, then straightened quickly to turn to admonish the two visitors. "That's enough, you've upset him. I told you he can't handle excite…"

"Gerald, look," Luke said, staring down at Randolph. Loretta looked up from her effort to gather the tin and journal just as Gerald turned back to look at his father, the old man now making what appeared to be writing motions on the arm of his chair with his right hand, the expression of pain still frozen on his face. The three stared at each other then back at Randolph. "Looks like he… looks like he wants to write something, Gerald," Luke said as they watched the shaking hand make small imaginary circles. "Do you think it's just the palsy, maybe?"

"Dad? Do you want to write? Can you hear me? Is that what you want?" Gerald asked his father, amazed at what it seemed he evidently was asking to do. "I'll get you something to write with, wait," he said, rushing to a small dresser by the back wall and taking a pad and pen from the top drawer. "He hasn't tried to write for years, not since his last stroke. I don't know what this is about," he said, walking quickly back to place the pad on the wheelchair arm and wrap the pen with the frail, shaking hand hovering over it. The three of them looked on in amazement and apprehension for almost a minute before scribbled words started to take shape on the paper. Loretta bent to try to decipher the writing as it was appearing, but gave up and stood again next to Luke.

"We'll have to wait until he's done, I can't make it out," she said as they waited for Randolph to finish. Though continuing to shake, the hand ceased writing, dropping the pen

386

to the floor with what appeared to be a deliberateness not caused by his palsy. Gerald lifted the pad from under his father's arm and brought it up for the three to study.

Loretta was the first to interpret the wild scratching and covered her mouth as she quickly turned away to face the windows of light. She walked toward them and stood looking to the outside, away from the three men in the middle of the room. *Goddamn it, we should never have come here; we should never have done this*, she thought, now angry with herself and Luke.

Luke realized the content next and muttered lowly at the words Randolph Martin had managed, in all his frailties and limitations, to convey to his son and these two people, whoever they might be. "My God, Gerald, look." Gerald took the pad and turned to let the sunlight brighten the lettering.

NOW you know too

Luke walked to Loretta and stood next to her in the bright sun streaming through the window. They looked at each other in silence, neither being able to formulate the words to ask the questions that somehow should be asked. Turning back, they watched Gerald standing silently, sadly looking down at his father; a pained, sympathetic expression on his face. They walked the short distance back to stand beside him again and remained quiet, waiting for him to tell them it was time for them to leave.

"Let's leave him be now. I'll see to him after you go, he'll be alright for the time being, I think," he said softly, motioning them toward the doorway.

Nearing their exit from this room of such bright light and dark memory, Loretta let the two men pass her and paused just long enough to turn to look at Randolph Martin one last time. She saw his elbow resting on the arm of his chair, his spotted forehead sunk deep in the open palm that supported it; his gray, luminescent eyes staring blankly out into the emptiness of the room and a distant past. She could see the bright sunlight glistening in the wetness on his cheeks. *What have we done?* she wondered. She wished again they had not come here, naively armed with such long lost emotional devastation. Her brief seconds of observation ended and she caught up with Luke and Gerald.

The three walked slowly back through the house toward the front door until Gerald suddenly stopped at the doorway to the study and looked down at the tin and journal he held in his hands. "Excuse me for a moment," he said, and walked into the room to approach the bookcase. Loretta and Luke could see him silhouetted in the window light, standing in front of the great collection of literature, looking up to the top shelf. He reached up and, pushing books aside, made room for the small leather volume and neatly slipped it in. As he turned from the case, his expressionless eyes caught those of Luke and Loretta. Without saying a word, he walked to a small table against a wall and slid the colorful tin onto a shelf hidden by a doily that covered the tabletop and draped down over the front. He stood looking down at the table while a strange sensation came over him; a 'pleased' feeling he could only describe, if he were pressed to do so, as a sense of closure he did not fully understand. Oddly content, he walked to join his two departing visitors.

Gerald looked spent as he stood in his front doorway, his irascible manner defeated for the moment. Luke searched for words to convey how sorry he was for bringing back the journal and its memory to an old man who should not be troubled with such thoughts so near to his end. "Gerald, I'm really sorry…"

Gerald reached out and put his hand on Luke's shoulder, avoiding eye contact, and simply shook his head. In that moment of complete and silent understanding, all was forgiven. "I 'spect he always thought something like this might happen. He just never really talked about it," Gerald said. "He always said his own 'burden' was still out there somewheres waitin' on him, fixin' in its own time to come back to him."

Loretta extended her hand to Gerald, softening her attitude toward him as she spoke. "Thank you, Mr. Martin, for giving us the chance to do what we felt at the time was a good thing, the right thing," she said, trying to smile. "I guess, perhaps, it wasn't after all."

"It's okay, you're welcome, missy… Ms. Carmichael," he said as he looked directly into her eyes. His expression was neutral, but that suited Loretta; she knew then she would never be 'missy' to him again. "He'll be alright after a while. Maybe he'll rest easier from now on… till the end comes." Leaving him in his doorway, the two turned and walked to the top step and were about to walk away from this sad mistake in judgment until Gerald's next words stopped them. He leaned hard against his door frame, slumping, with his arms folded in front of him. His eyes reflected a sadness and there was a defeated sound in his voice as he spoke his next words. "I knew some of those women; went to their funerals. Saw some of their babies, too, before they were... before they died." Gerald's parting words were riveting Luke and Loretta where they stood, preventing them from moving on. "I remember, back when I was pretty young, my father taking me to one of the funerals. He looked sad for a long time while the preacher eulogized and he finally bent down and said something to me I've never forgotten, even though I was just a boy. Would you two like to know what that was?" he asked in a matter-of-fact tone.

"What was it, Mr. Martin?" Loretta asked him, almost spellbound in apprehension.

"He said, 'Evil soaks into the Earth with the blood it spills; but in time the blood, by God's grace, will wash away. Evil is that strong. When you're old enough to have your own young'uns, come talk to me.' I didn't know what he meant then. It appears like you two must've stumbled onto the part of all this he never wanted me or nobody else to know about, and I can see now, after all these years, it's in that little brown book y'all brought back to him. I don't *want* to know what happened to cause all this, not now. You know, just maybe... maybe this'll end it somehow."

The enormity of his words spellbound the two, and without being able to respond, they could only watch silently as he turned to disappear into his house, closing the door behind him.

As the door to the Martin house closed, they both turned to walk to Luke's truck and got in to start back to Loretta's house. They were quiet as Luke started up the truck and turned around in the street, and they avoided looking at each other during the pensive ride back to Bessemer Court.

CHAPTER 44

Loretta's somber mood slowed her and kept her in the truck as the engine died to a sputtering silence in her driveway. Luke exited and made his way in troubled thought as far as the left fender where he chose to stop and lean, putting his hands in his pockets, staring down the street. Shutting the door and walking toward her steps, Loretta looked back at him, sensing his mood was keeping him where he was, and turned back to attempt to clear the air with an invitation for coffee. "Hey, you coming in? I'll make coffee. What's wrong?" she asked, walking back to lean next to him on the fender.

"What just happened, for starters. That was not the right thing to do. I feel bad about doing it now. And something else I need to tell you that I feel bad about doing," he said, turning to face her.

"What?"

"I'm leaving," he said, the apologetic tone evident in his voice. "For a while, anyway."

Loretta let herself absorb the verbal blow that just knocked the wind out of her by tightly crossing her arms and avoiding looking Luke in the face. She stared down at the ground while she stammered out her comment about his announcement. "Oh, um… yeah, I can… ah… where… where are…"

"Florida. See my folks for a while. They've been calling most every day for the past week. I had told them to stay down there when all this happened; told them not to come up unless things went bad, then I might need them, but I'd let them know. My dad said if everything turned out well, and them being devout and all they been down there praying their ass off for me, if things worked out for me, to come down and rest. I figure it might be a good idea to change locales for a spell, just… you see where I'm coming from, don't you?" Luke asked her, badly wanting this little woman with whom he had been through so much in such a short time to understand his need to leave Ocoosa County, if only temporarily.

"I can understand that," she said, nodding her head, still staring blankly at the ground, considering the very real and immediate possibility she may never see this man again. Finishing her sentence, she continued to unconsciously nod and stare, not knowing exactly what to say next.

Luke could sense he had put her walking along the edge of a place she didn't want to be and tried his best to take the sharpness off his plans. "It's only for a while, really… I mean, I've got responsibilities here, jobs to finish; yours, for instance," he said, motioning to her soffits.

"Uh-huh, uh-huh," she replied, still nodding and avoiding his eyes. "Yeah, that's true. So, when do you… how soon will you be leaving?" she asked, trying unsuccessfully to sound nonchalant.

Luke took a deep breath and sighed as he gave his reply. "Tom's picking me up at my place in an hour. He's taking me to Hartsfield. Loretta…"

Loretta turned quickly and stood on her toes to give him a brief kiss on his cheek, retreating before he could realize what she had done and respond. She backed away and met his eyes furtively now with her own as she talked to him. "I want you to call me, alright? I mean… please, just to let me know how you are, you know? Okay?" she managed to say, trying to sound merely polite and concerned. It didn't sound convincing to her. She hoped inside it didn't to him either.

Luke stood not knowing what to say to her and even less precisely what to do. His reflexes told him to take her in his arms and hold her, reassure her he was coming back, let her know he would miss her. But the last five years had been a time in his life without a closeness to anyone, and he stood by his truck fairly immobilized, confusion mixed with concern on his face. "I will. Really. I'll let you know what's going on. Well… goodbye… take care," he said as he turned hesitatingly and climbed into his truck, starting it without ceremony and backing into the street to drive away.

Loretta stood rooted with her arms still held defensively across her chest, releasing one just enough to tightly wave to him as he drove off, not even sure if he saw her. It didn't matter; they had said what goodbyes they could manage and now he was gone. Gone. He was gone.

Turning quickly, she climbed the steps and entered her house, moving hurriedly past a materializing Peach to open a pantry and take out a new box of Kleenex. Peach, strangely being ignored, sat watching her human flit purposefully back and forth through the house, putting her purse down then picking it up to move it somewhere else; sitting down to take off her shoes, then getting up to start another menial project before she had taken them both off, each time grabbing another tissue from the box as she quickly passed. When Loretta had finally performed every time-consuming activity she could think of, she grabbed the cat and the tissue box and sunk down into her couch, the box close by her side and a confused but appreciative Peach on her lap. It was time to explain to this cat, a cat happy to be stroked as rapidly and forcefully as Loretta was now doing, the difference between really 'crying' about something important or serious, and 'sniffling'.

"You see, Peach, I'm not really crying. There's nothing going on for me to cry about. I'm just sniffling. 'Sniffling' is something human girls, 'grown up' human girls, do when they feel someone, in this case a man I have no claim on, no actual relationship with but have been through *so much* with, leaves on such short notice. Just up and fucking drives away out of my life, maybe forever," Loretta calmly told the cat sitting on her lap while reaching down for a dry tissue. She forced a weak smile onto her face for the sake of her conversation, trying to show the oblivious feline on her lap that her human was taking all this fine, just peachy-damn-fine-son-of-a-bitch. Loretta took a series of deep breaths to keep herself from crossing the imaginary line between sniffling and crying and continued her rapid, rhythmical stroking of the cat, all the while staring blankly into space, dabbing at her eyes from time to time, trying to imagine how a Marlboro Man would occupy his time in a Florida beach town.

CHAPTER 45

November 18, 1995

L oretta felt this was as good a place as any to stop as she slowed her car and pulled to the side of the dirt road. Turning off the ignition, she stared out the passenger window at the rolling field for a long minute. *This is the day it all started,* she thought to herself, her jaw tightening. *By God, this is the day it ends.*

Getting out, she walked around the car to the edge of the pasture that stretched out for hundreds of yards to end at a wall of thick, tall forest. She stood motionless at the barbed wire fence that ringed the pasture, her hands shoved in her coat pockets, with an unblinking stare fixed out across the field. The sun was setting in a clear pink sky and the trees were casting shards of light and shadow across the tan, fallow earth. The gentle breeze that had blown all day was quickly dying. It was going to get cold, just like they said it would. Gazing at the distant tree line, she felt the anger at the past two months rising up inside her, filling her throat, her breathing deepening and getting quicker.

"Stop it! Goddamn it, stop it!" she screamed out into the darkening pasture, the intensity causing her to lean forward to yell with all her strength. They needed to know Loretta Carmichael was tired of this killing of the innocent. *"It's over!"* she screamed again as she shook with anger, the veins bulging in her neck. *"It's ov..."* she attempted to yell once more, this time her words collapsing in her throat, reducing her to heaving sobs.

She covered her face with her hands, letting loose the pent-up flood she had been holding back. The sounds of her crying mixed with the cawing of blackbirds that had been silent in the bare trees lining the road until their frigid peace was shattered by Loretta's outburst. She was vaguely aware of their raucous retaliation to her disturbance. No other sound invaded the chilling quiet of the pasture and trees but her sobbing and the annoyed squawking of the hundreds of birds flying from bare trees to telephone wire and back again.

Loretta took the few short steps to her left to grab the top of a weathered fence post and rest her forehead on the backs of her hands. She wept with an abandon she had not known for years, a cathartic crying, an unrestrained outpouring of release of the grief and stress of the last two months. She raised her head to look out again into the pasture through watery eyes, her face flushed and hot, yet cooling from the wetness of her tears. Her breathing was coming in deep shudders as she scanned the fading distant tree line, wanting, needing to glimpse just a shadow of an apparition toward which to focus the anger that was taking control of her once again.

Backing away from the fence, she screamed again with rage out into the darkness. *"You want stones? Is that what you want? You need more? I'll give you stones, you murdering bitches!"* She looked around her and saw the outcropping of small rocks in the washed-out side of the shallow ditch in which she was standing and fell to her knees to crawl toward them. Tugging on the exposed portion, she loosened a softball-sized rock caked with cold red mud and heaved it as far as she could into the pasture, barely clearing the top of the barbed wire fence. *"How's that? Is that a good one for a baby? Here, here's another one, you goddamn..."* her breaking voice carrying out over the cold ground into the gloom as she pulled another rock from the freezing mud. Bigger than the last, her throw bounced under the bottom wire.

Loretta attempted to pull a third stone from the red earth, but this one would not budge, its true size buried unseen in the side of the ditch. She struggled in her fury, a crazed woman in a shallow roadside gully, on her knees grappling with a stone too large; a rock, she felt if she could free it, might just somehow end the Ocoosa burden once and for all. Not wanting it to let it defeat her, she clawed at it, scraping the flesh from her cold, numb fingers until they were raw. Nails were breaking on both hands but she continued digging at the rock like a dog after a buried bone.

Loretta abruptly stopped, her energy spent, and began to pound the cold clay and dead grass in front of her with balled up fists in exhausted frustration. Her stamina gone, she slowed to a stop and stared down at the inanimate symbol of 130 years of grief and horror for this small Georgia county. It had won. The steam rolled off her face and out of her nose and mouth. She rose up on her knees, her chest heaving from exertion, her face streaked with red mud and tears. She pointed out into the darkness and shouted, with the maternal authority of an angry, living woman, *"This is the end of it, do you hear me? No more! It's done! No more!... I'm sorry!"* Like a mother admonishing an ill-behaved child, she didn't want any backtalk. She knew there would be none.

Exhausted, physically and emotionally, Loretta slowly rose unsteadily to her feet, her breathing gradually slowing to near normal again, her head pounding from the raw emotion and crying. She turned to walk slowly back to her car, and stopping just short of the road, turned one last time to face the fence and the dark-obscured field beyond it. Her stare arced back and forth, as though she were silently praying she would see at least something out there, someone to which she could give one final warning. "Oh Jesus, that's it!" she said out loud as she her swollen eyes opened wide in sudden realization. She covered her mouth and retraced her steps halfway back to the fence as what few tears were left started to flow once again. The anger she had felt now suddenly dissolved into understanding for the ghosts she knew were out there somewhere, watching her, wanting her to voice what her mind was now grasping.

"They never knew! The people of Ocoosa County never knew! Only Randolph Martin and he didn't..." she said half to herself, her eyes alternately peering into the growing blackness and looking down at the rocky, uneven ground in her path as she approached the fence once more. "What you suffered; what happened. These people have been paying for something they never knew about! Oh God! Oh God!" she blurted to the field and the souls she felt surely were out beyond the tree line somewhere in the darkness. *"No one has ever told you they were sorry! That's it, isn't it? Nobody has ever apologized for what happened to you!"* Loretta shook her head slowly in profound amazement and a sadness only another woman could reach down and summon for the suffering of her own gender. She felt her rage peel away and fall to the ground like dead skin that needed to be shed to reveal the raw sympathy that was underneath. "I'm sorry it happened, I truly am. We ALL are. But it has to stop. I expect this to be the end of it. They've paid for it for too long. It's over," she said in a normal tone, as though she were addressing one of Gerald Martin's ghosts standing right in front of her.

She turned again from the field, this time in hesitation, allowing this revelation to work through her consciousness, walking slowly toward her car once more. Loretta stood looking at the door for several seconds, not wanting to open it at first; almost afraid that if she got in and left this pasture, she would be abandoning something that somehow needed her humanity, her living connection to the people of Ocoosa County. *Strange*, she thought as she stared at the door handle, *me never believing in spirits. First my grandfather, now this. So here I am, Loretta Carmichael, standing in the middle of nowhere feeling like a link between the living and the dead.* She opened her car door and got in, turning the key and letting the engine run for a minute while she collected herself. One last long glance at the blackness of the land and she headed down the long dirt road for home.

The land, indifferent as always, acknowledged silently what had happened, and watched as the tail lights disappeared into the darkness.

***

Yards back into the gloom of the distant forest, flickerings of dim light gradually appeared one by one, pulsing and growing steadily into misshapen human forms the color of misty moonlight. Nearly two dozen torn and broken females, old and young, coalesced into a jagged, uneven line, hovering just above the freezing ground. Young Nicollete, her face so long transfixed in pain and fear, turned to look up at her sister as the expression of horror began to fade into a calm smile. Abigail approached her and, putting her hands on the child's shoulders, felt her own countenance changing from that of agony into one of peace and contentment and, at long last, forgiveness. Gazing down at Nicollete's regained wholeness, Abigail returned the child's look of tranquility, then turned to the rest of them, they too now complete and restored, giving the slightest nod to her left and then her right, signaling to them a serene finality. It was all that was needed. It was the culmination for which they had yearned for the last 131 years.

The spirits, fulfilled and acknowledged after so many years of pain and anonymity, turned and slowly melted back into the dark of the forest.

CHAPTER 46

The beams of headlights were receding from the front of Loretta's house as she turned onto Bessemer Court and drove the short distance to her drive. The shape of an old white pickup materialized in her own lights and she honked her horn several times when she recognized it as Luke's. The truck stopped at the end of her drive at the sound of her horn, Loretta pulling alongside the curb to park on the street. Luke emerged to stand next to his door and Loretta exited her Camry, an excited, muddy little girl, running up her drive to throw herself into him, flinging her arms around his heavy-jacketed torso as much as she could. He had no choice but to catch her and swing her around, lifting her off her feet to break her momentum and keep them both from falling. "You're back!" she said, still hugging him and beaming up into his face. "When did you…"

"Just now," he responded before she could finish her question. "I just now picked up my truck and thought I'd come by to see you before I went home. "I… I missed you, Hon. I wanted to come by and tell you. It… it was important to me."

"I missed you too," she said, now hugging him with all

her strength, trying to encompass as much of him as she could while turning her face to press it hard against his leather jacket. Luke continued to spin her until the porch light illuminated her face. He suddenly stopped and positioned her in the light in order to examine her more closely. Holding her at arm's length, shock flooded his face and voice. "Loretta! Look at you! What the hell happened to you?"

Loretta stood in front of him and thought quickly about what she would tell him. She looked up into his concerned face, a face she had missed seeing, a face that deserved an honest answer to his question. *Maybe I can be honest and not have to tell the whole truth,* she thought. "I... was out in the country... and I... I broke down," she told him, thinking while she spoke, realizing then that was exactly what had happened.

"You broke down? Loretta, you look like hammered shit! Hon, are you alright?" Luke asked her, wiping at the mud on her face with his fingers.

A slight smile came to her face along with her next answer and she looked contentedly up into his as she spoke. "I think I will be from here on."

Luke was at a loss as his head turned from Loretta to her car and back again. "I'm confused here, Hon," he said, taking her hands to look at them more closely in the light.

"Don't be. I think I'm going to be fine now; I think all of us will be," she said.

Looking back at her car for any apparent damage, Luke asked, "Is it okay now? Did you fix it?"

Loretta took a step back from him and, turning to face the south from where she had just driven, her eyes narrowed into a thousand-yard stare. "Yeah," she said calmly, looking down the length of Bessemer Court back into the past of Ocoosa County. "I really think… I might have." Her stare came back to Luke and focused again on his face. "Hey you, give me another hug!" she said as she wrapped her arms around him again. "I thought you were going to call me regular while you were down there! What the hell you been doing all this time, boy?"

Luke's concern over her appearance faded as he hugged her back and gently swayed her from side to side while he answered. "Not much of anything, really; mostly gettin' older day by day, you know, layin' around, doin' a lot of thinking."

"I can understand that," Loretta said, thinking back over what they had been through.

"A lot of my thinking lately has been about you," he told her in a low, steady voice. Mentally, he was surprised it came out as smoothly as it did.

"Me?" she replied, the side of her head again plastered against his jacket, her eyes opening wide and staring past him to the porch in anticipation for the rest of what may follow.

Luke separated himself from the mud-caked little woman in order to look down into her face. Holding her cold, raw hands in his, he forced out the words he had been going over in his mind for the last month. "Hon, I've had the chance to do a lot of thinkin'…"

Loretta's heart was quickening and she knew in her mind what Luke was about to say was going to sound good to her, no matter what it was; she knew it deep inside. His characteristic 'jitters' were appearing and she knew what he wanted to say was not coming easy for him. A little tension breaker was called for right about now. "Hey, I been meaning to ask, where'd this 'Hon' thing come from? Just when did *that* start?"

404

she interjected, intentionally throwing off his timing.

Luke looked down at her, bewilderment on his face. Not only had she broken his concentration, but now some sort of apology seemed to be in order. *Damn it!* he thought. "Loretta, I... I'm sorry," he stammered down to her, his confusion blending with concern.

Loretta beamed up at him and, grabbing the lapels of his coat, pulled herself close to him again. "I'm kidding!" she said, looking into his face with a smile she hoped and felt at that moment would never go away. "I never said anything 'cause I liked it, it sounded good! Hey, wait a minute!" Loretta buried her nose into his exposed shirt, sniffing strongly, then proceeded to examine the front of his coat and his sleeves in the same manner. "You quit smoking, didn't you!" she declared with enthusiasm.

"Yeah, I did!" Luke replied, surprised at her discovery. "How do you know?"

"I can't smell it on you anymore."

"You mean you could before? I thought you said you couldn't tell!"

"Yeah, I could tell, pretty much right off," she confessed. "I just didn't want to hurt your macho feelings, you were so smug about it. Anyway, good for you! Oh, I'm sorry, I interrupted; you were saying something about something? Go on!"

Even though part of his past he had thought he had gotten away with was now compromised, Luke smiled down at her, realizing what she had just done was for his sake. He knew he could now finish what he wanted to say.

"Hon, like I said, I been thinking a lot about you... us...

for a while now, and you know, if you think about it, we haven't known each other for much more than a couple months…" Luke said, pausing to formulate what he had to say next and waiting momentarily for any feedback she might have to add so far.

"Uh-huh, go on," Loretta agreed, encouraging him to continue.

"But we been through more together in that time than most couples…"

"Couples? You think of us as a 'couple'? I'm sorry, go ahead," she interrupted, a playfulness in her voice.

"Loretta, what I'm trying to say…" Luke attempted further, impatience appearing in his voice.

"I know, I know, I'm interrupting. I'm sorry, go ahead, finish what you were going to say," she said, feigning apology and patience.

"*Look*," Luke said, exasperated enough from her interruptions that his planned speech was at this point almost irretrievable. "What I'm *trying like hell* to tell you here is that… I like you, I like being around you. The whole time I was…"

"Mr. McClain, are you asking me out?" she broke in again, pulling herself even closer to him and looking up into his eyes.

"Hon, don't call me 'Mr. McClain', please. I already feel like a damn cradle robber!" he said shaking his head painfully. "Hell, I'm old enough to be your father!"

"Bullshit!" Loretta replied defiantly, "you'd have had to have had me at fifteen!"

"Well, you've got to remember, Hon, this *is* rural Georgia

we're in! That stuff happens all the time!" Luke responded, causing both of them to laugh. "But yeah, I am. Asking you out, that is. How about supper for starters? I'm starved!"

Her giggly, impish façade melted and Loretta replied with all the sincerity she possessed. "I'd love to, Luke. Anyplace you have in mind?" She could see the relief on his face and saw the tension fade from him with her acceptance.

"Oh, great! Good!" he stammered, "uh... well, I see there's a new Italian place on Main... it's... uh, it's new since I've been gone..."

"Calvani's," Loretta offered. "I haven't been, but I hear it's good."

"Then Calvani's it is. How long do I need to give you to clean up? Have you seen yourself?"

Loretta looked down at her muddy knees and realized for the first time just how filthy she had gotten in the roadside ditch. "How about coming back at 8:30? That good? Give you enough time?" she asked him.

"Oh *hell* yeah," Luke replied, "I'm a guy! Quick shower and change and I'm good to go. Are you sure 8:30 gives *you* enough time?"

"I'll be ready!" she promised, still all smiles.

"Well, Miss Loretta... oops! Sorry!" Luke said, remembering her dislike for the prefix.

"Oh, it's okay now," she replied deadpanned, nodding to him, shifting her weight from leg to leg and swaying her hips in an exaggerated manner as if simulating a dance. "I started dancing while you were gone."

Luke's mouth dropped open in dulled confusion.

"Wha...?"

"*I'm just kidding!*" Get out of here so I can get ready!" She grabbed him again, giving him as much of a hug as she could manage and looked up into his face as she backed away. "I'm really glad you're back," she said.

"Me too, Hon," Luke replied, turning to get back into his truck. He smiled and waved goodbye through the windshield, backing out onto the street and then driving away toward his house.

Loretta watched until he had reached the end of her court then bounded up her steps, her numb, raw hands twice dropping her keys while attempting to unlock her door. Fumbling the door open, she rushed inside only to halt in front of her hall mirror and turn for a sobering assessment of her appearance. "Whoa, I *do* look like hell! He asked me out looking like *this*? Good sign!" she mumbled to herself and the fast approaching Peach. Loretta reached down to acknowledge the cat with a single stroke on her back, then pushed her gently away. "No, baby, Momma's dirty as a little pig; don't rub on me now," she warned the cat with a little girl giddiness in her voice. "Okay now, let's see: gotta get out of these clothes, shower, do something with these nails, and find something to wear. Damn! Do I *have* anything to wear?" she said out loud to herself and Peach, who now sat patiently in the bedroom doorway thinking of food, listening out of necessity and cat curiosity to this little Atlanta nurse who had always had a difficult time finding clothes that fit her right; clothes that didn't make her look at least a bit... "undone."

THE END

ABOUT THE AUTHOR

Arthur Heath was born in Newport, Rhode Island and moved to the South at age fifteen.

After a stint in the Green Berets in the early '70s, he has worked as a craftsman for a renowned cutlery company in Orlando, Florida for the past thirty three years. The inspiration for this story came from a journey to Georgia to see a newborn granddaughter. Arthur is concurrently working on four new novels.

www.ingramcontent.com/pod-product-compliance
Lightning Source LLC
Chambersburg PA
CBHW020832030726
47496CB00001B/206

* 9 7 8 1 6 0 2 6 4 0 0 6 1 *